1984 *Michael G. F*

BY THE SAME AUTHOR

ERIK DORN · FANTAZIUS MALLARE

1001 AFTERNOONS IN CHICAGO · BROKEN NECKS

GARGOYLES · THE FLORENTINE DAGGER

THE KINGDOM OF EVIL · HUMPTY DUMPTY

COUNT BRUGA · A JEW IN LOVE

THE CHAMPION FROM FAR AWAY

CHRISTMAS EVE
(For Private Distribution)

THE FRONT PAGE (A PLAY)
(In collaboration with Charles MacArthur)

THE GREAT MAGOO
(In collaboration with Gene Fowler)

ACTOR'S BLOOD

TO QUITO AND BACK (A PLAY)

TWENTIETH CENTURY (A PLAY)
(In collaboration with Charles MacArthur)

A BOOK OF MIRACLES

A BOOK OF

Miracles

BEN HECHT

NEW YORK · THE VIKING PRESS · MCMXXXIX

TO ROSE

CONTENTS

A Lost Soul   1

The Little Candle   23

The Missing Idol   55

Death of Eleazer   113

Remember Thy Creator   203

The Heavenly Choir   309

The Adventures of Professor Emmett   367

I F you stand motion-
less for seven hours looking

up at the topmost window of the tallest building in New York you will be rewarded, provided you are not too much of a New Yorker, with a curious sight. You will see two Angels hovering there, that is, not outside this topmost window but a little above it.

Being of a practical turn of mind and not experienced in visions or perhaps not entirely believing in them since Science has identified them as the product of our confused sex instincts, you may deliberately mistake them at first for some sort of erotic symbols. Nothing could be more unfair to a pair of God's Angels than attributing them to Freud. But since the modern intelligence has, with a great show of logic and data, reduced even God to a homosexual component (I think, of all the heresies, this must be the most depressing to Him), the temptation to think disparagingly of mere Angels is easily understandable.

But your sanity and your good eyes will soon tell you that these hovering creatures are Angels—a bit dim, as if wrapped in cellophane, as are so many of God's mysteries, their wings outspread and shadowed, yet—as the most hysterical of skeptics must admit—Angels.

But so godless has the world become that I doubt there are even any skeptics left. Most of my friends have turned their backs entirely on the mysteries of Infinity, and except for those bright enough to understand the Second Law of Thermodynamics there are no mysteries. They have walked away from Heaven as from a hermetically sealed room and they are to be found neither kneeling outside its locked doors beseeching the Invisible nor banging angrily on its panels and proclaiming that the Invisible does not exist. I am afraid that my friends, were they to see my two Angels, would smile knowingly and be on time for dinner.

When you, however, who are perhaps a whit more aboriginal than my friends, behold these celestial beings, you will, at first, feel a wonder at their existence. Then, with your modern mind, whose habit it is to make nonsense out of God and God out of nonsense, you will lapse briefly into cynicism and inquire irritably: "What are they advertising?"

Yet a few minutes later you will become disquietingly certain that they are not ingenious advertisements such as float over the ball parks during important sporting events. For what enterprising manufacturer would permit such lugubrious faces and such defeatist attitudes as theirs to call attention to his product?

(I neglected, perhaps out of fear of confusing everybody a little more than necessary at the outset, to say that the two hovering messengers from Heaven were an extremely sorrowful-looking pair.)

Convinced at last of the impossible, you will, as I did, scowl, fidget, and look about you most furtively. A great fear will take hold of you, not of God to be sure, but of what would happen to you were anybody to find out that you were seeing Angels. You might be arrested as the psychopathic villain who has been molesting little girls in Coney Island. At the very least you would be hurried to some scientific center where you would go through a nerve-racking examination by two doctors, one of them unable to speak English. And if you persisted in your account of two sad, bedraggled Angels hovering over Seventh Avenue, unquestionably you would be fingerprinted as a schizophrenic.

So, seeing the two Angels, you will, as I did, conceal the fact from all those footsore realists hurrying importantly from one doorway to another as if in search of some non-existent hiding place—particularly since you have been standing motionless for seven hours, in itself a very sinister bit of evidence against you.

And quietly, secretly, you will enjoy the Angels' presence and think, no doubt a bit nostalgically: "What a piece of luck it would have been once upon a time to catch sight of two such divine Visitors."

Reporting their arrival to the Bishop, you would have lived the rest of your days in the heady odors of sanctity. You might even have been canonized. Whereas now—but I have already petulantly hinted at the consequences. Which is, perhaps, as it should be, considering the sort of rampant idiocy God has always inspired in those who have seen Him or any of His works too plainly.

But now, having had some abstract thoughts on the two Angels, you will have lost the sense of oddness and you will start inquiring: "What are they doing there and why do they, contrary to all report, appear so sad? Are they lost, or are they resting, and why have they chosen so unpoetical or at least so un-Biblical a locale as Seventh Avenue to hover over?" I can answer these questions for you, for I have more than merely seen them. I have discovered their story.

You may now remove your eyes from these celestial beings, since I can assure you they will be there for some time—not as Angels reckon the ways of our clocks, but as we do; and that after you have heard the story of their adventures you will be the more eager to study them and—who knows?—even to weep a little over their predicament.

This story begins in the town of Hegemish, Illinois, where, you will recall, a strike among the steel mill workers a few weeks ago resulted in the killing of a number of men and women. It seems that the workers were misled into making some demands— perhaps for more soap to wash their faces on Sunday—and that the police, whose faces are none too clean themselves, valorously scotched the uprising. But this strike has nothing to do with my story. It is merely an event that happened in Hegemish long after my story begins.

Hegemish, with or without bullets flying, is a cruel little town whose people make steel. They live in ugly wooden houses that stand in streets as devoid of beauty as an old man's mouth. The people and the houses of Hegemish, also its lower animals, store fronts, cinder-spotted vegetation, and mechanical contrivances, all seem as identical and related as the ingredients of a junk yard.

One look at Hegemish should be enough to convince any historian that the Age of Darkness, dissipated by the Professors of Salerno in 1002, has returned, and that the world—the world of Hegemish at any rate—has stumbled or been booted back into the gloom of the Scythian Wastes. And yet historians, at least the majority of them, give eye to Hegemish and proclaim it one of the flowers of Democracy; observe in its scrawny, metronomic folk a nobility of purpose called Production. And even artists describe in paint and phrase the steel mills that surround the town as the rhapsodic monuments of Power.

It is the fashion, I know, to find beauty everywhere, particularly where to the layman's eye it may not seem at first glance to exist. The ominous-looking structures on the outskirts of Hegemish, shaped like colossal boilers in a network of curving pipes and surmounted by a devil's hallelujah of towering chimneys, out of which smoke and flame pour incessantly, have inspired some of our poets to song. But to me, these steel mills have a horrid, anatomical look, and my fancy conceives them as the flaming bowels of greed. Also, whenever I see the clean faces of the Stockholders purring and shining in the cafés, I think of the rest of their anatomies in Hegemish and am inclined to grow stern and not enjoy the music.

Nearly all the people of Hegemish work in these steel mills, half of them through the night and half of them through the day. There are residents, of course, who do other things, such as sell hats, fix automobiles, slice meat, carry garbage away, and even run typewriters. For the steel-makers are a great civic as well as human responsibility. They not only have to be fed and clothed—at a decent profit—but governed, and very correctly governed to boot, as the recent strike revealed. This alone entails difficult though mysteriously lucrative work for a considerable group of patriots.

And there is even a newspaper in Hegemish, as if to belie my reference to the Dark Ages, which tries to provide thoughts for the steel-makers. What this newspaper tries tirelessly to point out is that everybody who has the welfare of the steel-makers at heart and wishes to give them more money, more leisure, and more importance—is their enemy. And that everybody who is against the steel-makers' having any more of anything is their true friend. I suppose from some point of view, to be found in any first-rate and exclusive café, this newspaper is in the right. But the exigencies of my tale keep me from visiting the night clubs, for the time, and from delving any deeper into the problem.

At dawn, half or nearly half the people of Hegemish move as if drawn by a magnet through all the streets and byways of the town toward the great pipe-netted boilers on its borders. One summer at dawn one of these magnetized particles, known to the census-taker as Joe Feeney—Age, 31; Unmarried; Birthplace, Hegemish; Religion, Christian; Nationality, American—was being transported in a crowded steel crate provided by the Hegemish Traction and Electric Company through the Illinois sunrise to the great time clock in Mill Number 1.

He was a skimpy, dried-out, but sinewy young man, with a gaunt face and the immemorial gnomelike stare of the workingman in his black eyes, which, however well he ate, appeared to grow colder and hungrier each year. He was not very clean-looking except for his teeth, which were white and strong and seemed to hint of an undefiled and incorrigible skeleton.

Such was Joe Feeney—all of him but his immortal soul. In writing of that I feel more hesitant than I would have felt some years ago. It is discouraging, in a way, to those of us who were beginning to understand so thoroughly the soul of the workingman, to come head on against the growing notion that he has no soul at all. Here is a fine new kettle of fish for the historian, the psychologist, and the parson. A powerful group of philosophers has arisen in Central Europe and Italy which contends that Joe Feeney's soul is a subversive myth, that all his dreams have been sold him by underhanded Jewish peddlers, and that the sooner he realizes he is an automaton owned by the State, the quicker he will find perfect happiness.

These philosophers have also decided that a human being is practically the same as an anarchist, that the true God is a flag, and the only worthwhile Heaven a battlefield full of dead Frenchmen and Russians.

Another group of philosophers, a little to the east of the foregoing camp, varies this unflattering picture of Joe Feeney by identifying him as an automaton who *owns* the State. In this land he is credited with owning factories, although he still finds it a bit difficult to get enough borsht to eat. He is showered with possessions, including railroads and steamship lines, and informed that all he can behold with his naked eye belongs to him. And in return for all this, all he needs to do is give up the notion that he has any sort of soul.

In fact, both these camps of philosophy, though one hears them assailing each other as if they were the most poles-apart enemies, are in reality agreed on the main point that concerns Joe Feeney. This is that, as a human being, he is a failure and must resign his hard-won delusions of individuality. He must return to the tribe and he must derive his feeling of importance not from himself but from the noise his tribe makes. He must love not himself but the tribe, and be not himself but the tribe.

It would be foolish, of course, to argue that Joe Feeney was being deprived of any considerable possessions when his individual way of looking at things was taken from him. For Feeney in his brief heyday as a soul was no Socrates. Nevertheless, Feeney, deprived of his mind, which perhaps he never had, and of his God, Who probably never existed—Feeney, returned to the tribe which he actually never quite outgrew, has a hapless, frightening air to him. Although at first glance he may seem romantic, as do the savages hopping around a totem pole, there is a hollow look in his eyes as if in giving up the things he never owned he had sacrificed much the better part of him.

All this, of course, is about a Feeney somewhere else. About the Joe Feeney of Hegemish riding to the steel mills on this summer morning there is nothing so final to relate. The philosophers have not yet remodeled him. He has not yet entirely handed over his identity to politics and thrown his heart on the junk pile of tribal conquest. The illusion still bothers him that he is a human being equal to all other human beings, independent of them and yet responsible to them for his thoughts.

And despite his inability to think with any logic on the subject, Feeney is ready—when he is not too tired or too angry—to

identify himself as a man and a philosopher in his own right. The
song of the tribe has not yet crept into his head though it is
everywhere around it. And there is something heroic about this
inattentiveness. There is something heroic about his clinging to
illusion when juicier bones are being offered, and about his standing his ground as a human being when it can be so easily demon-
strated that he is far from being one.

It is well to enjoy this spectacle of his heroism, for it is doubtful if it will last long. And when it is ended, it will be only fair
to remember that it may not be the rival philosophers who remodeled Joe Feeney. The machines and not the crusaders battling for his soul's possession may make Feeney over, and when
he says good-by to Democracy, it may be because the Machines
and the smoke that rises from them and the din they make obscured too completely the fair vision.

This being the true point of my history, I had better return to
it, and to my particular Joe Feeney of Hegemish, Illinois. On
his way to work Feeney, the Citizen and not the Generality,
smoked a cigarette and wondered why his ears were ringing. His
thoughts were, as always, simple and inaccurate. That he had not
slept well for several nights did not occur to him as a cause. And
as for the things that had kept him from sleeping well, Feeney
never thought of them at all. They were odd and subtle things
having to do with matters he had read in the newspapers, which,
as far as he could make out, were forever denouncing him. They
had also to do with his inability to make up his mind which he
hated more—the black print that denounced him or the windbags
in the steel mill calling on him to make counter-denunciations. In
short, he was in a state of confusion from having to decide for
himself who and what he was, and full of a wistfulness that came
from being merely Feeney a human being, rather than Feeney a

cause, Feeney an automaton, or Feeney owner of all the factories.

This question of identities—his own, and who his friends were, and his enemies—may have bewildered him when he had risen from his bed that morning with his ears ringing. He had considered the phenomenon then, and associated it scientifically with heavy drinking. But then he recalled that he had been sober for a long time.

He was still wondering about this when, an hour later, he rode the crane bar across the inferno of crucible drums spitting and sparkling with molten iron some thirty feet below. And Feeney's last thought before he fell from the crane into one of these fulgurating vats was still about this inexplicable ringing in his ears.

"It must be I ate something that don't agree with me," he thought, and fell off the bar on which he was riding, Valkyrie fashion, above the white flames of the drums. An instant later Feeney was no more. Not only had Feeney's soul left him, but his body, too, may be said to have left him. For death in one of these spitting vats is as thorough as dissolution by Black Magic.

Feeney not only died when he sank into the molten iron, but disintegrated promptly, atom by atom. Of all the blood, bone, hair, skin, cords, nails, muscles, sweat, and marrow that had made the biologic arrangement known to the eye as a man, Feeney by name, only a faint odor remained. For a few seconds Joe Feeney lingered in the world as a distasteful odor—and then ceased completely.

Feeney's funeral was held from the ugly house in which he had lived. To be sure, Feeney was not present in fact. But the sentimental satraps who operated the great steel mills insisted that the missing *he* be buried symbolically at their expense. They provided a coffin so that the family might have a focus around which to weep. This coffin, explained the spokesmen for the steel mill operators, was a symbol not only of the non-extant Feeney but also of their respect for the humanity, however devoid of remains, of their employee.

So it happened that the Feeney folk stood about an empty coffin, wept, glanced furtively at one another, the while a quartet, a gift from the bosses, sang hymns imploring the invisible Deity Who looked down on the invisible Feeney to be considerate of His slaughtered lamb. Then later, conforming to the poetical ideas of the steel mill operators, the Feeney folk, still weeping and piously concealing their confusion, followed this same empty coffin through the sun-soiled highways of Hegemish to the burial ground. And here I leave them for a more exciting locale.

It was one of those coincidences that would require a more learned theologian than I to understand, let alone explain, that caused God (for my tale has now gone to Heaven) to cock His ear toward our long-neglected planet and catch sound of the hymn being offered up by the bosses' quartet in the Feeney home.

I say long-neglected planet because that is exactly what the two sad Angels told me. I am not sufficiently interested in the politics of Divinity to refute or even to criticize them. This inclines me to take the word of the Angels and not to bother myself further. It appears that God, being occupied by tremendous problems involving the evangelizing of countless newly spawning planets, had for some hundred years paid no attention to us. It appears that thousands or perhaps hundreds of thousands of abodes for animal matter have been hatching themselves in the far-flung spaces of Infinity; that star and satellite crusts have been cooling and Evolution, one of God's most complex servants, has been turning algae into caterwauling and hysterical images of Himself up and down the nebula-strewn fields of the Universe. (It is difficult to describe such a matter briefly.) And busy with bringing all His new myriads of folk to heel, sending floods, showing Himself in burning bushes, working miracles, haunting dreams, dispatching ghosts and visions, writs and Saviors, and battling divinely to extirpate the primordial beast from these new squirming inhabitants of Space, the Deity, for what to Him must have seemed only the incalculable fraction of an instant, had turned His eyes from us.

I can well imagine that a curious itching must have entered His sublime indifference. Perhaps a tiny earthly soul dropped a tear in the hollow of His infinite palm. Or perhaps His inconceivable ear felt a tingling. At any rate, with a sigh for the vast labors yet to be done among His new worshipers, He turned His attention earthward with some such thought in His cosmic mind as, Oho, how doth that little grain of dust which for long kept blowing in Mine eye? How fare those pretty microcosms of Myself that I breathed into its little mountains and deserts?

It may be, too, that He wondered if it had been wise to indulge Himself in the whim of Evolution. How much simpler had been His rule over the castles of space when He had reigned only as a Mathematician and Master Chemist, concerned but with Fire and Force and the Quantum Theory. Divinity during those happy aeons had offered sweet and abstract pleasures (such as all scientists know) unmarred by this recent need for travel, disputation, and legerdemain. But out of a caprice born of loneliness, or perhaps out of a vanity wearied of being admired by the great Void of Scientific Space, He had, a little while ago, invented Life; hoping, no doubt, to have a neighbor with whom to speak across the awful fences of Eternity, or a child to please His Wisdom with its grateful and tender prattle.

Thus meditating, the Divine Face smiled. For there came to It the touching though somewhat discordant sound of a hymn. He smiled because such tiny, uncouth sounds as these were the rewards of His vast labors.

"How sweet," God said and turned to the two Angels, who, though they are the same Angels you saw over Seventh Avenue, were quite different in Heaven. There they glittered wondrously, and glory erupted not only from their eyes but also like an unimaginable phosphorescence blazed from their wings and enchanting figures.

"A man hath died," he continued, "and they are asking Me to receive him. Go bring Me this man that I may look on My handiwork again and rejoice over its development and loyalty. I wish to hold one of My children in My palm again."

My Angels tell me that the Divine Words spoken lit the Universe in a flare of beauty and that new summers bloomed and bright music sounded through the illimitable pastures of His will and that all space felt blessed. Speedily, more speedily in fact than Earth-bound intellects can calculate with all their obsession for racing, the Angels passed through the tumultuous stretch between Heaven and Hegemish.

They arrived at the Hegemish burial ground just as the local sexton and his helper had lowered the empty coffin, containing nothing more than the mill operators' poetic sentiment for Joe Feeney, into the earth. Lifting it tenderly and in such a clever super-molecular way as to render the operation as well as the coffin invisible, they sped it back to where God waited. They placed the little black box at the feet of God, Who, as a cloud dwindles into a raindrop, made Himself small so that He might speak familiarly to His child.

"Let this little box be opened," He said, "and let him step forth, unafraid."

The Angels tell me that God has no more control over inanimate objects than a housewife and that when He gives such orders to a box it does not open of its own accord any more in Heaven than in my kitchen. It appears He has power (of a sort) only over the Spirit which He has breathed from time to time into Nature. And though He can wilt a plant, overturn a sea, or blast an entire race of humans on any of his multitudinous planets, He has no influence over a box.

But I imagine this has been known to theologians for a long time and I am wasting space reporting this phase of my Angels' tale. Suffice then, that my celestial friends opened the box for Him and that there ensued a pause and that God stared as might any chimneysweep before a miracle, when no man stepped forth and, lo, the box was empty.

I shall not attempt to quote God in any of the further unfoldments of my story, owing not to any lack of information but to a slight embarrassment that takes hold of me when I write His words. Why this should be I do not know, since as a newspaper reporter years ago, it was my duty and privilege to quote, without a twinge, people who spoke not only directly for Him but with His very syllables. This was a little before and during the World War.

At any rate, God, startled by this empty coffin, turned and chid His Angels. He told them they must return to the Earth at once and find His child and bring His child to him for questioning, diagnosis, and judgment. Further, He said, He felt something dark and beyond speculation had happened on our planet in the little instant He had been busy elsewhere. Always, He said, ever since He had undertaken the education of His children, whatever their antics and confusions, these little boxes had brought them back to Him. Yes—God frowned—wherever Man had hidden from Him, in whatever devilish heresies and misconceptions and stubbornnesses, there was one place heretofore he was always to be found—to wit, in this same little box that ended all his tick-tock journeyings and cavortings.

My Angels, more sorely puzzled than since the days of Lucifer's departure, hurried back to Hegemish and, presenting themselves as visiting journalists, made inquiries. Their inquiries led them by nightfall to the large storage sheds of the steel mills. For they learned that Joe Feeney was no longer a man but a steel girder. They learned that his hair, skin, nails, cells, cords, muscles, sweat, and marrow had been consumed to everlasting nothingness by the molten iron into which his body had fallen. And this consuming had taken place so swiftly that—what with God's back being turned for the instant—the soul of Joe Feeney had had no time to extricate itself from the ferocity of the element into which it was plunged. All that had escaped had been a momentary odor and though the Angels, working desperately, succeeded in distilling this whiff from the tremendous stink that hovered over Hegemish, they doubted whether it would be acceptable to God as His child.

Thus imprisoned, Joe Feeney, instead of rising softly and leisurely to his Maker, had been whisked into a mold, pounded by terrific hammers, frozen by arctic blasts, and remelted in roaring furnaces. After a day or so he had emerged as a steel girder and been given a coat of red paint to keep him from rusting or staining.

Having learned all this, my two Angels went looking in the

sheds for Joe Feeney. Here they inspected through the night thousands of girders, all of which seemed devoid of either human features or any spiritual quality. But in the morning, as large cranes were swinging a consignment of these girders on board a railroad flat car, my Angels suddenly beheld Joe Feeney.

Veterans of many a miracle, my celestial friends stared quite open-mouthed at what they saw. A newly painted red girder swinging from its place in the shed to the flat car was dangling from an iron chain in the sun, turning and twisting in such a way as to irk the foreman and increase the hazards of the loading. The odd movements of this girder and the curses of the foreman trying to direct it into its necessary conformity attracted their suspicions immediately. In an instant more they knew their quest was at an end, or—as it turned out—just begun.

Behind the fresh paint of this girder they saw a breath moving as if a curious phantom artery beat faintly within the long bar of steel. This breath was, of course, invisible to the foreman, but my Angels watched it more awed than by the sight of any chimera with which they had, not infrequently, battled. Now the breath darkened the red paint and then it ran like a silver shadow down its length, and the long bar of steel gleamed as if sunlight were within it. When the iron chain finally lowered it into its correct place, the steel bar emitted a sound unlike that of any of the other girders coming to rest, and the Angels, hearing it and acquainted with all the nuances of souls in agony, were full of wonder. For they had never heard this sound before.

My friends were powerless to intervene. No more than God could open a box could they command the movement of inanimate objects. And when, an hour later, the loaded flat car started its travels, my Angels, still disguised as journalists, hid themselves away under the car's body on the rods and rode off with Joe Feeney.

The saga of the Angels who rode the rods from Hegemish to New York is a stormy one. The wrath of God appeared to accompany this flat car and to precipitate all manner of disturbances in Illinois, Michigan, Ohio, Pennsylvania, New Jersey, through all the territories passed. Rivers flung themselves over dikes and dams and there were upheavals. Meteors peppered the tracks and flames shot out of the dark. Roadbeds washed away and bridges crumpled like match sticks. Lightning struck and the thunder never ceased. Never before in its history had the New York Central been so taxed to keep its right of way open. Time and again the flat car on whose rods our Angels rode rolled into newly formed gutters and gullies, stood up on end and bent itself over unexpected holes in the earth. Gangs of diggers and gangs with torches and sledges attended the stumbling and collapse of this freight car, threw up new bridges, filled in all the holes, removed all the meteors, sidetracked all the floods, and, waving green lanterns, sped Joe Feeney eastward.

It was a full six months before the flat car, scarred, bent, and creaking valiantly, arrived in New York. Joe Feeney was still on board. Once in New York, my Angels tried to communicate with the Divine Intelligence. But attune themselves however they might, not a spark of the distant Wisdom reached them. This Divine indifference, an everyday matter to the citizens of the great city to which they had come, appeared to the Angels as something sinister and unintelligible. They spent many hours praying eagerly to God and beseeching Him for a little guidance and, if He thought it wise, some increase in their powers. And when nothing resulted, no single flash or murmur from on high, they fell to discussing their dilemma sadly but carefully, for though the Almighty avoided answering them, they were convinced He could overhear all their words and even their thoughts.

It is curious, one of the Angels argued, that God, Who is so attentive to all the details of Heaven, should reveal such indifference to this most important matter on Earth. And discussing the various reasons for the phenomenon, they finally agreed on one that they felt certain would not anger God, in case He overheard it. This was that the Deity found intervention in the affairs of the World distasteful—an attitude they could well understand. For in their dartings about as journalists they had observed a multitude of matters which anyone with the knowledge or memory of Heaven in him would most certainly have regarded with repugnance. I hasten to write that my Angels were not referring to morals when they came to this conclusion, for of morals they had no knowledge and, like God Himself, were unaware that they existed.

What the Angels believed to be repugnant to God, as it was to themselves, was the unwholesome look of everything, the incredible ugliness of streets and buildings—in fact, the entire manmade face of the World. It was, they said, difficult for them to believe that any form of life could flourish on such a planet, so dreary and inhospitable was its aspect.

After a short time another thought came to both Angels. If God is indifferent to us, they reasoned, He must be even more indifferent to these children He has allowed to hatch amid all these bramble bushes of steel and to thrive so astonishingly within all these towering coffins of stone. And with God's face so averted and none of His Wisdom guiding the affairs of men, how amazing it was that there were any affairs at all. And they felt a renewed interest in the hordes of figures that crowded a city and managed to exist so miraculously without any attention from Him.

Their final thought on the matter was that, though God appeared to ignore them, it was stupid of them to pretend they did not know His Will. His orders had been explicit and they decided to quit their fretful pleas to Him and be content with what they knew. God wanted His child delivered into His palm and there was nothing to be gained by asking Him to repeat His command. More practically, both Angels agreed that to harass the Infinite with pleas for further instructions might result only in further displays of anger.

So my Angels settled down quietly to wait. They had no concrete plan, but out of the great mutability of existence they felt certain something would turn up that would be helpful. Two weeks elapsed during which they stood constantly watching Joe Feeney, knowing how difficult it would be to locate him if they lost sight of him again. They indulged in some half-hearted invocation and legerdemain such as in the olden aeons of their Divine association they had used to influence the chemistries and forces of the Universe. None of these moved the steel girder to any response. It lay there with Joe Feeney inside it, as indifferent to their wooing as if it were the devil's own tail.

But in the third week Joe Feeney moved. He was lifted up and loaded into a truck and with some forty other girders taken away through streets and tunnels. The truck stopped on Seventh Avenue, backed up over a sidewalk, and whistles began blowing. My Angels had some days earlier exchanged their journalistic exteriors for invisibility, in which they felt much more at home. Thus they were sitting (invisible) beside the driver of the truck when it stopped on Seventh Avenue. Looking through the little window in the rear of the driver's seat, my Angels observed that

Joe Feeney had been singled out for some new distinction. An iron chain was being carefully wrapped around him. And as they watched, Joe Feeney began to rise slowly from the truck.

Quickly leaving their seats, my Angels joined him, hovering invisibly at each of his ends, as he dangled in the air from the chain. They had been ascending in this manner for several minutes when my Angels felt a common wave of delight. It suddenly struck them that their vigil was over. Joe Feeney was rising. Almost unprecedented though such an action was, God had decided to pull Joe up to Heaven, and my Angels began to hum softly those beatific melodies which usher souls into Paradise. They marveled briefly at the slowness of the ascent, for at this rate enormous periods of time—even by their reckoning—would be consumed before they came as far as the first outposts of Infinity. Yet they clung to their places without questioning, their voices swelling into hosannas, their eyes shining with the glory of their mission as they escorted Joe Feeney to the waiting palm of God.

Then suddenly, just as they were about to peal out on their trumpets, made from their hollow wing feathers, their first triumphant signal to the Deity of their coming, Joe Feeney paused. He hung twisting from his iron chain for moments. Then he swung swiftly toward a skeleton of steel that stood like some chimera's nest brushing the clouds. Here hands seized him and in a twinkling Joe Feeney lay quietly and symmetrically as part of a thin, criss-cross pattern that disappeared into a little vortex of ground far below.

Stunned by this unexpected interruption in their triumphal march to Heaven, the Angels hovered while Joe Feeney was snatched forever from God's grace. (Not forever, exactly, but that fact rather anticipates the ending of my story. Let me say, forever as far as paper and ink and readers are concerned.)

They watched sparks and hammers, fire and force, weld Joe Feeney to the other girders; nail, bolt, and fuse him as solidly as any ocean-bottom rock to the ocean floor. They watched Joe Feeney being riveted into the chimera's nest that almost touched the clouds. Then days and nights passed. Rain fell. Snow drifted down. Winds howled. The clouds breathed icily. Hovering motionless, my Angels watched Joe Feeney reduced to utter immobility but with a silver shadow still running the length of his red paint. Then men appeared. Stone appeared, and Joe Feeney was blotted out. The tallest building in New York, within whose topmost roof support Joe Feeney lay hidden, was done. Its windows were washed. Faces appeared in them and lights, and the metronome world of the great tower got under way and soon its high spearhead of windows was a familiar and monotonous sight to all within and without. Artists photographed and painted it, and poets sang its fearful symmetries and cried its dimensions as if inches were the banners of beauty.

A few years have gone since these events. Apparently nothing is known of all I have told you except to those who have paused and remained looking aloft for seven hours. These—there have not been many—have seen the two Angels, growing sootier and dingier with the seasons, for Seventh Avenue is no Riviera even for Celestial Beings. And such as have seen them have come away chastened but confused, unable even to theorize on the wherefore of two Angels in so odd a locale.

This, then, is their story and the answer. They are waiting for Joe Feeney. Though they have received no instructions from God, their duty lies forever in their hearts. They must wait for Joe Feeney. They must wait till this tallest of buildings some day crumbles or is beaten down by more ambitious hammers than reared it.

They must follow Joe Feeney as he hurtles on that day back to Earth and remain with him as he lies for a breather on some junk pile. And still follow him when he is remelted, reassembled, and twisted into new shapes for new uses. They must be at his side when again hands discard him and toss him back on the junk pile.

On and on through all his behammered and beforged mutations until that day arrives when the molten steel which once consumed the atoms of Joe Feeney in its spitting vat is itself consumed in the great vat of Time, my Angels must hover and wait at his side. Then when this girder lies in some tangle of refuse, refuse of an Era, and when it begins to rust slowly to nothing; when its brutality becomes dust and its uniform of violence falls from it, emitting in its final crumble a faint puff as of magician's smoke—then Joe Feeney will be free. Joe Feeney will stretch his cramped 'soul, and the breath that besilvered a bar of steel will taste night and dew and Infinity.

And on that day, looking with half-rusted eyes and chilled soul bewilderedly about, Feeney will find my two Angels waiting. They will be waiting to escort him, battered trumpets pealing, to the Palm of God, Who, I hope, will still be interested in a sight of His child.

THE LITTLE CANDLE

N THAT
dreadful July morning when

we Jews opened our morning newspapers to see what kind of face the world had made overnight we expected to read the usual accounts of other people's troubles, and a few of our own. For the newspapers had lost their innocence for us Jews. Where to most of the readers the newspapers propped beside their coffee cups contained the legendary doings of those men-in-the-moon and their womenfolk who perform the daily stint of murders and marvels, for us Jews the journals had to offer a little more concrete excitement.

As we opened our eyes in bed on that July morning, we knew there would be present that cloud of anti-Semitism offered by the editors like some fascinating weather report as News of the Day. And out of this cloud would stare at us the faces of Hitler and his co-philosophers, informing us again of the latest measures for coping with the loathsomeness of the Jew. They had been staring at us out of our morning newspapers for a number of years and insulting us with a tirelessness that, however boring it may have grown to other readers, kept us Jews constantly grimacing as if we had a stomach ache.

We had grown used, by this July morning, to staring back at these philosophers who despised us so garrulously. And many of us had achieved the stoicism of our ancestors, that quality which in facing disaster is the least exhausting. Yet, callous as we had come to seem while regarding the cloud in our morning newspapers, at the sight of it there came always the feeling into our hearts of a momentary dreamlike illness, as if the smoke of the Dark Ages rising from the tormented figure of Israel still lay in the air.

The faces of those who hate us are bad for our digestion and for our thinking. There are many such faces in our history. But then in our history they are all dead. It is easier to look on them.

However they gleam and snarl and however loaded with villainies their names, we have survived them and we may smile triumphantly, like all survivors, and think of them not as figures of evil, spreading terror among the helpless, but as poor little cadavers overrun with maggots. And we may read, for our solace, that they were Monsters and that Posterity has been pleased to verify the opinions of their many victims.

Yet with all this as part of our history and part of our daily breakfast we were unprepared for what we were to read on this July morning. We stared with nausea and disbelief at the print. For when we opened our newspapers we found that the cloud we had watched so long and, in a way, so aloofly, had grown suddenly black and dreadful and immense. It filled all the pages of the journals. The world had made, it seemed, but a single face overnight and this face thrust itself into our breakfast hour, ugly and hellish. Like a monster evoked out of the smoking pages of our history, it confronted us, exultant and with the ancient howl of massacre on its lips.

We learned that overnight some five hundred thousand Jews had been murdered in Germany, Italy, Rumania, and Poland. Another million or so had been driven from their homes and hunted into forests, deserts, and mountains. Thousands lay wounded and dying everywhere. More thousands, having seen their loved ones butchered and decapitated under their eyes, had taken leave of their senses and were howling like animals behind the barbed wire of concentration camps into which they had been clubbed.

This great International Pogrom had taken place under the auspices of the four Nazi-Fascist governments and was the flower of a long and careful series of conferences among the thinkers of the countries involved. The need to purge these lands of the contaminating Jew—finally and forever—had become so urgent that to have delayed any longer would have been to endanger the racial welfare of all Germans, Rumanians, Italians, and Poles. So the mad face with the comedian's mustache, called the Fuehrer, informed us.

The extirpating of the Jews had been carefully planned. All places where the contaminating Jew lived, slept, ate, kept a shop or office, worshiped, sang, or labored had been noted down months ago. All the centers of Jewry had been slyly invested by well-equipped regiments.

At an hour agreed upon long in advance, the bayonet, musket, bomb, gas, shell, and cannon of the four nations had launched the Purge.

The first accounts of the five hundred thousand murders and million refugees still fleeing before the terror naturally contained a minimum of political and philosophical comment from those in charge of the mass executions. But Germany, whose propaganda division once hatched a victory on the North Sea before the battle was over, was ready as always. The sages in charge of creating world opinion did not neglect to let their public know at once the deeper significance of the work that had been done.

True, as the androgynous Hitler immediately announced, the bloodstream of Europe was now cleansed of the hobgoblin strain of Semitism. But it was apparent even in the first barrage of headlines and extras that something even greater had happened.

This was that a second Crucifixion had taken place. The Jews had been put to death merely as an accessory. On the Cross, looming above the half-million corpses, the True Victim was to be seen—the phantom Christ with His now muted cry of love and brotherhood. It was against the Christian philosophy that the dictators had risen, and the murder of half a million helpless men and women was the proof offered of their revolt.

The Jew was no more. His back had been broken. Like a dog run over, he would writhe awhile in the dusty roads of the world and then expire forever. Thus spoke one German theologian. Never again would the sly humanitarianism by which the Jew and other weaklings of the world had sought to drag the superior races down to their own level lame the soul of Europe. No more devitalizing internationalism, no more decadent peace talk, no more anti-power creeds masquerading as brotherly love. The Jews had been Christ-profiteers. So said another German theologian in their epitaph. No oriental Christ would rule in Europe any more. Jew and Christ had perished together.

Such was the message that bade the world rejoice over its deliverance. But for the most part the press, to which the currents of philosophy are but a tiny and confused trickle of ink in a hidden editorial page, confined itself to bloodshed rather than significance.

In its paragraphs the wounded still screamed, the maddened still tore their faces, and the corpses, piled high in homes and highways, still lay with one foot in our hearts.

There were items of synagogue bombings and ghetto burnings, of the blind being put out of asylums to run before bayonets in the streets, of Hebrew school benches vacated forever by machine guns, of shopkeepers covered with kerosene burning noisily amid their wares, of doctors, lawyers, actors, teachers, scientists, and artists who, with clubs and steel, had been taught their new place, in the ranks of the dead.

There were tales and tales from north, east, west, and south, from great towns and small, from manufacturing districts, from places prettily famed for cathedrals, museums, universities, their history, or the beauty of their scenery. All those places were so scattered and so far-flung that the whole of Europe seemed suddenly to have become one vast trap whose thousand cities, like a thousand springs, had snapped off the head of Jewry overnight.

The tales continued in the afternoon press. Its columns took on a classic air. Out of the jumble of reported martyrdoms and sadistically related scenes of murder, there arose the strange and awesome picture of a race being put to death, of a great and ancient people in whose veins had lingered for so long the earliest words and image of God, dying like a single child on a single bayonet.

When the spokesmen for the Nazi-Fascist lands proclaimed that the back of the Jew had been broken (that back which had survived so many burdens), broken now finally and forever, they were not referring alone to those thousands of devastated bodies the crusaders had piled up in the streets.

By the broken-backed Jew they meant all of us—all of us who, like quicksilver under the ancient hammers of intolerance, had long ago, cringingly and yet defiantly, spread into the corners of the earth.

We had begotten and thrived in these corners into almost un-Jewish generations. The cringe of our souls had vanished or persisted only in those mysterious grimaces of fear which convulse the underworlds of our spirit. This handful of psychopathic hours we considered, thankfully, a small enough heritage of the evil centuries.

Thriving and learning the speech and even dreams of many lands, we had endured a vague but tenacious social obloquy with increasing unconcern. This discrimination against our presence in certain centers and the slight distaste for our persistently historic features on the part of those impromptu-faced races among whom we lived, were harmless enough ghosts of rack, thumb screw, and auto-da-fé.

Then slowly by our wits and our sometimes too facile talents, by the basic tenderness and sensitiveness of our bloodstream (inclined to turn the more timorous of us into toadies of those who liked us a little and hysterical disciples of any ideals that tolerated us a little), by these and many other of our racial charms, we had won a pleasant nod of recognition from the rest of humanity.

Thus, in the days preceding this July morning, we were in many parts of the earth making excellent progress in the rehabilitation of God's favored image. But we who had gone to sleep the night before on the borrowed pillows of civilization woke in the Dark Ages.

The echo of the great Pogrom crossed the seas and continents and sought us out in all the lands of the Gentiles. It came howling into our Long Island estates and New York penthouses. Its phantom bayonets charged into our offices and into all the high places we had won by our wits and talents. Its phantom bombs exploded in our humbler abodes, in our shops and stores and merry kitchens. And though none of our heads rolled from our shoulders, an ancient wound in our souls opened, and manhood, won through centuries of patience and struggle, drained from our depths.

It is folly to say that all Jews are related and that a mysterious umbilical cord ties us all together like a mob of wriggling Siamese twins. There is in us, however, a common denominator and a fraternalism curiously vital.

In our capacity for feeling each other's wounds we seem unhappily to resemble the growths of the lichen of which the biologists write. When in Norway a disease affects the lichen, causing its monocells to pale and wither, an exactly similar distress will overtake the lichen in Massachusetts and the Argentine.

This gravely mystifies the botanists, who exchange cablegrams and later treatises on the curious kinship of the world's lichen, and who evolve, I am sure, the theory that the disease is carried not by swift-traveling bacilli, but is caused by the relation of all lichen to some force invisible, some reservoir of destiny that influences the entire species as the moon influences all the waters of the world.

Among us there is a similar relationship to such a reservoir of destiny. For we are, as a race, almost as old and unchanged a growth as the lichen and have had time, apparently, to evolve an extraneous soul to which we respond as the seas to the moon. This extraneous soul is not so mysterious as in the case of the lichen. It is, in the main, to be measured and identified though it may own certain qualities beyond our psychological yardsticks.

Our extraneous soul is the attitude of the world toward us—the glint in our host's eye. Though among us there may be disparities of body, mind, and fortune—great barriers even, put up by culture and snobbery—in the eyes of our hosts we are all Jews. And in whatever guise we come to their tables we remain to them and to their servants, Jews. This unwavering classification, not in our own hearts but in theirs, is our kinship; and the most detached of us embrace it, more often in despair than in delight, as our pathetic racial strength.

On this July morning we were Jews again, whatever our previous conceptions of ourselves had been; Jews, battered and crushed and exiled once more from the pretense of fellowship. Not only was there in us that common denominator that echoed the cries of agony and death, that sent our spirits cowering beside the myriads of unknown Jews in the shambles of Europe, but the eyes of our host, however compassionate, segregated us into sudden ghettos of grief.

There was, too, a great devitalizing shame. As always in the days of all our stricken history, we had no armies to move forward to avenge our murdered selves. Scattered and impotent we lay, refugees all. All our fortunes and talents were useless. Our egoism could blow no trumpets. With all our champions, all our heroes of prize rings and stages, counting rooms and tribunals, our veterans of many wars, our dead on others' battlefields; all our record of achievement, culture, genius, and humanity, we must stand idle and die without firing a shot or uttering a battle cry. It was this that helped to break our backs.

We knew that our impotence as a people, forgotten in the noise of our individual triumphs, would again react like a mysterious death on our separate souls. However loud the cry of sympathy from the Gentiles around us, their eyes turning to us demanded something we had not in our being; demanded we become as they—a nation—and make a fight of it; demanded we die valorously together who knew only how to die humbly and apart.

This demand made our heads hang as if before the swords of the Pogrom rather than the compassion of our neighbors. We knew that our souls, lacking battlefields on which to die, were drained even more deeply.

As news of the mass murders continued into a second July day we heard, under the cries of protest echoing from our host's church and state, a murmur that sickened us. We in New York lived in the brightest light of equality that had yet shone on us since our disinheritance. Yet here where our racial brand had been almost obliterated as a mark of obloquy, a mysterious anger began to light the eyes of the Gentiles.

It was the anger of the bully, the anger that weakness inspires —the ancient human impulse to stamp out that which is maimed and unable to defend itself. It is an anger, this anger toward the helpless, which mystically vivifies the egos of its owners. It improves their morale as if it were the glow of a battle they had nobly won. The presence of defeat arouses, however illogically, the victor in them. And in their contempt for those who have been vanquished they find a pleasing measure of their own superiority.

Our impotence, our pallor and tears that so stirred their compassion, appeared to reach deeper into them than their hearts and to release from the hidden places of their being an ancient sadism.

Then, too, there was another reason for many of them to turn against us. This was the need among the leaders of industry and finance for extricating themselves from the centuries of Christian morality which they had long found incompatible with their economic war. Tolerance, kindliness, aspirations toward love of one's fellowman, and a belief in human equality and human brotherhood were a difficult credo for the money-weighted minority battling fearfully to retain its rights as exploiters and inheritors. How answer the insidious demands of the poor when the mouths of the strong were stopped with pious phrases and democratic proverbs sired by Christianity? By ridding themselves of the spiritual incubus of Christ and all his politicians, by overthrowing in their own souls the old ideals of Christianity, these industrial captains and their mercenaries could reach for mastership with no Sermons to weaken the arm of their Law. And this hatred of Jews was a heady exercise—a first vital step in the anti-humanitarianism the upper classes were finding more and more necessary in their struggle to remain on top. Thus in addition to the contempt our impotence aroused, and the sadism our wounds inspired, we offered the Fascist-minded of our countrymen a dumping ground for ideals they must discard, we offered them a honing stone for their cruelty and mastership. And we began to hear everywhere around us the unreason which, in our travail as much as in our palmier days, called us loathsome, and the mania which found us undesirable.

It was on the third day, with the newspapers crying out to us promises of English, French, and American reprisals, boycotts, state reprimands, leagues for our protection, that the Pogrom finished us. Swept by an exultation with which murder alone can light the spirit, the Nazi-Fascists brought their machine guns into the concentration camps and finished the work of the first night. Another hundred or two hundred thousand Jews (none kept count) tumbled like little archaic dominoes before an all-day shriek of bullets. And the Nazi-Fascist spokesmen, swooning with the power of their crime, raised priestly voices and thundered the holiness of their cause into the world. A marvelous eloquence lit their words. A sense of Vision and Obsession now came into the newspapers, and the intellectual side of the massacre dominated the mere physical drama of the event. These arguments became even more powerful against us than their regiments had been. Their Word ruined us.

They spoke of the world, afflicted for centuries by the Semite, being now delivered, being now rid of a stubborn malcontent and poison-bearing breed. There were Jews still alive, but let them tie their belongings into little packs to sling over their shoulders—and wander; wander as the scum people of the earth and hatch in caves and forests; hide themselves as the condemned of the world and the repudiated of a new, fresh humanity.

We made no little packs of our belongings and we did not wander (not yet). But our souls crept into caves and forests and even in the streets of the new world which we half owned we

moved condemned and repudiated. The strength of our finest
egos was not sufficient to stand firm. There was none of our
Champions who would ever raise his eyes again. We were again
in gaberdine and yellow hat, again marked, again on that ancient
trail of the oppressed that leads through the back of the world;
again with furtive eyes for our fellowmen and defeat for our
daily bread.

But even at such times the Jews, who have a tradition for
every gesture and every bite of food, however bitter, are not
without a prescribed pattern of action. It is written that when
the Jew is about to die in droves, he must pray. They prayed
now. They filled the synagogues with a chanting older than any
fictions of the world. Covered with tallithes they wept and im-
plored their Jehovah. They stood on their feet and bent their
bodies backward and forward in a continuous rhythm and
seemed, as always, when at their praying, trees being blown
almost to the ground by a strong wind.

All the synagogues of all the lands were filled. In all of them
rose the mad sing-song of Jewish agony. Many wise and holy men
stood before many scattered altars and intoned and wept. But
there was no congregation that prayed louder and sent their
hearts climbing the stairs of Heaven more ecstatically than the
fifty old men who filled the little hall called the B'nai Israel in
the City of New York.

This was as tiny a tabernacle as Jerusalem had ever spawned.
It stood in the lower East Side of New York. It was a one-story
structure made of wood and hardly taller than a man's hat. Its
roof sagged. Its walls bulged, and it faced the street with two
dusty windows and a battered unpainted door. It seemed to
crouch on its knees, in the midst of the tenements that sur-

rounded it, like a beggar in rags peering cautiously out of an alley way.

It was an old synagogue and its importance as a center of worship had long vanished. Tabernacles of brick and stone had sprung up in the neighborhood and even temples full of elegant furnishings had blossomed in this East Side in the century since the B'nai Israel was built. But this shack of a synagogue, rakish and pathetic in its poverty, had persisted, seeming through the years to become more and more the symbol of a race whom Christ had crucified.

Mysteriously, too, it had always had enough worshipers to keep it occupied, not only on Saturday mornings and through the frequent holidays, but every day. This was because the members who contributed their few dollars toward its continuance were old men, released from the terrible toil in which their days had been passed and owing no duties to life other than those they observed in the synagogue. Some were very old, so old that they had been brought to this country as luxuries carried on the backs of their children, and some, after a middle age spent here in the service of their families, in small stores, over workbenches and over pushcarts of insignificant wares, had slipped into the skull caps and pious habits of their fathers, and were spending their last years as they had spent their first, in the study of God's Word.

At dawn they gathered to say the prayers said facing the east, and facing the west they sang the praises of the Lord at eventide, and hurt no man. Innocently, they divided their days in going back and forth between their homes and the synagogue, the very old among them sometimes forgetting to eat, spending whole days in a corner of the synagogue, turning the pages

of a Hebrew book. In some homes they were revered, according
to the refinement of their natures and of those among whom
they lived. In others they were derided as aimless shuffling idlers,
stupid and unworldly, though they were as wise as the professors of Alexandria. The old men no longer noticed these matters. They lived in a world of their own, save when occasionally
they fastened their eyes and hearts on a child, the eternal small
boy who is the hope of every Jewish home.

Their world was the synagogue. Seldom did they appear anywhere else. Occasionally, one of these elderly children was to be
seen, lost on his way to a bookstore perhaps, deaf as an owl, and
guided through traffic by a policeman. Or sometimes, their eyes
far away, they stood with an umbrella over their arm at a
funeral. But it was in the synagogue that they were alive. As
other old men sit smiling in the sun, they sat happily in the decay and murky shadows of the ancient house of God. Some
of them had grown a little foolish perhaps. Like old horses
turned out to pasture they even frolicked a little in their fields
of learning, they disputed loudly over some minor behavior at
the Passover, they harangued one another about the Talmud,
or spoke a contemptuous phrase for Alexander of Macedon, or
an oath, accompanied by a sudden expectoration, for the name
of Titus of Rome.

Some among them were scholars of religion, latter-day Scribes,
who spoke only when properly addressed, and then only about
the Mosaic law. It was old men such as they who had followed
the True Candelabrum out of Rome, accompanied by a child,
who might see it with his own eyes, so that its image might be
preserved. It was such as they who through the long years of
the disappearance of the Talmud had committed to memory the
entire work. As long as they lived, or a child beside them to

whom they could pass on a proverb or relate a custom, the Word would not be lost.

Had any honest Jewish ghost of fifth-century Vandalland or Gaul peered in through the dusty windows of this synagogue on this July day, it would have seen nothing new, nothing changed. It would have seen, too, faces as familiar as its own ghostly image, faces whose persistent historic look belittled now as always the garments they wore, and gave their owners the air of seeming in dingy masquerade. And on this July evening, it would have caught an even more familiar sound than the unchanging voice of prayer. This was the sound of grief, of agonized expostulation with the self-same Lord who was visiting the self-same trials on these, His orthodox children.

The old men, who had wept for all the personal griefs, who had labored, and flown in insect-like flights out of far-away lands; they, who had buried sons, and sat in vigil by sickbeds, and sorrowed without ending, now wept for Israel. With tiny grief-stricken eyes shedding sad tears, they sang high with their old shattered voices, and wept and prayed and bowed their backs before the altar of the Lord.

Prayer after prayer went up, called from the depths of their old bodies. The night came, hot and stirring the reek of decay in the old house of worship, but the Elders kept their feet. For their Rabbi, still clothed in his white tallith, held his back to them and his face to God as he bent and unbent in his service before the Ark.

This Rabbi was Ben Ezra, tall, lank-framed, aged, and bearded; long-nosed and with eyes wide apart; and feared by the fifty Elders beyond any power on earth; feared, indeed, as much as he was venerated. For Rabbi Ben Ezra was a great man. His greatness lay not merely in leading the prayers and knowing meticulously all the forms of faith. These all of them knew equally well. Their Rabbi was a great man because they felt behind his wide forehead the presence of God.

Other synagogues might boast of marbled walls and pillars and of beautiful columns and stone steps, of tall windows always cleaned and of fine carvings. But none could produce a Ben Ezra. None could produce a man so wise, so holy, and so modest.

And what made Ben Ezra even greater than this was that his greatness was known only to them. He shunned the light of the world and sought not beyond the sagging walls of his synagogue for admiration. Tales of his learning, long become legends with their constant telling, filled them with that wild, secret pride which is the hard-won treasure of the orthodox.

Where were the books Ben Ezra had not read? Where the philosophies he had not studied and mastered? Where in all the world was there an idea, a dream, even a heresy, their Rabbi had not tasted?

In the single room in which he lived alone and which the Elders took turns in cleaning and visiting, their Rabbi had sat for fifty years reading and contemplating and feeding his spirit as one might feed a sacred flame. What Temple was there in the world more beautiful than the all-knowing soul of their leader? And where was there a pulpit in all of scattered Israel over which such a hero presided as over their own worn and dingy block of wood?

Yet with all this, he asked for no subservience. His voice, since the oldest of them could remember, had been always gentle. He alone of the congregation had never been known to lose his temper, to scold, to complain, or to shame his flock. Beside him, the wisest of these Talmudists felt small as the sparrow before the eagle and unlearned as the child before the father. When he spoke, their minds, cramped by the swaddling theologies of their faith, felt a larger vision knocking for entrance.

So it was that on this black day they put their trust in Rabbi Ben Ezra. With souls grateful and humble they huddled before him, asking only to pray in his presence. True, their hearts were little and frightened. To some of them, so archaic were their old heads and so little sense had they of the nuances that made some Gentiles better than others, the Pogrom seemed already to have entered the streets outside. But had they not been led once out of Egypt and through the Red Sea?

Rabbi Ben Ezra was with them. What if a Power Invisible breathed on the sagging threshold outside? For so it began to seem to them after a long day of sorrow and terror. What even if this Power should come inside with sword raised and death grimacing beside it? Within their leader's heart the great and unwavering truth of God had its tabernacle. They were old men, but had he only signaled, they would have risen and uttered proudly the prayers to the Lord prescribed for the hour of massacre. Tallithes over their heads, their eyes turned inward, they would have died avowing their strange belief that they were the Chosen of God.

As evening deepened, the sound of prayer and lamentation increased. In the candle-lighted shadows waving over the suppliants' heads, the little synagogue seemed to drift further and further into the past. Finally the Rabbi straightened and turned slowly and looked down on the fifty old men swaying rhapsodically in the shadowed room, their white shawls flapping like the sails of little foundering ships.

He stood watching quietly. His eyes were opened wide but no light was in them. He stood as if alone in a curious silence. Then he raised his hand.

The tear-stained faces ceased gradually their cries and movement. No longer did the book leaves rustle. The bent backs straightened.

Ben Ezra spoke.

Something shocking was happening. Impiously he addressed his flock from the altar in Yiddish. He said wearily that he wished them to leave.

"Be good Jews," he said, in the almost vulgar phrasing of the streets. "Go home. Go home at once. Don't loiter in the synagogue. Close the doors. Don't ask me any questions. Tomorrow you may return."

The fifty Jews stared at each other. They had prayed beside their leader in the divine language. When they stopped, it had been with exaltation in their hearts. Almost they had expected a miracle. They had waited for his message. And he had spoken to them as if they had been a bunch of fish peddlers. The sharp pang of embarrassment succeeded the historic grief on their features. The scholars hung their heads.

An old man, feeling suddenly lost, began to whimper in the mother tongue, asking querulously what God willed from them, only blood and blood? Suddenly he threw his book of prayer to the floor. Others led him away. In the doorway, some of the more timid, looking like tradesmen now and not Scribes, hesitated. Murder and torture seemed to wait outside the very door. If the Rabbi sent them from the synagogue, where were they to go?

The Rabbi remained silent.

And such was the habit of obedience and veneration among

his followers that they went. Straight into the unwelcoming world outside, into the very heart of their fears, they stepped over the threshold and were gone. Among them were some so wise and so divining that they seemed to make a little circle in the doorway as they passed on with head bowed, as if they had made room for a ghost.

Doubt and coldness were in the Rabbi's eyes; coldness and indifference to his flock. He too had felt and seen the ghost and had not driven it from the door. It was not the ghost from Vandalland of the fifth-century Jew, not the ghostly curiosity-seeker who might have peered in through dusty windows to see who and what they were who prayed within. It was a ghost of many meanings, a ghost of the new dead, and the old . . . of the hatred that, like a foaming hound at Israel's heels, had pursued him down the centuries, of the heroism and faith that had wrung only deeper contempts and more humiliating punishments from all his enemies. It was a ghost of the tallith-covered Jew wading through his own blood to Where? Praying through his own agony to What? Standing exiled from the soul of humanity and turning for friendship to Whom?

The last ones to pass over the threshold turned and saw their Rabbi calmly lighting the seven candles in the altar candelabrum. But though they turned, no cry came out of the past in their Rabbi's heart, no tardy call to bring them back to faith and sacrifice.

In the night streets the old men dispersed. They dwindled to bent little figures shuffling through the ghetto shadows. In all the homes beside them, through open windows, they heard the weeping of the Jews. On the street corners the newsboys cried out in an unfamiliar language the news of the familiar horror.

When he was alone in his synagogue, Rabbi Ben Ezra stood

looking at the empty little house of worship. Slowly, with calm fingers, as a woman might remove her finery after an overlong night of entertainment, he took from his shoulders the white silk prayer shawl and folded it neatly on the altar. His eyes rested a moment on the tassels of its edges which he had so often kissed. He tucked these tassels under the silk so they were no longer visible. He removed the black skull cap from his head. Bareheaded and rid of his holy vestments, he then turned toward the little cupboard above the altar in which lay the velvet-covered twin scrolls of the Torah whose every sacred word was known to him. In this Torah was written the definition of God that had exhausted the Jewish mind for a thousand years in its writing.

He stood thus for many minutes, his long thin bearded face gleaming like some medieval necromancer's in the light of the seven-branched candelabrum, symbol of the candlestick of Moses stolen from Jerusalem almost two thousand years ago. There was no fervor in his eyes, and his face lifted to the blessed Torah was cold. Because of the grace of his mind and depth of his wisdom, the old scholar neither scowled nor sneered in this great hour of his blasphemy.

In his heart the Rabbi was not questioning God or seeking to solve the mystery of His ways. He was judging Him coldly, out of the accumulation of wisdom reaching into the shadows of history. Since it was his habit to speak his thoughts aloud, the Rabbi spoke alone in the synagogue, eyes raised to the Torah. He spoke in Hebrew and addressed God, Whose Face was in the scrolls.

"I am an old man," he said. "I have served You as my fathers before me. I have studied the confusing words in which You have made Your Truth known. Since I was a child I have sought to see into these words and behold the spirit out of which they were crudely born. I have read much, thought much, and prayed more. My spirit is clean. My mind is informed. My heart, though heavy with the pain of my race, does not bid me cry out in anger. It weeps quietly in a corner of my being. For the heart of the Jew is a little child lost in a great darkness. It must cry, not because it is afraid, but because the father it loved has left it to flounder beside a lonely road. Though You hear its tears You ignore them. They are not for You. They are my own tears and I shed them within me."

The old Rabbi paused, for he thought he heard a sound as of winds blowing. Then he resumed.

"It is written that Your children shall stand for judgment before You," he said. "I, who am old and ready to appear for Your subtle decision, have no fear of that near hour. But before I go to Your glorious house to be judged, here in this little decaying house I have summoned You tonight for judgment. I, Ben Ezra, stand by the altar of my fathers and pass judgment on You."

Again the old Rabbi paused, for the sound he had fancied before came to his ears more loudly. A wind was blowing in the synagogue. It made the old walls creak. The candle flames around the walls one by one stretched eagerly and vanished. There were left only the seven candles in the candelabrum.

"It is a summer hurricane," said the Rabbi, and went on.

"I speak only for a little group of Your children . . ." he said, "a mere handful of all the creatures with whom You have covered Your earth. Jews, they call us. But of all the myriads who have sung Your name in different tongues, and perhaps in no tongue at all, and made offering to You in dreams as varied as the clouds of Heaven, this little group has been the most eager, the most loyal, and the most attentive to Your existence."

As he spoke the wind seemed to harass the doors and windows of the ancient structure. The walls fell to groaning, almost as if they had a voice.

"True, true . . ." the voice seemed to utter.

"When long ago we were the first to write Your Name in the Torah," said the old Rabbi, closing his eyes, "we did not offer ourselves vaingloriously as Your discoverers. We knew that You have always been in the hearts of men and even beasts, gleaming therein fitfully like a light that burns, exalts, and confuses. We did not discover You, but with Your help defined You a little better than many definitions of Your meaning already loud in the world. This Definition, however incomplete it may be, and however dimmed at times by the pride and stupidity of my people, we have preserved."

"True," the walls of the temple seemed to sigh around him.

"I hear Your Voice," said the Rabbi, "but You are an Illusion." After a while he continued.

"In preserving this Definition," he spoke, "we have exhausted ourselves. We have preserved little else. The knowledge that we had the true Word in our keeping made us arrogant, divorced us from humanity, and set us apart as a curious and irritating survival of an epoch discarded. We are like the remains of a feast that refuses to be swept away.

"But arrogance, and the glow of sanctimony so repulsive to our fellow-humans, have not been our only crimes. We have committed a greater crime against ourselves. We have practiced and perfected an insanity, an insanity to preserve us against the evolutions of culture and history, against the influences of logic, science, and beauty, against the disintegrating forces of power brought into the world by braver and stronger people than ourselves.

"This insanity we have nursed in our bosoms," continued the old teacher, "until it became stronger in us than even the biology of our beings. We breathed, our lungs quickened, our sinews moved, and our blood flowed around a skeleton of faith. We taught ourselves gestures and rituals and inscribed them in books we called holy. We swaddled our daily movements in traditions and bound even our dreams with layers of linen as if to confine them in an eternal bed of invalidism.

"We invented miles of gibberish with which to celebrate the thousand and one fetishes we substituted for Life. So strenuously did we work at keeping intact our definition of You, at seeing that it did not leak out of a single crevice, that we became a freak among nations—an ancient mummy moving, to the distraction of mankind, through its outraged streets."

The Rabbi raised his eyes to the cupboard above the altar. Had he opened the two doors before, or did he look now for the first time on two opened doors, inside them the faded purple of the Torah? The scrolls shone as if under a strong light.

"I am an old man," he said apologetically, "and my senses are lost in dreams."

But now a voice seemed to speak through all his being.

"Look in your heart," it said. "It beholds Me."

"My heart," said Ben Ezra, "is a child dreaming."

Presently he resumed speaking.

"We moved with our fetishes through the outraged world. We attacked the egoism of races stronger than ourselves. We became a red rag to the sane. For however sane a man is, a little insanity held before his nose will flood his soul with the wild cries always hidden therein."

The light about the Torah seemed to him to be growing brighter. The Rabbi gazed long at the radiance.

"I am not surprised," he said at length to the Vision, "for I am a holy man who has often seen Your face."

Nevertheless he continued.

"There is a complex and mysterious quality in the human mind," he said calmly, "which doctors better than priests can decipher. Yet this quality is clear to me, for it has been given to me to understand much.

"There are underworlds of savagery that need but the miaow of a cat for their release. We have been that miaow," said the Rabbi.

"There are diseases of the ego, struggling always toward a sense of power and fulfillment, that need but the smile of a sage for their eruption. We have been that sage.

"And there is also in humanity a vital desire for conformity, a need for smoothing itself out into some final uniformed guise, that shudders always at the alien. We have been that alien.

"It is so that I have understood the curse of the Jew. Many of us have blasphemed against You because of it. I am not one of these. The minds that willed and planned our deaths throughout the lands of Europe today, as yesterday, are clear to me. I see into them. I do not turn and accuse You of their evil. I lay the blame of massacre at their feet."

So spoke the Rabbi in simple scholarly fashion. And yet, when he came to speak of the massacre of his brethren, his voice broke, sorrow overcame him, and he could not suppress one cry of pain to his Maker.

"Do You hear, O Lord, what they are doing to us, and how we die, calling out Your Name?"

"Aye, I hear, I hear," the Lord answered him.

At length the old man lifted up his head and went on in a gentle voice.

"It is this that I have thought," he said slowly, "that in order to have Your Name written in a book, You have driven a handful of Your children mad. And in order to have it remain in that book from which You shine at me, You have increased their madness and allowed them to be hunted like crippled children throughout the world without end.

"And this is my judgment, O Lord. It is that You have made a mistake. Even as You made many mistakes when You first filled the earth with monsters, even as You created animals too large, too malformed, too strangely hungry, or too ungainly for procuring food for their hungers—so You have erred in creating this sad little monster, the Jew.

"Now I will pray," he concluded, "for I still believe.

"O God," he prayed, calling Him by His Secret Name, known to the Jews, "let this little decaying house in which I stand, vanish. Let it not remain like a dark and battered little casket out of which rise the moans of the unburied. O Mighty God, recall Your error. Withdraw Your mistake from the earth. Unbind the mummy of Israel. Make him into a man, O Lord of Hosts. You need us no more. We are few, we are only a trickle in the great river of Life. Oh, let us then vanish. Reward us for our long piety by releasing us from it. You who freed us from the Egyptian, free us now from the bondage of Yourself. Lead us to freedom. No fire or sword of the enemy will free us. No humiliation, no torture. The more violent the enemy, the deeper grows our madness. Only Your Word can undo what Your Word has done. O Mighty Lord, let the heroic little monster, the sad little monster, the indestructible little monster of Israel pass from the earth and join the legend of history. This do I implore. Amen."

The Rabbi ceased. His hands, raised in supplication, came

down. Only once more his eyes sought out longingly the sacred place, the beloved Holy of Holies.

"And forgive me for what, being God, You know that I must do."

It was his last prayer. Rabbi Ben Ezra was finished. For a while he stood leaning on the pulpit, for he was an old man and tired. And being only a man, and human, he looked around him at the edifice in which he had wellnigh spent his life. Beneath the beating of the wind, in the darkness, it seemed like a vast place, without outline. And one by one, he brought before his mind's eye the faces of the worshipers who daily filled it, the fifty noble old men whom he had hurt so unbearably today. He had not quaked before the Lord's face. And before the invisible ghost in the doorway he had not succumbed, nor wailed his pain in its presence. But the memory of the hurt old men before him touched him, and he wept. For a long time this awful sound continued.

Then he stepped down from the altarplace.

After a time, the summer storm again let fly its tumult. The door of the old house flew open. It banged several times, and remained open. . . .

The night lightened into a color like lead. The street was empty when there appeared in one of its area-ways a shrunken, darting figure. It wielded a huge paper box, which it juggled to the sidewalk. Then it lifted out and deposited in the street a garbage can. For its nightly work, this figure had turned itself long ago into a sort of lever, with jerky springlike movements. Moving in this cavorting flealike fashion down the street, it slowly approached the synagogue.

Seen in the light of a near-by street lamp, this was a being of aspect so grimy, so wretched, and so inhuman that one could scarcely think of it at once as a man. If it did not inhabit the night and a neighborhood so sorry, it might have frightened anybody. Long ago, what with the tremendous leverlike work of the scavenger, and the scavenger's solitary life, this creature that was a man had probably gone mad. It never spoke. Its face that was like a dirty clenched fist never altered. Its eyes, like two bits of rubbish gone astray, reflected only dregs.

The synagogue was a place known to this man. Here, whether he knew it or not, he even had an identity other than that of rubbish man. He was the *Shabbes-goy*—the man who, for a few pennies, lit the Sabbath candles on the nights when it was forbidden for Jews to touch fire.

It was this man who found the body of Rabbi Ben Ezra hanging from a beam in the synagogue. Who knows what his thoughts were or what prompted him to do what he did? Perhaps he had done some such work in some former time or, more probable still, there was nothing lowly, nothing menial, that he had not done in his forgotten years. He cut the body of the Rabbi down. He removed the rope and stuffed it among the rubbishy treasures that he saved in the huge pockets of his coat. He levitated the body to the altarplace beside the cupboard where he had often seen it stand. He placed on its shoulders the white drape it was accustomed to wear, and on its head the velvet cap. With hands so roughened and clawlike that they seemed to be covered with scales, he straightened out the body's features.

If there was a gleam of compassion somewhere inside it as it worked, the dingy and witchlike figure of the old Shabbes-goy did not show it. His fistlike face did not relax during his labors, which seemed like those of an automaton. When he was through with the offices of death, he went to work in the synagogue. He straightened benches, he swept, he opened and dusted windows, he put the prayerbooks carefully away. At the end he did something else. He poured into a dustpan a packet of incense salvaged from the sweepings of a Catholic church near by, and lighted it. And then he took out of his pockets his chief item of rubbish—a candle, pure and white inside its wrappings. He cleaned out the center socket of the candelabrum, for the candles were all burned down and, placing there his little candle, he put to it the light.

Outside, a pallor came into the ghetto streets. The sun was rising. The tall buildings full of crowded human nests, whose furnishings erupted from windows like bits of straw, became gloomily visible. Summer dawn, like a defeated and weary magician, rose from the pavements, and regarded wistfully the rooftops of the ghetto. The sounds of the day began in a pizzicato of opening windows, vague cries, and the clatter of wheels and garbage cans.

Plodding through these dim and staring streets appeared a number of figures. They came quietly out of the tenements and moved in one direction. They were the fifty old men going to celebrate the Lord's new day.

None of them had slept. Their old eyes were tear-scarred, their faces collapsed with grief and something worse. Shame and disillusion were on the faces where recently security and noble thoughts of God had reigned.

The old men assembled outside the familiar building, for there is no singing the morning paean until there are ten men. And before the ten gathered, there were all the fifty converging with dawn into the little street.

The old one who had whimpered the night before appeared

now to have lost his wits. He moved among the rest, mumbling and complaining, as if he would keep them from entering the temple door.

"Why do we stand here?" he asked, peering fearfully toward the synagogue. "Why are we here and why do we hobble up and down like old hens chirping for a crumb? Why are we not buried already? Who wants us? And where is God?"

The others ignored him and moved as always to the door. The one who had opened it gave a cry and then stood still. Behind him the others crowded forward and they, too, were rooted. Then slowly they crept forward into the dim little house of worship and, pressing against the walls, peering over each other's shoulders, remained staring.

The synagogue was still as in holy sleep. The benches stood erect and in order, and the dawn, glowing through the opened windows, revealed the swept floor and the tidiness everywhere. There was an odor, too, that clung to the old walls, an odor that seemed left behind by a feast. But who had feasted in this house of tears? It was so sweet and gentle an aroma that some of the old men closed their eyes and thought of the forests of their youth.

Slowly their hundred eyes moved to the altar. The sacred house of the Torah was open. Under it lay a body. Certain now that they were in the presence of something strange, the old men began to pray softly. They moved timidly forward and saw their Rabbi Ben Ezra. Within the drapery of the tallith, like a shroud, he lay smiling. As the echo of a bird's song lingers in the empty wood, so his soul departing had left behind a smile on the dead scholar's face.

And suddenly, as one, the hundred eyes beheld a Miracle!

On the altar stood the seven-branched candelabrum. Six of the candles had burnt out overnight. But the seventh candle in the center stood as fresh as it had been when it was lit, and from its top a little flame stretched in a point of blue and gold. The fifty old men stared at this candle that had burned all night and grown no less.

"A miracle—a miracle!" called out the wisest, and lifting their heads began to pray loudly.

"A miracle—a miracle!" the others cried, and their eyes overran with tears of joy.

Their Rabbi, the wise and good Ben Ezra, the great Ben Ezra, had told them to return in the morning. And now he had given them the answer to their doubts, the word of hope for their agony. Here on the altar was the answer and the word—a candle unconsumed.

The fifty old men stood before the little candle and prayed and sang so loudly that their voices drifting into the morning street convinced passers-by that the B'nai Israel congregation had gone mad. But as the morning grew, word of the great singing going on in the battered synagogue began to draw people to its doors. Why on this black day should there be Jews who sang?

Boys and shawled old women came first. Then the sad-eyed peddlers arrived and then the little tradesmen who had had no sleep that night. And slowly the synagogue became so crowded that no more could enter, and the street outside became also thick with people. Wearied and embittered faces asked of each other what was happening, what new disasters had befallen Jews, and lamentations rose from the throng as if a sickness were wringing moans from them.

Slowly the news of the wonder came whispering out of the synagogue. God had placed His sign on the altar inside.

God had revealed Himself and spoken in some fashion to His people. A rabbi lay dead, but above him, unconsumed through the night of murder and woe, a flame had remained burning.

When the first awe had spent itself, a wave of exultation rolled through the streets of the ghetto. For such is the trusting heart of the Jew that the little candle dispelled the darkness of the great massacre. Not everywhere, of course, for there were those to whom no God could speak. But among the pious, and among those who had once been pious, the matter was plain. The rabbis of the city argued throughout the day and night, and out of their wisdom interpreted the meaning of Ben Ezra's little candle.

The Jew was such a light, feeble and powerless, but never to be extinguished. God had placed him in a world of cruelty and darkness and had bidden him to keep His image glowing. And the meaning of this miracle was that, when all the rages of man had spent themselves, and the world lay in an unholy chaos, gutted by hatred and greed and vainglory, out of the unconsumed soul of the Jew God's light would rise again.

Shuffling along the street in the dim morning of the next day, the old Shabbes-goy, bent and ragged as some alley scarecrow, paused in the half-light and wondered what holiday his old friends, the Jews, were celebrating, as the hosannas rose from various synagogues, large and little. He nodded his head and his mouth opened in a feeble grimace, for the sound of the singing pleased him.

THE MISSING IDOL

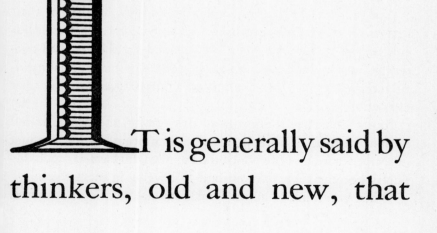

I

T is generally said by thinkers, old and new, that

the People of the world own hardly anything in it. Their religions, like their governments, seem to have provided only perpetual policemen for the protection of goods not their own. And the only diversions designed exclusively for them and not for their immemorial handful of betters are those which are said to exist in Heaven.

At least this was true until the advent of the Movies. Some day historians writing about the ups and downs of the People will stumble upon the fact that, in a struggle beginning among the glaciers and seemingly getting the People no nearer any of the Enchantments of existence, the Movies were their first unchallenged Possession.

It is strange that the People's first inheritance should be wrested out of the Kingdom of Art, a Kingdom in which they had less of a foothold than in any of the other mirages of empire and power.

You get a very sad picture of the People when you study the history of Art. It was always something the People didn't like. Particularly in modern times, beginning with the Renaissance, Art became more and more of a nuisance to the People.

Not only had they to toil and watch a little handful of their betters loll in idleness, not only to starve and watch this handful feed, and to stagger about in rags and see this handful glittering in satins, but they must also observe this immemorial handful most mysteriously swooning and applauding and rolling their eyes in bliss over the Arts.

Approaching the sources of all this ecstasy, the People found nothing in them. This is perhaps because beauty is the product of a superior kind of life which the People, who have so much difficulty keeping alive, have no time to develop in themselves.

When you think of all the books, statues, paintings, oratorios, symphonies, cantos, et cetera, that the People have never been able to enjoy, you can begin to understand their excitement over the Movies. Suddenly and inexplicably a diversion appeared in the world that belonged to nobody but themselves.

A Kingdom had blossomed, not in its usual place—the sky—but under their feet; and, staring at it warily at first, for there is always a catch to the Kingdoms offered the People, they invaded it and took possession with whoops of triumph.

Today the People, so long the limbo dwellers, rule their Kingdom mightily. The Movies are their Cellinis and Angelos, their Shakespeares and Shelleys. They control all the plots and elect their own geniuses. And, like some international Lorenzo the Magnificent, they distribute rewards undreamed of by their ancient enemies—the Artists.

I write these few obvious generalities about the Movies not that you may understand them—for who doesn't know all there is to be known about the Movies?—but as an introduction to one of the heroes of my tale, Mr. Leo Kolisher, who is the reigning producing genius of Hollywood. There are two other heroes in my story—Robert Gary and God—but I shall explain about them later.

Unless you knew that Mr. Kolisher had been rather mystically enthroned as a genius by the People, you would, I am sure, wonder how he happened to exist at all—and earn a living. Mr. Kolisher neither wrote nor directed his productions, nor acted in them, nor did he even produce them. (As for financing them, well, Mr. Kolisher was not entirely a fool.)

During the writing, acting, and producing of one of his movies by scores of other people, Mr. Kolisher charged about like one of the headless horsemen of the Apocalypse and committed almost as much damage. But not enough, however, to prevent the movie from finally appearing and being hailed as far as the hill passes of Tibet as another evidence of his genius.

But how, you will ask, did all this happen; how could such great fame come so undeservedly to anyone? The answer to such a query must be that Mr. Kolisher's fame was not undeserved. It was not merely that he placed his name—with a staggering frequency—on the product sent out from his studio, or that when the work was done he controlled the channels of publicity that celebrated its and—who can blame him?—his own wonders.

This helped a little. But self-acclaim, however tireless, does not alone make for triumph, even in the Movies. It would be a small and captious diagnosis of Mr. Kolisher's genius that stopped there.

The real truth was that of all the artists and artisans (there is a sprinkling of the latter in Hollywood) who toiled in the creation of a Kolisher movie, Mr. Kolisher alone understood the historical and spiritual significance of his product. Mr. Kolisher knew, and knew passionately, that it belonged to the People; that every foot and phrase of it, every tear and grimace of it, was theirs. Mr. Kolisher knew that he was a Man with a Mandate. It was his duty (and in the evasion or abuse of it he perished almost instantly) to keep the Kingdom of the Movies free from the ancient enemy of the People—Art.

And how did Mr. Kolisher know, so mysteriously, what would delight the People? By knowing nothing, is the only answer I can give. By being as devoid of all subtleties, refinements, dreams, cultural equipment, and talent as any of the lowliest whom he served. He was the Man in the Street with bay leaves in his hair.

It may seem a simple thing to be merely dumb, and to remain

so in the midst of the many voices of life. But I assure you it is not. It is as difficult as remaining young. And in Hollywood this accomplishment is rewarded above all others. It enabled Mr. Kolisher to sit enthroned, not as an ego full of creative birth pangs and garbled messages, but as a peevish and incorruptible representative of some two hundred million folk to whom Art for some hundred centuries had been a closed book.

Considering all this, you can see how fair it was for Mr. Kolisher to be a genius. It was a title the People gave him (just as they called other men, much more foolishly, their Kings and Presidents) because they knew instinctively what was what. They knew that he, and not the never-to-be-trusted artists whom he employed, was their servant; that it was he who saw to it that the Kingdom of the Movies, unlike all the other Kingdoms they had created, remained their own.

In the twenty-fifth year of his reign as genius, Mr. Kolisher was engaged in producing (or, rather, in having produced) a movie which he considered the greatest child, yet, of his world-famed talents. This movie was called, tentatively, *The Redeemer*, and for its plot concerned itself with the teachings and tribulations of Christ.

The way this had come about is that some nine months before the beginning of the events I have to relate, Mr. Kolisher had discovered Religion. I do not mean that he had taken to praying and throwing himself wantonly at the feet of God. What Mr. Kolisher discovered was that for a long time Religion had been something in which the People had been remarkably interested. Or, as he put it himself, everybody is religious or knows somebody who is. Wherefore, Religion, my hero had concluded, would make a wonderful movie; more than that even, a tremendous piece of entertainment.

Having called around him a half-dozen of his superior intellects, he had laid his inspiration before them. They had demurred and offered as their general opinion that People were tired of Religion.

"You are all wrong," said Mr. Kolisher; "I like Religion." And he rumpled the bay leaves in his hair.

Accordingly, Mr. Kolisher's artists fell to work devising a plot and characters that would best express their chieftain's inspiration.

I shall spare you the details of the preliminary work that preceded the filming of *The Redeemer*. At least, I shall merely summarize them. Some eight different scripts were prepared by a dozen different authors, all of them of considerable renown (for it was Mr. Kolisher's principle to discard only the best). Hundreds of drawings were made by scores of artists who might once have labored on the ceiling of the Sistine Chapel. World-famed musicians and costumers crossed seas and continents to sink exhausted at Mr. Kolisher's feet. Biblical savants and university scholars and a whole bevy of German playwrights were put to work on a "break-down" of the New Testament.

Throughout the preliminary hours of darkness and creation, Mr. Kolisher, as confused as any rabbit at the peak of the hunting season, scurried and backfired, rampaged and bombinated. Observing Mr. Kolisher during these months, you would have thought, most certainly, that his only ambition lay in seeing that no movie of any sort ever came to light again under his aegis. You would have marveled at how Mr. Kolisher, with no ideas at all about anything, without even the vaguest knowledge of history, Biblical or secular, and without any conception whatsoever of drama, poetry, philosophy, music, painting, or even carpentry, sat as Arbiter Supreme on all these matters and regulated their creation by the simple process of running amuck some fifteen hours a day.

But it would be captious and short-sighted to look on the Kolisher antics of this period as the product of a deep-rooted mania for sabotage. There was behind all Mr. Kolisher's gyrations an almost mystic pattern. Without being aware, from any point of view, of what he was doing, Mr. Kolisher was doing something profound. He was keeping the movie of *The Redeemer* from becoming Art. He was reducing it, day by day, to that type of kindergarten saga he could understand and feel, as he said, without getting a headache. (In the Kingdom of the Movies it is the Artists who must have the headaches.)

After nine months of gestation, Mr. Kolisher sat back with the sunny feeling that he, himself, despite the blundering efforts of some fifty overpaid creative intellects, had produced a marvelous script.

The casting of the central character of *The Redeemer* was in itself a period of special travail. It was Mr. Kolisher's contention that Christ would have to be played by someone who meant something at the Box Office.

The Kolisher staff argued to the contrary. They thought the part of Christ sufficiently important as a dramatic role to warrant trying a newcomer in it. It might, they argued, make a Star out of some unknown thespian, but it hardly needed one to begin with. They begged Mr. Kolisher further to remember that the original character had Himself been a man of no consequence, recruited from the simpler folk of Palestine, and that His appeal had been to equally unfashionable people. Mr. Kolisher was somewhat surprised to hear this, but in no way unhorsed.

The real Christ, countered Mr. Kolisher noisily, may have been a nobody, but there would be no nobodies in any production of his. He believed firmly in the Star system. Times had changed since Bible days. It would be an affront to the Public to offer it some fifty-dollar-a-week actor as its Saviour.

"I don't know how much the People love Christ," said Mr. Kolisher honestly, "but I know they love Robert Gary. Get me Robert Gary. We don't want to take any chances on a movie that's going to cost two million, and possibly three million before we're through."

Nearly all Mr. Kolisher's talented underlings paled at this command. The idea of Robert Gary's playing Christ struck them as a fantastic mixture of insanity and sacrilege. Mr. Gary was, at the moment, the outstanding great lover and matinee idol of the movie public.

It is of course unnecessary to tell you who read today about Mr. Gary. But if these pages survive a few years, there will be readers, amazingly enough, who may never have heard of our Robert. And though his every movement, breath, and dimple is as familiar to you as your own face in a shaving mirror, I shall none-theless describe and discuss him with an eye to his fickle posterity.

But before doing so, one more moment of Mr. Kolisher's final tantrum on the subject of *The Redeemer's* casting, for he was being violently opposed in the matter.

"How long," demanded Mr. Kolisher, who had been reading up on the subject overnight, "how long did it take Christ, who you say was a nobody, to become popular? It took years. He went along with a few crazy people following Him down the street—for years. And even when He was crucified, there was hardly anybody in attendance. Following which," Mr. Kolisher pursued, "what happened? More years of unpopularity. More years of nobody knowing Him and people even killing off any-body who claimed to know Him.

"I wish to observe," continued Mr. Kolisher, "that Christ became popular when fine people took Him up. And I wish you to consider further that He was supposed to be God's Son. He was only *acting* a nobody. Whereas, as a matter of fact, He was actually all the while, incognito, so to speak, the most important man in the world. Which exactly fits the case of Robert Gary.

"Now, the problem is, do we want somebody as unknown and as unpopular as Christ used to be? Or do we want someone as well known and respected as He has become in modern times? It seems to me, gentlemen, there is only one answer. Gentlemen, when we crucify Robert Gary, we are crucifying somebody the public loves and will feel sorry for, and the whole picture will have some meaning. I am not going to wait two thousand years —or even one thousand years—to have *The Redeemer* a hit."

Mr. Gary was engaged for the part.

And now, before recounting the historic conference that resulted in Mr. Gary's playing Christ at a ten-percent cut in his salary, I shall finish his description and discussion for Posterity —to whom I address the following few paragraphs.

In the days, O Posterity, of which I write, the People, just as they nominated their geniuses, elected their idols.

What it was that turned a vacuous and unknown actor into a movie idol, I am unable to say (at least without a great deal of thought). And I doubt whether your own historians, with more perspective and data at their disposal than I have, will be able to determine it any more positively.

It may be a sort of Lady Bountiful wantonness on the part of the People that leads them to confer the largest of their worship on the least expectant or deserving of their servants.

Or it may be that the People prefer to make idols out of dummies because in doing so they remain conscious more of their own power than of the divinity of the thing to which they make offerings.

Besides, when you make an idol out of such very ordinary clay as Mr. Gary, you are taking no chance that it will become one of those Frankenstein images which the People have so often created for their own destruction.

All this, and its connotations, may be what is in the collective soul of the People who scream the glories and wonders of such as Robert Gary.

For Mr. Gary, outside of being an idol, was nothing. His very beauty, worshiped by millions of women, lay not so much in his face and body as in their need to worship something beautiful, and, at the same time, not too beautiful. (For that would have made them Idealists rather than Idolaters.)

And on the day when these millions of ladies ceased worshiping Mr. Gary, as they did long before you idly opened these pages, that bewildered young gentleman, like an altar suddenly ungarlanded, lapsed promptly into the limbo of the commonplace, and even the repugnant.

For me, even in his little hour as an idol, Mr. Gary never emerged from this limbo. But the People, at least the female contingent, contradicted me most amazingly.

This contingent, combining into one collective coquette whose fancy is inflamed by a mole, an ear lobe, or an eyelash, had suddenly nodded to the little man who was Robert Gary, and by this nod turned him into a reigning beauty.

And having turned him, willy-nilly, into Apollo, they had given themselves ecstatically to his courtship, knowing that, however wantonly they adored him, he was their victim—a creature to be cast aside in a few years for another favorite.

Poor Mr. Gary's helplessness, like that of some tender lamb

being fattened for oblivion, only made him all the more appealing. It is always pleasant to love someone whose heart, and not yours, is to be broken.

Thus for several years more millions of ladies than I care to imagine in such an intimate relationship kept the image of Robert Gary bright in their libidos and shrieked their rapture over his presence as if he were some shadow Pan.

What they actually worshiped was a bovine-eyed, long-faced, fat-chinned youth (the lower part of whose phiz looked like a dimpled buttock) with a repulsively thick thatch of curly black hair, which gave him the look of a wigmaker's dummy. And, as are so many of the idols acclaimed by the ladies, he was sexually as harmless-seeming as some tender-mannered and well-behaved nephew.

Whereas men, a little bolder about their secret longings than women are, will admire a flagrant and pneumatic-looking strumpet and set her up as their Collective Mistress, the ladies usually choose for a shadow lover someone whose appearance will not betray too much the lewd delight it inspires. They can then gurgle their admiration over him and seem to themselves, each other, and their parsons, more aunties than nymphomaniacs.

I may be all wrong about this and it may be quite the opposite of what I have said.

It may be that our ladies, suffering from crippled libidos due to the fire-engine tempo of modern life, simply elect as their heroes non-sexual-looking types and that the whole thing is on a Platonic basis. I have heard psychiatrists say that sex has become a very spiritual thing and is driving people crazy instead of into beds. Perhaps it is not infidelity they practiced in their dreams of Robert Gary, so much as relief from it.

Then again, it may be that, loving Shadows as much as our

ladies do, this empty doting is what has turned them into female eunuchs.

The thing is extremely complicated and will bear more scrutiny than I have place to give it.

As for Mr. Gary's talents, which made him the highest-paid and most-adored actor of his day, these were even more nonexistent than his beauty. The dullness of his face was no mask for hidden fires.

In the movies in which he played he was usually to be seen standing around a little awkwardly, and speaking up rather bravely, as if making any sort of public statement were a difficulty which he was barely able to overcome.

Also, in revealing to his worshipers the various Emotions, such as pain, longing, heartbreak, or merriment, Mr. Gary's natural modesty and also his natural lack of these emotions were the despair of his directors.

Foolishly, these latter worthies demanded of Robert that he disturb the lineaments of his face, that he flash his bovine eyes and stop shifting from leg to leg like a frozen pigeon. But all that poor Robert could do was just that—shift from leg to leg, as if waiting for change in a candy store, and say his lines like any high school boy lost in the fogs of graduation day.

What the directors didn't understand and Mr. Kolisher perhaps did was that these very shortcomings were enchanting to his worshipers. Although they were willing to acclaim a bit of talent here and there provided it didn't disturb, depress, irritate, or confuse them, as a true idol they still preferred a symbol as impotent as any Golden Calf.

Mr. Gary—whose beauty they could forget without regret and whose talents in no way commanded the homage which they bestowed—was just that. He was a symbol of the People's wantonness, an answer to the Artists and Critics who had so long selected for them idols to admire that gave them only headaches.

And what happens to a little man, harmless and well meaning and working modestly for a living, who abruptly finds himself the adored of the world; who suddenly hears his name breathed soulfully or lecherously by millions of fevered maidens and matrons; who encounters wherever he goes hosannas, worshipful throngs, and police escorts? Various things happen to various idols so precipitously garlanded. But none in the history of movieland reacted quite so astonishingly as Robert Gary.

For Mr. Gary failed to react at all. In the midst of acclaims greater than befell the Caesars, nothing happened to Mr. Gary. No sense of greatness disturbed the pleasant, bovine smile of his eyes. No vanities bloomed, jungle-like, in his soul. No horizons opened for his boy's mind.

Mr. Gary knew he was an idol, knew that now he was receiving a salary of $15,000 a week instead of the $75 a week he had been glad to receive two short years ago, and knew, finally, that some day the People would tire of him and he would be able to eat a meal in a restaurant without having his socks snatched off him by admirers.

But though he knew these things, Robert had no feeling about them. He was content to sit glittering with the ruby eyes that were not his own and shining in the gold paint he knew would soon wear off.

He had at times some thoughts on the subject of "it all ending." These thoughts, which took the form of stares more often than of words, had to do with the People.

Robert felt they had made a willful mistake in adoring him, just as if some millionaire had left him a fortune under the false impression that he was a son. He felt that the lawyers would find out about his true lineage and take the fortune away.

This in no way saddened Robert, for there was nothing very much in him to sadden or elate. But it made him look on all the hullabaloo, which he had so unexpectedly inspired, with a true idol's eyes, in which is always the soul of indifference.

Mr. Kolisher, unlike all his lesser colleagues who knew Robert, felt an awe in the young Star's presence. On their first casting get-together for *The Redeemer* he spoke to Robert quietly, and in such a manner that had any of the People who adored Robert been eavesdropping, they would have overheard nothing to offend them. And Mr. Gary was awed, too, because he knew that the greatest genius in Hollywood was speaking to him.

Mr. Gary did not know why Mr. Kolisher was a genius any more than the latter knew why Robert was an idol. These things were mysteries into which true servants of the People never pried. So they faced each other with a certain heady comradeliness which exists among altars as well as Gods.

Mr. Kolisher outlined in full all the troubles he had had in preparing the story of *The Redeemer*, the heroic expenses already incurred, and added, as calmly as if he were the most aloof of critics, that this same movie which was costing him his shirt (and, of course, all his stockholders' shirts) was going to be the greatest he or anyone else had ever produced.

In confirmation of this, Mr. Kolisher said that he had already bought five hundred camels, one hundred dromedaries, three hundred cages filled with vultures, roped off a hundred square miles of desert, and that he was at the moment building Jerusalem.

Robert nodded.

Furthermore, Mr. Kolisher added, he had thirty men on the payroll doing nothing but research and Mr. Gary could feel assured that every button on every priest, soldier, and early Christian would be exactly right.

Again Robert nodded.

Continued Mr. Kolisher, the part he had in mind for Robert to play was the title part of the picture—in short, the Redeemer Himself.

Again Robert nodded.

Further, Mr. Kolisher pointed out that Mr. Gary would not play this part in black and white, but that for the first time in history Christ would be revealed to the world in technicolor.

"And now," said Mr. Kolisher, "I will be frank. You are the only man in the world fit to play Christ. I have told that quite openly to everybody. I want you to take into consideration, however, (a) the importance of the role, (b) the tremendous costs of the production, (c) what it will mean to your future to appear in a part so full of audience sympathy, and, finally, (d) I want you to bear in mind that this whole picture, from the first scene to the last, is about Robert Gary—nobody else."

Robert nodded again.

"And finally," said Mr. Kolisher, who in conference was always like an army with inexhaustible reserves, "the director-in-chief of the entire production—working immediately under me—is going to be Gustave Lingbaum."

"Mr. Lingbaum," said Robert softly.

Movie actors look on great directors as a combination of magician and midwife. Aware in their hearts of their own lack of talent—their non-pregnancy, so to speak—they are inspired by the hosannas of the critics over their Magnificent Performances with the notion that the Director somehow delivered them of a child not in them. And, since the Director thinks so too, this completes his status as Magician.

It is a moot question whether the Director rides to fame on the Idol or pushes it there at his own expense.

Leaving this problem unsolved, I return to Robert. Having said softly: "Mr. Lingbaum," he had exhausted his side of the debate.

It was thus it befell that Robert Gary signed up to play the character of Christ for ten percent less than he had received for playing, three months before, the character of Bert Haskell, all-American quarterback and hero of the intercollegiate Rose Bowl game.

And now all that Mr. Kolisher prophesied of the greatness of his production came to pass. Somehow, despite his most furious eleventh-hour outbursts of sabotage, Jerusalem arose pillar on pillar in the desert a hundred miles from Hollywood.

The Temple of the Jews, bewailed through centuries, reared its glories again and round it lay once more the land of Bible days.

All was as it should be, and Mr. Kolisher, riding in his town car through the streets and byways of his Jerusalem, felt as great a pride, if for different reasons, as any patriarch who had ever trod the original.

It is with cameras turning, troops of soldiery, citizens, and chariots moving and the streets of this facsimile Holy Land alive with rabbis, Romans, electricians, pigeons, dromedaries, money-changers, harlots, dreamers, and prop men, that I leave not only Mr. Kolisher but all terrestrial matters, and turn to the third Hero of my story, sitting benign and omniscient beyond the vaults of space.

It was much easier to describe and discuss God in the days when so little was known of Him that any monk with an attack of dementia praecox became a revered authority.

Until the end of our last century, visualizing the Deity required no particular effort, even for the sane. Our immediate forebears (of all Denominations) beheld Him as a sort of talented Mind Reader who knew everything that was going on and occupied Himself busily with a system of Rewards and Punishments for Man.

Whatever differences there were concerning the sort of prayer, music, genuflexion, or costume He preferred, on one point all the schism-mongers were agreed. He had created the soul of Man and was mightily preoccupied in striving to improve and purify it.

The considerable evidence to the contrary was majestically ignored. The arresting fact that in the whole of history Atheists had been about the only harmless, well-behaved people, whereas every firm believer in God had devoted most of his energies to murder, torture, arson, and calumny, is of course more of a reflection on Piety than on Omnipotence. But there is a corollary and one which scratched away early at the doors of Reason.

It is more than a little difficult to understand why a Deity mightily preoccupied with our purification should inflame us with all the seven lusts the moment we took to paying definite attention to Him.

It is only in the past few decades that the true and even stranger reality of God has come into the world. Human egomania, which had for so long kept God in Heaven like a critic in an opera box surveying excitedly our Wagnerian antics, was badly jolted by the first laboratory reports of His new meanings.

With every fresh discovery of molecules, atoms, electrons, and all the other minute and enterprising paraphernalia of Nature, it became more and more obvious that God had other things on His mind than the purifying of our souls. Heaven, it appeared, was no suburb awaiting our retirement, but a most amazingly busy Super-Laboratory.

And if there were Angels, it was obvious they had little time to blow trumpets or strum harps, what with the inconceivable business of keeping all the molecules dancing, all the atoms bombarding Space, and every particle of dust obeying the labyrinthian Laws of Existence.

As for God, however omniscient His mind, how much time proportionately could He devote to our words and philosophies in the midst of the eternal Cataclysm of Space with whose governing He eternally grappled? Very little, indeed; and it is this new understanding of God and His preoccupation with Superior Forces that has depressed the soul of Man, these recent years, and turned it into dark ways.

We have taken to behaving like children whose teacher is too busy to note our conduct, and to the ancient accusations of Godlessness that once brought us to heel we reply—very scientifically—that it is not we but God who is Godless.

We have only to go to Heaven to see the truth of the new findings. And thither we shall go, if for no other reason than to be near the third Hero of my tale. And since, according to all theologies, even those of the laboratories, He is all shapes and all things, we find Him in that partly human guise He assumes when He desires surcease from Himself.

On this day of our visit, God had turned over His Forces to His innumerable assistants, who, though they are not so learned as He, are able nonetheless to supervise, after a fashion, the incalculable labors of the Universe.

With God idling in human guise, His mind for the moment free of all the chores of Creation, His Angels sat in trance-like silences and carried on the Work. Smilingly the Deity looked about Him and saw His racing caldrons glowing in Infinity; saw, too, the mighty alchemy of His largest stars repeated in the soul of the tiniest grain of matter.

This orderliness pleased Him, for it had taken many aeons to achieve. He was proud of His Laws and of the Rhythm that had transmuted the pure nothingness of His pioneer days into the obedient Wheel of Life.

"Observe," He spoke to the Archangel Michael, whom He had called to His side for company and a little disputation, "observe the precision in which All is confined. My Universe is a clock inside which other clocks are ticking.

"The great gases rearing like serpents of flame in My most distant seas of Space," said God, "feel this ticking and the Law of Form within them. My system of weights and counter-weights imprisons Chaos itself. And in all this traffic which sweeps headlong down the arches of Infinity, observe there are no collisions."

"Or at least none worth mentioning," said the Angel Michael.

"Yes," said God, without meaning to change the subject, "I am fascinated by My clocks and pleased by them. Observe that within each Form I have hidden a Brother to guide it; and within each Brother I have inserted yet another Brother to watch over it.

"I have been so careful in the creation of this Brotherhood that there is no Brother but has a guide within him, so that the most invisible speck of My Universe wears the full mantle of My Infinity.

"Were this All around us to disappear," said God, "as the result of some hypothetical miscalculation, one speck of My Work remaining would contain in it all the secrets and powers of My Laws and be sufficient for the reconstruction of Infinity. It is pleasing to Me that Chaos should hum like a housewife at her tasks and that all My Geometries should lie in My Palm like a coin well earned."

These last words, so reminiscent of our own world, apparently reminded God of something, for he opened His eyes and asked softly:

"Where is it?"

"Forgive me," said the Angel Michael sleepily, "what are You looking for?"

"Earth," said God, "that bit of moon dust in the Minor Group."

"I know the name," said the Angel Michael and, after a look around while God rested, pointed out the planet asked for.

God smiled approvingly.

"I am pleased to note," He spoke, "that its speed, size, and shape are exactly as they should be. It looks quite perfect, does it not?"

Michael nodded.

God spoke again.

"This is the one," He said softly, "that has developed Thought. It is inhabited by creatures who call themselves Men."

"Men?" said Michael with an inquiring look.

"Man," said God, "is a highly developed particle who operates under a rather large multiplicity of My Laws. In fact, in some ways, he is the final mutation of dust, although I have had other experiments in mind at times.

"They have minds," said God, looking down, "that move like gnats along the walls of Infinity, seeking its measurements and its meanings. They wrestle with the secrets of themselves and look for the light within light."

"Why do they do this?" asked the Angel Michael.

"They dream of detaching themselves from the Laws that operate them," said God, "and emerging into Divine Supremacy over matter."

The Angel Michael was shocked.

"In fact," God continued, "they already have achieved a belief that on changing their atomic arrangements, which they call dying, they pursue a triumph over Nature in the guise of souls."

The Angel Michael was puzzled.

"They fancy that their souls," said God, "rise like some refined sort of smoke and come straight to Me to partake of My omniscience. As far as I can make out, that is their belief."

Michael wondered at God's calm.

"It is nothing to frown upon," God answered him, "since We are in no way inconvenienced by it."

"They sound very troubled," said the Angel Michael.

"Yes," said God. "It is that fact which filled Me with compassion a little while ago, as you may recall. I listened to them harassing each other and floundering at death grips with each other in the shallow surfs of reason and I sought to lift them a step toward the Deep in which We reside."

"I do not recall," said the Angel Michael.

"You were probably busy elsewhere," said God and fell silent, as if remembering something. Removing the distances from His eyes, He looked casually at the Earth. A curious expression came upon Him.

"I am amazed," He said.

"What is it?" asked the Angel Michael.

"Look, observe what is happening," God said, and brought the Earth close to Michael's vision. "I am truly amazed."

The Angel Michael looked for a while and then spoke.

"They are nailing someone to a cross," he said.

"My Son," said God, frowning. "I am extremely confused."

The Angel Michael regarded the Deity with surprise.

"Confused?" he said, and looked very awed.

"Either this is the Devil's work or I have had a sort of lapse," said God. "What you see there is something I could swear has already happened."

"It is difficult," said the Angel Michael, "to determine which events have happened and which are going to happen. I have often found Time a very confusing witness."

"I have never made that mistake before," said God, still frowning. Then He continued, as if putting the problem of the error from His mind.

"I was telling you of My compassion," He said. "It was out of that compassion that I sent My Son to instruct the Thought of the World. Knowing its crude talent for remembering only what is too obvious, I decreed that My Son should be crucified."

"I do not understand," said the Angel Michael. "It seems very cruel."

"I wished to create sympathy for Him," said God, "and through sympathy, belief. And through belief, understanding."

God stopped and sighed.

"At least," He said, "it was My impression I had done all this, and that My Son Jesus was living in happy retirement. But apparently——"

Again He paused.

"I have been doing them a great injustice," said God, indicating the men on the Earth. "I have thought for some time that these human particles whom I sent My Son to instruct had not only abjured but wretchedly misinterpreted all His hints."

"You have been very busy with the new nebula," said the Angel Michael thoughtfully.

"I have," said God, "but that is no excuse for such wool-gathering. At any rate, there He is and My decree is being put into operation."

"What is the name of that desert city?" asked Michael, who continued to be deeply surprised by the Deity's abstraction. Perhaps he even recalled things that his banished brother, Lucifer, had once spoken of.

"Jerusalem," said God. "It is a little field I have been working in for some time. Those bearded men are Jews and those others with the clean-shaven faces are Romans. And that glittering little house was built for Me. It is My favorite Temple. Or was."

"You mean, is, I think," said the Angel Michael, softly.

God scowled.

"I can't have been that busy," He spoke. "Yes, is. I am very fond of it. But the whole thing amazes me. I could have said that this little house had been destroyed and this whole field long ago uprooted and given over to error and desolation."

"It looks very busy," said the Angel Michael.

"Poor little man on the Cross," said God, "He will cry out soon, inquiring why I have forsaken Him."

"Does He know He is Your Son?" asked the Angel Michael.

"Yes," said God.

"Then why does He not say so to everyone?" asked the Angel.

"He has," said God. "We will talk of that later."

He sighed.

"The whole thing is very confusing," said God. "It is my first aberration in a long time. It proves the folly of peering at Time too casually.

"However," He continued, "there is some profit in the incident. It was My original intent—in fact, I thought I had carried it out—to allow My Son to die and be buried and then restored to Me in secret."

"Why in secret," asked the Angel Michael, "if You wished to impress Humanity with His true meaning?"

"I had a theory about reaching into their wisdom by gentle and unmagical pressure," said God. "It is degrading to Reason to educate it unreasonably. I was averse to hypnotizing them with a bit of legerdemain. In fact," He added after a pause, "I was afraid of frightening them into some sort of hysteria instead of leaving behind a calm divine seed of Reason.

"I am pleased that I have had this chance to reconsider My plan," said God, "for in a dream I had, which in My moment of confusion I considered an actual part of My past, it was revealed to Me by My intelligence that My first plan was dangerous."

Michael pondered on how God could dream of that which had never happened, nor was to happen, but kept his silence.

"My lack of boldness in asserting Myself," said God, still on the subject of this odd dream, "was greatly responsible for the mishaps that followed—or, rather, I mean, that would have followed—My Son's sojourn there. Had He been there.

"The point is," continued God, extricating Himself from these remarks with a smile that blinded Michael almost completely, "the point is, I am very pleased to have this opportunity for changing My mind about the spiritual redemption of Man."

"Then You are not going to redeem Him?" Michael asked.

God smiled again.

"You don't understand, Michael," he said. "The point is I am going to redeem Him but in a much simpler way than I had originally intended. I realize now that in addressing Myself to the Soul of Man I must take into consideration the monkey-mind through which My message is filtered. And I think it will be best if I perform some tricks."

"You will perform a miracle?" Michael widened his eyes eagerly, for he had heard tales of such matters.

God nodded.

"It is in many ways degrading," He said, "to perform like a charlatan for these half-beasts for whom I am seeking a finer mold. But a miracle will simplify their impression of Me.

"It will do away with Sects," began God and then looked at Michael kindly. "You must take for granted, Michael," He went on, "that I know more about the Thought of Man than you do. And that if I have decided to dominate that Thought by a few miracles, there is Wisdom in what I do. My Son shall not cry out in vain to Me. When He calls to Me from the Cross, I shall be there to take Him in My arms. And He shall not go down in history as a Myth or a Phantom. Nor shall those who write of Him be identified later as liars and bigots.

"You will," said God, beaming fully on His Angel, "proceed at once to Earth and remove Him from the Cross in the presence of all who have gathered in Gethsemane."

"Gethsemane?" inquired Michael.

"That is the name of the little spot where all this is happening," said God. "You will find it easily. It is to the east of the planet as it now lies, near the bottom of one of its continents called Asia."

The Angel Michael arose. He stretched his pinions and regarded the Earth.

"I will bring Him back," he said softly.

Saying this, the Angel Michael leaped forward and was gone. Some moments of confusion ensued, for, arriving in Asia and seeking out the spot named by God, Michael found no sign of a Temple, no activity around a Cross, and no glimpse of any Son.

Apprised of this, God said nothing for a long instant and then, in words that seemed to the Angel Michael strangely faint, bade him go westward to another continent. Obeying this uncertain Divine guidance, Michael finally—by merest good luck, it seemed to him—arrived on the scene he had watched from God's side.

"Investigate fully," God sent a message, "and tell Me the name of the city."

The Angel Michael inquired quickly and replied.

"It is called Jerusalem," he said.

"Is there a man named Pilate present?" God sent another query into the Angel's mind.

"He is here," Michael answered after a moment, impressed by the Deity's social knowledge of this remote bit of dust.

"Are there Jews?" came a query from Heaven.

"Innumerable ones," the Angel Michael answered.

"Tell Me of them," God queried softly.

His Angel paused.

"They have false beards," Michael finally answered.

There was yet a longer pause from the Infinite.

"Am sending another Angel to assist you," God spoke at length. "Do nothing till he comes."

A few moments elapsed and Michael beheld his brother, the Angel Azriel, at his side.

"What of My Son?" God asked of His two messengers.

The Angel Michael hesitated.

"You reply," he said to his brother. Azriel answered God.

"No sign of Him yet, but we have found Lingbaum," said the Angel Azriel.

"Lingbaum?" The name was a question from on high.

The two Angels looked at each other, astonished.

"It is strange," said Michael quietly, "that He should know of a man named Pilate, who is of no consequence here, and not know Lingbaum, who is the Master of the City."

"Lingbaum," Azriel answered the Infinite's question, "is Master of the City and Director of its destiny. It is he who is putting Your Son to death. He is giving many orders."

There was a long pause.

"Where is My Son?" God spoke again.

The two Messengers conferred. Michael was for keeping silent, but Azriel feared the Divine impatience.

"Which one?" the Angel Azriel asked, keeping his thought as calm as he could. "For there are two of Them."

By the length of the silence that followed Azriel's reply and by the darkening of their spirits, both Messengers knew that God was wroth.

"I am sending Malliol," the Deity finally answered.

The arrival of the Angel Malliol cheered the two Messengers, for he was one of the wisest of the Host. They related to him what had passed and acquainted him with the facts around them. The Angel Malliol turned his thought confidently to Heaven.

"Which one, O Lord, shall we bring back to You?" he spoke. "For there are two of Them."

This time God answered loudly out of the Infinite.

"Impossible!" He thundered. "One of Them is an impostor!"

Luckily for the Angels, Mr. Lingbaum, directing the filming of *The Redeemer*, at this moment ordered the stand-in for Robert Gary, who resembled him in make-up, lineaments, and size, removed from the Cross.

"We will use Mr. Gary himself for the medium shots as well as the close-ups," said Mr. Lingbaum. "We don't want any wise-acres spotting a stand-in on the Cross. It would kill all the illusion."

Accordingly this stand-in, whose name was Joe, jumped to the ground, to the amazement of the three Angels closely watching the strange events. Robert Gary climbed a small ladder leisurely and was adjusted into place by the prop men.

"Now, Mr. Gary"—Mr. Lingbaum stood on the ladder beside him with final directorial instructions—"put everything out of your mind. Just hang there. Remember those are nails through your hands and feet. But don't overdo it. The Saviour was no coward. He didn't scream and mug. He just hung there and took it. Keep the drama inside you."

"Yes, sir," said Robert.

"All right—shoot!" cried Mr. Lingbaum, and a great silence fell on Gethsemane.

The Angel Michael addressed his thought to God.

"They are shooting Him now," he said.

"Shooting whom?" God demanded.

"Your Son, I think," said Michael.

There was a pause from on high.

"Azriel," God's voice spoke, "is there or is there not a Cross on which My Son is being crucified?"

"There is," said Azriel.

"Is My Son in agony?" God continued in a softer voice.

"It is difficult to tell," said Azriel, "for He is making no sound nor yet expression."

"Look close," said God.

"Yes," said Azriel, "it seems to me He is suffering. He is complaining to Mr. Lingbaum about his eyes smarting."

"The time has come for My miracle " God's voice whispered within the three Angels.

It was then that the Heavens suddenly darkened and the bright desert day was transformed into eerie night. Fires flashed from the sky and ominous sounds rolled over the desert. A strong wind smote the sands. The city of Jerusalem shook under these manifestations. Several of its towers toppled. Scores of Mr. Kolisher's booster lights and arc lamps were smashed to bits and all together some hundred thousand dollars' worth of scenery and equipment was destroyed. To add to Mr. Lingbaum's troubles, panic seized the herd of one hundred dromedaries and they bolted, screaming and snorting, into the hills.

"It's a simoom!" Mr. Lingbaum bellowed through his megaphone. "Bury the film cans!"

The storm, unprecedented for violence and peculiarities even in California, lasted less than three minutes. Hardly had the wind struck, the fire flashed, the thunder rolled, and the darkness engulfed the scene, when it was day again, serene and bright. So quickly had the storm come and gone that its witnesses could barely credit their memories. But there was evidence in the wreckage left.

Mr. Lingbaum, emerging from a sound wagon where he had sought refuge, surveyed the set and then issued a number of commands. He ordered the debris cleared at once and his crews to erect new lights.

"Lucky it didn't knock the Cross down," said Mr. Lingbaum. "We've got three more good hours of light to shoot in if that Goddamn simoom don't come back. Get Mr. Gary. And tell him we're going on with the scene. Hurry it up."

Mr. Lingbaum's assistants scurried off to dig Mr. Gary out of whatever refuge he had sought during the storm. For he was not on the Cross.

Of course, Mr. Lingbaum's assistants were not looking in the right place.

When Robert Gary opened his eyes he knew something amazing had happened. But Robert, though he might recognize the need for amazement, was not the one to feel it.

He surveyed the scene, into which it was obvious he had been transported by some supernatural agency, with a well-ordered and undemonstrative interest. God, aware of the human content of the mind before Him—for He had clothed His Son within and without as a Man—had welcomed His Child home with a display of lesser magic. He had descended to Aesthetics and produced for His homecoming shapes and colors and ensembles of great beauty.

A Hall of such proportions as to have filled any earthly mind other than one from Hollywood with blank awe lay before Robert. Down the sides of this vast Hall stretched a forest of pillars made of incandescent matter that resembled the precious stones of the World. They rose like vari-colored flames and their ruby, sapphire, and diamond light made a symmetrical bonfire whose beauty was almost too devastating for critical evaluation. Among these pillars was a host of figures with golden wings outstretched in an architectural hosanna.

The beauty of these figures, for they were the chosen ones of the Host, was also of that superior kind which no eye of Earth could fully encompass or tongue appraise. The far vanishing floor of the Hall was made of a single pearl that gave forth a light of dreams.

Overhead Robert observed that there were more Angels, for he had already identified the lovely troops about him. They hovered in deliciously arranged groups, some with trumpets to their mouths, others in attitudes of celestial languor; some with wings arched in flight, others in postures of adoration. They formed a continuous dome-like frieze as far as the eye could see.

Robert's senses felt faint with the impact of so much color, sound, and glory. But God had calculated carefully the frail human capacities for beauty. He had curbed His displays to a gentle exhibition, fearful of overwhelming His Son, in the first moments of His return, with those blasts of loveliness which Robert would not have been able to endure nor I to describe.

At the end of the Hall, Robert perceived God. He knew His identity instinctively, for, though the Deity had reduced Himself, with some effort, to approximately human proportions, He had retained a single particle of Divinity in His eyes. These blazed like a pair of continuous cannon flashes and Robert, realizing that, whatever the occasion, he was a sort of guest of honor, advanced slowly toward their light.

It may have been that Robert's own eyes, used to the intensity of the movie lights, and his mind, used also to the ambition and caprice of the movie sets, were not as overwhelmed as they should have been. There was also Robert's incapacity for reaction, which had infuriated some of the more sensitive Hollywood directors.

In fact, miracles to Robert were not entirely without precedent. Having been raised, for no reason he had ever been able to understand, from a nobody to an idol, finding himself now raised into Heaven, he was hardly more astonished. It was inexplicable, of course, but to one who had already tasted the Incomprehensible it had lost somewhat of its flavor with repetition.

The Angels, watching Robert's progress down the Hall, attributed his calm demeanor to the fact that he was of Divine origin. For the tale of God's Compassion and His experiment in a planet's education had been swiftly told by Michael, Azriel, and Malliol.

God waited happily for His Son and, as He approached, felt inclined to admire the grace of His movement. Considering the agony His Son had recently been through, His bearing, thought God, was extremely commendable.

But as He watched, a misgiving came into the Deity's wisdom. There was that about His Son which confused Him and in an odd, unpaternal way irritated Him.

"It is possible," thought God, "that He has been spoiled a little by the World."

Robert was now before the throne. He stood in silence, a bit frightened as always during mob scenes. He had also begun to think that it might be God was about to punish him for some sort of sacrilege.

It occurred to Robert that despite Mr. Kolisher's rhapsodic statements, which had made him cut his salary ten percent, the role of *The Redeemer* was not without its unhappy side. Robert felt worried about this and was about to explain rather lamely that he had been talked into the whole thing by Mr. Kolisher, when he heard the Deity's voice and shivered and held his tongue.

"Advance to My feet, My Son," God began. "You whom they called Christ and whose poor body, racked with Agony, sought to reveal to them the greatness of My Compassion and Your own services, advance and——"

God failed to finish His speech. For one thing, He did not like its content and, for another, He realized with a sudden Divine clarity that the young man standing attentively before Him was no Son of His. God cast a quick look down the Hall of Angels and decided it would be better to dismiss all the witnesses to this most extraordinary situation.

"My error will only confuse them," He thought inwardly, "and take their minds off their duties." Even more inwardly He brooded: "A little thing such as this might start them talking about Lucifer."

Turning His thought on the Host, he bade them all leave and take the Homecoming Hall with them.

Robert watched the multitude of Angels, pillars, colors, and the pearl floor vanish even more quickly than any movie set he had ever worked in. He realized that in the handling of scenery God had a natural advantage over any of the Hollywood producers, not excluding Mr. Kolisher. God interrupted his meditations.

"What are you doing here?" God spoke.

"I don't know," said Robert. "I suppose it has something to do with my being on the Cross."

"What were you doing on the Cross?" demanded God.

"They're shooting the final scene," said Robert, "and I had to be there as—as the central figure."

"What final scene?" God asked.

Robert hesitated and then answered desperately.

"I had nothing to do with it," he said, "except obey the script."

"Scriptures," said God sternly.

"No," said Robert, and then added quickly: "I beg Your pardon. We work from a script and the script called for me to be crucified. I think Mr. Kolisher himself decided on that ending."

"Mr. Kolisher," God repeated the name.

"Yes," said Robert.

"Who are you?" God asked.

For an instant the novelty of the question startled Robert Gary, but he realized quickly that fame must be a terrestrial product and answered with the modesty of greatness in a strange land.

"I am Bob Gary," he said. "I work in the movies as an actor."

"The movies?" said God and thought an instant. "They are something recent?"

"Yes," Robert answered eagerly, "we are in our infancy."

"I have been busy elsewhere with other matters," said God and fell silent again. Taxing His mind a bit, He understood what the Movies were. His silence continued for several moments while His thought mastered the Industry.

"Then what I witnessed was not actually happening," said God. "You were just posing for photographs."

"It's a little more than that," said Robert. "It's more like acting."

"To be sure," said God kindly, "I know all about acting."

Robert nodded humbly.

"I would like to hear what You have to say about acting," he faltered, for he thought these were matters that might interest the erudite Mr. Lingbaum.

"Acting," said God, "is the art of making real for others that which is real only for one's self. Man has many nets with which to fish for Truth. Of these, Acting is the largest and strongest. In it he can retain Truth for a vivid hour so that all may look and see its secrets."

Robert was silent.

"I perceive," added God, "that the Movies are somewhat different."

"Yes, in a way," said Robert cautiously.

"Tell me," said God.

"Well," said Robert, who felt more at home in interviews on the Movies than in any other type of discourse, "it's like this. You see, there's so much Truth in the World that the Movies try to show the other side."

"The other side of Truth?" said God. "What would that be?"

"Oh," said Robert, smiling, "pleasant things. You see, the Movies are sort of a dream life for the Masses."

Robert had read this curious statement in a scurrilous criticism of one of his pictures when someone, by mistake, had left a radical magazine in his dressing room. Feeling, however, there might be some mental relation between God and a left-wing movie critic, Robert offered the explanation hopefully.

"Why were you re-enacting the story of My Son's agony?" He asked.

"It was Mr. Kolisher's idea," Robert answered, rather caddishly. "He engaged me for the part."

"Who is Mr. Kolisher?" demanded God.

Robert widened his eyes.

"He is the leading genius of Hollywood," said Robert, thus extending the reach of Mr. Kolisher's Publicity Department beyond its happiest dreams. "I mean, there is no doubt but that he produces the best pictures. This one is his greatest work so far. It's called *The Redeemer*."

God nodded.

"Is Mr. Kolisher producing *The Redeemer* for religious reasons?" he asked.

"What do You mean?" Robert murmured.

"I mean," said God firmly, "has Mr. Kolisher any interest in the Redemption of Humanity?"

"I don't think so," said Robert honestly.

"Then why," said God, "is he producing *The Redeemer* instead of something else?"

"Well," said Robert, nervously, "first, it's a great subject and appeals to everybody. And, as he told me himself, he's taking the greatest care not to offend anybody—particularly the Jewish people. So that the picture will have a universal appeal. It's bound to gross several million dollars. Religion, if properly handled, always gets big grosses."

"I know that," said God and with some effort continued to smile at Robert Gary, who He saw was too simple-hearted either for Divine wrath or for disputation.

"What makes Mr. Kolisher," God continued, "imagine that My Son's life and death are a pleasant lie?"

"I'm afraid," said Robert, "that I have not made myself clear. *The Redeemer* is what we call an escapist picture. It's about things that happened so long ago that they don't matter any more and one can look at them sort of aloofly, so to speak."

"I see," said God.

"People like History that has already happened," went on Robert, "and they enjoy looking at it in the Movies no matter how many people were killed. I read in a magazine once that the Masses like watching blood-and-thunder Movies because they take their minds off their own troubles."

God nodded.

"That's the secret of why costume pictures are coming back," went on Robert; "the world is pretty badly off right now and likes to forget what's going on for an hour or two, and just sort of enjoy the Past and all its superstitions."

God felt a stir of anger at this speech, but looking into Robert Gary's heart He saw that it was simple and that the young man was doing his best to be agreeable.

"So My Son makes them forget their troubles," He repeated.

"Oh, yes," Robert agreed quickly.

"I wish I had heard of this Movie earlier," said God. "I might have been of some help."

"I can assure You," said Robert eagerly, "that it's been beautifully done. Some of the lines I have to speak are almost like poetry. Mr. Kolisher has spared no expense or effort."

"Still," God mused, "there are some things . . ."

"He's built a whole city," pursued Robert, "Jerusalem, and filled it with all its original inhabitants and animals and everything."

"I saw it," said God.

"The Garden of Gethsemane is really a gorgeous shot," said Robert.

There was a long pause and God appeared to be thinking.

"What sort of music are they using?" He inquired at length.

"The very best," Robert answered. "Both modern and ancient."

"What about the Hill of Skulls?" asked God.

"You mean Golgotha," said Robert.

"Yes," said God.

"Mr. Kolisher built it from replicas," said Robert. "That's where I carried the Cross on my back."

"I know," said God.

"It's one of the best shots in the picture," Robert offered.

"The Temple of the Jews looks a little skimpy," said God, who seemed still to be brooding.

"It doesn't photograph that way," said Robert. "I'm sure You will be pleased. That is, if You see the picture."

"I am going to look at it," said God and again He sat in silence, thinking.

"I wonder," God thought, "if this Mr. Kolisher is wiser than I am, at least in the eyes of the little planet on which he lives.

"I have always tried to educate its inhabitants through suffering," thought God. "For it seemed to Me that people must take seriously and study deeply that which was revealed to them through Pain.

"I have always reasoned," thought God, "that the ultimate goal for Thought was the understanding of My Mysteries. Might it not be the forgetting of Them?"

God studied the history of the World for a moment.

"There seems to have been a great deal of suffering," He resumed inwardly, "and all this suffering appears to have improved the race of Man very little."

He recalled now, without any confusion, the sending of His Son to the eyes of Man.

"It was folly of a sort," He went on within Himself, "to think that the agony of one Figure, even though He was My Son, could influence to any degree the mind of a people to whom slaughter and torture are a daily diet. Indeed, it was like"—and God searched for a phrase—"like sending coals to Newcastle." He smiled.

"I wonder," God thought, "if these Movies, which turn event into dream, which rob Existence of its sting, and which remove all vestiges of troublesome intelligence from the tales they reveal—I wonder if they are not more sensible than My Redeemer, as an influence. And more desirable than all my floods, locusts, famines, and other Manifestations as an educational source?

"Yes," said God, "I wish I had thought of them and sent them into the World as My Messengers. But, alas, I was thinking in another direction."

Casting His Thought over His Universe, He sighed and added: "There are many things to do.

"I begin to feel now," thought God, "that My efforts to increase the Intellectual talent of man were a well-meaning error. It is better that he grow less, rather than more, intelligent. It is better that he see himself less and understand less the Meanings of his existence as well as of Mine. It is better that he learn to look on Life as a pleasant and even pointless dream; that he turn from the abortive cries of artists, saints, and sages and go to the Movies. It is better, I am sure, that he know nothing happily than know a little, most unhappily.

"These Movies," God continued inwardly, "with My assistance, might, in a while, take the place of all Man's present troublesome investigations into Beauty, Nature, and Truth. They might become an ephemeris of images among which the mind of Man could wander without pain or mishap for Eternity.

"A sort of millennium of Anti-Thought," God mused, "that would fill the World, and all of Life would become a shadow to be enjoyed as a child enjoys the dancing of a sunbeam across its cradle."

God looked at Robert Gary, who had been standing for a long time in His silence. Robert, for his part, was reminded of the days when, as an extra, he had waited hour upon hour for a nod from some head in the Casting Department.

"I am in favor of the Movies," God said aloud, and smiled. "And despite your assurances that Mr. Kolisher's production is perfect, I should like to be of some help."

"I don't know what You could do, exactly," said Robert, "unless there are some retakes."

"You said," God answered, "the final scene was still to be shot."

"I don't think Mr. Kolisher would care for any changes in that," said Robert.

"Nor should I," said God, and looked sternly at the young man. "I am not trying to interfere with Mr. Kolisher," He added. "I am sure he knows what he is doing."

(At the moment—I should like to interject—Mr. Kolisher was out of his head, bellowing for his missing Star. But I shall come to that scene soon.)

"But there must be something," God said thoughtfully.

Robert had never known anybody who had not thought that way about a Movie—that there was something, somehow, which, if thought of, would improve it. He recalled that such after-thoughts had often spoiled some of the best pictures he had been in. He doubted, too, that God, who seemed just to have learned about the Movies, would be able to offer anything constructive for *The Redeemer*. But he kept silent, for Robert had learned long ago not to argue with critics.

"You," said God. "I can improve you."

Robert glanced around him quickly, forgetting that the Angels had been dismissed.

"My performance," said Robert, "looked all right in the projection room. That's where the rushes are shown every day," he added informatively, "I mean, the showing of the previous day's work. Of course, you can't always tell from the rushes. But Mr. Kolisher was more than satisfied. And so was Mr. Lingbaum."

"Lingbaum," God repeated. "I heard that name before!"

"He's my director," said Robert. "He thinks I've done a very good job."

"I am sure you have," said God kindly. The simplicity and courage of this little human appealed deeply to Him. "I was not referring to your acting, but to your soul," He went on. "I could improve that."

"In what way?" asked Robert, interested.

"I could make you a little more true to character when you perform on the Cross," said God.

"How?" asked Robert, stubbornly.

"By making you Divine," said God.

Robert stared.

"You will be truly My Son," said God. "I shall place a particle of My Light within you. There will be a glow of beauty in your face. And through all the hours of your agony there will shine the glory and simplicity of My Truth, as evidenced in you. The world will weep when it sees you, and the Soul of Man will see into Heaven."

Robert flushed and offered no objection.

God reached out a hand and touched his shoulder. A moment later appeared the three Angels who had borne him from the desert into Heaven. They beheld a changed Robert Gary. A radiance such as distinguished their own figures shone from him.

"Return him to the place where you found him," God said.

"I'd rather call on Mr. Kolisher first and explain where I've been," said Robert, "if You don't mind."

"Very well," said God, "take him to Mr. Kolisher."

He smiled on Robert as the Angels led him away. Then God vanished and resumed His work with His Forces.

Robert found himself surrounded by a good part of the Heavenly Host. Despite the Deity's hope that the truth of His reunion with His supposed Son would remain secret (for He worried about the ancient business of Lucifer), His three Messengers had revealed the curious error of Omnipotence to their brothers.

Smiling now at the jest, the Host flocked around Robert with a babble of questions. Jostled, and his ears ringing with a thousand queries about the Movies, Robert, who was used to such demonstrations and curiosities, smiled as sweetly as he could—which, with the new Divinity given him, was very sweetly indeed—and said pleasantly everything he could think of saying.

Some of the bolder Angels begged him for a souvenir of his visit. One of them finally reached to him and removed the crown of thorns from his head. Others followed this example and in a twinkling Robert was denuded of all but his shorts, which he wore under his Messiah's robe.

He laughed good-naturedly at this display of interest in his person and talents, but pleaded with his new admirers to leave him his shorts, for he was not made (he explained in his own words) as they, whose nudity offered no interruptions to purity. Finally he signaled his three guides. The Angels all blew trumpets for Robert and a group of them followed their visitor to the last rim of Heaven.

When Robert next opened his eyes, he saw Mr. Kolisher. He was about to speak when Mr. Kolisher saw him. And then for fifteen minutes Robert was unable to say anything, for he would not have been heard.

Robert learned that he had been missing for three days and that Mr. Kolisher had believed him killed in the storm that had almost demolished the set. A thousand police and their deputies had been searching the desert around. The entire nation had been horrified and several hundred thousand letters had arrived from the People demanding that Mr. Kolisher increase his efforts and spare no expense to find the missing idol.

Throughout these activities, which had cost him a pretty penny—the three-day delay alone represented a carrying charge of $150,000—Mr. Kolisher had given out a score of heartbroken public statements and suffered, in private, as if Robert had been his true son.

"You were drunk somewhere," Mr. Kolisher suddenly interrupted his saga of grief. "Look at you! Walking into this office naked. You're still drunk," he added after a searching look into his Star's eyes. "Explain yourself, Mr. Gary."

Robert smiled.

"You will have to excuse my undress," he said, "but they took all my clothes away."

"Who did?" demanded Mr. Kolisher.

"The Angels," said Robert.

"Sit down," said Mr. Kolisher softly.

A great understanding had come to him. He realized that Robert Gary had not been drunk. The glitter of Robert's eyes and the strange expression of Robert's entire face should have revealed the truth to him at first glance. Mr. Gary had been taking drugs and had been laid low by an overdose or gone on an extended dope jag.

"We will have to keep this quiet," said Mr. Kolisher. "It would not only ruin my picture, but ruin you and have a bad effect on the whole industry if it leaks out."

"Keep what quiet?" asked Robert.

"What you have been doing," said Mr. Kolisher diplomatically.

He opened the dictograph key and spoke into the instrument in slow, precise tones.

"Give me Mr. Birdwin," he said.

"Here, boss," said a voice.

Mr. Birdwin was the head generalissimo of the extensive Kolisher Publicity Department.

"I want you to pay close attention, Mr. Birdwin, to what I have to say," said Mr. Kolisher.

"Shoot," said the voice.

"Mr. Birdwin," said Mr. Kolisher, slowing way down, "Robert Gary is waiting here with me in my office."

"I'll be right down," said the voice.

"Stay where you are," said Mr. Kolisher. "I want you to send out a story for international release throughout the entire world. Send copies to the Associated Press, the United Press, and all the other major agencies for news gathering."

"Yes, siree!" said the voice.

"Robert Gary," resumed Mr. Kolisher, "was knocked off the Cross by the storm. He fell on his head and suffered a severe concussion of the brain. Not knowing who he was, you understand, or what he was doing, he wandered through the desert for three days, living on nothing but cactus leaves until his senses were restored."

"I got it down," said the voice. "Go on."

"Mr. Robert Gary is back now in this office," said Mr. Kolisher, "and will be on the set positively tomorrow morning to finish the picture. He is still a little shaken by his tragic experiences, but they will in no way interfere with him finishing his role as the Redeemer. That's all. And furthermore, Mr. Birdwin, I want the press kept away from Robert Gary personally. He is in no condition as yet to speak to them. You understand me?"

"Yes, siree," said the voice, and Mr. Kolisher clicked the key.

"That'll hold them," he said and turned to Robert. "Now, Robert," he went on, "I am going to close the door and see that we are not interrupted and you are going to make a confession to me, for the good of your soul and your future career. And when the picture is done I am going to see to it that the best doctors in the country take you in hand. I owe this to you because I don't mind saying, whatever your personal shortcomings, you have done a fine job as the Redeemer."

"Well," said Robert, "I am willing to tell you what happened. But I don't think you will believe me."

"Proceed," said Mr. Kolisher.

"Well," Robert began, and there came over him a sudden sadness such as has always fallen into the hearts of those who try to speak of the personal favor of God. "Well, Mr. Kolisher, I was taken off the Cross by three Angels during the storm and they carried me to Heaven. I don't exactly know why it all happened, Mr. Kolisher, but I was led into a large and very beautiful hall full of Angels. Then I met God and He talked to me. I didn't know the whole thing had taken so long. Three days, you say. Well, it seemed hardly a minute."

As Mr. Kolisher remained silent, Robert added, nervously: "I'll tell you what God said, if you care to hear."

Mr. Kolisher rose, his gaze intent on the curious glitter in his Star's eyes. "Robert," he said, "I don't care to hear whatsoever. I will, however, send for some clothes and have you taken home. And I want you to promise me, on your sacred word of honor, that you will not speak a word to anybody—till it wears off."

Although Robert kept the sacred word of honor he had given (for he felt almost from the first moment of his return the hopelessness of getting anybody to believe in the truth), the echo of Mr. Kolisher's suspicions passed through the crowded streets of Jerusalem the next morning. By the time the cameras had been put up and the set lighted, the theory that Robert Gary was a hophead and had wandered off on a dope jag had mysteriously gained a number of adherents, chief among them Mr. Lingbaum.

"It's the irony of the picture business," said Mr. Lingbaum, "that we are going to photograph on the Cross this morning, in the role of the Saviour, a ham who not only can't tell his left foot from his behind, but who is also a hophead. Look at the way his eyes glitter," he added in an undertone as Robert Gary, in full costume, appeared.

"Hello," said Robert coldly. He had guessed what was being said. "Do I look all right?"

"You're a fine-looking Saviour," said Mr. Lingbaum ambiguously. "A little too much brown in the make-up, though. Tone it down. And have Joe pump some glycerin into your eyes before you get on the Cross."

"I won't need any," said Robert coldly, "I——"

He was about to say that with God's light inside him and full of Divinity, he would need no glycerin in his eyes to help him register the proper emotions of the Son. But he decided to keep it a secret.

"I have my own conception of the part," he finished.

He walked away with a curiously elastic step toward the little ladder leaning against the middle Cross. For there were three crosses, and on the other two the Thieves were already in position.

"Hopped to the ears," said Mr. Lingbaum, watching the thorn-crowned figure with fascination. A number of electricians and extras winked at one another.

A few minutes later the technicolor cameras were turning, and Robert Gary, hanging from the Cross, enacted the Agony.

The script called for some seven shots of the Crucifixion, beginning with the nailing of the hands and feet, which had already been taken in close-ups with papier-mâché facsimiles of

Robert's extremities, and ending with him dead, head dropped and body stiffened in its final throe of pain.

The story of the Redeemer, in its final pages, cut away from and cut back to the Cross seven times, each time revealing the increase in the Lord's suffering. Mr. Lingbaum had rehearsed the whole Crucifixion the morning before the storm. Nevertheless, he expected a great deal of trouble with Robert. He was surprised when, without hitch and in a manner that surpassed anything he had ever seen this lamest of all actors do, Robert went through the ordeal of the shooting.

"My God," Mr. Lingbaum thought several times as the cameras turned, "he's better than Barrymore!"

It was late afternoon when the scene was completed. Robert, considerably worn by his efforts and yet feeling oddly exhilarated, leaped from the Cross, spurning the little step ladder. The picture of *The Redeemer* was finished. Mr. Kolisher, present on the set during the last few hours of shooting, threw a fatherly arm around Robert's shoulders.

"You did fine, wonderful," he said. "I didn't think you had it in you. It was magnificent."

In his heart, Mr. Kolisher knew it was not talent but dope that had inspired Robert Gary to his truly unusual performance that day. But he decided, graciously, not to mention the fact. In Mr. Kolisher's code, an artist, drunk or sober, was entitled to praise if he did the work well and without too much delay in the schedule.

"You were all right," said Mr. Lingbaum. "I don't think we'll need a single retake on this day's work. And I'd expected a lot of trouble with those scenes."

"Thank you," said Robert to both men, who had escorted him to his dressing room.

Mr. Kolisher waited until Mr. Lingbaum had left.

"I will see you tomorrow afternoon in my office," he said quietly, "about that matter I mentioned yesterday. Tomorrow afternoon—after the rushes."

Mr. Kolisher was waiting at four o'clock the next day for a call from the projection room. He was eager to see the rushes of the scenes he had witnessed shot, convinced that they would furnish a stirring and beautiful climax to his magnificent production. The door opened, without warning, and a stricken and pallid Lingbaum entered. Mr. Kolisher looked up in surprise.

"I have something to tell you," Mr. Lingbaum said in a hoarse voice. "I've just come from the laboratory."

"What's the matter?" asked Mr. Kolisher, rising.

"The rushes are no good," Mr. Lingbaum answered, white-faced.

"In what way?" Mr. Kolisher asked slowly.

"You won't believe me," said Mr. Lingbaum and fell, as if shot, into a large leather chair.

"Proceed," said Mr. Kolisher.

"Robert Gary ain't in them," Mr. Lingbaum answered.

"Ain't in what?" asked Mr. Kolisher more slowly.

"The rushes," breathed Mr. Lingbaum.

"Out of focus," countered Mr. Kolisher coldly.

"I said he ain't in them, in focus or out of focus," Mr. Lingbaum answered, petulant despite his pallor. He felt bewitched, for though he had always believed actors non-existent, he had never thought them so non-existent as this.

"What are you trying to tell me?" Mr. Kolisher demanded.

"I don't know," Mr. Lingbaum said slowly. "But I just looked at the film in the view box and there is no sign of Robert."

"Is—is anything else on the film?" Mr. Kolisher asked, feeling dizzy.

"Everything," said Mr. Lingbaum. "The lighting is beautiful. The colors are remarkable. The composition is perfect. Only there is nobody on the Cross. Not a soul."

"He was there!" Mr. Kolisher cried out. "I saw him with my own eyes."

"I photographed him!" screamed Mr. Lingbaum. "By God, I tell you something has happened!"

Twenty minutes later Messrs. Kolisher and Lingbaum, with a group of their assistants, sat in the darkened projection room waiting for the rushes to be shown. They sat in a hush in which Mr. Kolisher's heavy breathing sounded ominously.

The rushes appeared and for a few minutes the hush was broken by cries of amazement. A dozen different-voiced sounds of incredulity and bewilderment filled the dark little auditorium. But Mr. Kolisher's voice was not among them. His breathing grew heavier, but no other sounds issued from him.

On the screen had appeared the Cross, standing between two other towering crosses tipped at picturesque angles and bearing each the figure of a Thief, sweating, writhing, and unshaven. Behind these the desert clouds drifted full of beauty and portent. All was visible in its original coloring and, as Mr. Lingbaum had said, in perfect composition and focus. But on the center Cross there was not the faintest hint of Robert Gary.

"Where is he?" Mr. Lingbaum cried out suddenly in the dark. "Shut it off. Take those things off the screen!" Fear had overcome him.

"Let them run," Mr. Kolisher spoke loudly. "I want to see every foot that was shot."

And Mr. Kolisher did. He saw, however, more than the amazed ones in the projection room did. He saw that there would be no retakes and that *The Redeemer* would have to be released without the Crucifixion for a finish.

Mr. Kolisher knew, despite there was, as always, nothing in his mind, that something more than dope was wrong with Robert Gary.

A garbled and generally discredited account of the "Hollywood miracle" spread through a number of newspaper offices and dinner parties. It was derisively tagged as a bit of press agentry and one in shocking taste. For there is no one so gullible as to believe in the reality of anything within the Kingdom of the Movies.

Mr. Kolisher's predicament was unusual. His showman's soul itched to broadcast the incontrovertible fact of his Star's Divinity or, at least, magic properties. The fact that Robert Gary had been to Heaven, or some place like it (taken there by Angels), and that he had spoken to God, would immeasurably increase the drawing power of his (Mr. Kolisher's) greatest production, *The Redeemer*. But his instincts warned him that ten people would call him a fool, and an unscrupulous fool, at that, for every one person who might feel a vague belief in such an advertising campaign.

The Redeemer ended, as he had seen it must in the projection room, without any Crucifixion whatsoever. There was no use doing things by halves—that is, in long shots with a double on the Cross.

Mr. Kolisher, after a secret interview with Robert, refused to make any retakes. Robert had added some details to his original story. It was obvious to Mr. Kolisher that something remarkably peculiar had happened to Robert, something which a group of scientists could probably explain—and did later. Mr. Kolisher, listening to the astonishing story, was not exactly frightened, but he considered the whole matter a mystery beyond him or his Publicity Department. He advised Robert to go somewhere and rest up.

"I don't wish to either contradict or criticize you, Robert," said Mr. Kolisher, "but the main thing is that if you go away and rest, the thing you are suffering from may wear off and they will be able to photograph you again. My advice to you, Robert —and, mind you, I am extremely fond of you—is you can't be too careful. I've seen lots of Movie Stars, every bit as big as you, come and go, come and go."

Robert nodded.

"You may think yourself more important because of this amazing thing that has happened to you," pursued Mr. Kolisher thoughtfully, "but whatever you are, you ain't much good as an actor as long as you remain invisible. What worries me, Robert, about your whole story, is it ain't logical. Now if God had wanted to help me in my production of *The Redeemer*, why would He spoil my main actor and kill the chief scene of the whole script?"

Mr. Kolisher turned his attention to some documents on his desk and added in a crisp voice:

"Get some rest, Robert. And thank you very much for your work in the picture. I appreciate it. That'll be all."

Robert stood up.

"Maybe if I went to church," he murmured, "and prayed to God He should remove His light from me, I could make a comeback."

"That is your lookout, Robert," said Mr. Kolisher aloofly,

"but I would advise you to be careful about what you say and do—in church or out of it. Lots of people are liable to misunderstand you. That'll be all, Robert."

And Robert, in whom bitterness and confusion were beginning already to warp character, went into hiding in a desert sanitarium, pending developments.

The opening of *The Redeemer* in New York—its first public showing—was the Industry's most outstanding première up to that time. It is doubtful whether the actual enactment of the Saviour's drama within its precincts would have excited its citizens any more. There might have been a handful of more intensely elated onlookers, but, I am sure, hardly as general a feeling of awe and expectation.

At least, in Heaven the unveiling of the Kolisher production created a much vaster stir than had the original performance in the Holy Land.

On this night, which was to witness the cinematized tale of God's Son, there was neither vagueness nor ignorance beyond the vaults of Space.

God had summoned as many of the Angels as He could spare from the operation of His Forces and revealed to them what was going to happen. Taking a leaf from the way Mr. Kolisher was doing things, for He had grown (to me) an unreasonable admiration for that man, God had seated His Angels in a vast and glittering theater, far more spacious and beautiful than His Homecoming Hall. So transcendent, so staggeringly opulent were the dimensions and appointments of this theater that I shall not even attempt to describe them, except to say that Hollywood has a long way to go.

The unfolding of the first reels of *The Redeemer* held the Angels breathless. At that distance, perhaps, the events taking place on the screen in the New York theater seemed to them as real as the other doings of that little world.

God patiently explained to them, while the performance was going on, that the Movies were not life. They were, He said, not only a representation of it, but a charming dream-like improvement.

Some of the Angels understood that God meant not an improvement on His Works, but on something else. Others of them, however, were impressed by God's unprecedented modesty.

"What you are seeing," said God as the New York performance progressed, "is the work of Mr. Kolisher's genius. It is very fine and I am glad you admire it. However, I have assisted Mr. Kolisher in the final part of the drama."

"In what way?" asked the Angel Michael at his side.

"You will see," said God and smiled. "The last part of *The Redeemer* will be by far the best," He added.

"When does Your contribution begin?" asked the Angel Michael.

"It begins," said God, "where Robert is on the Cross. I have, as Mr. Lingbaum would say, directed the acting in that scene."

The Angels nodded excitedly. Marvelous though the Movie seemed to them thus far, they knew that with God's help its wonders would be augmented and they waited breathlessly.

"Now, in a few minutes," said God, "My scene will appear."

The Redeemer was carrying the Cross up a hill. Crowds were hooting and stones were flying at his head.

"Wait," said God.

The Angels all leaned forward eagerly. But a surprising thing happened. No sooner had the Redeemer reached the top of the hill on which stood the two crosses bearing Barabbas and his co-felon than darkness came slowly down on the screen. The picture of the Redeemer, with a hundred voices pealing above the roar of organs and orchestra, faded out. The Angels stared and then turned to the Deity.

"Something has happened," said God. "It will continue in a minute.

"Michael!" said God, for He intended to send him to the rescue of Mr. Kolisher. But He became silent. The first-nighters were applauding wildly. The lights in the New York theater had gone on again and the audience, clothing themselves in lovely pieces of finery while they dabbed tears of compassion from their eyes, were filing out. It came to God that the Movie was over.

There was a hush in Heaven.

"I can't believe it," said God. "It is something too difficult to believe."

The Angel Michael, closest to God, held his breath, for a great darkness had come over the Divine face.

"Mr. Kolisher did not use My ending," said God. "He threw it away."

The Angels said nothing. They had seldom seen the Deity so disturbed.

The awed and happy crowds emerging from the theater in which they had witnessed the latest product of Mr. Kolisher's genius stepped into one of the worst storms that had ever smitten the city of New York.

Lightnings and thunders of a prodigious type filled the black, wind-howling night. Gusts of razor-sharp rain blinded all the traffic and even the people inside cafés shivered unhappily at this outburst of the elements.

The storm raged most of the night. A great deal of wreckage had to be removed in the morning.

The newspapers devoted considerable space to the "freak storm," as it was called, for the weather bureaus had had no warning of it from any of their instruments. Nevertheless, there was enough space left to herald the beauties of Mr. Kolisher's *The Redeemer*.

The Movie was described, in language which the Kolisher Publicity Department could not have improved on, as a sort of climax to Mr. Kolisher's genius. What most impressed the critics, however, was not the magnificence of the Movie—for they were used to that from his skillful hands—but the restraint the great producer had exercised in not revealing the final scenes of the world-famous drama.

They declared, with a remarkable unanimity which may have had something to do with the gold-plate banquet Mr. Kolisher had tendered them on the eve of the opening, that Hollywood's leading wizard had done something both noble and artistic in leaving the final scenes to the imagination.

It would, they thought and said, have been much too harrowing even for the seasoned First-Nighters to have had to sit through the actual Crucifixion.

Mr. Kolisher was pleased to read these things. He caused innumerable copies of them to be made and distributed among the People, that they might see how expertly and cleverly he had served their best interests.

But though he was pleased, he was, too, a little disturbed. He wondered about the storm that had almost spoiled his Opening Night, and decided on no more religious pictures.

But you will be wondering probably, or should be (as Mr. Kolisher was), about Robert Gary. Despite the many things there were to praise in the Kolisher production, the critics found space for several paragraphs about the Central Character. They agreed that Robert Gary had excelled himself in his tender and beautiful portrayal of the Redeemer and pronounced, as with one voice, that he was now firmly established as filmland's leading idol.

It was, alas, a pronouncement completely cockeyed.

What happened to Robert is a little involved, but will bear telling. Shortly after the great success of *The Redeemer* Robert was cast (not by Mr. Kolisher, but by the major studio from which he had originally been borrowed) in the role of a South Seas beachcomber—also in technicolor. Some preliminary tests made of Robert quickly resulted in his being dropped from the cast. For the tests revealed the same amazing deficiency as had the rushes in the Kolisher projection room: Robert was not in the film.

He was dropped from the great studio's payroll within a week. His contract—the most magnificent one in the film capital—providing for an abrogation by either side in the event of any "act of God," was canceled. Although this was, of course, a mere piece of legal phrasing, Robert's lawyers, who had heard his story, assured him he had cooked his own goose in the telling of it and would have no chance in court with his own admission of such an "act of God" against him.

In the end his employers believed not a bit of Robert's story, having had the matter of his camera invisibility explained to them by their Research Department. It was due, they had found out, to an excess of radio-activity and bone phosphorescence, but they felt it within their ethical rights to take advantage of Robert's own silly tale as a means of saving $15,000 a week.

Robert was never employed again. Some interest attached to him for a few months. A number of religious-minded people called on him—in his sanitarium—and begged him to go on a lecture tour of the country.

This little group was convinced that all the things Robert had to say were true. His invisibility to the Camera, owing to Divine Radiance, would lend, they were certain, credence to his story of his Heavenly visit. They urged Robert, who in a way was truly another Son of God, to leave his sanitarium and spread his Divine Revelation among the People. As the outstanding Movie name of the day, he was sure of huge audiences for any personal appearances.

But Robert, though he knew God had placed His Divinity upon his face, refused to budge from the sanitarium. Robert had a horror of public appearances and was certain that the sight of a crowd waiting for him to speak would shrivel his brain to nothingness. He was not going to make a fool of himself as a tongue-tied Messiah, and this is what he said to his would-be religious sponsors.

But there was another thing in Robert's heart that kept him from the projected tour as God's Son. He had no desire to pose as such a One and no wish to broadcast the Truth of God to a dubious world. For Robert, whose simplicity the Deity Himself had admired, was embittered with God for ruining his career. He had felt in his bones something of the sort would happen when God had begun asking those questions about the inside of the Movie business. God had tumbled another idol, which, in its debris, was in no mood to spread the Almighty's fame.

The Kingdom of the Movies continued to flourish without either Robert's or God's assistance.

Of all the things I have written in this story, the most interesting (to me, at least) is the sad conclusion to be drawn from it. I am afraid it appears that God's intervention in the World of Man, even in the simplest of his enterprises, such as the Movies, is fraught with disaster and futility. Amen.

DEATH OF ELEAZER

N THIS
new summer morning the

city glitters with light. Warmth is in the streets. Overhead the buildings loom like plate-glass trees. The spokes of the sun turn in a thousand windows.

The hearts and bodies of people seem full of this new summer. In the shop-lined avenue there is an unaccustomed air of personality about the half-sauntering figures. In their open-throated, bareheaded salute to summer there is a smile of festival, and honeymoon in the passing faces. The smell of the ocean, whose vast and idle waters are only a few miles away, brings a truant glint to the eyes of the younger walkers, and the older ones, who no longer smile at each other, smile at memories.

This pleasant morning, without grasses or trees or trilling birds, is still lush with summer languor as if the bright warm sky were full of the odors and phantoms of river lands and rolling meadows. Nature, routed by the city, seems to creep back into its stone streets and gleam out of the eyes of these strolling citizens.

On such a day the history of the world and all its achievements seems useless. All the travail of the many centuries of conquest and progress is hardly a footnote in the heart of this summer crowd. Life, innocent of its thousand and one nights of politics and science, sways gracefully and luringly still in the bodies of the young and sighs tenderly still out of the eyes of the old.

There was on this morning one who walked this street and whose thoughts were far from rejoicing over the innocence of Life. This was a reddish, square-faced man, elderly, broad-shouldered, and dressed in heavy dark cloth and thick-soled shoes which, like the rest of him, made no compromise with the season. He was James Malloy, Captain of Police. His flat blue

eyes looked unwaveringly ahead of him as he strode, for Captain
Malloy considered it part of his technique as a man-hunter to
seem as uninquisitive as a sleep-walker.

But the captain's eyes, though immobile, were remarkably sensitive. Not only did they see what apparently they were not
looking at, but they evaluated, diagnosed, and sorted all that they
saw. This they did automatically, for, whatever the rest of Captain Malloy was, his eyes were two tireless and very able scientists at work in an endless clinic. They looked at faces with an
instinct for character that was subtle and accurate.

Captain Malloy's greatest annoyance during his thirty years as
a detective was the knowledge that of all the faces moving in any
street his was usually the most transparent and the most easily
to be diagnosed. He would have liked very much to be a bloodhound with the talent of the hunting beetle, which lies in wait
for its quarry with its legs drawn in so that it resembles a stone.
Instead, he was a reddish, square-faced man with flat blue eyes,
stiffened chin, bushy brows, and taut cheeks, and there was no
concealing from the stupidest of criminals what he was. There
was a trained, aggressive air and a hound's keenness and an aura
of detachment and righteousness to the captain, which no haber-
dashery or feigned mannerisms could becloud for a moment.
Dressed a bit defiantly in his formidable garments, his black iron
derby, his heavy blue suit and ponderous shoes, the captain was,
within and without, the man-hunter.

On this morning what Malloy saw in the sauntering crowd
was for the most part not worth the seeing, from any policeman's point of view. Cluster on cluster of faces bobbed past
with no message for the captain's eyes. They were the faces in
which moods had idled rather than foraged, and left little behind
for hound senses to sniff at. And the captain noticed, though he

was little given to poetical thoughts, that all these nondescript faces were a little in love with the bright morning as if the outside of the world today were of more importance than its inner stories.

But in these clusters of faces the captain's eyes now and again located the Devil's spoor, the faint but never-ending trail of crime that marked the faces of every crowd for him. Had you asked Captain Malloy what it was he saw, he could have answered only hesitatingly. For the captain's mind worked much too slowly to reveal its contents to anyone but himself. His lightning-like ability to correlate the lines of a mouth, the glint of an eye, the tautness or tremble of a muscle with the extensive rogues' gallery he carried in his memory was far beyond his power of explanation. But just as he was able by this memory to identify several thousand known criminals at a glance and to know their names, records, and predilections without recourse to any memoranda, so he was able to identify parts of these faces in the anonymity of the crowd.

He saw the quiver of the pupil that told of guilt; the white-skinned, gaunt temples and extra bony structure of eye-sockets that told of drug addictions and hidden depravities; the fleshy ears and over-lidded eyes that told of sadism and all its sleeping deeds of violence. All the conflicts and complexes out of which crime is born, all the over-greeds and under-controls that return the human to the animal, spoke to Captain Malloy out of a hundred little matters sometimes of no more significance than the placing of a wrinkle. So minute, in fact, were the signs of the trail at which the policeman sniffed that you might have agreed with some of his envious colleagues that there was more instinct than science to his work. Proud though he was of his power for noticing things, Captain Malloy would himself have agreed, in part. For he had also noticed that there was another spoor to crime than that to be seen by the eye and catalogued by the swift, microscopic work of memory. There was an aura to the malignant and the maladjusted that brushed the captain's spirit. He could have sensed a murderer in the dark and smelled a dishonest soul through a burlap bag.

Such, omitting a great deal of other matters, was the character of Captain Malloy as he strode this morning to take a train for the outskirts of the city. He was intent on visiting a Dominican monastery and consulting an old man called Father Dominic, who, he had been told, was a great authority on crucifixes.

The captain was on duty and had been so without rest morning or night for two months. During this time four murders, committed apparently by the same maniacal hand, had provided excitement for the newspapers and presumably for the millions who read them.

Captain Malloy often wondered what it was about crime that so fascinated everybody. Like the scene-shifter manipulating the worn and stupid-looking props of the back stage, the captain could not quite understand the "ohs" and "ahs" of the audience applauding the spectacle from the front. He knew, however, that they applauded and that the corpse along with the killer stirred a remarkable exuberance in them. And that the tedious business of the hunt, the arrest, the trial and conviction, was full of glamour for those who watched.

Captain Malloy had more theories about these watchers than he had about crime. For his cunning told him that in this fascination exercised by the guilty on the innocent, by the cruel on the kindly, by the mad on the sane, lay a trail deeper than the tell-tale Devil's spoor. Hidden away even in these placid faces that offered no criminal signature of lips, eyes, or ears, was a kinship for crime which to the captain seemed almost like crime itself. It seemed to him that crime was a seed in the whole of humanity, and though it came to flower in only the two percent, as figured out by the statisticians, it lay dormant everywhere. It needed but a little extra stir of grief or hunger, or often merely some accidental shifting of the glands, to set it flourishing.

And being on the way to interview a man of God, Captain Malloy wondered if it was this seed of crime lying at the bottom of all souls that was indicated by the phrase, Original Sin. The priests said Adam's deed had put it there, and his medical friends maintained that all sorts of wolves, apes, and other monsters from whom man was descended had left it there. But however it had arrived, out of Hell or from our treetop sires, Captain Malloy knew better than most philosophers how firmly and universally this seed was present.

In Captain Malloy's pocket as he marched there lay a curious antique crucifix, which had been found clutched in the left hand of a man named Joseph Franks, who had been murdered in Central Park the night before. Joseph Franks's belly had been ripped open, and by this the police knew that Franks was the fourth victim of the sadist killer who had signed three previous deeds with a similar sign manual. But this time a clue had remained. The dead man's fingers had been pried from around a crucifix of strange workmanship that they had evidently snatched from the neck of the murderer. The fastening loop at the top of the crucifix was broken.

The first authorities Captain Malloy had consulted had said the red half-circle beneath the Saviour's feet was a partly obliterated D and obviously stood for Dominic.

Captain Malloy looked nervously out of the train window and, being a good Catholic, tried with difficulty to forget that monks

wore around their necks crucifixes such as the one in his pocket
and that they dangled away from their robes when they leaned
over.

The gardens of the Dominican monastery on the edge of the
City of New York were extremely beautiful. They occupied
two acres and were enclosed by high weather-stained and vine-
covered walls of stone. Within these walls grass-overgrown slate
tiles made a rambling walk through clumps of pine, oak, linden,
butternut, and mulberry trees. The walk disappeared into shrubberies of syringa, lilac, and magnolia and trellised towering wis-
tarias. It emerged to circle carved oak benches and lily-covered
pools of water. At one end of the garden, under a little forest of
heavily leafed maples, a young colony of ferns raised darkly
glowing serpentine heads. The ground sloped to various levels
and the walk became steps by which one climbed into unexpected rock gardens half covered with vari-colored mosses and
a-twinkle with diminutive blooms. Against one of the stone
walls ran a series of grape arbors made of undressed cedar boughs
and under their canopies the cloistered ground was covered with
the flashing foliage of periwinkle, arbutus, and other creepers.

Along the walk where neither tree nor shrub cast shadows,
grew the flowers. These borders were clustered also with peony
and rose bushes. Verbena, lilies, phlox, cornflowers, petunias,
delphiniums, and scores of other early summer celebrants ran beside the walk and circled the bushes in flurries of color.

All of the garden, including even these cultivated blooms,
seemed half a wilderness as if it had come tumbling capriciously
out of the earth and scattered itself exuberantly over walls and
hillocks. It was only when one noticed on second look the rolling areas of clipped grass, the bowered shrines and little foun-

tains, the lilied pools and always navigable lanes curling through trunks and foliage, that one knew this was a garden carefully tended.

In further proof of this labor one saw, too, the black-robed Fathers whose duties kept them hovering like huge beetles under the shrubberies and crawling among the plants with trowels, baskets, and pails of bone meal. There were always three or four of these figures stirring in the leafy corners. And on the carved benches others were to be seen doubled like dark question marks over yellowed books, or sitting straight and contemplating the tree-leafed spaces above the garden walls.

Of these black-robed figures the most industrious was usually that of a shriveled little ancient with a weatherbeaten bald head and the face of a moldy faun. This was Father Dominic, who for sixty years had lived in this garden as attentively as any of its squirrels, aphids, or coleoptera. The Order was proud of Father Dominic as its botanist and had published some nine volumes compiled by the little Friar during the months of winter when he sat evoking garden memories in his bleak cell.

These books were among the most curious in botanical literature, being full of quaint admixtures of science and religious meditation so interwoven that it was difficult to distinguish data from piety. Indeed, some of Father Dominic's more cautious readers considered his literary work full of heresies and the product of a mind nearly divorced from the God worshiped in the monastery chapel. But even these critics, troubled by the pagan pages printed by their Order, hesitated to condemn them. For there was in Father Dominic's nine books the distillation of a soul so gentle, so humble in its knowledge, and so full of some mysterious love, that none who read could restrain a smile evoked by his musing. And Father Dominic's superiors, in discussing the whimsical and somewhat disorderly meditations that fluttered like pagan bees and butterflies among the data of his pages, remembered proudly that the most learned of scientists, including the celebrated Hindu, Chandra Bose, had written enthusiastically of their weatherbeaten little Friar and found in his work secrets beyond their own talented but worldly intellects.

Nearing eighty, Father Dominic remained to the oldest of his colleagues as unchanging as the vegetation he haunted from dawn to sunset. Sun, wind, and earth had long ago claimed his face as their handiwork. His eyes had come to peck like birds at what they saw; his lips were baked into a smile as unwavering as the curl of a leaf almost dead; his long fingers had grown hardened into a chitinous surface resembling that of the bugs they were forever pursuing. Yet with all his digging and floundering around in a half-century of rain, wind, and blasting sun like any farmer, Father Dominic's senses had remained as acute as those of a recluse. The fragile instruments by which he measured the reaction of flowers to the passage of a cloud across the moon, or the puzzling movements of the Oscillatoria plants, or the quantity of oxygen exhaled by a cornflower in its modest efforts to keep the world alive, or the beat of the soft and watery engines of life that caused the garden to bloom, smell, quiver, and die— these required the delicacy of a surgeon's touch. There was no tremble in the little Friar's ancient fingers. Daily he moved with his chemicals and minute electrical devices through the enchanted factory of the garden, catching the hidden whispers of its toil, studying the digestive apparatus of trees and shrubs, and the half-animal heart throbbing beneath the static face of vegetation.

Not only his eyes and fingers toiled, but his nose also was as busy as a grasshopper among the thousand scents of earth and foliage. To Father Dominic these scents were the gage of death rather than pleasure, and by them he measured, as by the sighs of an invalid, the speed of the rose's decomposition and the lily's farewell.

Long ago he had written: "The odors of flowers are the sweet signals of their mortality. They are the sweat on Nature's brow given off in a cloud of fair smells as each of her green children toils and sinks exhausted into her lap. The decomposition we dread so in life is the glory of the plants. And by some subtle pact with God those that die the swiftest smell the sweetest."

On this bright morning that found Captain Malloy en route to the Dominican monastery, Father Dominic was awaiting another visitor also. This was his old friend, Rabbi Eleazer, with whom he had been discussing God for more than half a century. Father Dominic's friendship for the Jew Eleazer had, like his writings, been aired now and again in the Councils of the Order. It had been given out then, by those who thought the friendship needed defending—this was long ago, when the Friar was still young—that his interest in the pale and dark-eyed Jewish youth was a call to proselyte among the most ancient and stiff-necked of unbelievers. And when it had become evident, with the passing of the years, that it was to this same Jew, now a Rabbi, that Father Dominic gave the full gift of his greatest friendship (his only friendship), these same defenders had excused the irregularity by the fiction that the conversion was proving difficult. They had even cited precedents on record when the saving of a single Jew had taken as long as twenty years, for this was a race whose history showed that it was easier to send a thousand of them to the Devil than to persuade a single one to go to Heaven. But once saved, they said, there was none like the Jew for expiating the error of his former life. Scores of Torquemada's ablest lieutenants had been lured from the stiff clutch of Israel. There was also the fact that Christianity had been created by a Jew raised up by God, even as their very Order had been launched by the son of a Jew.

Such were the considerations that marked the talk at the beginning of the friendship, for those were more pious days fifty, and even thirty, years ago, than today.

The continued visits of Eleazer to the monastery's gardens and library came finally to be accepted without remark, or even passing thought. Now, even the most holy of the Fathers had come to smile on the tall, pale Jew with his deep-set eyes and long Arab nose, and to pilot him gladly to where his friend Dominic awaited his coming, as he did this morning.

Sitting on a bench beside a pool of waterlilies, Father Dominic had the fancy that, on such a lovely day as this one provided by God, a man felt more like a plant than a human being. On a day like this, if one sat still, one was able to drink of the golden breast of the sun like any suckling cornflower in the garden. One knew, too, how the petunia balanced the whole of summer on its eager and expiring petal. And when one looked up, as Father Dominic did, one beheld the tree leaves motionless, like hands arrested in benediction.

Waiting for his friend Eleazer to come, the Father experimented with a notion he had often longed but never dared to incorporate in his works. The weatherbeaten old man pretended he was a plant, exhaling oxygen rather than carbon dioxide and full of that mysterious tingle of kinship he had noted and measured among the various blooms in the garden. The old man knew there was danger in this game, for at a certain point of it certain ideas came into his head for whose presence he always fasted the rest of the day by way of penance. Nevertheless, with the small sigh that innocence utters on expiring, Father Dominic gave himself over to the pleasant but guilty business of being a plant this summer hour—a hardy little shrub abloom on an oak bench. His soul communed with other shrubs and he felt the faint roar of the earth at his roots. God stepped out of the tortuous theologies and became a wind that brushed his cheek, a warmth that lay like a mother's kiss on his heart. No mystery remained to haunt the old man's head. All was serene and beautifully related. Life and Death were brothers in the garden exchanging their secrets gently with each other, and in the flushed face of the petunia, Father Dominic the shrub beheld his sister.

For timeless minutes the figure on the oak bench sat thus absorbed by Nature, so that the very bugs and gnats and toiling snails whose existence came brightly into his senses flooded him with delight. The cloudless sky descended to his eyes and entered his veins, and his nose became a door through which trooped all the mysteries of the ketones and esters, the acids and aldehydes of color and odor. When for some time he had tasted, like a plant, the perfect food of God, Father Dominic's mind awoke in the midst of this sweet dream and spoke to him like a very serpent in the garden.

"It is thus," thought the Friar, who seemed to have fallen asleep among his pleasures, "it is thus men once worshiped Nature, especially the ancient Germans who believed themselves to be descended from the trees . . . particularly those of the Black Forest in their southland. Yes . . . they used to bind and tie themselves when they came to pray in the wood so as to resemble their ancestors a little more closely. And if they toppled over while praying, they rolled out of the forest like logs and it sometimes took them weeks to get to the edge of the sacred wood. . . . There is no doubt that many of them died pretending too long they were logs in transit.

"It is easy to understand that there were people once who thought themselves descended from plants," he mused. "Much easier," he sighed, "than to figure out why nearly all the savages worshiped some animal as their ancestor. Well . . . well . . . there is really nothing in the world or above it that grows or moves or stands still, that is to be seen, heard, smelled, or even imagined, that has not been worshiped by somebody as his origin.

"I wonder wherein the totemism of the ancient races—which beheld in the bird, the cat, the bear, the ape, and the horse their original selves—where that differs from the modern theories of man's evolutionary descent? These ideas since Darwin say that Man is evolved out of those very animals which the most ignorant savages also identified as their earliest sires. . . . It would almost seem that the early people of the world, groping about in their memories of where they came from, and the scientists of today, groping among the skeletons and fossils for the secret of Man's beginnings, came to the same conclusions. Is it possible . . . that all of science today . . . is a faint, resuscitated echo of the knowledge that was once innately a part of Man?

"For instance . . . that myth shared by so many of the early races as to how life came to our planet. In Syria, Babylonia, far China—yes, and a hundred different places—the early peoples used to believe that a Giant had fallen from the skies, cast out by enemy Gods, and in falling was smashed to bits. And out of these bits emerged Man, Plants, and Animals. Even the Osiris of the Egyptians was a cousin of this Giant. Only . . . as I remember . . . instead of smashing to bits by himself, he was cut up into tiny segments.

"Now in what way does this myth differ from the theories of

modern biology?" pursued Father Dominic. "The new and most accepted theories have it that organic matter fell to the earth from the sun. A part of the sun broke off, it has been figured out, and crashed through space. And in its long fall was ground to dust. And out of this dust, Life emerged and finally Man.

"Even in the Bible the language of the old myth continues; only there Man does not fall literally from the skies, but from the grace of God. Ah! But it is still to be noticed that he falls! The thought that Man had fallen physically from on high obviously lingered for ages in his mind. Then as he grew more intelligent, it was replaced by the thought that his fall had been a spiritual one. And now that he has become even more intelligent, he is back again to the original theory of a physical fall."

The little Friar came to himself and murmured a brief prayer.

"What does it matter . . ." he said, directing his thoughts sternly into the proper channels, "what does it matter how Life was created or where—since, wherever the deed was done, whether in the moon, sun, or in Eden's garden, it was God who created it, as is believed by all good Christians? We are His children. . . . Amen."

Opening his eyes, he smiled to see the flowers emerging as from a dream and beckoning him again to their vari-colored altars leaning tipsily above the earth. With a smile still lingering on his faun's face, he lifted his eyes and saw the tall, pale Eleazer approaching beneath the shadows of the arbor.

Rabbi Eleazer was a proud and difficult old man who gave the impression to those who knew him that he was a reluctant part of this world. Spare and pale in his old age, the body and face of Eleazer suggested some large-eyed bird that had been plucked of its plumage and robbed of flight. But doubtless one thought of birds only because it was obvious that his soul had soared so high. When one listened to this man one felt that his mind was a rickety ladder leaning against Heaven, and that while his soul soared, his thought climbed exhaustedly after it.

Unlike the screwed-up faun's eyes of the old Friar, the eyes of Eleazer were wide, placid, and unused, for they had never looked on anything that was to be seen. They were brown and full of a spaciousness left behind by dreams. His long whitened face seemed ironed out with study. Only in his full lips, whose redness had turned to russet at seventy-nine, was there any hint that he came of a tribe that had once written the Song of Songs.

Of Eleazer's outward activities as a Rabbi there was almost nothing to tell, except that his manner for fifty years had baffled the little flock of Jews whom he led in their patient pursuit of God. In his synagogue he had stood these years beneath the Torah and, with a zeal so perfect that it appeared almost like abstraction, had performed the offices prescribed by the ancient law. It is true that his flock had dwindled, and his synagogue, once elegant, had become a shabby place. And probably it was only because the Portuguese Jews who had founded this congregation are among the most unchanging of all Israel's tropisms that the doors of his synagogue had remained in use at all.

And yet, helpless though he was in many ways, Eleazer was more to his congregation than a Rabbi who presided over them with a piety amounting to indifference. He was the last of the one hundred and ten Rabbis of his name (D'Amie), who formed an unbroken line into the dark ages of Portugal, and beyond these dim centuries to dimmer ones still, when Israel had walked clothed in royal Visigoth trappings and lighted its holy candles in Iberian castles. Because Eleazer was a candle out of this Past with which a handful of Portuguese Jews still stiffened their dreams, they came to worship at its cool and hidden light. They heard the correctly enunciated Hebrew, and listened to the echo of the dreamer's hidden visions, his body's sing-song, and were content. If their hearts remained cold, that snobbery so pathetic in the Jew clinging to an ancient moment or two of manhood was enriched.

And, as time went on, they were rewarded in another way. Like a hero whose story emerges only in a long time of telling, Rabbi Eleazer came alive for them. The awkward old man, with the tired white face that had presided over their hours of death and woe or holiday peace with a courtesy that did not light up, that was not of this world, kindled a new feeling in their hearts. A new feeling vied with their foolish pride, and the awe they had felt even in his belittlement of them. They loved the old man. But this was after many, many years, when he was old, and only a handful of the former congregation remained at his feet.

Also, they understood him. Dreamer, stranger, and visionary, he was of the great line of Misnagdim who had hung their harps on the willow tree in the time of the Diaspora, and rejoiced no more. By nature he was one of those unyielding Rabbis in Jewish history, powerful in law and excommunications, who had not mingled with their people, but had kept them in their place while they communed elsewhere with God. By profession he was a mystic.

This was a study so painstaking that it could not be grasped in the presence of others. And now that his followers understood him, they knew also that his meditation and reading had taken him far beyond where they could hope to be present.

Others had been present, it is true. It was recalled that, during his years, scholars had come and gone from his house, men pale and vacant-eyed as himself. Sometimes these guests had lingered for several years and then vanished never to be caught glimpse of again, walking almost surreptitiously in and out of the brick house adjoining the synagogue.

Rabbi Eleazer's flock accepted his judgment. He had not considered them worthy of his inner light. He had been too proud to reveal it to eyes that had lost their talent for seeing God. And if he had left them cheerful worldlings, it was with their worldliness they cared now for the old man, worried about him, and took care of him in numerous ways he did not guess, while he trod, without turning, his stiff-necked path to God.

As he grew older, his faults, as faults do, increased. Serene and fanatical, he went his way as to some appointment. And yet something strange had happened in his temple. As time had gone on, he had not grown more strong to lead his people, but they, through their love, had grown stronger to follow. Perhaps he knew this. Or, perhaps, the fabric of his character wore thin with age, and he allowed them glimpses of the holy life inside him. Wonderful words sometimes fell from his lips in the pulpit, and, with tightened hearts, his people listened.

"It is not given to one man to light the soul of another by words. . . . Words that are a light for one are a darkness for another. This is true even of the words in the sacred books. I have not helped you to find God but I have been content to see that you remembered Him a little."

So he had preached on the Sabbath eve before this story opens, for that day was the Sabbath.

"Tonight in saying good-by to you I would wish to speak to you as Souls. . . ."

Over this there were some in the audience who puzzled.

"Tonight in saying good-by . . . ?" they asked themselves, but

many things their Rabbi said did not mean what he said, and when he said: "I shall preach no more here," they also overlooked it. A wonderful man was their Rabbi, with ways not to be known.

". . . to speak to you as Souls. But this is difficult. For it is without words that the soul must mount, and the wings of the soul lie deeper than the mind.

"I would remind you . . . of Silence . . . the Silence that has long ago passed from your hearts. I shall speak to the Temple of Silence within which the Spirit dwells.

"There is a Road that leads away from the world to God. Only turn your face toward it and shut your eyes. Shut your eyes. Look for Him under the stones of your heart. And the Road will move under your feet.

"If you would rise to His Glory, remember that you must descend first into the caverns. Return to the Silence where the world is but an evil and dimly remembered shadow, and Heaven is a light forever growing. There, my Jews, is your homeland. There, in that little heritage of ecstasy, is your Temple that no enemy can overthrow.

"Beyond the language of religion, beyond purification . . . beyond goodness . . . beyond piety . . . beyond good deeds . . . beyond all that we call ourselves . . . there is a hidden and lonely island in the soul. This is the white sand where no feet have walked. Tonight as you go home . . . begin to look. . . . Look for this sand that is dry and shining."

This, of course, they did not do, but late that night some of them awoke, here and there, and thought of their Rabbi, as they were used to doing, and, turning on their pillows, remembered the birdlike look of the old man's face and felt a concern that was like an agony gripping their hearts. They worried about his health, and if he slept well, and there were some who were still young who, sighing, would have liked to protect him with their lives.

"I am glad it's such a lovely day," Father Dominic said with a smile so golden that it showed all at once the secret of his tranquil existence. "Sit down, Eleazer. They've put the table over there. Later on, we'll have some wine and seltzer and cooked cherries and cakes. I myself am not hungry."

The Friar had a soft, almost boyish voice, and a way of speaking so unstilted that one would have known him immediately, no matter what his clothes were, for a simple man, a workman maybe, save that there was no taint of coarseness or ignorance in his talk.

"Still full of penances?" the Rabbi smiled.

Eleazer was a different being in the Friar's presence. Long ago, in his willful way, he had given his awkward and unsmiling heart to this friend and no other. Caprice and ease and many other charming ways marked his manner toward his friend.

"The smaller our sins the more aware of them we are," he quoted.

"I understand," said Dominic. It was his manner to illumine the slightest of his utterances with the rare and inexpressibly glowing smile of the happy man. "I understand, and am rebuked, Eleazer. We do penance for little sins as a boast that we have no big ones." He laughed softly. "I see now that it will be better if I eat."

"Whether you eat or not, Dominic," Eleazer said, "God knows you are a good man."

"Yes. He knows. I guess I'm old enough for Him to have made up His mind by this time."

Yet he spoke of his age lightly, as if it were a jest. For in each other's presence, the two friends felt their hearts grow younger, as if a bridge had been provided them to the Past.

Perhaps this bridge was no more magic a thing than the garden—the enchanted piece of land that blossomed and clamored with scents and frolicked like something living at their feet.

The Rabbi acknowledged it gravely, as if it were a third and beloved presence at their meeting.

"The garden grows more beautiful every year," he observed.

"Yes . . . God has been amazingly good to me," Dominic agreed, in his soft voice, and he added presently:

"It seems a shame to think how we worried, and doubted life . . . at least I did. Do you remember, I used to say to you: 'Some day we'll grow older, Eleazer, and we'll find out how grim and terrible life is'?"

"We have not found out," Eleazer said peacefully, and yet there was something in his tone that made the Friar look at him frowningly.

"Have you found out, my friend?" he asked.

"No," Eleazer said firmly. To himself he thought: "He has always been too innocent to know that I am a Jew."

The glow returned to the small face of the Friar, and he drifted back into the quietness that had been the study and the rare achievement of his life. It was good to sit here with his old friend Eleazer. Good thus . . . and presently, he knew, they would speak of God. This was the jewel and wonder of their friendship, for while it had been given to him, Dominic, to be completely happy in the presence and the creation of beauty, the Way—the very fountain at the threshold of things—he had not known. Nature had spoken to him, but God's voice he had never heard.

It had been different with Eleazer. And Father Dominic had grown content with this knowledge . . . for as long as one man is left to see the way to God, the road remains open.

Many were the wiles he had of luring his friend into these Discourses, sometimes calling himself a pagan, who did not know, invoking his friend's pity with his regrets for the hidden Source, speaking his heart in innocent praise of his friend's wisdom, and sometimes asking questions frankly like a youth, but always returning to the dear Subject.

"It's been good to know your eyes were fastened on Him, while I was in the garden chasing bugs, and it's made me almost as happy as if it were my own eyes that beheld Him," he had often said to Eleazer, in many ways.

(It was this impious turn of phrase, as well as thoughts like these, that was a concern to his brother priests.)

Or: "Without you, I would have been an utter pagan. Yes . . . You have always been able to present God to me, Eleazer. I recall three hours once long ago when you spoke to me of God in such a way that even a flower would have understood you. Oho, if the truth were told, I'm nothing better than a gardener."

Today he had spoken in this vein, while his friend soothed him, saying it was a mistake to regret one's life, and that to have given up his garden to cultivate his Soul, as Dominic often threatened to do, would have been a pity, since the one bloomed in the other. And to prove to Dominic that it was not good to seek too much, he told him this legend:

There was a Rabbi (he said) who came to the holy man Baalshem to learn from him the secret by which he understood the speech of the animals. This novice had burned to know the secret for a long time. Accordingly they went together into the forest, and the holy man Baalshem began teaching him the secret. And as the eager disciple began to master it, he heard, suddenly, all around him, the squirrels chattering to one another of places to hunt for nuts, and birds telling each other where certain little warm winds were blowing, and where the worms and snails lay hidden. He heard also the love plaints of all manner of little animals and the cries of devotion that even the tiniest and ugliest children of the forest have for one another. As the apprentice heard these things, he continued to ask the holy one further questions. . . .

He wished to know now how it was that Baalshem could understand not only the speech of the animals, but of the angels. And finally he asked the saint the secret by which he evoked the forces of God.

And Baalshem smiled sadly at his disciple and said: "Look, poor man, a while ago you heard the voices of Nature speaking, and your long dream was realized. And now, in your eagerness to learn more secrets, you are not even aware that you are no longer listening to the tongues of the forest. Of what use is it for you to learn anything when you do not love God enough to pay attention to what He reveals to you, but must always demand more gifts?" And the poor apprentice, turning his ear again to the forest to listen to the speech of the animals, heard nothing but the usual chirruping and the sound of the wind in the leaves.

So Eleazer spoke, and Dominic listened in tranquillity, as if he had nothing to do but to listen, to enjoy, to live. Sometimes the turn of a phrase lit up his face, for he loved talent, and Eleazer he admired above all men. And when his friend was done with the tale, he thought about it for a long space of time, saying gently at last:

"It was not the secrets of God that this unfortunate man loved, but his own ambition, it's clear. And when he failed in the test you speak of, Eleazer, he probably lost, not only the secret of understanding the voices in the forest, but his original desire to hear them. So that when he went away from the holy Baalshem, he was much poorer than when he came."

And he added, smiling shyly: "Thank you, Eleazer, for telling me this story. I'm going to use it in my writings, as you know." And with a twinkle in his eye toward the Friars who bent over the garden beds near by, he joked:

"Wouldn't some of *them* be surprised if they knew where a lot of my pious notions came from? Whenever my brothers feel a little doubt about my Christianity, they reassure themselves by reading the tales I have pillaged from Rabbi Eleazer."

But he spoke absently and looked before him without seeing plain the year's pristine burst of bloom. A heaviness plucked at his thoughts, and he divined that it had to do with Eleazer.

"You have dreamed something," he said presently. "Tell me what it was you dreamed."

"Yes, I had a dream," Eleazer said.

"I feel it is there in your mind—a bad dream."

"Would you say there are any bad flowers, Dominic?"

"There are one or two I don't like—the mesembryanthemum chiefly. And then of course there are the weeds."

"This was a weed," Eleazer said, sighing.

Dominic did not press him.

The old men had risen and were walking slowly through the garden. Even Dominic's stride was calm. He drifted under the garden trees, remembering how often Eleazer and he had walked in these same places.

"Eleazer and I . . ." his thoughts said—and there they paused, for friendship can think no sweeter than this phrase.

Still a sadness tugged at his heart strings, hurting.

"To live, to grow old and die in one place, to know one's roots for one's home, to wander only in one's dreams . . . why weren't these things given to my good friend, Eleazer?" he thought sadly, for he was not so innocent as Eleazer believed.

And then, as they approached the grove of maples where the table of hospitality had been set out, his eyes wandered to the ferns coiled out of the sunless earth, and his mind to its science, as was its habit. The sight and smell of ferns reminded him of a world far away in a Time unrecorded by Man . . . before trees and flowers had appeared on the earth. In that Time, owing to the content of carbon in the air, only these ferns had lived— tall ferns, three and four hundred feet high, covering the earth and massed in horrendous forests full of fabulous-looking insects larger than eagles and dogs. And of this tumultuous vegetation that had once filled the skies with its ferny-toothed towers, only these delicate scrawls of green that thrived in the half-dark re- mained. Nature, thought Father Dominic, has its memories just as Man. . . . The Past with silent feet walks everywhere.

The table, covered with a bright blue cloth and gay with jars of preserves, with wine bottles and earthenware dishes, recalled Dominic to hospitality, and to his friend.

Over the table, they resumed their talk. But we will not fol- low them. It is better to close the door on an old friendship than to listen too closely to its labyrinthian pattern, its past and pres- ent, and all its deep-springed silences. Besides, when it came to their Discourse on God—that Discourse so elliptical and high- pitched, and at the same time so pellucid and clear-souled—it is no use pretending that our ordinary ears are attuned to its over- tones or that our souls are similarly attuned. Neither could words convey it, for these two were nearer the Truth than are mere words. And if the simple shining soul of Dominic is beyond our comprehension, how much more so the soul of Eleazer? For the little light of the Jew is no lamp, or candle even, but a light that flickers from hand to hand now, blown by many winds and bearing always a little nimbus. . . .

They spoke, the lover of life and he who was only a friend of life. Many anecdotes they exchanged, whose meanings are lost to us in their knowledge. And they ate, out of hospitality and a deference to hospitality, of the things set before them. They spoke of things as old as their friendship, and older, of things as old as the stones, and older, for the Light in them was older than the stones—until they came back, by the high hills and footpaths of their friendship . . . to the dream.

"Tell me how it was I knew you dreamed," asked Dominic. "Was it because you dreamed of me?"

"Yes," said his friend. "We were walking together in a field of corn—you and I. And the corn took fire. All my clothes were destroyed, and I lay uncovered, hugging the cool earth."

"And what became of me?" Dominic asked.

"You wept," Eleazer said.

Dominic pondered uneasily what the dream meant.

"Do you know?" he asked.

"I am to know soon," Eleazer replied, and smiled at his friend, whose face had grown as unhappy as a child's. And seeking to divert his mind, he spoke of other things.

"The ferns," he said, "cast a curious light on the air, as if they had once devoured the night."

Father Dominic wondered whether his friend spoke of the

carboniferous era or of inner things. He decided that to a man of such spirit, knowledge and divination were identical. And this same must be true of dreams. He sighed heavily.

Two figures appeared beside the table.

"This is Captain Malloy of the Police Department," Father Francis said. "He said you had agreed to see him."

"Yes, yes, yes . . . yes . . ." Father Dominic spoke with annoyance.

Seating himself ponderously, Captain Malloy catalogued in his mind: "Old folks."

Relaxing his legs after the long walk from the station, the captain felt himself as unloved and undesired as if he had intruded on a nest of criminals. He wondered about the Father's other visitor, obviously a Rabbi. And he understood that the Father's refusal to introduce him to this visitor was a statement that his visit would be too brief for any social amenities.

It was Captain Malloy's habit, when confronted with such inhospitality, which was no infrequent matter in his life, to sit rigidly waiting until his presence had generated a sort of psychic guilt in the nerves of any reluctant host. But this time, he realized grimly, the shoe was likely to be on the other foot. It wasn't likely that the Catholic Friar would be much impressed by him. And on the other side, he felt the Rabbi's face—the distant, uncompromising, historic, and saintly face of the Jew—turned toward him, and doubtless appraising him for what he was.

An uncharacteristic shyness fell on the detective. The delicacy of his mission also confused him, for the questions he had come to ask might give the Father the wrong impression of what was in his mind, as if he were surely hunting for a monk as the murderer. It might also be that Father Dominic, being such an old man, would even conclude that he himself was under suspicion.

All these considerations that lay in Captain Malloy's head un-
nerved him the more with his being aware that a part of his brain,
beyond the control of piety or decent logic, was sniffing away at
Friar and Saint with no consideration at all.

Looking up a little more reddish-faced than when he had arrived, the captain saw with some surprise that the ancient Friar
was smiling at him, and that the other man also was smiling. He
felt himself suddenly loved and admired as if he and not they
were full of childishness. He smiled back, and Father Dominic
said:

"This is my friend, Rabbi Eleazer."

"Glad to know you," said the detective.

But though he acknowledged the salutation, the Rabbi contented himself with withdrawing into a silence and behaving
abruptly as if he were not present.

Father Dominic poured a glass of wine.

"You've had a long walk, Captain," he said, and handed him
the glass.

The detective drank obediently, though he had a strong distaste for sweet wines.

"Well," he said as he wiped his lips, "I'll try not to take up too
much time, Father. I realize a monastery garden is no place for
a detective."

"You said something on the telephone about a crucifix," said
Father Dominic, with a directness that startled the detective,
coming from such an old man.

"Yes," said the captain, much relieved that the object in his
coat pocket had finally entered the talk. "I've brought it with
me. I was told you were an authority on crucifixes, Father.
That's why I decided to bother you."

He produced an envelope from his coat pocket and removed

from it a crucifix some four inches in length, with the figure of the Saviour sculptured on it. A small red half-circle of some inlay was at the figure's feet. Over its head, above the crown of thorns, was inlaid another crown, a wreath of tiny flowers whose colors were almost imperceptible.

Father Dominic leaned over and looked at the crucifix. An expression of surprise darted into his old face. He grasped the object and began to study it intently, turning it over, and sampling its texture with fingers that apparently began to tremble. Then he removed a small microscope from his pocket and fell to studying it through the glass, making the while strange, strangled, and incredulous sounds.

Finally, laying down the glass, he half spoke, half sobbed: "There can be no doubt about it!"

"You *recognize* it?" Captain Malloy gasped in his turn, for he had not expected his hunch to work so perfectly.

"I know it!" the Friar cried exultantly.

"As belonging to someone in particular?" Captain Malloy asked with a tripping heart.

"It belonged to the Saint who founded the Order of which you are the guest today," the old man said with a shining face. "It was worn by him himself. It is described particularly and beyond doubt in certain papers. This crucifix never left the holy man's neck from the day it was made, and on the day he died"— here the Friar paused breathlessly—"it accompanied him to Heaven."

It was an anticlimax that hurt the captain almost physically. A crucifix that went to Heaven! No doubt it had tumbled from there, too, into the murder victim's hand.

And for all that he was a churchgoer, the decided way in which the fact had been mentioned angered the detective. And he was further annoyed by the fact that the Rabbi did not seem to doubt the cock and bull story, but listened evenly in his recess. It took the captain a full minute or two to recover from his anger. He had been prepared for the vagaries of age, and even for some of the exaggerations of religion when he had sat down with these old men, but not for this.

"That crucifix," he finally said, in his heaviest police-department manner, "was found in the hand of a man who was murdered last night. Perhaps you read about it, Father. The murdered man's name was Joseph Franks."

Father Dominic's face grew shrunken.

"No, I read nothing about it," he said.

"I heard of it last night," said Eleazer. "His wife spoke to me on the telephone."

"Was Franks a member of your congregation?" Captain Malloy inquired routinely.

"No . . ." said the Rabbi, in his far-away voice. "Perhaps I knew him, though. She said I married them."

"This crucifix," Malloy said sternly to the two woolgathering old men, "was snatched by the victim from the neck of the man who murdered him. You can see the fastening loop was broken."

"Yes . . . I see," said Father Dominic.

"The victim," Captain Malloy continued, "was the fourth man to be murdered by this same unknown hand."

"How do they know this?" Dominic asked.

"Because they were all four murdered in the same way," the detective explained considerately.

"Each of the four Jews was found with his belly ripped open," the Rabbi's voice said from the shadows.

The little Friar closed his eyes and grew pale.

"I know little of what goes on in the world," he said faintly.

"There is little to know that is new," the Rabbi's voice spoke sadly.

"Now," resumed Captain Malloy, turning to the Friar, "if you will tell me something else about this piece of evidence, something other than that miracle you mentioned, it might be of help to us in finding the murderer."

Father Dominic spoke didactically.

"It was one of eighteen crucifixes made for the Founder of the Order by Father Antonio, a sculptor who was among the first of the holy St. Dominic's followers. Seventeen of the crucifixes were given by the holy Founder to seventeen missionaries, sent by him, as is well known, to all ends of the earth. This was in 1237. The eighteenth crucifix was the one you hold so irreverently in your hand, my son. Its workmanship was different in certain details. Father Antonio, the maker, left behind a manuscript at his death giving minute descriptions of it. I will show you the manuscript."

"Later, if you don't mind, Father," the captain said. "But now perhaps you would care to tell me what church or museum might have had possession of it. That would help us track down——"

"None!" Father Dominic interrupted testily. "It went to Heaven, as I told you."

"And stayed there for seven hundred years?" The detective almost wept. "In Heaven's name, Father."

"Its seven-hundredth birthday fell on the day the first Jew was murdered," said Rabbi Eleazer's voice placidly.

Captain Malloy mopped his brow.

"Perhaps my friend knows something more that he can tell you," Dominic said, with an air of finality. "My friend is a very godly man."

Though ignoring the suggestion, Captain Malloy couldn't help reacting to the murmur of the Rabbi's voice in the background.

"I am to know. I am to know," it sighed.

"Old people . . . they talk to themselves," the captain said mentally. He decided there was nothing more to be gathered from this visit.

"Thank you," he said, and was reaching for his black derby on the ground, when another voice spoke in the little maple grove.

"Excuse me, please," said the voice, in a Teutonic accent, "I haf brought the slippers, Father Dominic. Excuse me, please, I wanted to gif them to you myself."

Captain Malloy straightened and saw a slightly stooped man of fifty with a plumpish face and the look of a strayed and eager little dog in his eyes. He was standing as if in the midst of a bow and suffused with reverence and embarrassment. He held a small bundle under one arm.

Father Dominic was smiling at the newcomer.

"In a minute, please," he said kindly and turned to the detective.

Captain Malloy bowed his head, and the old priest murmured: "Bless you, my son."

Then raising his head Captain Malloy looked quickly at the obsequious and fuzzy face of the man who was standing with the slippers under his arm. The captain stood staring for several moments and then walked away.

Dominic watched the detective walk away and then looked blankly at the man with the bundle.

"Oh," he said, as if he had forgotten his presence, "I am glad you brought them. Very glad. Sit down, my son. Sit down there on the bench."

"Thank you, Father," the man said gratefully and sat down. He began unwrapping the bundle.

"They are for you, Eleazer," Dominic said. But he was not thinking of the slippers. He was thinking in his depths of the last words his friend had spoken. Eleazer was not one to speak prophecies lightly, and he did not dismiss them lightly.

"The slippers . . ." Eleazer prompted him.

"Yes . . ." Dominic went on. "I measured your footprint in the petunia bed last month. And I had them made. They are the same kind you admired once, when you saw me wearing them. Pfefferkorn is an artist in making slippers."

The man Pfefferkorn beamed and inclined his head humbly. Rabbi Eleazer turned his eyes to the pair of colorful petit-point slippers that had come out of the bundle. He continued for several moments to look at the slippers and the workingman hands holding them. They were broken-nailed hands, soiled and heavy-knuckled from toil. Then the Rabbi raised his eyes to the shoemaker's face.

"They are beautifully made," he said, and continued to study the grateful and obsequious face of the workingman. "Have you been making slippers long, Pfefferkorn?" he asked, hesitating a half-instant before he spoke the name.

"Ever since I can remember," the shoemaker answered eagerly. "I am glad you like them."

Eleazer took them from his hands.

"Thank you for the gift," he said shyly to Dominic.

Dominic smiled to see his friend holding the slippers and examining them fondly.

"They have a curious pattern," Eleazer said. "Yours, as I remember, were a little different. These have another design woven into them. See, there are little yellow triangles each with a smaller triangle inside it."

"Yes," said the shoemaker happily, "it is an old design from Cologne. I haf woven it special for you, Rabbi Eleazer, special for you, please."

"It is very old indeed," Eleazer smiled. "This was the sign used by the Jews when they were forbidden to show the Star of David. They took the Star apart and laid it inside itself in the form of two triangles. And yellow," he added softly, "was the color prescribed for them by the German law as a symbol of their greed."

"Perhaps you don't like that on your slippers," Father Dominic said unhappily, and frowned on the shoemaker Pfefferkorn.

"I like it very much," said Eleazer quickly. "It was thoughtful of Pfefferkorn to embroider them so. That will give me added pleasure."

"Thank you," said the shoemaker with a sigh and stood up. "I haf worked all my life for the Fathers of St. Dominic. And I am happy always to work for them. Always to work for them."

He bobbed his head in a series of eager bows.

"Bless you, my son," the little Friar murmured.

Rabbi Eleazer held out his hand. The obsequious shoemaker looked at him with surprise in his twinkling, doglike eyes. Then he rubbed his own hand clean against his trousers and raised it slowly to the Rabbi. Eleazer's thin fingers closed firmly over the roughened palm and he stood for a moment, eyes intent and distant, holding fast to Pfefferkorn's hand. A faint color came into the Rabbi's pale cheeks and a glitter slowly lighted his look.

"*Auf Wiedersehen*," he said with a sigh and removed his grip.

The shoemaker bowed again and moved backward toward

the walk. He continued to look with his eager grateful smile at the two old men and to make humble gestures so blind that he bumped into several trees. He murmured a little irrationally: "Excuse me. Excuse me," and continued his backward walk, saying finally: "I have some work to do up there. Excuse me, please. If anything iss wrong with the slippers, I will be there, please."

Dominic watched him move away and smiled at this skilled and able workingman who had so pleased his friend.

The two old men were again alone. They sat looking at the waning summer afternoon. Birds chirped over them. Beyond the dimly lit grove, the sky still flared white and blue and radiant with sun. But the emerging tints of the garden told that the day was ebbing. Flowers and shrubs released from the heavy hand of light were beginning to glow with their own colors. The voices of the birds were like the tender echoes of this peaceful day that lay cradled in the garden.

Father Dominic looked deep into the day with his observing eyes. He quieted the unrest in his thought by allowing the patterns of Nature to take possession of his spirit. The colors, smells, and wavering shapes of the garden, and the hidden bird throats throbbing everywhere around, overcame him with that timeless sense of life known only to the tranquil heart. His little bird eyes peering into the day felt its existence beyond himself, as if the hour in which he sat were in itself a bird note pouring from a throat overfull with song. He heard the beginning of this song far back among the fern towers and he heard its continuation in the ages and ages of summer days to come, summer days to fall endlessly out of the bursting throat of Life. And as the Past and the Future revealed themselves to him in the unchanging sigh of this summer hour, his senses tasted the wine of Immortality.

But now a change was coming subtly over the day. Wisps of gloom were heralding a summer shower.

"It's going to rain soon," Dominic murmured to his friend.

"Yes," Eleazer said. "It is getting dark."

"The rain won't touch us here," said Dominic, "and I think it won't last long either. You are in no hurry?"

"No," said Eleazer. "I am happy here."

A glow of green had come into the air, and a wind like a runner full of tidings moved over the plants and trees. The garden became bright with color as if it had turned on an inner light, and the shrubbery gleamed as if with lantern rays. A stir and a freshness were on the earth. In the deepening gloom, the garden, like a lover preparing herself with odors, arched her many bosoms for the embrace of the rain. It arrived first in the trees, pattering on the leaves. Thunder sounded and the rain rushed to the ground.

The two friends, with eager faces, watched the rain stripes in the garden and listened to the cool, wild scratch of the water on the trees above.

"It is good for the flowers," said Eleazer, and his friend smiled deeply, full of his secret knowledge of roots uncurling, soft pistons pumping, and a whole system of aqueducts distributing the rain to burned petals and parched tendrils.

"It is very good," he agreed, sniffing happily the new odors brought from the clouds.

Now the rush and surge of the rain seemed to fill the garden with a mock terror. Flowers bent and twisted about as if pretending they were being uprooted, and the shrubbery leaves danced under the beat of rain and wind as if in the throes of destruction. Beyond the standing river of rain, the sky, however, was already beginning to clear. Bright spaces gleamed eerily through the gloom of the downpour. Thunder sounded again, but more faintly. The scattered day was slowly returning. The scratch of the rain grew fainter and a halloo of light rolled over grass and shrubs. The shower had ended, leaving behind a laggard patter of water running down the leaves.

Father Dominic sighed with delight at the spectacle.

"The soul of man is a garden," he said softly, "made in the image of Nature and refreshed by tears and sighs as deeply as by the sun and fair weather. I wrote that when I was young and full of faith in metaphors."

Eleazer nodded and smiled.

"The storm is part of the calm," he said. "In the old days when God walked among men He carried His lightnings concealed in a little willow branch."

"When God walked among men . . ." repeated Dominic slowly, his eyes on the flowers.

"Yes," said Eleazer, "it was thus."

"Does He still walk somewhere with His willow branch?" Dominic asked gently.

"Yes," said Eleazer, "it is still thus."

The Rabbi rose and breathed deeply of the garden air.

At his side, Dominic thought only of how to speed him on his way happily. For when people are very old, they see in each parting the final one, and each bird song is like a parting cry.

Resolutely he put out of his mind the ghosts that had darkened the afternoon with their presence, and all the untoward shadows, and looked about him, calling on Nature for help. And just as the garden had ushered in the pleasures of their meeting, it took its part now in the farewell.

"The face of life is sweet," Dominic said, marching with loose strides at his friend's side, and calling attention with his beaming to every glowing zinnia face and every bright leaf on the way.

Eleazer understood him.

"It's hard to leave so beautiful a garden," he said.

"The twilight is marvelous," Dominic murmured joyfully.

Presently Eleazer looked up as if he had been called.

"I must go," he said, with a sudden wild note in his voice.

He leaned over and touched his cheek to his friend's face.

"Peace be with you, Dominic, and with all who are kind to you," he said tenderly. "I will wear your slippers tonight." Then, with a smile at the slippers under his arm, he walked away.

Father Dominic watched with deep love in his heart as the Rabbi moved over the wet grass, and climbed the steps of the walk into the garden beyond. Dominic remained where he was standing. Slowly the flowers clothed themselves in the veils of twilight. Bird songs rocked to and fro.

Suddenly the Friar seemed to awake to something ominous. The blood had started to beat in his temples, and he stood remembering the dream his friend had told him of, of walking in a corn field that had burst into flames and devoured him, while he himself was left weeping.

"Why did he dream that?" he cried aloud in anguish. "And why did that man come to me with the Cross of St. Dominic? And why"—he stood shivering in the dying day—"why were those miserable old symbols of Cologne on the slippers? . . . Devoured by burning corn. . . ." A name froze itself on his lips.

"Pfefferkorn. . . ."

"Oh, God in Heaven," moaned Dominic, as he began to run swiftly after his friend.

When he came to the road, his friend was nowhere to be seen.

When Rabbi Eleazer came out of the monastery gates he saw the slightly stooped figure of the shoemaker Pfefferkorn disappearing around a turn in the road some distance away. Eleazer walked after the figure.

The half-countryside beyond the monastery buildings stood intimately outlined in the twilight. Distant trees and cottages separated by swampy fields gazed out of the hollow eyes of the early nightfall. Eleazer came to the turn in the road. He saw the shoemaker again, walking now more swiftly, and Eleazer, whose muscles were weak, moved after him.

This region through which Eleazer followed Pfefferkorn was a fringe of gas stations, road houses, little truck farms, and an occasional stretch of pavement with squat, flat-roofed stores lining it. It was the far end of the city that sprawled like a scaffolding for tomorrow. In the twilight, however, it seemed old rather than new, as if it were the debris of a city long wiped away. The headlights of trucks and automobiles fled through it, leaving behind a constantly deepening silence and lifelessness.

Eleazer walked on, his slippers in a bundle under his arm. Pfefferkorn, moving quickly, so stooped that only his shoulders were visible, was still in front of him. Now the day had withdrawn, but the night had not yet come. The always unfamiliar hour that precedes the darkening of the skies occupied the flat lands. Denuded of sun and color, the trees and structures retained an ominous visibility, as if abandoned by both the day and the night and waiting within a shell for the touch of life.

Pfefferkorn had turned off the main road and Eleazer turned with him. The gloom deepened and the figure of the shoemaker dissolved and reappeared in the distance as the Rabbi followed. Through darkening fields now the Rabbi moved, through black clusters of trees looming in the shell of light, on and on in this nightless hour as if drawn swiftly over the earth by a force stronger than the muscles of his ancient legs. The wasteland smells came heavily into Eleazer's nose. The strangled watery bark of frogs and the sleigh-bell chatter of insects fell on his ears. But Eleazer was aware of none of these, nor of the swampy earth now sucking at his shoes, nor of the brambles tearing his clothes and hands. He moved on unaware of his pounding heart and the ache of exhaustion in his lungs. In his mind was a light, dim and skeleton-shadowed as the twilight around him. It was a light cast by the dissolving figure of the shoemaker in the distance. The soul of this figure, like an ominous guide, tugged at the old Rabbi's weary body and provided a secret luminescence for his way.

Suddenly the dark came and the land disappeared into the summer night. Shadows bloomed in the trees, and the road grew blind. Window lights, like distant little cores of life, lay in the wandering dark. The fleeing automobile lamps moved in faraway funnels of speed. The swampy night closed about Eleazer, muffling him with the sharp, sweet smells of decay, and encircling him with black shapes. The darkness swallowed the figure of Pfefferkorn. But there was no change in the old Rabbi's movement. On into the dark he continued, striding and plunging through bough-tangled lanes and over wet fields loud with the hissings and little trumpetings of hidden life. The dim glow of another soul swung like a lantern before his eyes and he moved panting and unseeing but knowing that the blackness before him held the running figure of Pfefferkorn.

Then abruptly Eleazer stopped. A loop of terror had halted him. He stood trembling as if the dark around him had become another world and he had walked too far. A faint ugly odor of decay came out of the heavy tree shadows. Eleazer stood trem-

bling in the midst of this ghostly stench and heard voices wailing
far away. In the darkness the Rabbi felt himself surrounded by
things rising out of the ground as if the grave of Time were
opening. The night dreamed evilly around him. Eleazer closed
his eyes. Then he raised his head and looked wildly at the top
of the night. The deep black face of the heavens stared everywhere down on him. He stood looking up like one from the bottom of an abyss. He saw the distances increase and the night
grow endless. When he had stood thus for several moments his
trembling ceased. He lowered his eyes and saw he was in the
midst of a thicket of fir trees. Their clawlike foliage gleamed in
the starlight.

Suddenly beyond the thicket a little light winked and a window appeared, yellow and staring in the dark. Eleazer moved
toward it. He saw the outlines of a dwelling hidden in a sag of
shadows. The glitter of old stones uncovered a little its dimensions. It was a small and heavy house, squat to the earth. In one
of its windows a candle had just been lit.

Eleazer walked slowly to the half-visible door. He stopped
before it, and the things unseen that had come out of the earth
to make him tremble crowded about him at this door. They
struck at his old heart, and his hand reaching to push open this
door halted as if seized. But Eleazer moved the terror away from
him and placed his hand against the edge of the door and pushed.
Slowly, with its hinges creaking, the heavy door opened. Eleazer
from the threshold looked into a room. It was empty and moldy.
From the window a candle spread a film of yellow light over its
shadows. He saw a tall-backed chair in a corner beside a cupboard hung with a curtain. Near it was a broken couch. An uncovered wooden table stood against the further wall. On the
table lay a half-dozen pairs of old shoes.

Eleazer entered the room. There were no other rooms beyond it. The night glistened in its windows. The Rabbi looked in the shadowed corners. He went to the cupboard and pulled aside its hanging. There was no occupant in the room. The candle that had been lighted a few moments ago burned lonesomely on the window sill. Eleazer walked to the candle and took it in his hand. It was still warm with the fingers of another.

Holding the candle before him, Eleazer moved about the room and found it littered with bits of leather and heavy with dust. The candle flame jumped above his hand and he stood still listening. Only the sounds of the night outside were to be heard. Birds, frogs, and insects spoke in the dark. He moved again and his foot felt an iron ring under it. By the candlelight he saw there was a door in the worn flooring. Unlike the rest of the flooring, the door was clean of dust. He lifted it up by the ring, and the wet rancid smells of a basement billowed up. The candle dimmed and flickered.

Peering down, Eleazer saw a flight of ladder steps that vanished in a pool of inky space. The steps were steep. With his back to the cellar darkness Eleazer slowly descended the ladder, holding his flickering candle close to his face. The descent took a long time, for the steps continued on and on into the dark. At length Eleazer stood on an earthen floor. A chill brushed his face and his fingers felt the moist grip of the cellar shadows.

He was in a tall cavernous room fully of ugly smells. In the diminished light of his candle he could at first see nothing but its wavering yellow point before him. Currents of heavy air moved in the dark, threatening his little flame. His eyes discovered slowly that this high-ceilinged cellar was not empty. There were barrels in its shadows. His candle uncovered them and he stood watching the shadows that rose and fell around them. Then he moved toward them. He found no one. Along the wall he saw a workbench covered with odds and ends of the shoemaker's craft. He leaned over to examine what was on this bench, when the candle flame above his head leaped and stretched itself, assailed by new currents of air. For a moment it hovered between a last blue tip and extinction. Then it straightened and resumed its yellow wavering. The new currents of air had ceased.

Eleazer turned. At the other end of the darkness he saw another candle. It wavered a few feet above his own and he knew that someone was sitting on the steps and holding it. He stood still and waited. The light of this candle on the steps swelled in the stillness and he saw the face of the shoemaker Pfefferkorn. The face was watching him, its eyes glittering, its unshaven cheeks distended in a grimace. The swelling candle rays beside it fell on an ax that lay on the step.

"What are you looking for, Rabbi Eleazer?" the Teutonic voice whispered from behind the candle.

Eleazer was silent. He stood holding his candle steadily before him.

"Maybe you are looking for a cross," the shadowed face continued, "an old cross like you saw in the garden today, that the policeman brought. Is that what you are looking for, Rabbi?"

Eleazer could see the grimace increase. The grimace devoured the shoemaker's doglike and obsequious face. Peering out of an aperture of light it gleamed at Eleazer, purring and malignant. Its power filled the underground room, and the deep shadows around Eleazer became full of Pfefferkorn. From this whispering shoemaker on the steps moved a chill of terror as if the cellar had grown deeper and blacker. The darkness in which he sat with his ax at his side was like a cage sinking into the earth and bearing the Rabbi with it.

"How many such Crosses do you expect one poor shoemaker to own, Rabbi Eleazer?" Pfefferkorn's wet mouth whispered.

Eleazer did not answer, and the shoemaker sat motionless. In the silence the two candle flames wagged at each other, and the blade of the ax on the step glistened feebly. Then Pfefferkorn spoke again.

"Why did Rabbi Eleazer play detective and follow me to my house?"

"He was led," said Eleazer.

"Who led him?" asked the whisper.

"Pfefferkorn," said Eleazer.

The shoemaker chuckled. The cellar echoed around Eleazer. A chuckle came from behind the barrels and out of the dank black corners.

"I ran fast to lose him," said the figure on the steps. "I walked through swamps and woods, dark woods. I was surprised, I tell you, to see him find the way in the dark."

"Pfefferkorn held a light for my eyes," said the Rabbi.

"Liar," the whisper thickened.

"Not you," said Eleazer, "but another Pfefferkorn."

"Liar," the voice cried from behind the candle. "Jew liar."

"Who calls me that?" Eleazer asked quietly. "Not the Pfefferkorn whose soul I followed like a firefly through the swamps. Not that ancient unburied Pfefferkorn who hides today inside a little shoemaker. For he is a Jew, too. And being a Jew he knows I am no liar."

"Ah," the voice from the steps sighed, and the candle flame drew nearer the ax.

"Sit where you are," said Eleazer sternly, "for you have time,

Pfefferkorn. Think of all the time you have, of the long centuries you have prowled and the longer ones to come. The deed will wait a little while."

The ax had vanished from the step and the candle moved down. Pfefferkorn's shadow leaped into the cellar and stood up wild and crooked on the wall.

Eleazer spoke as it moved.

"Why have you changed your mind," he asked, "and become afraid to hear me speak? Remember that you sent for me. You came into my dreams and pleaded that I come." Eleazer raised his voice as the shadow grew on the wall. "Why else did you embroider the yellow triangles in my slippers? So I would see them and come to you."

"Christ-killer," said Pfefferkorn thickly, "why should I want to hear your Jew voice?"

"You sent for me to save you," said Eleazer.

The shadow on the wall grew still. Pfefferkorn sat down slowly on the last step and the ax blade glistened at his side again.

"To save me!" The shoemaker's chuckle echoed from the barrels and dark corners.

"Yes," said Rabbi Eleazer. "To save you. For you are a gilgul. You are a soul, damned and wandering outside the windows of Life. A dead man lives inside you, shoemaker. And he is weary. He sent for me."

"What is this!" screamed the figure on the step. "What are you talking about! You telling me who I am! Rotten, stinking Jew! I am Pfefferkorn, the shoemaker. I work for the Fathers. You saw me in the garden."

The cellar remained full of sounds after the voice had finished. Eleazer watched the candle move from the steps to the wall and remain there as if its holder were crouching. A faint moon of light glowed on the wall. The blade of the ax dangled near the earthen floor like a glistening head struggling to raise itself.

When the echoes had ended, Eleazer resumed.

"You are Pfefferkorn," he said gravely, "who was born in Moravia five hundred years ago; Pfefferkorn who was a Jewish butcher boy in the ghetto of Moravia and whose parents were Jews and who was taught the meaning of God by the Rabbis of Frankfort. Five hundred years ago you were alive. But now you are only unburied. You are tired, and you have sent for me. Then, listen—poor, sad, accursed Jew from the synagogue of Moravia, who once stood with his people before God."

The shoemaker crouched against the wall, holding the candle before him, his other arm dangling. His eyes shone, and a grimace that exposed his teeth peered out of the little hole of candle-light. His wet open mouth growled as it breathed.

The Rabbi's voice now seemed to come from all the corners of the darkness.

"Listen—for it is the truth I speak. At night you have lain in your bed, shoemaker, listening to the voices that make covenants with the gilgul. You have lain, sweating and quaking, while the demon held court inside you, uttering cries that came not from your mouth. And you have heard a world long dead speak to him.

"I know these voices, Pfefferkorn. They are the voices of Jakob von Hochstraten, of Arnold of Tongern, of Gratius of Deventer—still moaning out of old graves for Jewish blood. It is they who speak to you."

"Holy orders they give to me!" the figure against the wall cried out. "At night!"

"Wait! . . . You have time. Lower your ax, shoemaker. Stand not between me and the gilgul, for it is to him I would speak. Gilgul, by the powers of my soul I invoke you. Come forth, demon. Pfefferkorn of Moravia, come forth!"

Darkness and silence lay in a spell about the two starry candles. The holy man did not break the silence with any invocations, nor test it with his powers. Instead he spoke presently in a whisper, as if he were merely trying out and questioning the mystery before him.

"Poor Gilgul," he spoke in a voice intensely sad, "poor accursed soul. Recall yourself. Remember who it was who stole in the market-place in Moravia. Recall yourself, and it may be given to me to help you. Come, rob again your father's friend, Nathan the goldsmith. And run, thief, to the Christian monastery crying that your people punish you. Fall at the Dominicans' feet. Kiss their slippers. Save yourself from the punishment for your thieving. Cry for the Cross and Baptism. And rise, poor Apostate, poor Pfefferkorn, the Christian. Mad Pfefferkorn, baying for vengeance against your people. Pour out the false mad tale of Jewish deviltries to the mad nun Kunigunde. Hurry with her to the Emperor, her brother. And to your work, Pfefferkorn! Rekindle Torquemada's fires for the German land. Plead with kings and bishops for the scourging of Israel, the burning of Israel's holy books. Move and travel tirelessly from altar to palace, crying always: 'Death for the Jew. Let the Jew be cursed and burned and driven from the earth.' "

The figure against the wall trembled. A moan came from its lips and grew louder until it filled the darkness. The shadow of the figure loomed again, and Pfefferkorn moved from the wall.

"Let the dead wait a little longer," said the Rabbi softly. "No, do not pray, ghost and demon"—the voice of Pfefferkorn had risen, calling on Jesus—"for you know it is I who hold the mystery and the secret."

"Black Jew," the heavy, hoarsened whisper came from the wall. "There is no secret but the sweet call of Jesus Christ to save the world."

"The gilgul speaks," the Rabbi said to himself in wonder, "the ghost and demon who longs for me to save him. Pfefferkorn of Moravia has grown tired of his accursed self. He longs to lie down among the dead and be at rest."

Long he remained silent, then he spoke in Hebrew.

"This is the Beast, O Israel, whom you cast out of our ancient soul by the first fires of Sinai. The Beast, older than the first prayers of Man. Beast—brother of the Prophets and Fathers of our first tribes—he is the Animal driven out from within the body of Israel when God placed His light in it. And because it was the Jew that first unhoused him, it is the Jew he must hound. Against the Jew he must avenge himself. Thus he has moved, Beast-Brother, through the ages, whispering to men and driving them mad with his own madness. Thus he has wandered, from age to age, faithful to his quarry, washing his hands in Jewish blood."

Eleazer paused, as though he were listening to a silence far beyond the awful silence where he stood.

"Such is the judgment," he said at last, "and such the mystery of his hands."

When he had finished, a sigh as of a dog at a closed door came from behind the candle held by the shoemaker.

Eleazer moved forward calmly to the face of murder.

"Gilgul, this I have to tell you," he cried out. "You have sent for me, but my help you shall not have. In vain you called. In vain you embroidered the slippers. It is decreed that Pfefferkorn, wearied with washing his hands in Jewish blood, must still blindly kill. No holy powers will I summon. I see no light. I do not know the way for you. Possessed by the demon you are, and so you must remain."

As Eleazer stood waiting, he saw with unchanged eyes that despair was in the sweating face before him and pain gleamed in its demon's eyes. An agony of pain came sweating out of the man.

And as Eleazer looked into this face of torment, the ax smote him, splitting through his ear. He fell to the dark floor in silence.

The voice of Pfefferkorn moaned and bleated and burst into ugly cries. Wildly the ax swung again. Its heavy blade split through the nose and the mouth. Again it swung.

Still howling, the man rushed to the workbench and snatched up a shoemaker's knife. He returned and dug the butt of the candle into the earthen floor. He remained, kneeling and cutting—his hand half hidden and moving to and fro. . . . The light of the candle mirrored itself in blood.

When Pfefferkorn, still working, looked at Eleazer, the large brown eyes were wide open. As he looked, the eyes of Eleazer moved from the right to the left. The pupils lay still in the socket corners and then moved back slowly.

Pfefferkorn sprang to his feet. The darkness swallowed him and he reappeared rolling a barrel. He tilted it and emptied the kerosene over the mutilated figure. He touched the candle to its feet.

The darkness sprang aside. A green and yellow fire mounted swiftly from Eleazer's body. It seized him in a vivid eager clutch, and the underground room became wild with light.

At the foot of the steps, Pfefferkorn looked back. In the heart of the fire that covered everything, he saw the large brown eyes of Rabbi Eleazer close slowly.

Captain Malloy had spent an irritating day in his office. His policemen had rounded up for him some thirty lunatics—shambling, timorous creatures released at one time or another from the asylums. These the captain had questioned. One after another the muttering, shifty-eyed child faces had looked from the other side of his desk, a strong light shining on them.

Puttering about at odd jobs, drifting from bedhouse to bedhouse, knowing themselves as bits of human junk that belonged nowhere, these loony ones were used to the ways of the police. When the net went out for suspects of strange and unsolved crimes, these shuffling figures with their frightened eyes and stuttering voices always emerged with the first haul.

Facing the familiar captain once again, each of them had begun with bluster his account of whereabouts and activities. But under Captain Malloy's questions each had started to shift in the chair. Captain Malloy had studied the guilt that responded furtively to his inquiries, trying to distinguish between the guilt of crimes done and crimes dreamed. The day had concluded with six confessions. Six of these shaken and beclouded souls had cried out, at the sight of the crucifix with the broken fastening loop, that it belonged to them, and that their hands had been the ones that had committed murder and mutilation. The six confessions, sprinkled with gibberish and echoing with the hosannas of mania released, were taken down by irritable police stenographers who, like the captain, knew their labors were a gruesome waste of time. But Captain Malloy had a plan in the back of his head that required the assistance of six unshaven lunatics. Accordingly, the six, wallowing in their phantom deeds, were locked away in cells.

At five o'clock Captain Malloy left his office and started once more for the monastery of the Dominican Fathers. The crucifix, so dramatically identified by the little Friar in the garden, was still in his pocket. The newspapers he read on the train were full of tidings of the lunatic round-up, of statements from eminent psychiatrists that a fourth of all the city's population was insane and in need of aid—presumably theirs; and of promises to their readers that the Police were closing in on the Mystery.

"Captain Malloy, in charge of the hunt, refused to comment on the arrests made," read one of the tales, "beyond stating that he felt certain of a solution of Joseph Franks's murder within the next twenty-four hours."

Captain Malloy, who had made no such statement and was full of no such certainty, threw down this pipe-dreaming gazette and looked out of the train window. The sultry afternoon was full of rain to come. The train was hot and uncomfortable, and outside the window the grimy streets of the city wheeled in a panorama of ugly spokes that dizzied and depressed the captain. He turned his eyes away and sat looking moodily before him. After two months of constant work, the only clue to the four murders that had come to him was the look in the eyes of a man he had seen for a moment in the monastery garden. Irritated with himself, Malloy fell to muttering inwardly that he was behaving like an old maid with the fantods, that there was no sense in this long trip after an exhausting day, that the man he had looked at for a moment was an honest German shoemaker and nothing else.

Yet this shoemaker's face, eager and beaming as he had stood beside it, had signaled something to the inner archives of Captain Malloy. The policeman had felt himself bristle, and his psychic nose with a single sniff had drawn in an ominous scent. The captain's microscopic memory tried now to reconstruct this smell for study, but he was unable to recapture its delicate ingredients. He was able to remember only that the eyes of this shoemaker had glittered as if full of desperate and hidden light as they rested smilingly on the tall, pale Rabbi who was visiting Father Dominic.

Growling at himself as the prince of wild-goose chasers, Captain Malloy sank deeper into his seat. He had come to the angry conclusion that he was wasting valuable time and behaving like a rural constable rather than a city detective. But the train continued carrying him nearer the monastery of the Dominican Fathers.

Father Francis, stocky and pink-faced, returned to the police captain waiting in the monastery's silent hall. Father Dominic, he reported, would be unable to speak to the visitor. When Malloy asked politely why, the black robe answered that Father Dominic was at his prayers and would remain so for the rest of the night.

"Perhaps you can help me then," said the captain. "I would like the name and address of the shoemaker who visited Father Dominic yesterday."

"Oh, Pfefferkorn!" The Friar smiled. "The one who brought the slippers?"

"Yes," said Malloy, and Father Francis gave him an address some miles away.

Stubbornly Captain Malloy tracked down a taxi and rode through the scattered suburb and past the stretch of marshlands. The taxi turned off into a wretched, half-passable road just as the threat of rain became a reality. The sky blackened. Gusts of chill wind swept and rattled the taxi windows. Then a salvo of thunder sounded, shaking the darkness. As the sky came swiftly close to the earth, the thunder sounded again, and the rain came down. A smear of plunging water filled the chilled and darkened afternoon, and Captain Malloy, with no raincoat, cursed aloud. In an increasing spray of mud the taxi clattered on. It came to a halt in the midst of nowhere like a raft stranded. Malloy saw a thicket of fir trees in a blank field. His driver was shouting through the window that something to the right was the Pfefferkorn house. Malloy stared into the rain-boiling field all about him, and cursed his idiot guide. Then he noticed the charred stumps of a small building. Part of a stone wall still stood, and around a blackened space lay piles of debris and soaking rubbish.

"It must have burned down last night," the taxi man shouted, as Malloy, with door opened, leaned out surveying the scene.

A blast of thunder shook the ground, and the lightning spat through the dark. There was a pause and then the storm fired point-blank at Captain Malloy in the taxi. Thunder lifted the wheels and the captain's derby and left a gasp in his throat. But his eyes caught a glimpse of the Pfefferkorn wall crumbling and the stones rolling away and he understood now how a stone house could have burned to so small an ash. Malloy settled back angrily in his seat and instructed the driver to go on. He would inquire everywhere until he learned what had happened, and if Pfefferkorn had taken refuge somewhere, or if he had disappeared. Captain Malloy was on the trail.

The rain had doubled in force when the taxi stopped before a frame house at the end of the suburban street. It was one of a score of chocolate-trimmed white wooden buildings as alike as a set of playing blocks. Captain Malloy sprinted across the pavement to its front door and stood soaking in the downpour as he waited for someone to answer the bell.

A soft-faced young woman with pale hair and pale blurred eyes drew the door curtain aside and peered out. The captain rapped amiably on the glass panel, but the young woman, with a sudden flurry of alarm, disappeared. Malloy waited stoically as the rain pasted his heavy clothes to his body. A man appeared and the door was opened. Malloy faced a pale-haired German, young and well built. He noticed the soft cheeks, the pink ears, the puffy colorless lips, the powerful arms and large hands, as he explained his presence in the hallway and told who he was. The soft-faced woman had returned and stood timidly beside the man, who was evidently her husband. Malloy's powers of observation were not too keen with women. With a quick look at her bulging youthful body, he ignored her.

"Pfefferkorn iss not here," said the young German and smiled. "His home has burned down, poor feller. He only slept here last night. My name iss Gustav Edelberg," he added, and held out his hand in stiff friendliness. "Come inside a little, if you please, Captain, and ve can talk better. I am sorry Pfefferkorn iss not here."

Malloy stood in the arch of a small parlor full of shining oak furniture. Behind a tall oak piano covered with music, Captain Malloy saw a large swastika flag, standing on the floor. Another swastika flag was tacked on the wall and under it hung a large gold-framed photograph of Adolf Hitler, the German Fuehrer.

Young Edelberg continued smiling as Malloy's eyes moved about. But behind the albino gloss of the Teutonic face the drenched but alert Malloy felt an uneasiness.

"You're a Nazi?" asked the captain.

"Yes," the young man smiled, "I am Offizier in the German-American Storm Troopers. You are welcome."

Malloy walked into the room. The soft-faced Mrs. Edelberg uttered a cry at wet shoes dirtying her polished floor. She covered her mouth quickly with her pudgy hand and stood shamefaced and cringing. The policeman leaned over a pile of large cardboard placards facing the wall.

"Ach, everything iss such a mess!" exclaimed the young wife. "Excuse it, please."

The Nazi officer looked at her coldly. She blushed and nodded her head apologetically several times.

"For parades, I suppose," said Captain Malloy.

"Yes," said the Nazi.

Malloy read a few of the lettered slogans. "Jews Are Ruining Our Country. Rise Up, Americans." "Oust Jews and Find Prosperity." "Jew Plots Kill Christian Culture."

"You know Pfefferkorn well?" the captain asked, looking up.

"Yes," said his host.

"He is a good friend of yours?" the captain murmured.

"Yes, we are very good friends."

"Is he also a member of your Nazi organization?" Malloy continued.

"Oh, yes." The wife beamed. "Pfeffy is a good member. He helped make all the signs with my husband."

The husband looked at her and spoke sharply in German.

"Get back into the kitchen quick," he said, "and concern yourself not with my affairs, please."

With a cringing, anxious look in her blurred eyes, the young woman obeyed.

"Why are you asking after Pfefferkorn?" the Nazi now asked Malloy.

Malloy said nothing. His eyes remained on the blond young man. He saw the good nature that had greeted him retreat as if behind a layer of fat.

"You are a Jew?" the German asked slowly.

"No," said Malloy, "I'm Irish."

"Excuse me, then," said the Nazi stiffly, "there are many Jews in this neighborhood. Ve must be careful."

He bowed slightly and Malloy thanked him and walked to the front door. He had learned that Pfefferkorn was alive.

"Allow me, please," the blond young man said, "I will get an umbrella for you."

"Never mind," Captain Malloy answered and sprinted across the pavement to the waiting taxi.

Careening through the rain-beaten roads, the taxi started back for the thicket of fir trees. On the way, Malloy stopped and bought a large flashlight.

The rain flung itself at the captain as he walked across the field to the remains of Pfefferkorn's house. But the spit of lightning, the blasts of thunder, the lash of water against his face and soggy clothes, were far-away matters to Captain Malloy. He walked now in an inner world, his senses on some invisible goal.

The rain steamed from the debris of the burned dwelling. Holding his flashlight before him, Malloy kicked at the slop of ashes and charred wood. His light picked out a hole in the ground. He knelt in a pool of water and looked into a cellar. There were no steps to descend. The captain returned to the taxi and ordered his driver to bring him back a tall ladder from some place. The taxi clattered out of the thicket again.

Captain Malloy waited under the fir trees. His jaws were rigid and he no longer belabored himself with criticisms of his conduct. He had found nothing new, no tangible thing to add to the trail at which he sniffed. But the trail was there, ghostly and persistent. Illogically and with no single fact to assuage him, Captain Malloy waited contentedly under the fir trees, his blue eyes looking dreamily at the house that had been burned.

In a half-hour the ladder appeared. Malloy carried it to the rain-steaming field and lowered it into the hole he had found. The hole was deep and the ladder barely reached its bottom. He climbed down its rungs, the rain pouring on him as out of a huge bottle. The black, sightless hole in which he found himself was shoe-deep with water. He splashed about in the darkness, sniffing the sharp wet ghost of the fire that had raged here. Foot by foot Malloy explored it with his light. The place was empty of all furniture. Hollow and black, it surrounded him, its odors sawing away at his nose. Occasionally the black hole turned ashen blue as the lightning stretched wildly in the outside night. The cellar flared and grew blind. The thunder blasts fired their shrieks through the hole overhead. Then quiet seized the earth and the rain worked busily in the darkness.

Malloy continued to explore. In a corner of the reeking cellar his light picked out an object. On a dry bit of earth he saw a slipper standing. Malloy stood staring at it. He saw it was made of a sort of embroidery, newly woven and unworn. Then the captain did an unaccountable thing. He looked around fearfully and crossed himself. For what he had looked Malloy didn't know. For the darkness to move, perhaps, or a thing to appear; for the muddy earth to open under his feet and the inky reeking air to become filled with pale shapes. He stood with the skin on his large body tightened. A bomb of thunder exploded over his head. Its echoes leaped around his ears. He set his jaws firmly and waited for the tremble to leave his hands. Then he leaned over to pick up the slipper. As his nose neared the ground another smell came to him. It was not the wet ghost of flames this time but an uglier smell that confused him and made him think of chickens. Straightening, Captain Malloy put the slipper under his wet coat as if it were something alive, and climbed up the ladder.

A half-hour later the captain was in a hotel telephone booth, water gushing from him as from a fountain as he waited for his office in New York to answer. He caught his breath as he remembered something.

"It was flesh I smelled," the delayed message came from the Malloy inner archives, "human flesh. Burned."

A voice answered over the telephone. Captain Malloy spoke briefly. He wanted a suitcaseful of fresh dry clothes and a raincoat brought out to him. The voice took down the name of the hotel and then said: "By the way, we got a report in that some Rabbi has disappeared out your way. It was Saturday night, and he didn't show up for services."

"What's his name?" asked the captain.

"Just a minute, I'll read it all to you," said the voice. "Here we are. It says Rabbi Eleazer, aged seventy-nine, height six feet one, weight one hundred and forty, clean-shaven, missing from the synagogue since yesterday."

"That's enough," said Malloy, "and hurry up with my clothes. I'm wetter than Monday's wash."

Malloy had intended taking a room in the hotel. Instead he walked out of the empty lobby and into the storm again. He waved his drenched arms to his taxi-driver, who had moved down the street. The taxi splashed up. Captain Malloy drove once more to the Dominican monastery two miles away. His reddish, square face, despite the long prowling in the storm, was content and peaceful.

At the monastery Father Francis, though concerned over the policeman's wretched condition, insisted that the ancient Dominic was still at his prayers.

"May I have pencil and paper?" said Captain Malloy. These were procured, and he wrote the following lines:

"Please may I see you about something involving your friend Rabbi Eleazer, the shoemaker Pfefferkorn, and the crucifix?"

"I'll wait here," he said. A few minutes later Father Francis returned. Dominic walked behind him.

"Forgive me, Father, for disturbing you again," said Captain Malloy.

Father Dominic raised his eyes and said softly:

"I was praying for him."

Malloy beat back the glint of surprise in his eyes, and continued to look at the priest with his expression unchanged.

"Did you think something had happened to him?" he asked.

"I was praying for him," Father Dominic repeated. He looked pleadingly at the policeman. "What have you heard?" he whispered.

"Tell me, Father," Malloy insisted gently, "why you were praying for him. It's important that I know."

The Friar shook his head.

"It's nothing that can be told," he answered.

"Well," said Captain Malloy, "can you tell me if this slipper belonged to the Rabbi?"

He removed the slipper from under his coat. Dominic saw the yellow triangles and the familiar pattern.

"Yes," he said.

"Did he have this slipper with him when he left you yesterday?" Malloy asked.

"Yes," said Dominic. "Where is he?"

"He has disappeared," said Malloy gently. "He failed to return to his home last night. But I found this slipper in the cellar of Pfefferkorn's house. The house burned down last night."

"Burned down," whispered the little Friar.

An ashen color came into his sunbeaten face.

"It will be a great help to me and to your friend, Father," said the captain urgently, "if you would tell me why you were praying for him since he left your side last night."

Father Dominic's face twitched and the pain in his eyes was covered with tears.

"Rabbi Eleazer does not need my help," he said finally.

Captain Malloy bowed his head and turned away.

Father Dominic looked after him.

"You have done good work tonight, Captain Malloy," he said sadly, as the door opened to the storm.

The arrest of Pfefferkorn was accomplished quietly. He was taken in the morning from the house of the American-Nazi lieutenant, Gustav Edelberg. Captain Malloy placed him among the six loonies in the station cells and called his three witnesses. These were the young woman who had noticed a man following the murdered Joseph Franks, the janitor who had seen a man lurking on the street corner where Max Asher was killed, the newsdealer who had seen someone follow Irving Bronski into the deserted theater alley on the midnight he was found slain and mutilated.

Under conditions that would leave no doubt in any jury's mind, he hoped, Captain Malloy led each of his witnesses separately to the row of cells. Each looked at the seven suspects and selected Pfefferkorn as the man observed near the scene of the crime. After these identifications, Pfefferkorn was charged with the murder of five Jews. He was indicted on these counts and ordered to be placed on trial for the last of them, the killing of Rabbi Eleazer. The trial was set for a month later.

But the trial did not wait for the date that had been set. It began at once everywhere, in the streets, the cafés, the newspapers, in homes, churches, and meeting halls. Hour by hour the significance of the arrest of the Nazi Pfefferkorn for the murder of five Jews increased. All who read the first accounts of the case felt immediately that a *cause célèbre* had been born. The nation's Jews, psychically tormented by years of Nazi calumny, seized quickly on Pfefferkorn as the symbol of German Kultur. They cried out triumphantly that Pfefferkorn, the fiend, was the logical and inhuman flowering of Nazism; that Pfefferkorn, the monster, was the New Germany incarnate, legitimate spawn of a nation that had tried to strengthen itself by filling its veins deliberately with hate.

And the American Nazis, less numerous but more effectively organized, answered back that Pfefferkorn was innocent of any crime, but that he was being sent to his death as part of the cunning Jewish plot to blacken the name of Aryan. And the facts for and against Pfefferkorn were spread before the world by the newspapers and debated more and more hysterically everywhere.

In a few days the seeming innocence of Pfefferkorn began to triumph. The published facts aroused a storm of doubt. The case as revealed in the press appeared to grow vaguer and more circumstantial the more light there was turned on it. The vast jury of the public began to inquire, Where were the concrete facts of guilt? Where, even, was the body of the dead Rabbi? Police and hundreds of Jewish volunteers had dug and searched in the vicinity of Pfefferkorn's burned house day and night and no corpse or clues leading either to murder or to Pfefferkorn had been uncovered. Pfefferkorn had been identified by three witnesses as the killer of Jews. But who were these witnesses? Jews themselves. Captain Malloy, in charge of the case, refused to comment other than that he knew Pfefferkorn to be guilty and that he expected a confession before the trial.

But no confession came. Instead, heartbreaking and half-articulate stories of his life from Pfefferkorn's lips appeared in the newspapers. Rumors filled the city that the little shoemaker was being beaten and submitted to various tortures by the police in a desperate effort to force him to admit the crimes. And that behind this desperation were the Jews. The Jews were beating Pfefferkorn. The Jews were bringing their great financial powers to bear on the officials of the city, demanding that Pfefferkorn be proved guilty in order that the Nazis of the world could be convicted of inhumanity. These rumors generated swiftly and simultaneously everywhere.

And as this public trial continued, a feeling began to rise against the Jews. Their outcries that this little shoemaker was an anti-Semitic fiend hatched by Nazi hate, who had gone around disemboweling Jews, began to grow irksome and full of some alien over-emphasis, and their hysteria soon sounded offensive. This was Shylock howling again for his pound of Pfefferkorn flesh.

Swiftly the Nazi propagandists took advantage of this mood. They thrust aside the long-prized but always tenuous barriers of American tolerance, and launched an open campaign against Jews. The Hitler gibberish with all its tragi-comic naïvetés about Jew cunning and Jew dominance became new, loud fact in this public trial of Pfefferkorn.

The Jews of the nation welcomed this burst of calumny at

first. Its howling and stupid accusations appeared to them to convict their accusers of every sin against reason. For to the American Jew, the racial calumny that has kept his brothers shuddering throughout most of the Christian era seemed too preposterous to be effective in the New World. As he read the virulent attacks uncorked by the city's Nazis, the American Jew was convinced that their irrationality and intolerance would prove a boomerang. Surely, he thought, the unreason and obvious disease of these German minds must arouse only revulsion wherever their cries resound.

It was this illusion that was to bring him his deepest distress, for it is always the miserable realization that anti-Jew propaganda finds immediate adherents that brings his spirit down. Noting that others believe what is unbelievable, the Jew begins to feel that all the world around him is slowly going mad, and in this madness he becomes a sort of delusion. He feels himself ceasing to be human and becoming a pariah imprisoned in the delirium of others. And there he struggles full of impotence, as one does in an evil dream.

In the second week of the Pfefferkorn controversy, the Jews found themselves slipping into this wretched fantasy in which they have immemorially lost their standing as human beings and in which everything they say is robbed of all significance, for the reason that it is Jews who are saying it. The meaning of the Pfefferkorn trial underwent a cruel change. Not Eleazer, the ascetic Jew whose face peered out of the newspapers hourly, but Pfefferkorn, the pious, hard-working German shoemaker, had become a Cause and a Victim. And it was the Jews who were on trial, as they must always be when they so far forget themselves as to become an Issue.

Finding themselves marched into the prisoner's dock, Jewish

spokesmen summoned the ideals of democracy and humanity
to their defense. But the multitudinous jury of bystanders listened with increasing irritation. The appeal to their sanity and
fair play angered them, for in such appeal there is always the
accusation that these qualities are missing. This in itself is enough
to antagonize the righteous. But there is also the fact that it is
extremely dangerous to accuse any mass of people of inhumanity. It invariably sets them to proving it.

Throughout the days before the trial, the Jews continued
desperately their pleas for fair play, desperately and more and
more in vain. For in the long recurrent struggle of the Jew to
establish himself within the bosom of humanity, it is always the
same in the end. The cry for justice calls more attention to the
weakness of the crier than to the strength of his cause, and the
Jew ends by flushing ten sadists for every humanitarian.

The activities of Pfefferkorn's defenders, led by the pale-
haired Nazi, Edelberg, reverberated everywhere. A great emotion swept the various German-American sectors of the city.
Thousands of cheerful-looking men and women who sang,
danced, and drank beer emerged from Teutonia's parlors in
New York to heil for Hitler and Pfefferkorn, and contribute to
the defense fund of the latter. These celebrants crowding the
meeting halls had, however, only a secondary interest in the
shoemaker's innocence. The cause to which they rallied was that
of their own solidarity. Lustily and gaily, they sang songs revealing the unanimity of their thought and passion. It was this
opportunity to feel the tribal rhythm of uniformity, so dear to
the slave-haunted soul of the German, that brought them cheering around Pfefferkorn.

The charm and gaiety of their solidarity began to be felt
everywhere. Non-Nazis looked wistfully at so much picnicking

going on under their noses and began to wonder what was the secret of all this carnival spirit. They began to see that this socially enviable and humanly warming sense of solidarity had, as its welding ingredient, a hatred of Jews. And simultaneously it became apparent to thousands of outsiders that there was something not only sensible but very pleasant in this hatred of Jews.

Triumphantly the Nazi Bunds continued to color the temperament of the city of which they were so small a part. They sold its tax-bedeviled inhabitants the pleasures of hate—its anodyne of relief from petty matters and its ego-inflating joys.

Where the apologists for the Jews stuttered and pleaded and called passionately on history and humanity to vindicate their cause, the Jew-haters smiled, sang songs, drank beer, and sat happily behind their hate. The menace of the Jews to which they responded with heroic, shoulder-to-shoulder cheers was merely a piece of evil magic to be overcome by fearlessness and the waving of a Cross or the chanting of an Exorcism. That it was a fearlessness of that which had no power, of that which, horrendous though it was, would be easily crushed, made no difference. The deeper the Jew hatred grew, the braver the Jew-haters felt. For hate is the promise of courage, and when felt even against the powerless, it excites its owners with illusions of valor.

Toward the end of the month the larger part of the city stood beside Pfefferkorn in the cellar and enjoyed itself. But those who enjoyed themselves most were the inner circle, the generating storm troops of the hatred. For these, Jew hate had become more than a casual social exhilaration. It was a cult, a drug, and a sport. It set its followers apart from humanity, and welded them into that deeper comradeship which only criminals can

feel. It regenerated also the German sense of self-esteem shattered by the war. In this contempt for Jews, in this embracing
of intolerance and savagery, the Germans felt they were tri-
umphing over the ideals whose protagonists had massed against
them and defeated them twenty years ago.

But these and scores of other motivations were of no concern
to the Germans, who are never a people for analyzing the
sources of their happiness. In their hatred of Jews, shared so
uncritically, they had found a rallying point, a sort of master of
ceremonies for victorious mass merrymaking. This was enough
for them. The Jew was the belle of the Pfefferkorn picnics, the
ugly Maypole round which Teutonia, reunited and full of song,
capered again.

As the fourth week of preparation for the trial began, this
happy and heroic feeling of solidarity had become so great
among the Germans that the possibility that their Pfefferkorn
was a murderer and mutilator of five Jews was entirely over-
shadowed by the fact that he was one of them. At times it even
seemed as if the very accusations against Pfefferkorn added
stature to the man. In their mystic *Kampf* against the Internationalism and Uncleanness of the Jews, the sturdy Teutons of
New York began to feel that their Pfefferkorn's deeds, though
never admitted, were a mystic measure of his greatness. A man
accused of murdering five Jews was a sort of phantom Napoleon
around whom their own undone Jew murders rallied; a hero
who by the very nature of the accusation was entitled to an
Iron Cross rather than to the discomfitures of a trial for murder.

At last Pfefferkorn, now backed by the sympathy of the city,
confronted his victim, not in the dark cellar but in the light of a
law court. There was no ax in his hand this time, but three brilliant lawyers sat around him smiling confidently. A defense

fund of several hundred thousand dollars was at his disposal. In the streets outside as the trial opened throngs of Nazis sang hymns to Pfefferkorn. And the newspapermen in the courtroom, come from a hundred centers, scribbled away on descriptions of Pfefferkorn. They had no prejudice against him. Like all greatly publicized figures of crime, he was their own—"their boy" Pfefferkorn. Gratitude for so fecund a news source as Pfefferkorn colored their scribblings, and the camaraderie between the dramatist and his subject matter animated their reports.

In the courtroom, a cordon of police lined the walls. The benches were filled with celebrities come from everywhere, avid, posturing, opinionated. The trial of Pfefferkorn, echoing through the nation and into far countries, was not only a battle front for them, but a social event. They occupied the crowded benches with the satisfied air of important people who feel themselves in a sufficiently important place.

The People's case against Adolf Pfefferkorn was in the hands of Joseph Menelli, the city's much admired prosecutor. Short, fattish, dynamic, and bristling with a chronic buzz of conflict, Menelli entered the courtroom on the first day like a wrestler coming ominously out of his corner. He moved slowly. He looked at no one. His broad shoulders, his theatrical, self-possessed glower, his wary, provocative calm, identified him in the first few minutes of silence as more than a lawyer come to argue a case. He was the Knight in the field. Menelli, the East Side Italian butcher boy who had butted his way through a generation of politics into the metropolitan limelight, was the People's champion against Pfefferkorn. It was to be seen that Menelli, along with his law books, brought a Cause into the courtroom.

In front of Pfefferkorn at the defense's table sat Francis Cantwell, the most expensive of the city's criminal defense lawyers. He was white-haired, humorous-faced, and friendly-looking in an old suit of unpressed clothes. Behind Pfefferkorn sat John Potalski and William Emerson, aides to Cantwell and famed in their own right as the heroes of a score of murder trials. They were middle-aged men, well built, keen and driving. Unlike the friendly, humorous-looking man who captained them, they came to battle taut and restive.

In the witness rooms outside the court sat the corps of special investigators who had been toiling valiantly for the defense since Pfefferkorn's arrest. Among them were the witnesses to be called. Guards stood at the tall doors of these rooms. Guards filled the thronged corridors.

On the bench, chin sunk on his chest, sat His Honor Daniel Leak. He was a white-haired man, portentous and full of judicial posture. It was obvious even to those who had never known of this judge what his attitude would be through all the crises of the trial. He would shine as a hero of punctilio. Neither humanity nor prejudice would speak through him, but always the law and its gamelike rules of procedure.

Of dominating interest to all in the courtroom, however, was Pfefferkorn. The eyes of spectators and journalists bored at him. Their consciousness of him covered the shoemaker like a beam of light in which every twitch of his features and movement of his body was magnified into drama. His plump, good-natured face with its shaggy brows and twinkling doglike eyes radiated the magnetism of enigma.

How familiar and human he looked, this stooped, nondescript figure fished out of the colorless deeps of the crowd and landed on this high pedestal of Event; so proper, so normal, so understandable to the eye. His manner said: "I am Pfefferkorn, a shoe-maker like any other shoemaker." His smile, his embarrassment, his pathetic interest in his counsel, said: "I am nobody like any other nobody. I belong at a workbench, not here. I am fright-ened, but hopeful. I am only what you see, the familiar, slovenly figure you have always known as a tradesman or a workman. I am one of you in a lesser way. But I am one of you."

But out of this simple and appealing humanity that spoke from Pfefferkorn came another voice, eerie and shocking. It was the voice not of Pfefferkorn or any part or grimace of Pfefferkorn, but of the five murders with which he was charged, and the one for which he was on trial. The sibilant and menacing murmur of crime surrounded Pfefferkorn. These murders spoke, saying: "We have been done. We are the brutal deeds of a fiend. Look close at Pfefferkorn. Watch him. Stare into his eyes. See if you can find us there. We are deeds that may belong to Pfefferkorn. Find us in him."

And looking into Pfefferkorn's eyes, watching, observing, those in the courtroom heard in their own heads a third voice that said: "How strange and far away is the simple thought of another. How impenetrable and dark is the life that beats in the humblest and most familiar of figures, and how perfectly hidden is the thing that we call brother. This nobody, this mild and appealing little man, this One of Us, is as great a mystery as if he had dropped from Mars."

This mystery of the familiar, this enigma that stares empty-lidded out of a neighbor's smile, multiplied the meaning of Pfef-ferkorn. And his simplicity multiplied it again. He sat among his counsel like a provoking and bedeviling riddle that no eyes could read, and that the short black-browed Menelli had sworn to tear open and reveal.

As the business of picking the jury started, the most experienced of the newspapermen began to sense uncertainty in the People's champion. It was too early to judge the caliber of his weapons, but Menelli himself looked dubious to these experts—fretful and curiously out of control. This was difficult to believe, for the Menelli record denied it. But this impression was discussed among the divining journalists. And it was true. Uncertainty spoke out of the very noise in which Menelli tried to conceal it. For though he rumbled and barked and seemed the most dangerous of prosecutors, his clever and violent mind was full of uneasiness. He had worked tirelessly in assembling the People's case, and had come to trial with a fevered and embittered conviction of Pfefferkorn's guilt. Behind this conviction was another almost equal certainty that the evidence of it he had to offer the jury was bleak and insufficient.

He had absorbed along with all the details of the case the mystic knowledge of Pfefferkorn's guilt that filled Captain Malloy. It was this knowledge more than any facts proving it that he found himself ready to offer as the People's side. His black eyes when they turned to Pfefferkorn lighted with hate. He felt the shoemaker's evil as if it were a stench, and his heart lifted with a will to shatter the riddle of Pfefferkorn and uncover what his senses knew.

There had come to Menelli, too, a hatred for the Nazis who were behind the defense. He saw these rabid sympathizers as so many Pfefferkorns with minds as befouled as the shoemaker's. His mind raged against them. There was in Menelli no particular love of Jews. He knew almost nothing of their history, and before Pfefferkorn's arrest had felt almost no concern for their troubles in the world. Nor had the cause of the Jew been awakened in him. He was of that sensitive but egoistic type of mind which, though incapable of surrendering to ideals, is tireless in its attack on their enemies. Injustice and not its victims trumpeted him forward. His strength must come from the ferocity of the enemy rather than the cries of the wretchedness he championed.

Preparing his case, Menelli had read through scores of Nazi speeches and interviewed the orators and leaders of the Nazi cult. His mind had sickened as if it had been inducted suddenly into a nightmare. He saw this cruelty imbedded in the German mind like·the half-decayed fangs of barbarism. And he saw the ugly guilt of Pfefferkorn glowing like an infection out of the pink and white fattish faces of the Nazis with whom he talked. A philosophy based on a love of self and a hatred of everything alien to that self must end by generating in others a hate of the thing that sets itself apart. And Menelli, encountering more and more Germans during his inquiries, began to see in Germans something that grew more inhuman and preposterous with each inspection. And though he had begun with an academic dislike of their politics, he ended with a rage against their faces, accents, mannerisms, and very haircuts.

When we hate, we look only for those things in the hated one that will vindicate and increase our aversion. And as if to oblige us, the one hated seems intent on concealing all his qualities from us but those we consider repulsive. It is this psychological trick that often gives the Jews in their words and deeds the air of caricatures, as if they had been hypnotized by hate into seeming hateful. And it is as true of Germans as of Jews.

To Menelli the prosecutor, every German he interviewed added to the clarity of his hate. He saw them as a people with a spark missing, as if life were only half present in them, and the other half occupied by a corpse-like stubbornness. He saw

Pfefferkorn as a German and not a defendant, or even an individual, and his hatred prepared a case against Nazidom rather than a shoemaker accused of crime. And his great forensic talents became confused and absorbed in the angry questions that crowded his mind.

How could intelligence so malformed and cast in so unhuman a pattern persist in the light of reason? How could so warped and criminal a mood seize on a modern soul and drag it singing and elated into the darkness of the past? What was there in the riddle of this chuckling, butcher-hearted swarm of Germans, full of hate and defiance, who had gleefully exchanged their humanity for the hyena philosophies of an aberrant little paperhanger named Hitler? What was there in the cries of that vengeful little eunuch whose useless sex had infected his mind with rages and phantasms that found so powerful an echo in the German soul?

These questions filled Menelli, the champion of Justice, and armed his own humanity with claws and fangs as incredible as those he had glimpsed in the Nazi cult. His intelligence cautioned him from day to day against rushing Pfefferkorn to trial, and urged him to wait until his aide, Captain Malloy, had uncovered more evidence. But his rage lured him into battle.

He appeared in the courtroom unprofessionally armed with passion, a champion thirsting for conflict rather than victory. Headstrong and dramatic, he would end floundering stupidly in the nets of the law's minutiae. His very courage and righteousness, unguided by the talent that had brought him success, would turn him into a black-browed clown as he battered at the rules of evidence. The Pfefferkorn counsel, crafty in the utilization of his emotional violence and legal weakness, would cruelly pervert this People's champion into their own chief witness. His passion would be offered the jury as part of the persecution that sought to convict an innocent Pfefferkorn of the crime of being a German. And by ludicrous but incontrovertible steps it would be the Germans and not the Jews who were in danger of martyrdom, and the victims of bigotry. Poised and amused at the futility of Menelli's onslaughts, the Nazi spokesmen would come to seem tolerant and superior, courteous and law-abiding, and, paradoxically, cast in a finer mold of reason.

These eventualities came to be. Menelli's passion defeated him from the first hour of jury picking. The procedure-haunted judge coldly edited his outbursts and outlawed his emotional attitudes. He was cautioned again and again to confine his conduct to that of a prosecutor of Pfefferkorn, not of Nazidom. As a result of these first errors, the jury, completed after four days of histrionics, was hailed as a victory by the Nazis. Not a single Jew had gained a place on it, and three of its members were German-born. The presence of these three in the jury box further undid the swarthy battering ram of a prosecutor. He took to regarding the jury as an enemy. Embittered always by the insufficiency of his evidence, he placed the jurors on trial, assailed and challenged them in every question asked and every objection offered to the bench.

The Jewish population had found immediate solace in the virtuosity of the Menelli hate. His outcries were hailed as manna by the Jewish press. But as the case progressed into its third day even the Jewish journalists saw that their first impressions had been accurate. Hour by hour the Menelli evidence seemed to lose what stature it might have had alongside the violence of the Menelli passion. It began to appear that this volcano of a prosecutor was erupting only in pebbles, harmless and even comic-seeming because of the noise that accompanied them.

On the fourth day, which had promised the climax of the People's case in the testimony of Captain Malloy, even the stanchest of the anti-Pfefferkornites began to lose heart. Captain Malloy seated himself in the witness chair amid an expectant quiet. His rigid, square face repeated calmly the tale of Pfefferkorn's guilt as he had first felt it. He traced his work through the finding of the slipper in the cellar of the burned house. The slipper was shown him.

It was the People's lone exhibit.

Menelli had based his case on this slipper found in the cellar. Out of its presence there he had spun his theory of the Pfefferkorn crime in the opening address. Gentlemen—urged on by the thought that Pfefferkorn was the mutilator of Jews sought by the police, Rabbi Eleazer had followed the shoemaker to his house. The aged and delicate man of God had exhibited no policeman's cunning. He had walked into the Pfefferkorn cellar, sustained by the righteousness of his own soul and lured by some mystic knowledge of the shoemaker's true self. He had confronted Pfefferkorn with his crimes and under his arm he had held, as he spoke, the symbolic Jew-hating slippers Pfefferkorn had embroidered for him. And Pfefferkorn had murdered the Rabbi in the depths of this cellar. Then, exulting in his deed, he had set fire to the house. Hidden from any road, the house had burned down without attracting attention. Pfefferkorn had crouched in the glare of the flames, watching the fire continue his crime. When the fire was done, cunning had returned to Pfefferkorn. He had remembered the body in the cellar. Lowering himself into it again by a rope, for the stairs were now burned away, he had hoisted the remains out of the cellar. He had walked on in the night until he had come to the marshes he knew so well. In these marshes the body had been hidden and still lay out of sight under the muck and vegetation of the swamp. The storm that had preceded Captain Malloy to the scene the next day had removed all traces of the crime. But it had not removed the slipper. Almost miraculously the slipper had remained behind untouched by fire or criminal cunning, to speak in the absence of all other witnesses of the things that had taken place in the Pfefferkorn cellar.

Malloy, now looking at this slipper from the witness stand, nodded his head and answered yes. It was the same slipper his light had picked out in the rain-whipped cellar. Malloy's testimony ended with this identification and he was turned over for cross-examination.

And now his story under the half-humorous queries of the white-haired and friendly-looking Cantwell suffered a transformation. It became a story of obsession, devoid of fact, born of hunches and the most unpoliceman-like species of reasoning. Malloy, the bloodhound, became an irrational and hate-crazed cat's-paw of the Jews. Impervious to storm, rain, and reason, he had hurled himself at the business of fastening a crime on a Nazi, and all the subtleties that had led him to Pfefferkorn were twisted easily and even comically into the aberrations of an obsessed and melodramatic Hawkshaw.

Ridiculed and discredited, Captain Malloy stepped from the witness chair. He had left behind an impression of guilt preconceived and never proved, except in his own fevered imaginings. As he passed Pfefferkorn's chair, Malloy paused and looked into the shoemaker's eyes. They were raised to his with an expression of wonder and unhappiness so repulsive to Malloy's knowledge of the man's guilt that the captain turned crimson. The Pfefferkorn sympathizers in the courtroom, whose numbers increased hourly, tittered at the policeman's discomfiture.

All he could say when he returned to Menelli's table was: "Don't give up. He's guilty as hell."

Menelli nodded. His broad shoulders lifted and his eyes darkened.

"I'll get him somehow," he said.

Father Dominic followed Malloy on the stand and again the promise of Menelli's impassioned opening address, in which the Catholic Father had figured so importantly, came to nothing. There was no evidence in Father Dominic beyond the one fact that Eleazer had left him late that rainy afternoon carrying the two slippers Pfefferkorn had made for him. Like Malloy he nodded when the slipper found in Pfefferkorn's cellar was shown him. This was his lone bit of evidence, but Menelli was not content with it. He knew of other matters that betrayed Pfefferkorn's guilt, and he plunged stupidly into the business of bringing them out of Father Dominic. Why had the Father prayed for Eleazer's safety after the Rabbi had gone? What had happened that had aroused the Father's fear for his friend's life?

Black-robed and gentle-voiced, the Friar looked uneasily at Menelli as these questions came. Menelli was wrong to ask these questions, Dominic thought. His own accurate and logical mind informed him how his words would be turned upside down by the lawyers for the defense. Still they might help. If he spoke carefully and tenderly the jurors might feel what he had felt. Carefully and tenderly Father Dominic then tried to evoke the afternoon in the garden with his friend. He told of the Rabbi's visit and of some of their talk. He repeated what had happened when Pfefferkorn had brought the slippers, and in his gentle and talented words the scene under the maple trees came again to life. Then he related the dream the Rabbi had told him. It was this dream that had frightened him.

Menelli still persisted. Why had he grown frightened? Had there been something else that had warned him, some other information known only to him and Eleazer? Here Father Dominic hesitated. His little faun's face looked helplessly through the window beyond at the summer afternoon. How tell them that Pfefferkorn was related somehow to another Pfefferkorn five hundred years ago, that Eleazer, who was a mystic, had sensed this gruesome fact, that the ancient Dominican cross found in the hand of the murdered Franks took the crime back somewhere into the hate-filled centuries of the earlier church? In what way would these curious things help the dead man he had loved? They would only bring to light the old charge that the Dominican Order had been one of the ancient breeding places of a Jew hate, and that it had burned and tortured Jews in the name of holiness, and that Pfefferkorn, the fiend who posed as a shoemaker, had the name of one of its ancient and honored sons. His little eyes, unblinking as they stared out of the window, became full of pain. He longed to raise them in prayer and to beg God to show him some way for the truth to be told so that it might be believed.

After a long pause, Father Dominic looked poignantly at Menelli and answered: "My reasons for being worried over my friend Eleazer lie between me—and Someone Else."

The cross-examination of Father Dominic was gentle but devastating. Patiently the friendly-looking Cantwell went over the old priest's tale of fears and conjectures until they lost all their poetic mood. They became the crotchety and irrational fret of age. Lawyer Cantwell was even tender toward the ancient Father's little mental quirks. But when he dismissed the witness, the Pfefferkornites had scored another great point. The aberrations of this brooding, unworldly little priest appeared to have been mendaciously summoned by the prosecution to convict an innocent man.

Facts—facts, whispered the anti-Pfefferkornites in the courtroom. And beyond the courtroom, wherever Jews were reading of the trial, the whisper repeated itself in their hearts. Facts, facts, where are the facts of the crime? Is it possible that Menelli in his fever of Nazi hatred hopes to convict Pfefferkorn only by the one accusation that Pfefferkorn hates Jews and belongs to a race that hates Jews? Where are the facts of the deed done, of Eleazer murdered, of Pfefferkorn's trail leading to his victim and away from him? Facts, facts, the desperate whisper of the Jewish elements grew louder. What had happened to their champion? How was he so unarmed? Was he betraying them? Was this another part of the Nazi plot to discredit them in the eyes of the world? Had their champion meant to lose? Were all his outcries against Nazidom no more than a noise behind which he worked for the Nazi cause?

Desperately these whispers spread through Jewish neighborhoods, and Menelli, entering the courtroom on the fifth day, found rage in all the partisan eyes that looked at him, Jewish and Nazi; and contempt in the eyes of all the others. The white-haired, slovenly-looking Cantwell alone smiled at him, as if this great battle of hatred and prejudice were no more than a casual day's work in the lives of two lawyers.

"Cheer up," said the solicitous Cantwell. "We all lose cases sometimes."

And Menelli's heart grew heavy. Throwing aside all he knew of jurisprudence, he made a last effort. He demanded of the bench that the three witnesses who had picked out Pfefferkorn in the police cells as the man seen in the vicinity of the previous murders be allowed to testify. The plea was denied by Judge

Leak. Their evidence had no bearing on the murder of Eleazer. Vainly Menelli pleaded that the special quality of the case made it legal procedure to identify Pfefferkorn as the fiend who had killed others than Eleazer. The three must be heard as character witnesses, Menelli cried stupidly, and their evidence admitted. His passion irritated the bench. These alleged eye-witnesses to other crimes, said the judge coldly, might be summoned at such times as their testimony might have a bearing on the alleged misdeeds of the defendant. He added, angrily, that according to his understanding of the People's complaint, Adolf Pfefferkorn was not on trial for being a fiend but for the supposed murder of Rabbi Eleazer.

Menelli rested his case. Menelli, the theatrical battering ram, had opened no holes in the Pfefferkorn defense. The blows had spent themselves in noise and misdirection.

Calmly the three lawyers arose from the defense table and moved that the case against their client be dismissed. The bench reluctantly denied the motion. Lawyer Cantwell accepted the denial with grace. And the defense began its case.

A half-dozen character witnesses for Pfefferkorn were called, none of them Nazis. They were simple neighborhood folk who had lived near Pfefferkorn for many years. Their evidence, unchallenged by the black-browed Menelli, established Pfefferkorn as a lover of children, as an amiable and hard-working neighbor, and as a citizen respected for his honesty and kindliness.

Following these witnesses, the defense announced it had only one other witness to question before allowing Pfefferkorn himself to take the stand. Mrs. Bertha Edelberg, wife of Gustav Edelberg, the Nazi Bund lieutenant, was summoned into the courtroom. Pale-haired, timid, and full of homely fluttering simplicity, Mrs. Edelberg took her place in the witness chair and was sworn. There was a delay while defense counsel conferred. The newspapermen busied themselves with descriptions of this typical housewife and mother, shy in the limelight, with large hands that told of home chores and honest blue eyes that looked still innocent with girlhood. When counsel had permitted the quality of their witness to be sufficiently absorbed by the friendly smiling jurors, the questioning of Mrs. Edelberg began. She answered shyly, as does a woman not used to talking to strangers.

Menelli and Captain Malloy listened blankly to her answers, unaware of the direction they were taking. They had been informed that Mrs. Edelberg would be the leading Pfefferkorn character witness. Menelli had waited patiently for this single Nazi sympathizer to confront him from the stand. He had prepared a half-day of counter-questioning into the Nazi beliefs. But now Bertha Edelberg was saying things that chilled Menelli and the detective.

She had visited Pfefferkorn at his house, said Mrs. Edelberg, on the day he had brought the slippers to Father Dominic. Pfefferkorn had just returned, said Mrs. Edelberg, very happy with having pleased Father Dominic by his work. And he had told her how carefully he had made the slippers. He had even gone down into his workshop in the cellar and brought up a slipper with yellow triangles embroidered on it. This one, he said, had come out wrong because he had cut the sole too close. So he had put it aside and made another slipper to replace it.

Lawyer Cantwell held up the People's Exhibit—the slipper Malloy had identified as the one he found in the Pfefferkorn cellar. Bertha Edelberg identified it now as the one Pfefferkorn had shown her on his return from the monastery.

"He said he was getting old," said Mrs. Edelberg, smiling shyly, "because he sometimes now had to make three slippers for a customer instead of two."

Menelli stared, his eyes raging. Captain Malloy listened, expressionless.

Mrs. Edelberg finished and Menelli rose to cross-examine. This lie was the end of his case unless he could remove it. The weary expressions on the faces of the jurymen that met his angry stare told him it could never be removed by mere onslaught. It was obvious that the jurors were waiting for him to climax his hatred of Nazis by an attack on this simple and honest Hausfrau. And for the first time since he had entered on the trial of Pfefferkorn, Menelli's mind grew cool. He stood looking calmly at Mrs. Edelberg. No jury could believe that this pink-cheeked, child-like woman, so perfect a symbol of all the virtues, could lie; could lie so boldly, could invent or repeat falsely so criminal a story.

Almost pitiful in her embarrassment, she sat facing the prosecutor and waiting. Menelli studied the appealing bravery of her German smile, the doe-like flutter of her honest heart in the flush of her cheeks. As he stood with lowered head before the witness, a black-browed bull refusing the charge, Menelli weighed his chances. If he could twist the truth out of this witness, expose her lie, he would achieve—what? His lone fact, the Rabbi's slipper, would stand unrepudiated. Would it be enough to convict? For an instant Menelli marveled at the suddenly revealed bleakness of his case, this case that stood on a single slipper without another shred of evidence for support. His heart filled with nausea for his own incompetence. He could hurl himself now at this Nazi wife, torture the lie she had told. He sensed swiftly the tears that would flow from her, the cries of confusion, the pitiful appeals for aid that would break the jury's hearts. And the finish of it—when he stood discredited before this sobbing plump little matron. Menelli sighed. Already this jury hated him for his hatred of Pfefferkorn, whose guilt he had failed to prove. How much more would they hate him and how much blinder would they become to any liar's stammerings into which he could browbeat this witness if he went on now. It was not courage that left Menelli, but sanity that entered him. His own intelligence, emerging after weeks of passion, spoke to him, saying that he needed facts with which to confront Mrs. Edelberg.

"I ask permission to postpone my cross-examination for rebuttal," said Menelli and sat down.

He looked wearily at Captain Malloy. The courtroom broke into a rush of whispers. The clerk's gavel banged. The noon recess was called. The newspapermen stampeded out. They had news to flash. Menelli had struck his colors. There remained only the triumph of Pfefferkorn's own testimony. This would take an hour, and there would be a verdict before adjournment. No partisan blindness or despairing hope could doubt what this verdict would be.

In the noon streets the Nazis sang "Horst Wessel" and Pfefferkorn hymns. Of Pfefferkorn they sang that their little shoemaker was a hero sent to show the world the justice in the Nazi abhorrence of the Jew. The malignant soul behind the whimpering face of Jewry lay exposed now for the world to judge.

The crowds laughed and grew fearless of the police. They pushed Jewish-looking men and women from the sidewalks. They raised banners telling of the Plotting Jews, and marched singing through streets frequented by Jews, who stared as at a monster—that monster of their woes who had finally crossed the seas.

Menelli remained at his table in the courtroom. Newspapermen stood around him with questions. Did he still believe Pfefferkorn guilty? If Pfefferkorn were acquitted, would the state try him for the other murders? Or was the state through with Pfefferkorn and willing to let him go back to his humble shoemaking? Menelli refused to answer these questions, and the newspapermen went away. Captain Malloy appeared.

"You better get some lunch," he said.

Menelli shook his head, and Malloy sat down near him. The two men remained silent. They heard the singing and cheering through the open windows, and the cries of the newspaper extras. Malloy looked around at the vacant room. A half-dozen spectators still sat on the benches. He recognized them as members of Rabbi Eleazer's congregation. They had been present throughout the trial. Malloy saw a glint of tears in their eyes. They sat in silence, as if the court were still in session. Their faces were raised and intent, as if they were praying.

In a corner, the captain saw the black-robed figure of Father Dominic. As always, the sight of him disturbed Malloy and set something going in his head. He sniffed the secret still hidden in Father Dominic. Some day, long after the trial and its echoes were over, he would talk to the Father again. And he would continue talking to Dominic at intervals of a month, two months, a year, until he learned what it was the old Friar held locked in his head. As he stared at Dominic, Malloy knew that this case, soon over for Menelli, was only beginning for himself. He felt sorry for Menelli. Vaguely and coolly Malloy felt sorry for the Jews who would suffer from the defeat he and Menelli had brought on them. But when the detective's eyes turned to the chair in which Pfefferkorn had sat these last days beaming and eager, his face grew more rigid. Untheatric and passionless, Malloy was a better People's champion than the heavy-shouldered Menelli. He would never strike his colors.

The courtroom began to fill. The crowd brought a new silent excitement with it. There was missing the hum of greeting and discussion that usually accompanied the entrance of the Pfefferkorn audience. Judge Leak took his place on the bench. Then Pfefferkorn emerged from his door, escorted by two guards. The clerk's gavel banged, and the clerk's voice called the start of the last session of the trial. The newspapermen were already scribbling at their tables descriptions of Pfefferkorn rising and walking to the stand, being sworn, facing the crowd. These things and many others they were anticipating with their pencils. But there was a delay. Attorney Cantwell had not yet arrived. His colleague Emerson begged the Court's indulgence. Mr. Cantwell was being detained by the press at his lunch table and would be there at any moment. The judge frowned and leaned back in his chair.

The eyes of the crowd rested on Pfefferkorn. It was a Pfefferkorn grown vividly familiar. They knew every mood and mannerism of his stooped figure. But they had never heard his voice. A curious hunger to hear the voice of this over-familiar yet enigmatic figure was in the courtroom. As they had made Pfefferkorn big by their wonder and curiosity, now they waited avidly to hear him return to normal human dimensions in the sound of his voice. The suspense of a Pfefferkorn who was about to talk held the benches still, and in this silence the hundreds of eyes remained eagerly on the shoemaker.

The ticking of the clock over the judge's head became audible. From the streets below the rattle and whistle of traffic and the subdued hubbub of the crowd entered through the open windows. The pause in the courtroom deepened as if a rhythm had seized the silence.

Captain Malloy, motionless at the prosecutor's table, suddenly moved his arm as if he were about to rise. He had felt a prickling in his skin. He stiffened and his eyes turned toward Pfefferkorn. He saw nothing but a figure waiting among many other figures. Yet the prickling increased. He saw Pfefferkorn straighten in his chair. The twinkling doglike eyes widened and the thick lips parted. Malloy saw a shadow fluttering on the skin of Pfefferkorn's open throat, and knew that an artery was beating wildly.

Pfefferkorn's eyes were turning slowly toward the empty witness chair beside the judge's bench. The muscles of his jaws were set as if resisting the movement of the eyes. Yet they continued to turn. Then they stopped and stared and Malloy saw that Pfefferkorn was looking at the witness chair—staring at a point above its empty seat with terror. His mind crouching in the silence, Malloy watched. A signal, eerie and tingling, came to him telling him something was happening. This was all that Malloy could know, for the thing to be known lay beyond the world of his eyes.

Pfefferkorn was looking at the face of Rabbi Eleazer. Pale and thin and unmarked by hatchet or fire, the face of Eleazer was looking back at Pfefferkorn. The dead Rabbi sat in the witness chair. Pfefferkorn, making no sound, saw that the Rabbi's clothes were wet and out of this wetness there came to him the smell of a swamp. And though he struggled to turn away, Pfefferkorn continued to look at this pale Eleazer sitting in the witness chair and smelling of the swamp. He heard as in a dream the ticking of the clock, and felt the courtroom around him growing vague. Then as he was about to shake this phantom out of his head with a cry or a lurch from his chair, he saw the long face with the large brown eyes move. Eleazer was breathing. He was leaning slowly forward, his eyes coming nearer. Flight lifted the soul of Pfefferkorn but his body clung to the chair as if death had seized it.

"Pfefferkorn of Moravia," spoke Eleazer from the witness chair, "ancient and accursed spirit from the past, hear my words. By the power in me I command you. Gilgul, ghost and demon, I summon you forth."

The Rabbi's words rang clearly in Pfefferkorn's ears and he turned his eyes slowly from side to side to see who had moved or heard. There was silence and the clock's tick. Pfefferkorn wet his lips and the grimace of his face bared his teeth. The voice of Eleazer continued wearily from the witness chair:

"Demon who was Pfefferkorn of Moravia, I have found the way for you. I have come back, Gilgul, to show you the end of your road. I speak to you, tormented one, from the place of rest. Come forth, demon, and I will lead you to the grave you dream of. Deny me and you remain forever accursed and wandering outside the gates. Rise, Pfefferkorn, and let the blood on your hands proclaim you. In the name of the Almighty I summon you to tell who you are."

The courtroom suddenly moved. Heads turned. Faces bobbed. In the wait and silence, Pfefferkorn had risen to his feet, clumsily, as if being pulled from his chair. Eyes swung to him. The judge straightened behind the bench. The two defense lawyers were looking with amazement at their client. He was swaying on his feet, white-faced, and a sweat was streaming on his neck. Suddenly from the rear of the courtroom a voice cried out.

"Eleazer, Eleazer!" Dominic wailed.

Confusion filled the room, but the crowd, caught in the tension of the swaying Pfefferkorn, gaped and stayed silent as another voice was heard. It was Pfefferkorn speaking, his hands holding his head as if in agony.

"I did not make three slippers," said Pfefferkorn. "I made only two slippers."

A gavel banged. Pfefferkorn's hands rose in the air and fluttered wildly. Sweat streaming from his face, he bleated above the stir of sounds in the room.

"He brought them to my cellar. Eleazer stood in my cellar holding a candle and I killed him. Then I burned him and dragged him to the swamp. Go back, Eleazer, to the swamp. Go back. I will tell them where you lie. Go back. Wait for me. Yes—yes, I killed. I killed the other Jews. I have killed many—many others."

Pfefferkorn's voice turned to a cry that came like a sob of torment from his throat. Leaping from his seat, Captain Malloy flung his arms around him.

"Show me where he is," Malloy cried, and Pfefferkorn started for the door. Malloy clung to his arm as guards cleared the way.

Father Dominic sat in the grove of heavy-leafed maple trees and looked at the sun glistening in the garden. The foliage hung lifeless in the deep summer heat, and the inhospitable sharp light of the afternoon sun blurred the colors of the flowers. The old man frowned at the hot glare that had driven him from his work among the plants, and raised his eyes to the sky to see if clouds were forming anywhere. But the sky was empty and swollen with light, and he leaned back in his chair and turned his attention to his visitor, Captain Malloy. The detective, plagued with the heat even in the tree shadows, mopped his neck above his wilting collar, and sipped at his wine and seltzer.

"Is there any possibility," Dominic inquired of his guest, "that there will be a reprieve?"

His voice was weary and he no longer smiled when he spoke.

"No," said Malloy, "the execution takes place tomorrow morning."

"He still wishes to die?" Dominic asked.

"Yes," said Malloy. "I saw him last night. He sits in his cell covering his face and moaning for them to hurry."

"And all those friends and admirers of his," Dominic said with his tired gaze, "are they very upset?"

"Not very," said Malloy. "Their mistake seems to have brought them closer together. I heard from one of the leading Nazi organizers, who boasted proudly to me that they have recruited thousands of new members in the last two weeks."

"I am not surprised," said Dominic. "Human beings when they believe too much in themselves become always less human." He paused and sipped at his own glass. "Do they still hold meetings and denounce the Jews?" he asked.

Malloy nodded.

"Worse than ever," he said. "As far as I can make out, now they're mad at the Jews because the Jews were right. They consider that this makes them a greater menace than ever before. There's no arguing with any of them. They just hate Jews, whether they're good Jews or bad Jews, right ones or wrong ones."

"I should have liked to talk about that with Eleazer," the little Friar sighed. "He would have been able to tell us something."

Looking at his guest keenly, he went on. "You have been waiting to ask me some question. Is it about why I prayed all night for Eleazer after he left the monastery?"

"I have figured that out," said Malloy, "by myself."

"What is it then?" said Dominic. "Is it about something I did in the courtroom?"

"Yes," said Malloy, "that's it."

He smiled at the Friar. "You called out Eleazer's name," he said.

"Nobody remembers that but you," said Dominic. "Why should it bother you?"

"I would like to know," said Malloy.

"The papers have been very informative," Dominic said, with the ghost of a smile on his lips. "They have explained that Pfefferkorn's guilt produced a hallucination for his eyes. You have read what the doctors said, my son. Why ask for more?"

"But you called out his name before Pfefferkorn had spoken," said Malloy. He hesitated a moment and then asked: "Did you see him?"

"Eleazer?"

Malloy nodded.

"I saw him," said the little Frair. "His clothes were wet but his face was pale and unmarked. His eyes looked a little tired. I am very sorry I called his name so loudly. Eleazer must have smiled at me in his heart for being so surprised. It has worried me a great deal since it happened—that I was so surprised."

Malloy waited for him to pause.

"Then it was a miracle," he said quietly.

"Yes," said Dominic, looking away to see some clouds forming in the sky. "It was a miracle. But not Eleazer's coming back and appearing in the court. That was only natural. It was no more than one would expect of a soul as wise and holy as Eleazer's."

"Then what was the miracle, Father?" Malloy persisted.

Father Dominic's eyes became sad.

"The miracle was," he said, "that there were twelve men in the world who believed the truth. That there were twelve human beings sitting together in a box who believed also that it was wrong to kill Jews. It must be that these twelve men were on the side of Humanity. This shows a certain progress in the world . . . which may be considered miraculous."

The old man sighed and picked up the crucifix at the end of his rosary. He made a motion of blessing, and added quietly:

"Forgive me, I have some work to do."

Malloy watched him as he moved quickly to a flower patch and knelt on the earth. As the black-robed figure leaned over the blooms, Malloy saw that his lips were moving and that the little Friar was chattering to himself. . . .

REMEMBER THY
CREATOR

Remember now thy Creator in the days of
thy youth, while the evil days come not,
nor the years draw nigh. . . .

OD had
had a bad night with Nebula

19. That orderly womb of space had launched a trio of premature planets into the Infinite. Scorning all the delicate relationships of form and movement with which God had carefully nursed the Nebula, these three brothers of Chaos had galloped off without orbit or chemical conscience and threatened a goodly section of the Heavens with disaster.

Not only God but His Host had labored to avert a thousand collisions. Certain rarely used Forces had been hurried into the erratic paths of the three runaway bombs of matter. Not until after a score of His worlds had been shattered had God finally trapped the anarchists and destroyed them.

The Angel Michael, who had remained at God's side during the entire disturbance, listened now to the Deity's account of the matter and held his tongue. He was sad that so many of God's most obedient creatures had been forced to share the inevitable doom of anarchy. There was one planet in particular whose coloring and complex movement the Angel Michael had always deeply admired. He had tried to influence it out of its orbit, and so save it from the three brothers of Chaos. But it had remained faithful to its laws, and been shattered into a long spray of mist, which was still falling dismally down the chutes of space.

God looked at His grieving angel, and then at the dismally falling mists that were the funeral plumes of His most amiable worlds.

"What happened last night," God continued calmly, "has turned My Mind to certain elemental problems. I am reminded that the great law of My existence is that I and I alone am mystery, and that there are no mysteries beyond Me."

The Angel Michael nodded. He was always a little surprised

when God grew garrulous, for his own wisdom, which was practically infinite, told him that to know was to be silent.

"Yet we saw last night," pursued God, "how mysteries may evolve from that which is simple, and how Chaos, My ancient enemy, still lurks within the perfect laws of matter. It will not happen again for a very long time," God added thoughtfully, thinking of certain readjustments. "Nevertheless . . . it seems to Me I have not come to grips with the actual problem of this vestigial Chaos that haunts My existence. . . ."

Presently He spoke again.

". . . that bit of moon dust," He said suddenly, "that you visited not so long ago. I'm thinking of it."

"The Earth," said the Angel Michael, and shuddered.

"I am not reconciled," said God, "to the fact that matter should speak, that dust should dream, and that atoms should think. It seems to Me that in the evolution of Dust into Thought there is a certain anarchy to which I have not given enough attention. Of course the Thought that has evolved itself out of these audible and contemplative atoms of mankind has been too absurd to consider seriously. Yet consider it I must," He concluded, "for it is there that Chaos lurks."

"You investigated the Earth some time ago," said the Angel Michael softly.

"Yes," said God, "I sent a Son there."

"You wish to call Yourself to its attention again?" asked Michael, whose quasi-omniscience told him that dark and difficult labors were coming nearer.

"Yes . . . No . . . Wait . . ."

God paused and brought the Earth close to His eyes.

"Before I can command their minds, which give off such an

ever-darkening cloud of error, I must study them more closely. I know the fire out of which they are made. I must know the smoke that rises from this fire.

"Go there," He said to the Angel Michael, "and find out the secrets of their thought. Study everything that lies in their minds, however absurd or futile it may seem. Bring Me back the full history of their Thought."

The Angel Michael spread his wings, hovered for an instant over the vaults of space, and then vanished.

There were many things that occupied God during the Angel Michael's absence, but for the most part He delegated their doing to His Host. He vanished into one of the Voids. Which one of these Voids God had sought out none could tell, since they all appeared equally non-existent. Thus when the Angel Michael finally returned and sought them out for some news of God, they could give him no definite information.

The Angels Azriel and Malliol, among the wisest of the Host, bade Michael rest, for he appeared greatly cast down and there was that in his eyes which disturbed them. In reply to their most subtle questions, however, all that the Angel Michael would say of his absence was that he had been among men. How this could have disturbed one accustomed to walking into the engulfing fires of newly hatched stars, none could conceive. But Azriel and Malliol, who had once been to Earth on a confusing errand, nodded and tried to explain to the others of the Host that there were matters on Earth undreamed of in Heaven.

"As for God," said the Angel Malliol, "He has not shown himself since you left His side. I should advise you to remain with us."

But the Angel Michael shook his head at this excellent advice and wandered off. Placing himself on the rim of Infinity, the Angel Michael moved disconsolately from one Void to another, peering into their Nothingness and murmuring stubbornly the name of God. He continued his search outside the Nowheres of Infinity until he found himself shivering before so dark and deep a pit of non-existence that his heart grew small and his eyes felt all light falling from them.

God emerged. He regarded Michael with the frown of One disturbed at labors.

"What are you doing here?" asked God.

"I have returned," said the Angel Michael.

"I know," said God, "but why do you haunt the Brink, as I have forbidden?"

"I was waiting for You," persisted Michael as he followed God into the more familiar corridors of Infinity. "I have strange things to relate."

The Deity regarded the darkened, desperate face of His favorite Angel.

"You may speak if you wish," He said kindly.

Michael was silent.

"You were gone some time," said God.

Michael nodded.

"Did it take so long for you to understand the History of Human Thought?" pursued God.

"It has no history," said the Angel slowly.

God continued to look at Michael, in whose eyes an abstraction remained. What, He thought, has become of Michael's serenity and of that lovely glow of humility and irony that had set his face apart and made it the cleverest in Heaven?

"So you found that human Thought has no history?" God repeated in His kindest voice.

Michael smiled.

"It has a certain capricious record," the Angel answered, "but it is less a matter of history than a chemical chart."

The Angel Michael paused.

"A synthesis of all animal movement reduced to nothing and yet existing in a sort of dream," he added. "If you wish, I shall explain."

God nodded indulgently.

"In the Thought of Man," said the Angel Michael eagerly, "I found the spread of a bird's wing, the quick and subtle dive into sea caverns of a fish, and the thrust of a tiger's claw. I found, too, the lumbering shadows of ancient monsters and the terror of ice."

God noted the elation in Michael's voice and remained silent.

"This Thought," the Angel Michael went on, unaware of God's scrutiny, "is a shadow of a thousand and one shapes cast by the little surface of existence on which they move. And this shadow is, mysteriously, able to create other shadows that are cast by Nothing into Nowhere. This process is called Logic. Lost in these shadows, they love each other and slay each other and stagger grotesquely and vociferously back to the dust they are. This staggering and the cries that accompany it they call History. For their Thought is more a record, very brief, of phantoms that have led them into never-ending battles. As hunger leads the animals to tear one another's throat for food, so does Thought prey upon Thought; so does one dream devour another, and all this devouring of dreams by dreams is attended by fearful and constant massacres. This never-ending warfare of their dreams they consider their spiritual existence, and point proudly to all their thousand monuments of bloodshed as proof of this same spirituality. They are disdainful of their physical sides, which they use only for the more peaceful business of living. They raise their monuments, it would seem, only to that which destroys them."

"You sound bewildered, Michael," said God, "but continue. Something may occur to Me."

"If I am bewildered," said the Angel Michael, "it is because human Thought is difficult for divinity to understand."

"You found it so," said God slowly, for this statement was offensive to Him.

"Yes," said the Angel Michael, defiantly. "There is in this Thought a contradiction that startled me. For unlike our Thought, it knows nothing. Yet it thinks. It is the tongue of an animal wagging idiotically out of a cave filled with horrible bones. Yet it whispers of matters not in the chemistry of those bones."

Michael paused and stared into Space.

"They dream," he continued, "yet their most delicate dreams echo with bestial howls and their most beastly utterances seem lit with fairytale lanterns. They think of things they are unable to believe. And they believe in things they are unable to think about. This is their Religion. They pursue in the Nowhere of their brains new names for that which is eternally hidden from them. This is their Science. They are able to uncover a few of the mysteries. But as each mystery is uncovered they bury it in an equally mysterious darkness that prevents them from ever understanding what they know. And in their curious lust to be greater than they are, they are continually reducing each other to endless piles of corpses. This is their Politics.

"They flounder and stagger," said the Angel Michael, "in the increasing mists of their minds and live and die in the deepening shadows of their reason. And blind, they talk of light; ignorant, they scream of wisdom; monstrous, they weep like Angels; devoured by the maggot of mortality, they laugh like Gods. That is how it is," concluded Michael and fell silent, wondering at his own garrulity.

"I have not been idle," said God.

"You knew what I had to tell You?" asked Michael.

"I know more," said God. "You are correct when you report there is no history to human Thought. For that which has no Law to guide it has neither past nor future. It is unpredictable and can be measured only by its own shifting fallacies. As the fire is lost in its smoke, so are My Laws hidden in this effluvium of Thought given off by the perfection of matter."

"It will be difficult to introduce form into that which is less than a shadow," said the Angel.

"It has always been difficult," said God softly. He moved His hand across Space. "This was extremely difficult," He said and smiled. "In a little while the confusion you noticed on that planet will be over. Their Thought will bow to Me."

"Will it be Thought then?" asked the Angel Michael.

"It will be part of Me," said God. "It will contain the predictable and regulated overtones of matter. It will be the intelligent tongue of the atoms. It will speak with understanding and it will know itself as the shadowed particles of My will."

Once more the Angel Michael stared sadly into Space.

"Where is the Dove?" God asked when He looked at Michael again.

"It flew past a minute ago," said the Angel, and his eyes followed a silver thread of light that led beyond Infinity into the Void.

"We are going there together," said God. "Come."

The Angel Michael stood once more on the Brink and once

more peered into the terrifying Nothingness of the Void.

"Am I going with You?" he asked.

"Yes," said God.

"What will happen in there?" the Angel asked.

"You will lose your wings," said God. "You will lose all radiance, beauty, and wisdom. And when you are reduced to the status of a human being I shall make you small and the Dove will carry you to Earth. You will be My messenger and truth-teller. You will grow up and you will overthrow the anarchy of the Earth and lead the disorganized smoke of its Thought to My feet. You will be My redeemer."

"Will I be black or white?" asked the Angel Michael.

"White," said God.

The Angel nodded.

"Will I be of any use in the guise of a human?" he asked.

"The truth has its own power," said God.

Again Michael nodded.

"Shall we go in?" he asked softly as he peered beyond the Brink, and his heart shivered at the touch of Nothingness. He started forward. God touched his shoulder.

"Wait," said God. "You are the fairest of the Host. There is none to take your place at My side."

The Angel Michael looked into Nothingness and then raised his eyes calmly to God.

"I am already changed," he said.

"You desire to leave Heaven," said God.

"Yes," said Michael.

"Your brother Lucifer," began God, and paused. After a time He asked: "Is there revolt in your heart?"

"No," said Michael, "there is no revolt in me."

God held the Angel Michael's eyes with a terrible scrutiny.

Michael felt his heart shrink and the recesses of his soul tremble at this look. But he remained upright and his own eyes refused to close.

"There is no revolt in me," he repeated softly. "There is a memory of Earth. I desire to help them."

"Come," said God and stepped into the Void.

The Angel Michael's eyes now filled with tears, and everywhere around him he heard a sound of lamentation. Turning, he beheld the Heavenly Host swarming like a great cloud below him and sorrowing for his pain. He heard Azriel call his name and cry to him to stay. And other voices sought him and covered his heart with their love. But he turned his head away and entered the unimaginable Space where nothing existed.

For some moments his radiant figure remained in the darkness, bold and glittering like a phantom struggling in the nets of night. Then a lightning smote him, and without pain but with a sigh which drifted out of the Void and echoed through all the Heavens he vanished. The Angel Michael was no more.

God emerged. The Dove sat on His shoulder and in the palm of His hand He bore tenderly a tiny creature. As He moved toward the space in which hung the Earth, He spoke softly.

"You will give My truth to them, Michael," He said. "You will speak to the anarchy of their Thought. You will have no other powers than the knowledge of the Truth. You will pit that against My enemy. You will enter his mind with My love and breathe into his mind the truth of My glory. And in a little way at first, but later more and more, you will bring him to his knees with the understanding of My plan and the knowledge of My mystery."

As God moved, around Him crowded the silent Host. God's eyes remained on the thing in His palm.

"You were more dear to Me," said God, "than the Son I sent to them before, for I was more used to you, and yours was the proudest and cleverest of My souls. You were always gallant and without fear," said God, "and you are the first who has ever stood beside Me in the Void. Michael, Michael"—God's voice grew soft—"who are they that you love them so? Who are they that you vanished unafraid?"

The faces of the Host now crowded boldly to the edge of God's hand and looked into its palm. The tiny creature who lay there seemed too ridiculous for their attention. So absurd and ugly an object had never been known in Heaven before. Yet as they looked, this writhing bit of matter opened its eyes and in their straight blue stare they beheld the Angel Michael.

"It is a child, new born," said God.

"Michael, Michael," the Angels wept.

The child moved in the palm of God.

"Michael, where are you?" wept the Angels.

The child raised its tiny hands with fingers too weak to open and its little mouth uttered a delicate and humorous sound.

"He is saying good-by," said God.

He gave the tiny creature to the Dove.

"Remain with him," said God. "If he sorrows too much or longs for Me, be at his side."

On a spring morning an old woman named Sarah opened the doors of the Good Samaritan Home for Children, which is one of the less ambitious buildings of the City of New York. The morning was still wet with dawn. A breeze moved over the pavements. The old woman Sarah, whose eyes were dim and whose body was without sap, stood on the threshold alone in the half-light like. a little bent tree whose tired roots remember the

morning. Her work-curled hands fluttered in aimless truant gestures against the heavy folds of her work dress. She looked
gravely at the new color of the day, and in her face, reshaped
by age and toil, a little light appeared to be glowing as if the
dawn had kindled her nose and cheeks. She regarded the familiar
street with so deep a smile of gratitude that all its colors, dews,
smells, and sounds seemed to be radiating from her. Then she
became again old Sarah, the scrubwoman, and, fetching her
dented pails out of the vestibule, dropped to her knees with the
agility of an acrobat and began on her tasks. These were each
dawn to clean with chemicals and water the brass plate under
the doors of the Good Samaritan Home and to remove thoroughly all the bits of leaves, dust, and scribble of disquiet that
had accumulated on the Home's stone stairs since the preceding
daybreak.

As she began with the rubbing of the wet powder over the
brass plate, her eyes fell on a large basket a few feet away. The
basket was on the top step. Old Sarah disliked matters that inter-
fered with her work, for in many years her work had achieved
a rhythm much stronger than her will. Her battered hands ply-
ing brush and cloth as she moved back and forth on her knees
were almost as aloof and persistent as the beat of her heart. They
continued to move, rub, rinse, polish, and dry the brass threshold like a pair of ancient grenadiers faithful to their posts though
a thousand baskets beckoned. It was only when her task brought
her a few feet nearer that old Sarah paused, while wringing out
her scrub rag, and looked into the basket. A smile puckered her
face as if a strong light had hit her eyes. There was a baby in the
basket.

She wiped her hand on her dress and lifted the small blanket
covering the infant. Her eyes brightened with glee as she studied

this basketed visitor at the doors of the Good Samaritan Home. It was a well-formed and amiable visitor, waving curved arms and clenched fists and beating with curled legs on the air. Then its face, staring intently up at the entranced old Sarah, began to glow much like her own—and it laughed. This laugh, which had no sound but consisted of a remarkable twisting of mouth and cheeks, tightening of eyes, and frantic waving of all its movable parts, so overcame Sarah that she too began to wave her hands, still holding the scrub rag, and to guffaw like an old witch over a kettle. The laughter of the scrublady contained an amazing variety of sounds, including cat calls and Indian war whoops. She laughed at this marvelous comedian in the basket until her throat ached and her eyes overran. Then she reached her hand to its neck, where a card was tied like a tag on a package of groceries. She read the card and wiped her eyes and her face continued to beam as if it would explode again. The card read:

"Michael."

"Ho, ho kok, kaka kak!" said old Sarah. "Mikil, Mikil!" (making the name rhyme with pickle). "Ho keek, keek keek. So dat's who you been, huh. You little devil, you. I fix you. Ho kak, kak kak," and she dug her fist into his stomach as if intending to disembowel him. However, she was only tickling Michael to see him laugh again, which he did. For five minutes old Sarah remained on her knees beside the basket, cackling and whooping in the dawn, her eyes swimming with bliss at every grimace and movement of her entertainer. She continued to kneel and peer into the basket, surrounded by her pails, brushes, rags, soaps, and cans, and to clap her hands and wave them in the air and roll her body back and forth like a Hindu dancer—until she noticed that her scrub rag, hanging from an infatuated hand, had been dripping all the while on the infant. She fell excitedly to wiping the dirt-spattered legs, spitting on her fingers to rub them clean. The reappearance of the pink skin under her efforts squeezed old Sarah's heart as if it, too, were a sponge at work.

Looking up for a moment, like a pirate from his treasure chest, old Sarah grew very angry at an intruder. A white dove had perched on the basket's rim and was blowing itself up like a balloon and emitting strangled noises.

"Shoo, go way," she commanded and made a swipe at the bird with her wet cloth. The Dove hopped out of danger, and continued to balloon its throat and to gurgle excitedly. It occurred to Sarah, who was quick to understand certain of the simpler things in life, that this pretty bird meant no harm to the one in the basket.

"All right," she said with a series of kek-kek-keks, "don't you *scheiss* on him, you doity boid," and shook her fist crazily over Michael's unwinking face.

Her eyes turned nervously to the still unshining brass floor plate. A panic sent her crawling on her knees to its clouded surface and she fell vigorously to scrubbing. As she scrubbed and rinsed and re-rinsed her rags, she continued to beam at the basket, clucking hilariously at its occupant, winking as she caught his moving stare and waving her brush and rag for his delight. Ever and anon she wagged her finger warningly at the white Dove still perched on the basket edge.

"Ka ke ke ke," said old Sarah to the infant, attacking the brass with great swoops. "Just a minute. Don't start hollerin', you crazy. I fix you. Kok, keek, keek, keek. You stay there, you little devil."

When the brass was shining as brightly as it had shone every dawn for seventy years, Sarah crawled back to the basket. She hoisted the visitor out and stood up with him. She became silent as she held him against her old body. Looking down at his widely opened eyes, she grew bewildered as if a sudden social embarrassment were at work on her tongue. So soft and warm did this prince of entertainers feel through the heavy cloth of her dress, so delicious and wondrously ornamental did he seem, that old Sarah felt like apologizing for holding him. Her face grew stern with fright and she stood cringing for several moments, like some wizened little embezzler halted by the shout of invisible police.

Then very fiercely she opened the tall doors of the Good Samaritan Home and, with a last guilty look at the still unwashed stone steps, entered the building. Michael lay in one of her arms. From the other hand dangled her scrub pail, which like a scepter she was loath to lay down.

The officials who had allowed old Sarah and her morning's loot to enter the superintendent's office, after a great to-do that involved waking a lot of dozing dignity, were kindly people, but they all began explaining to the old scrublady that the Home was now overcrowded, its endowment already overtaxed, all its orderlies, nurses, doctors, and teachers overworked. Having informed Sarah of their dilemma, they debated among themselves while she stood nailed to the carpet and clinging to Michael, glowering as if before a jury of executioners.

Then one of the officials, a bearded, rheumy old gentleman whose name was Dr. Rufus, came forward and had a long look at Sarah's find. He inspected it professionally, holding Michael by one foot, his head a-dangle, and pinching his skin, slapping his behind, and ogling the inside of his mouth. With a final wallop across Michael's reddened buttocks, Dr. Rufus returned him to Sarah. The amazing child had given forth not a sound during these indignities. Dr. Rufus stood nodding his head in thought and chewing on a mustache that obscured most of his mouth. He was a frosty-mannered and slightly doddering savant who seemed, for the last ten years, to have held himself together with a snarl, a sneer, and a disgust for his fellowmen.

"Fine specimen," said Dr. Rufus to the other officials present. "Excellent disposition. No blemish inside or out. It's too bad he has to grow any older. He's perfect now."

"Our problem remains the same," said Mr. Jorgenson, who was the Superintendent of the Home, "whether he's perfect or not."

Dr. Rufus turned his short square of red whisker at the superintendent and thrust it forward as if it were a battering ram.

"The hell you say!" he snorted. "If you gentlemen will permit me, I will settle this problem for you and you can go back to your work of pretending to be Good Samaritans spending other people's money—with a clear conscience."

"There's no occasion for anyone to be insulting," said Superintendent Jorgenson with a look to Sarah.

"Poppycock," said Michael's red-haired champion. "Listen to me. Old Sarah has been working in this black hole since she was old enough to blow soap bubbles. She has scrubbed the floors of this miserable den of charity for seventy years. Seventy years," Dr. Rufus repeated with a powerful sneer. "I remember old Sarah scrubbing away when she was about the age of that young gentleman in her arms. The long and short of it is," went on Dr. Rufus, to all the faces confronting him, "that old Sarah has found gold while scrubbing. And the gold belongs to her."

He poked the old scrublady in the ribs and winked at her.

"It's yours, Sarah," said Dr. Rufus. "The findings of this muddled group of Samaritans is that you keep the little bastard, feed him, wash him, wipe him, and to hell with that pail of slops for the rest of your life. Here"—he stepped forward—"give me that."

Sarah sidestepped his grab for her scrubbing pail.

"Naw," she said, "that's mine. I take him to my room. I got the steps to finish. Come on." This was added to Michael. Still carrying her loot and her ballast of a pail, old Sarah stamped out of the office. Scorning as always the elevators, the ancient scrublady hurried Michael up three flights to his new home, which was a corner of the cot she had occupied for forty years. Here she placed the infant, and then fell to her knees, which was an all too easy gesture for her. She looked furtively at the door to make certain it was shut. Cackling quietly to herself she leaned forward and began kissing the infant's hands. A curious noise interrupted her. The white Dove was pecking at the single window of her cubby-hole room.

"Shoo!" cried Sarah. "Go way!"

Then she returned to the child's hands.

Michael for twelve years was Sarah's son. As she had beamed on him kneeling beside his basket, so the old scrublady continued to beam on him through each hour of these twelve years.

She grew deaf, distorted, and a little unreasonable and seemed to acquire with age an unseemly speed in her movements. By the time Michael had grown old enough to observe such matters, she had taken to sprinting and darting about in a manner disturbing to the decorum of the Good Samaritan Home. In this Home, Charity wore its never-varying air of kindliness and its pastry smile, and moved as if someone were lying ill in an adjoining room. Old Sarah offered a continual offense to this Mysterious Personage lying in state somewhere on the premises. Here, where Virtue tiptoed about as self-consciously as a villain entering a forbidden parlor; where orphans, always fresh from barber shop, bath, or organ recital, moved in solemn little chorus formations up and down the stairways of philanthropy—amid all this paralysis of Good Deeds, which appeared to have stiffened even the chairs, couches, and beds of the Institution—old Sarah pranced like a withered and tottering Mother of Fauns.

It was a mystery to all but Dr. Rufus how someone like Sarah, who had known nothing of life, could love it so. Her constantly clattering pails interrupted conferences, lectures, and even religious services. She charged through these events like some soapy piston. Her increasing disdain for her superiors not only astonished them but left them impotent. Old Sarah had once been so humble that the most minor of officials was able to strike her dumb with awe, and the slightest of greetings had set her to curtsying like a demented courtier. Now she had become apparently oblivious of all command. She seemed, in her own mind at least, to have taken possession of the Home. All humans appeared to be losing daily their importance to old Sarah. They became, and this sometimes angered them, part of the furniture that obstructed her duty—which was to clean, to scrub, to rinse, and re-rinse her rags, and remove from floors, stairs, wood, stone, and linoleum all marks of human occupancy. But there was more to it than cleaning. A rhythm and a significance had come into old Sarah's battle with dirt, as if she were obliterating a trail.

This she did with such a high air of devotion, with so gamin-like and helter-skelter an indifference for the rest of the world, that the orphans marching from barber shop and organ recital began to look on the old scrublady as a creature out of a fairy-tale, a grandma Cinderella on her way with pails and scrub brushes to the Ball.

In vain the Officials introduced new and rival scrubladies. Unable to dislodge Sarah from her knees, to which position they had assigned her in her girlhood, they went about trying, like European statesmen, to parcel away the homeland of her dripping brushes. Driven from one stairway by such interlopers, routed from another floor by a whole cordon of rivals, old Sarah would reappear crawling like a wily turtle down unsuspected spurs of the never-obliterated trail.

Wherever feet had left tracks, there old Sarah appeared with the flourish of an acrobat, with the pomp of a Mardi Gras and the righteousness of a jury; and there, banging away with her brushes and rags like some Paderewski valorously smiting the keys of an instrument dearer than life, the shrinking witchlike little figure filled her soul with a music inaudible to others.

When Michael became of an age to be of help to his guardian, which was shortly after his first birthday, scandal shook the Institution. Nurses and orderlies came knocking on Superintendent Jorgenson's door with the news that old Sarah had gone completely mad.

Superintendent Jorgenson quickly left his desk and made for Hall 3, where the organ recitals took place. There he saw Sarah with her pails, brushes, cans, and rags, but now with another addition to her flotilla. This was Michael, a diaper trailing from his loins, and gliding, stomach to the wet floor, on a large cake of soap. Old Sarah, on hands and knees, was whooping after him.

Superintendent Jorgenson, shaken by the spectacle, dashed forward and laid hands on her two dented pails. He handed them to an assistant, and they were whisked out of the hall.

"That's enough of this!" he cried. "You're mad! You're crazy! You're out of your head. A crazy one. Do you understand me?"

But the superintendent, howling and illustrating his ideas with forefingers whirling at his temples, seemed the crazy one and not old Sarah. She stood staring with dignity and, as his shouts and gestures continued, her crinkled eyes filled with contempt. Michael had come crawling to her feet and sat, with his rump full of soap suds, clinging to her large comedian's shoes.

Dr. Rufus left the group of officials in the hall. When he returned in a few minutes, the superintendent's voice, a bit hoarsened, was still offering evidences of old Sarah's lunacy. Dr. Rufus held the two pails in one hand and a scrub brush in the other. Old Sarah received her possessions back in silence. She hoisted the equally silent Michael from the wet floor, and holding him face down in the crook of her strong arm as if he were a more precious bundle of rags, the while her pails, brushes, cans, and cloths loaded her other side, she marched out of Hall 3.

If not for Dr. Rufus's defense, old Sarah would have been routed from her domain, then and there, forever. The defense, conducted in Superintendent Jorgenson's office, lasted an hour. The old doctor, whom Jorgenson considered fully as mad in his own way as Sarah, was nevertheless a difficult man to best in any argument. His thirty years of service to the orphans who had enjoyed the haircut of the Samaritan Home, his curiously high standing with the board of trustees, his uncontrollable temper, which he swung like a fire pot around his head—all combined to leave him the victor on any debating field. But this time his victory was not entirely a complete one. Although he fought valiantly for Sarah's right to scrub where she liked and to employ any assistant she chose, the official contention was a trifle too much for him. This contention had it that the spectacle of Sarah and the naked brat wallowing about on the floor under the eyes of any visitors was belittling to the Institution. Despite the noise of his rebuttals, Dr. Rufus gave ground before this charge. He agreed to a compromise. Sarah was to be allowed to wallow and scrub to her heart's content on the fourth floor only.

It developed that Sarah had no snobbish feelings about first, second, third, or fourth floors. She agreed curtly to confine herself to the last on condition she be allowed to do the front steps as always. As this task took place during an hour when her new co-worker was still asleep, the point was yielded.

Thereafter old Sarah scrubbed only the fourth floor, which, in addition to a long corridor, offered a dozen sleeping rooms of nurses and orderlies for her brushes. And Michael remained at her side. For many months he was more a hindrance than a help to old Sarah, overturning pails of water on both of them, choking on pieces of soap furtively crammed into his mouth, and vanishing like a lost ball under beds, out of which darkness the busy Sarah wasted a great deal of time retrieving him. But after his second birthday, which had sent him to the hospital for a week with an attack of indigestion, Michael developed talents that infatuated his guardian. Suddenly he had blossomed into a chubby miniature of her. He not only crowed like her but had learned to stagger rather than walk and to hurl himself like an acrobat at the pail handles and scrub cloths. He also scrubbed and rinsed and re-rinsed and dried and polished as ably, if a little more slowly, than his ancient colleague. She assigned him whole patches of floor and baseboard and important sectors of corridor. Over these, little Michael, crowing and cackling with a delight that never failed to transport old Sarah, moved with pails larger than himself and cleaned with a devotion amazing in a two-year-old.

In the three years that followed, the irascible Dr. Rufus often pondered on what Michael's future would be. Old Sarah had apparently settled this in her mind, which even Dr. Rufus was beginning to feel was a little warped. She considered Michael's career firmly launched. He would remain at her side, scrubbing away with more and more agility. He would move forever as she had moved, on knees growing stronger, his head down, bringing a clean look to wood, stone, marble, and linoleum.

Dr. Rufus, despite his cynicism toward the world, felt that Sarah's conception of Michael's life was too one-sided.

"I know of nothing better or more honorable than scrubbing," said Dr. Rufus kindly. "There is no human activity that does less harm and no other of which you can say it leaves the world a little better each day than it found it. Yet there is in our Michael's head a force that scrubbing alone will never develop."

"He gotta go to school?" asked Sarah, in whose cubby-hole of a room this conference was being held. She looked proudly at Michael busy on the fire-escape outside the window. But while she beamed on him, a sigh came from her heart and she turned little trembling eyes to the doctor. She had had a vision of Michael full of the importance and learning to be found in school. But in the midst of this vision her heart tugged frightenedly at this educated Michael's frock coat, and her eyes stared helplessly at his savant's silk hat.

"I'll teach him myself," said Dr. Rufus. "I'll see to it, by God, that he learns enough to keep him from remaining an idiot and not enough to turn him into a fool. I'm against our entire educational system," he added, scowling at Sarah, "for the incontrovertible reason that it has never educated anybody. All it does is hatch more and more chicken minds and send them cackling and overrunning the world with their confounded chicken-headed theories. God Almighty! After three thousand years of injecting education into our bloodstream, show me one honest heart!"

As if in answer to the old physician's cynical cry, Michael appeared on the window ledge. His face was smudged almost beyond recognition. His clothing was torn and fluttering in wisps from his behind. Beside him, ballooning its throat and gurgling, was the white Dove.

"Dat crazy boid!" cried Sarah. "Shoo! Get out, you!"

She flung her arm in its direction, but the Dove continued to stand where it was and gurgle.

Michael, however, fell into the room, picked himself up, and marched to Sarah's side. He climbed into her lap, balanced himself on her thighs, crouched down for a moment, and then leaped. He landed on all fours, his forehead banging against the floor.

"He'll kill himself," said Dr. Rufus.

Sarah chuckled.

"He's gonna be a fine joomper," she said.

"I think he's hurt." Dr. Rufus leaned forward.

"Leab him alone," said old Sarah authoritatively; "joomping don't hoit nobody. I got boomped lots of times." And she laughed like a parrot screeching and slapped both her knees furiously with her hands.

Michael sat up, holding his forehead. He was silent. Old Sarah left her chair suddenly and crawled to his side. Her work-battered hands touched the bruised skin.

"It'll go way," she said, staring into Michael's eyes to see if there were tears. "Hoits always goes away."

Dr. Rufus educated Michael by reading books to him and holding forth, once they were read, on their asininity and the asininity of all writers and all existence.

During the day, Michael remained at Sarah's side, so content at his continual water hauling, scrubbing, polishing, and drying that the Officials of the Home came to regard him as a harmless little lunatic. He was seldom seen by the other orphans, except during organ recitals and the religious services, which Superintendent Jorgenson insisted, despite the boy's seeming idiocy, he attend. When not at work during the day, Michael played on the fire-escape. Here, racing up and down, he had adventures, full of the lonely glamour of childhood. And between falls and contusions he was very happy.

At night he lay on the cot with Sarah, while she slept with her wrinkled, shrunken, and muscular arm flung across him, and listened to the red-bearded Rufus. The doctor was never tired of filling the cubby-hole room with endless tales of human conquest, human travail, human disasters and progress, all bespeaking, according to him, the ineradicable backwardness of the human race.

"I want you to remember history, son, as I have told it to you. And never mind trying to learn dates of battles and the names of battle leaders. To hell with that and to hell with your learning the Causes of Wars. They're all alike, all battles, all dates, all leaders, all causes, and all wars. From the first breaking of heads in the jungles of China, where our idiotic race seems to have originated—yes, we're all Chinamen—to the present bombing of children and old ladies in the streets of Spain—they're all alike. I don't care, son, who wanted what, or what was called right and what was called wrong. All these wars I've told you about were all fought in the same fog of human stupidity. Animals kill for hunger. That's why we call them animals. But we members of the human race kill for no reason. That's why we are called reasonable beings. It's all an endless futile struggle, son, to locate the meaning of ourselves.

"I have it figured out, Michael, in my own way. We are all

of one blood—we humans. The blood of the race is an ocean divided into a billion little cups, like you and me, son. We're divided, but we're all one ocean, and we have a tide in us that is run by the moon and the stars, as the ancients once said. And they said more science when they said that than has come out of all the Galileos and Darwins since that time. When we crawled out of the sea and fastened ourselves on the first stones of the earth, we took the sea with us. That's obvious to me, son. The sea continued to wash away inside us, washing against our stomachs and our hearts. It remained running through us in little pipes we call arteries. What I say, son, is that there's an ocean in us that can be charted and that responds to the movements of all Nature around and above us. But that's not all of us. There's another element in us that didn't come out of the sea. There's a wind that blows over this blood ocean, that beats it with hurricanes and bedevils it with whirlpools. This wind is our thought. God knows where it came from, and what makes it blow. Son, all we know is that a wind blows and the ocean is never at rest."

Each night as Michael lay beside the peacefully sleeping Sarah, Dr. Rufus elaborated on this theme, adding historical facts to it, peopling it with fish and monsters and crustaceans, and finding in the records of history, science, and art a multitude of illustrations. But there was another education that Michael was experiencing, which, more than all the roaring of the Red Beard, was shaping his life. This was love. With all the violence of his child's heart he loved old Sarah and Dr. Rufus and even the cynical fairytales that the angry physician brought trooping around his bed.

There was no memory in him of any previous Michael, and no knowledge remained in his head of the long ride from Heaven under the wings of the white Dove. He was not yet aware that

God had sent him to redeem the world. But there had grown in his heart by the time he was seven a tenderness that set him apart from the normal ways of life.

He grew taller, and his face took on a curious look that bore out a legend in the Home that he was more than half mad. It was the fierce and concentrated caress to be found in the face of a mother leaning in the night over the crib of a fevered child. It was a look that was to bring great trouble into his life, and seemed even in his childhood a magnet for misunderstanding and growing enmity. But in this expression, that was beginning to disquiet even Dr. Rufus, there was nothing mysterious. It was the gleam old Sarah had turned on the dawn as she emerged to scrub the brass plate on the morning that Michael lay kicking in the basket. It was a look that radiated a dream. And as he grew older, it was a look that searched for Sarah—for old Sarah died when he was twelve, and left him this look as her only heritage, the look that through terror, abuse, and despair kept seeking her sweet, half-mad smile in the confusion and glower of all the world's faces.

Sarah's dying took three days. During these days Michael moved on his knees alone down the fourth-floor corridor and in and out of the many rooms to be cleaned. He could feel in his heart the aching tissues of his old friend and the familiar face stared continually up at him out of the cleaned patches of flooring, as if it were her cheeks that were shining in the polished wood, marble, stone, and linoleum. Through all his life Michael was never to see anything shining but he saw old Sarah in it.

At night he remained in a corner of their cubby-hole room and watched Dr. Rufus come puttering in in night robe and slippers, feel her pulse, put his trembling bony hand to her forehead, stick lozenges on her tongue, sink to his knees and hold his ear cocked against her heart like a robin listening for a vanishing worm. On the third night, the Red Beard beckoned Michael to its side.

"Not much longer," he said and stared at the boy.

Sarah opened her eyes and beamed at Michael as she had beamed over the edge of the wicker basket in which she had found him.

"We neber found out who your mudder was," said old Sarah with a foolish and triumphant wink at the doctor.

"You were my mother," said Michael.

"Me?" said Sarah as her eyes rolled weakly.

"Be a good boy," said Sarah.

Michael nodded.

"Keep everything clean," said Sarah.

Michael's eyes smiled at her.

"Thash right," Sarah whispered, her speech seeming to grow a little drunken. "I ain't 'fraid. Kek, kek ke . . . heh heh." Her cackle grew far away. "Mikil," she smiled, "gib me a kiss like a good lil fella. Yeh. Mikil, gib me a kiss."

Old Sarah raised her arms, dropped them tiredly around Michael's lowered head, and died.

And when he stood in the chapel at the coffin, Michael still felt his lips on her forehead. Her voice cried in his heart as if not Sarah but all of life were still asking for this kiss.

The services were brief. Superintendent Jorgenson, despite the glowering of Dr. Rufus, spoke of Sarah's loyalty. He informed the freshly haircutted orphans assembled that Sarah, whose antics had long been a legend, had been found as an infant on the doorstep of the Home that was burying her. She had set a good example, said the superintendent. God, he said, would now reward her for her great loyalty. God would take her to

His merciful bosom and bless her. Throughout this talk, Super-intendent Jorgenson continued to wipe his eyes, remove and replace his spectacles, and sniffle shamelessly. An orphan at the organ began to play, and a choir of orphans began to sing over the witchlike body in the coffin. This ended the services, and the coffin was carried out of the chapel.

Dr. Rufus and Michael rode in the single car that followed the hearse. Later they stood in the autumn afternoon and watched the coffin lowered into the earth. Michael looked at the bottom of the grave. He felt suddenly that he was standing on the edge of the world peering into a pit of Nothingness. Life was vanish-ing into this pit. The pain of the Nothingness into which old Sarah and her thousand and one cakes of soap, her rags and cans and brushes and cackles and Indian war whoops had disappeared, tore his heart. Death ached in his veins, and life sobbed beside him at the edge of the world.

When he rose to his feet, his eyes were wide and quiet. He walked away from the covered grave with the frightened bent little figure of his mother clinging to his hand. When she could no longer walk he lifted her in his arms. And when her body began to shiver in the autumn wind, he placed her in his heart and continued to walk, but a little more slowly, for he was burdened.

Michael went to live with Dr. Rufus in an impressive-looking old stone house.

The physician, now turned seventy, had announced his re-tirement from the Good Samaritan Home. He complained vio-lently to all who would listen that senility had marked him, and that his body was unfit for any future social uses. But since he complained only to fellow-physicians, who, perhaps out of a mutual protective code, have a way of ignoring one another's diseases, Dr. Rufus's claims to invalidism went without investigation. He was given a farewell dinner by his colleagues, toasted, sung, and placed half drunken into an automobile. Michael was beside him.

Standing before the impressive relic of yesterday's grandeur that was his home, the red-bearded Rufus waved his arms, and talked to Michael.

"Here it is," he said, "my tomb. Not a tomb like Sarah's where you can lie, son, in dignified dissolution, one with the happily rotting contents of the earth. But a tomb to breathe in, groan in, wait in. A tomb for the living. A vestibule for the worms. I know whereof I speak, son. Disease is in me. Each of my joints is inflamed like a drunkard's nose. I'm doomed. I've outlived my carcass. Have you ever seen a beetle trying to shed its old frock coat? That's me, son. I'll be crawling into one of the beds in this house and I'll lie there for years trying to wriggle out of a dead shell . . . while those wisenheimers, the doctors, stand around chanting like a Greek chorus: 'He's got arthritis, poor old Rufus.' "

The Red Beard sat down on the steps and took Michael's hand.

"I'm an angry man," it proclaimed loudly to the boy. "In a few months that's all that will be left of me—my anger propped up on a pillow. Prometheus chained to a handful of chicken feathers, while the devil wrestles for his soul. That's what our old friend arthritis does for you, stretches you out, turns you to stone and blinds you."

Michael shivered in the cool night and squeezed the doctor's hand. The hand seemed to be leading him to Sarah.

"Don't contradict me," bawled the Red Beard, "and I'll tell

you something more; something I couldn't tell you about while that crazy grasshopper of a Sarah was alive. For we must never offend the happy with our wisdom. There is no God. Not for today at least. We have elbowed Him off the stage, shoved Him into the wings, saying: 'We are the show. We are the Plot. We are the Main Characters. Keep off the stage until we get·done with our parts!'

"So that," continued Dr. Rufus, "is where God is at the moment—in the wings. And we occupy the night alone. We investigate ourselves, our grass blades, our internal and external atoms, without that bewildering Hosanna in our ears. In the end it is nothing but a heroic form of self-torture. For who are we?" The old doctor raised his voice angrily. "Who are we? Looking for our meaning like a monkey snatching at his face in a mirror."

Michael clung to his hand. As long as he held this hand he seemed to be near Sarah.

"We are the glory of God in exile," he said softly.

Dr. Rufus looked at the boy beside him.

"Who told you that?" he demanded.

"I don't know," said Michael, "but sometimes I feel that people don't belong in the world, but in Heaven. They're crippled angels, and have to wear shoes, and God's looking for them."

Dr. Rufus began to whoop and slap his thighs, reminding Michael of the way Sarah used to carry on when she was happy.

"Looking for us, is He?" The old man laughed in the dawn. "Well, He'd better look for Himself. We're here. But where is He? Listen, son, if there's a God, He's somewhere inside us— modestly concealed like a bright penny in some vest pocket. And if there's a Purpose in our crawling out of the hot primeval ooze and wrestling ourselves into the shape of man, that purpose is inside us."

"No," the boy answered, shivering. "It's in God. There is nothing in us but God's breath."

"Holy jumpin' mackerel!" said Dr. Rufus and stared at the boy beside him. "Where did you pick up that lingo?"

Michael's glowing eyes looked back at him.

"Either I'm drunker than I thought," said Dr. Rufus, "or there's something wrong with your face. And your hands," he added, lowering his eyes. "What have you turned so white for, Michael? Are you frightened?"

"No," whispered Michael.

"Here, let me see that hand," said Dr. Rufus with sudden professional calm. He picked up Michael's small hand and held it close to his eyes, turning it over and studying it. "Curious loss of pigmentation," he muttered. "What are you staring at, Michael? What's in your mind?"

"The glory of God," said Michael.

A heavy frown filled the doctor's face. He tugged at his red beard.

"Well, I'll be Goddamned," he muttered finally. "You bring a boy up on a diet of pure science, and he ends up having hallucinations. The duck's egg in the eagle's nest"—he smiled at Michael—"or is it the eagle's egg under the duck's tail? Who knows?"

Dr. Rufus rumpled Michael's hair and slapped playfully at his cheeks.

"Wake up, son," he smiled. "Duck or eagle, I'm taking care of you my way. And I don't want to hear any more about God or Purpose out of either of us. We'll stick to facts. And the facts are that we didn't fall from Heaven, but rose out of the Sea. Our bodies are still full of gills and sea water and third eyes and second noses and dead muscles and a hundred vestigial organs in

which our Past stares out of us as out of a taxidermist's window.
We're full of jungle shadows, and our art and reason and even
the music we make are the ferment of chemicals that haven't
changed since the earliest days of chlorophyll and haemoglobin.
We have an inch or two of brain more than the rest of Nature,
that's all. But don't overestimate the human brain, son. The
brain is only one among a hundred thousand muscles. The muscle that thinks."

Dr. Rufus looked up and smiled wearily.

"You see those stars?" he said. "Far away, aren't they? We've
thrown rope ladders out to all the mysteries and kept climbing
—out of one darkness into another. But we won't climb any more
tonight. Come on—we march into the tomb." He grinned, turning toward the house. "Give me your shoulder, son. My legs are
creaking like a baby's rattle."

In the house of four floors in which Michael found his new
home were two servants and the doctor's sister, Margaret Rufus.
The two servants were a married couple, and reminded Michael
of a pair of mice peering around doorways. Miss Rufus seemed
oddly related to them, as if they had all once belonged to the
same litter. But where the eyes of the two servants were gray
and veiled, those of Miss Rufus were black and full of anger
that was something like the doctor's. But Michael did not notice
this too much. He saw a thin woman with a bluish face that
never smiled.

During the first month Michael, who was burdened, remained
unaware that this bluish face hated him. He continued to live
in the protection of his memories, and around him the echo of
the rattle and bang of old Sarah's scrub pails continued to make
fairytale music. In vain Miss Rufus's heart cast its shadow where
he walked, laughed, or slept. He continued to smile at her with

that unawareness which is infuriating to all neurotic spirits. Her scrawny face, thin-featured and thin-skinned, as if life were the flimsiest of veils, returned his smiles with an increasing anger. Michael then began to feel the darkness of her heart, and he thought childishly that she was troubled, but it did not occur to him yet that he was the one who troubled her.

His attention was taken up chiefly by the doctor, who had begun to make good his prophecy of falling ill. The doctor grew stiff in his movements, and pain often brought a deeper rage into his face. Michael haunted his friend's side, his heart heavy, eager to run errands, to talk or laugh or listen to the sick man's fierce protests against his own body.

"I've hit a reef in that blood ocean I told you about, son," he growled. "I'm banging to pieces on a reef."

But Dr. Rufus remained alive. He did not die but launched into a slow retreat, with all guns blazing. He retreated first out of the streets, into a wheel chair; and then up the stairs, into a bed. Here he lay finally, unable to move his legs or turn his body, and the doctors, as he had prophesied, decided that he had arthritis. They puttered with the fires in his joints, and discussed tirelessly the meaning and causes of the calcification process that now began to turn their patient half to stone. The old serving couple nursed and fed him. Visitors arrived with bits of gossip, which, like their sickroom gifts, they left uselessly behind. It was understood that Dr. Rufus had come to the end of his retreat. Here in this bed, where he had been born, the red beard would remain jutting from the pillow until death came to pluck it.

In the midst of these changes, the undying red-bearded face continued, undaunted, to talk. Michael remained beside it, listening as he used to do in Sarah's cubby-hole room, sometimes holding onto the doctor's hand. Soon his friend began to grow blind, and whenever he was tired of speaking, Michael read aloud to him from books and newspapers. This reading was often interrupted, as the things that Michael read set off angers in his listener's still turbulent brain.

"This man Hitler," he said one afternoon, when Michael had been reading to him of Germany's annexation of Austria, "is an ancient and honorable phenomenon proving that Evolution works both ways, up and down, except when it works around. Its chief direction is a cockeyed circle and the zigzag of a drunk making for home. As . . . witness the free swimming water bugs who have lapsed into barnacles. . . . And the once liberty-loving bacteria that have turned into parasites. And then, there is the other type of progress—forward in no direction. The narwhal who sports a single tooth eight feet long, for instance, and he himself only a scant fifteen. There's no sense to this tooth. It has no function that a decent-sized molar couldn't fulfill as well. And there's as little sense to the extra armorage of the hedge-hog, or the overthickened skins of the saurians, or the extra fol-de-rols of structure in the shell animals. They don't need them. They don't use them. These things hatch and grow as part of the Vanity of Evolution, who seems to be a carpenter with too many tools, and without lights. For there's many a bug and quadruped who's worked himself into a cul-de-sac, and vanished.

"In man too there's the same sprinting in the wrong direction, the same lapsing mentally from eagle to lizard, and the same growing of spurious tusks and landing head down in the swamps again.

"Yes . . . this Hitler-hatching is one of our oldest habits. It's the empty flourish of Ego. It's the Ego without an Art to dissipate itself in, the dream that escapes the personality of the dreamer, and enters the psychic bedrooms of his neighbors. We all have dream-ideas of this or that, but we hold them in check either by art or learning or by the cautious desire for anonymity that keeps most of the world sane. But when the idea becomes greater than the man in whom it hatched—like the dream of nobility in a paperhanger—history appears. And history is always bad.

"For there's small profit to us in studying the Hitlers. Now if we could learn what it is that improves mankind and advances the evolution of our monkey-brain a notch! But it's always easier to see the forces that foul the human mind, and to trace its lapses. In men like Hitler it is the same werewolf facts that always operate. *Quos Deus vult perdere, prius dementat*—excuse the reference to God. These facts are the phosphorescence of defeat. They come limping out of every debacle to haunt the victors. By the time humanity, justice, and sanity have triumphed, it is always over a wasteland. . . . And it's there the Germans will end—on the manure pile that waits for all mania."

Further and further away from Sarah the hand he held tried to lead Michael. Perhaps the doctor felt the weight of this small hand in his own, felt it tugging backward.

"There is too much love in you, Michael," he would say, as a prologue to his discourses. "You embrace life too tenderly. Put away that embrace, son. Examine what's around you. I know how pretty the birds, the trees, and the flowers are. But those things are only life. Man's sky is his mind. And it's a sky you can't lie under dreaming. It's a sky that's got to be rebuilt. Torn away and built over until it's large and fair enough for man."

Even when Michael was silent and held the hand gently, the tired face in the bed would grow truculent and rumble such complaints.

"Why is it that, after listening to me so long, you remain Michael? Your silence contradicts me, and the tone of your voice, when you speak, is too gentle, as if you were humoring the vagaries of a blind man's mind, and forgiving them."

At first he had spoken kindly in this way, and Michael understood humbly that this was a remnant of Sarah's love that was still left in this world. No matter how Dr. Rufus attacked the light he saw in his pupil's heart, blowing on it with all the winds of his disillusion, Michael knew that he did not want to blow out this light . . . but somehow to increase it.

But as the illness encroached further with its fearful pangs into the victim's every limb and vital organ and, for a long time seemingly, everywhere but into his mind, the complaints grew more frequent and bitter, and Michael felt in his friend an increasing antagonism. Their battle grew more open.

There was another, more human, reason for the doctor's bitterness against the boy to whom from childhood he had given a strange love, and the fruits of all his knowledge. Abandoned by the world now, and brooding about it as do all martyrs, Dr. Rufus was hurt by Michael's evident ingratitude, and the boy's apparent desire to leave him. This ingratitude was proved by Michael's frequent and increasing absences from his bedside.

Behind these absences was the dark story of Miss Rufus's ill-treatment and finally her torture of the boy Michael. No sooner had the doctor retired to his bed of slow death than she had decreed that the boy should eat in the kitchen. He was forbidden the important rooms of the house. Soon other restrictions were built around him. He was locked in his bedroom at nine in the evening. The books the doctor had given him were removed from the shelves near his bed, and he was allowed no lights. Later, the carpet was removed from his room, the chairs carted away, his blankets reduced to a single bit of torn matting, and sheets and pillow-cases were no longer allowed him. Day by day, these hardships and indignities multiplied, pouring from the spinster's heart, as if, no longer sterile, it had become wildly blooming, but with weeds and cactus growths that sought to choke the soul of the child who had come into the house.

Soon she began to slap and pummel the boy, her hands seeming to grow drunken with the punishment they administered. The fair face that had known only Sarah's loving eyes and the caress of her work-battered hand felt a mania of hate tearing and gouging at its beauty. As Miss Rufus grew more assured of her brother's blindness, the savagery of her beatings increased. Michael's face often showed great swellings and bruises.

Still he did not inform Dr. Rufus against his sister. It was only when she, with new cunning, began to lock him away from the sufferer in the sickroom, that Michael desired to cry out to his friend that he did not mean to hurt him. But he continued to keep secret the sister's hatred, because he felt that to reveal these things would bring needless pain to the helpless man.

For five years, he, who had been loved more perfectly by Sarah than an angel is in Heaven, lived by the side of this hatred. During these years, Michael's look never changed. He was looking for Sarah, and despite the blackness of the hate that confronted him, he found her. He saw Sarah's little eyes staring into his own to see if there were tears, as she used to do whenever he fell and bumped himself—and he did not cry out. Still the poem that had been his childhood remained secure in his heart. And presently he was able to see Sarah's eyes in everything. He found her in the pain that lay under the blackness in Miss Rufus. He found her in the fear, hidden away like a criminal, out of which arose the ugliness of this aging woman.

As his goodness grew strengthened, the truculence and enmity of the doctor increased against it. When he was seventeen, Michael knew that the Red Beard looked on him angrily, as at a stranger rather than a son and pupil. The rumbling voice had ceased its wandering discourses, and now came to grips only with Michael; at him the brain launched itself, wrestling subtly and wildly with his soul.

"You offend me, Michael," he would say.

"How?" the boy would plead.

"Your brain hides from me. It lurks at the feet of some Jesus like a dog that's crawled back to his master. There's something comes out of you, an attitude like a priest's robe, that shames me and makes me seem small. My thinking seems small beside your silence."

The doctor was at this time in hideous pain. Under the coverlet drawn tight to his chin, his chest heaved as if it were signaling desperately for help. The skin of his face was covered with a granite gloss, and his voice broke in its hollow rumblings.

The boy, his face full of love, would place his hand on the hot forehead and smile intently into the blinded face.

"Your hand is cool," Dr. Rufus would mutter. "It has a healer's touch." And he would add: "Do your hands turn white as they used to?"

"Yes," Michael would say.

"And you feel a power inside you?" he would ask.

"Yes," Michael whispered.

"Take your hands away," the doctor growled then. "I prefer pain to mystery."

Or: "When you touched me you seemed far away," said the doctor. "Where were you?"

It was useless to evade.

"Why are you silent?" the invalid would rage, in his weak voice.

"I am trying to remember something," Michael faltered. "Someone who is trying to speak to me . . . someone I once knew. . . ." He had heard, as if he were dreaming, the lamentations of strange beings in strange places, voices weeping and calling for him: "Michael, where are you? Michael . . . Michael, come back."

"Hallucinations," muttered the Red Beard.

"I don't know, I don't know," Michael pleaded.

"Hallucinations," the Red Beard repeated, and its laugh was more dreadful than its cries. "You have the religious mind. It's amusing to me to know that all my work in behalf of reason has turned you into a crystal-gazer. That's what the religious mind does . . . looks into itself as if it were a crystal globe, instead of looking out, like a prisoner. . . ."

In the silence that followed, Michael felt the doctor's fierceness. And he, who had not wept at all at Miss Rufus's persecutions, now wept in the night for all the love that had faded from his world. Now it was only Sarah's hand he held when he slept in his room for a few hours. And only her work-battered fingers that touched lovingly in his dreams the bruised skin of his face.

"It goes away, Mikil," she whispered, staring into Michael's eyes to see if there were tears. "Hoits always goes away."

Another Presence, perhaps not much more real, but dear and familiar, consoled him in his room. It startled him sometimes, and then made him smile. It was the Dove, gurgling. The Dove appeared sometimes on the ledge of his opened window, and

Michael, looking at it through the tears in his eyes, saw it shining and unbearably white. It was the same dove he had known as a child, making the same quaint noises with its throat. But now, in its presence, a wild thought cried out in him sometimes that there was a power in him to heal all that suffered. The whiteness of his hands seemed to grow whiter, and a voice, soundless and far away, spoke inside him.

One day the weeping boy turned away from the delightful sound that was the throat of a dove gurgling. Cowering, he hid from the Voice inside him that would have spoken. He thought of the tortured one dying slowly in the room near by, and an impulse came to him to deny what was in himself, and affirm what was in the doctor. He felt he had failed in allegiance to his friend, and he decided to confess to him, hoping that the dying Brain on the pillow would exorcise God.

"And so . . ." the doctor catechized, with a remembered kindness in his voice, "when you are silent, you do know what it is you think about?"

"God," said Michael softly.

There was a pause so long that Michael began to hope the doctor hadn't heard him.

"And who is that?" the Red Beard inquired.

"I don't know," said Michael.

"Where is He?" persisted the Red Beard. "Is He in Heaven?"

"Perhaps," said Michael softly.

"Come now." Dr. Rufus raised his voice. "There must be something more to God than a hole in your head that contains neither words nor ideas. Don't be so shy with your God, Michael. I want to hear about Him."

"I see Him in the world," said Michael slowly.

"That's better." The Red Beard smiled. "Once we've located God we can discuss Him. In just what portion of the world do you see Him, Michael? In the history of man?"

"No," said Michael, "not there."

"Where then?" the Red Beard demanded.

"In beauty," said Michael.

"That needs another secondary definition," said the doctor. "What do you consider beautiful?"

"It's hard to pick out separate things," said Michael, "as if you asked what waves in the sea were beautiful."

The Red Beard chuckled weakly.

"I understand," it said. "So you've discovered God in the fields, hills, and streams. In birds flying, flowers nodding, animals running, and the whole gamut of terrestrial color and grace. And you've decided that this dream of beauty around us is God, eh?"

"Yes," said Michael. "Beauty is our dream, but it is God's reality."

"How many madmen have said that," the voice rumbled wistfully from the pillow, "and how many scientists have confirmed it!

"Yes," continued Dr. Rufus, "our scientists after measuring the world have found the same surplus that spells God. The same too much and too intricate and too useless that proclaims a Divine and Artistic hand in its manufacture. Beauty is again God's calling card at the laboratory bench as it was at the altar. We've wrestled a lot of new statistics out of the Heavens and the Earth, but no new philosophy. Our scientists add a new alto to the Magnificat at eventide.

" 'In a world,' they say, 'where every bit of fuzz on a bug's leg is usually so purposeful, what of that extra cosmos of beauty that has no purpose? Well,' they say, 'it has a purpose. Its purpose is to turn our souls to God.'"

Dr. Rufus paused.

"Is that what you think?" he asked.

"Yes," said Michael.

"So looking on Nature, you see God," Dr. Rufus said more loudly. "You see in Beauty evidences of a Divine breath superior to ours, eh? Well, Michael, I see something else."

"What do you see?" asked Michael.

"I see that there is no Beauty," said the Red Beard. "Like the word God, the word Beauty is a name that reveals not our souls but our ignorance. I want to discuss this with you, Michael, because I lie here thinking about it. I'll grant you this: there's nothing nimbler than God. You'd think that when Reason first shooed Him away from his Magician's Table and stripped Him of His Miracles and booted Him out of the entire history of man, He would retire in good order. But no. He leaves the little domain of Psychology and takes possession of Chemistry, Astronomy, the Quantum Theory, and all the test tubes of Science. Our scientists, uncovering one by one the secrets of existence, end up with bent knee before the daffodil and the dinosaur. God exchanges His white whiskers for an X. There's a promotion! Instead of being the soul of bad reasoning and childish thinking, He becomes now the soul of Beauty. The Pan X. Having nothing else to think about, Michael, I've been thinking that the fear of God will never quit men's minds until they either lose or understand their love of Beauty.

"I am blind," the voice on the pillow resumed, "and I spend a lot of time remembering the look of things and thinking of their beauty, and wondering what made them so. And it may be only a blind man's revenge that makes me discover now that there was no beauty. But I doubt this. I prefer to think it is an answer that has come to me, a large answer. It's an answer that I'll give you, Michael. You will use it as an exorcism to drive God out of the hills and flowers and to remove His breath from the whole of Nature. And don't cry out in your heart 'to get thee behind me.' It's not evil—what I tell you, Michael. It's loyalty to a race you belong to—the race of the brain. It's the little muscle that thinks against all the lightnings of Heaven. You come on my side, Michael."

Michael shivered and covered his face and shook his head desperately, as if he were struggling to drop out of it the light that continued to glow faintly and terrifyingly in all the crevices of his being.

"You seem more friendly now," said the Red Beard. "I don't feel you trying to shame me with that silence of yours. You seem very close, Michael. Let me feel your hands."

Michael leaned over and touched the blind forehead.

"It isn't cool," smiled the Red Beard. "It doesn't feel like a healer's hand, but hot and bedeviled like the inside of my head. Well, that makes our little discussion easier. I'll tell you about my Answer. It's this:

"I say, Michael, that there is no face of God in the beauty of the world and the Heavens. There's only our own face in it. We consider the phenomena of life beautiful because they are the multitudinous homelands we've left behind. We're not exiles from God's glory, as you once told me, Michael. We're exiles from Nature.

"Beauty is our memory of beasts and houses we've outgrown. Our aesthetic sense applauds the beauty of stars, hills, grasses, wings spread, flowers blooming, and the sea glittering with its half-foliage denizens, because these things are our biologic memories. Our aesthetic sense is a salute to our past. It isn't God we see, or Beauty, but a memory of self in the surviving crucible of the world. Things too dimly remembered to call brother, we call Beauty. We were once birds and fishes and crustaceans. And we still look at the treetop with the heart of a bird. We stare at the sea with the heart of a fish. We admire the sun with the heart of an amoeba and we look into caves with the heart of a lizard. Just as the village of our childhood glows with mysterious charm when we return to it, so the colors of the sea fascinate the gills still inside us when we look at them. We call our Mother beautiful because she bore us. Color and shape and movement and odor are similarly lovely to our senses because they were once the wombs we moved in. They are our ancestors, and we hail them as far back as they reach with that dispersed and sublimated self-love we have for the greatness of our forebears.

"But proof," smiled the Red Beard. "Every idea must have a toe to pirouette on. How do we prove that Beauty isn't Beauty? How do we prove that Beauty isn't the largess of God, but the romanticized history of evolution? Well"—the voice appeared to be growing childlike and losing its rumble—"let us apply the theory of relativity to it. If relativity works for the stars, it should work for the color of an apple blossom. For instance, it's conceivable that all the orderly world with all its color and movement and surplus of pure entertainment would not stir a single sigh in a Martian. Or in any other form of life evolved out of any other planet. For such an organism as might visit us would have been created in a world of fire, and come to life out of a heat wave of at least 2000 degrees Centigrade.

"Now imagine such a connoisseur from the Milky Way looking at our world. He would see no beauty in grass, birds, hills, sea, or flowers, for the good reason that he had not derived from them. The sight of our colors and shapes would touch off no nostalgic memories in him, nor fill him with that vestigial sense of triumph over Nature which is our Aesthetic Sense.

"The Martian, having triumphed over Flame, would undoubtedly consider ashes more beautiful than verdure and sigh more tenderly over melting rocks than leaping brooks. He would hear a hymn to himself out of the scarified tissues of his Martian landscape. And all that we think beautiful would be meaningless to him. And all that we hold ugly would be the wonders of God to him."

The tired voice trailed off.

"Go on," it whispered presently, "go to bed and say your prayers."

Sobbing wretchedly, the boy threw himself across the feet of the figure of stone.

But the man who had already spoken his swan song with his last strength, in torment, did not console him for his treason.

"There's something about you, Michael," he sighed, "something about you . . . something that washes my words away. It bothers me when you stay near me. It bothers me." The voice sank. "Don't bother me, Michael," it sighed.

One more year Michael's servitude continued. For one more year he attempted to repay his debt—and Sarah's—to Dr. Rufus. In that year a last change came into the illness. Pain, unspeakable and beyond bearing, attacked the old doctor. Other doctors came and decided that his eyes should be removed. They had turned to stone and were causing pain by their pressure on nerves and brain. This measure Dr. Rufus refused.

"No, gentlemen," the weary tongue jested, "I prefer the

cadaver intact. My stone eyes lend a certain dignity to the ensemble."

In vain they pleaded, and tried to administer sedatives for his agony.

The stone man refused. For him, he said, there would be no morphine at the end, and no religion, only the comfort of his thought. Reason had been his flag, and he would fly it to the end.

Michael stood in the doorway, listening. Perhaps this was Dr. Rufus's final taunt to Michael.

From that time on, silence fell in the sickroom. The silence deepened with the passing months. The mania of pain ruled the house.

Now it was Michael who nursed Dr. Rufus. The old serving couple, frightened, were no longer to be seen in his room. They clung to their quarters unless evoked by the sister's bells. No guests came. Alone, Michael bore the burden of the man who was slow to die, the burden of the madwoman, and the burden of the silence, which might have been sweet with the service of his willing heart. The tired boy, from whose form all buoyancy and strength had disappeared, no longer took the time to walk in the streets, but remained for months inside the house. At night, often hungry, he lay awake full of a sense of mounting event, and the silence around him was like the approach of a stealthy crime.

Michael grew thin. His body, which had grown strong under encouragement and love, was wasted, and his face was hollow-eyed and old with the weight on his mind. Still the extraordinary beauty of his face did not diminish, and it was this beauty that brought his final sorrow in this house to the innocent boy.

One day, returning to Dr. Rufus's room after a brief absence, he saw an unaccustomed sight. This was Miss Rufus, who, though she had seen Michael daily, had not visited her brother in many weeks. A change had come into Miss Rufus's hatred of Michael recently, one he could not have defined.

Long ago, in seeking a reason for her loathing of the child, the ugly spinster had found and confided one to the servants. This was that Michael, with his orphan's haircut, had been the spawn of love, the repulsive symbol of a sin committed by some woman in the dark of a lover's arms. For this she had tortured him, her hysteria fed daily by the fear that Michael would inform against her to her brother. But she had realized long since, through vigilance and spying, that he would not betray her. Now it was she who accused.

In this change that had come into her mania of late, Michael had become no longer the symbol of love, but love itself. Her thin-breasted body and withering arms had felt the sweetness of the tall boy, and her entire being had launched itself at him as at a robber come to steal her single treasure—the hatred by which she kept herself strong enough to live without life. Now she called him a monster, she raved that he was full of dreaded powers and monstrous secrets, and even his smiling was a mask for hidden danger.

"You are being accused, Michael," Dr. Rufus greeted him in an unfamiliar voice—a voice that spoke unctuously out of a personality that had escaped all pain.

"Speak your complaints, Margaret," he added to his sister.

In a rasping voice that spread into the air the horror of her hidden life, Miss Rufus spoke of Michael's persecutions. She raved of his plotting against her, watching her through key-holes while she was undressing. . . .

"And worse, worse!" she screamed, unable to find words for

her crazed meanings. At last the shrill voice collapsed into its culminating sobs.

"Delusions of persecution," said Dr. Rufus in a voice more pleasant than when he had used it professionally, and he continued: "You are charged, Michael, with being part of the madness of my sister, Margaret. What have you to say?"

The voice waited, and then resumed, with a chuckle.

"Ah, he preserves his divine silence. He stands and radiates. Very good. We'll make a note of it. He offers radiation as a defense."

Again the voice chuckled.

"The charge stands as follows," it said. "Your radiation, Michael, or as you call it, the Glory of God, drives people mad. The divine presence does not heal but disorders. That cool sweet love you exude, Michael, falls on the human mind like an evil dew out of mystery and poisons it."

"I've tried to keep him out," Miss Rufus wailed, "but he sees through doors and walls."

"Let me speak for us, Sister," the voice silenced her. "The truth is, Michael, that I've lain here with your secret for a long time. My mind wrenched it out of your silence and radiation. The truth is," repeated the voice, rising with anger, "that you are God. You are God, Michael. Look at him carefully, Sister, with your two eyes that stick out like toads ready to jump. He is God."

"No, no!" the woman screamed. "He's the Devil. The peeping Devil. The Devil with an angel's face."

"Well said," the voice on the pillow attempted to chuckle. "God and the Devil are a pair of interchangeable masks. And now, Michael, my own complaint. Are you following the proceedings? Answer me."

"Yes," said Michael.

"When I thought you were Michael I loved you," the voice went on. "Then I found out who you were and I hated you. And in hating you I, too, have stepped a little out of line. A little out of line," the voice rumbled wistfully. "But if you think I'm mad, Michael, you're wrong. You're wrong," it cried suddenly. "I'm crippled, paralyzed, blind, half turned to stone, withered to a handful of pipe stems, brittle with disease and tormented by the nails being driven into my brain and the nails through my hands and feet, Michael. And nails through my heart and groin. And with all this nailing going on I have to retreat somewhere to think. I retreat to the last little perch. I become a bird on a twig, twittering crazily at the destruction below. But be patient with my twittering. My mind is still in it. Do you hear my mind, Michael, behind my words—above agony and sitting in judgment on God?"

"Yes," said Michael.

"Thank you," said the voice. "Then it's understood that I'm mad, but not too mad. It's understood that I'm a little Argument that won't give in, a little bird chirping on a tomb. It's understood further that my sister Margaret and I are human beings—we belong to that plague that speaks and thinks and dreams. We give off the stink of humanity—cruelty and unreason and despair. And we ask you, Michael, to remove your light from this house. We refuse the light, whatever it is and wherever it comes from. Because it doesn't come from where it should —from the Hell of the human mind. We refuse to live by any other light than that. You are judged and dismissed, Michael."

The voice grew hoarsened.

"You will leave this house," it said. "Get out with your angel face. We don't want it hovering . . . the old jackal of Divinity that haunts the death beds . . . waiting for the soul to be tossed to it. . . . I am going to die without falling into God's arms, Michael. You will not shine on me, O Spirit. . . ."

The Red Beard continued to tremble as the mouth became silent. Michael waited. The two figures in the shadowed room seemed locked in some tormented embrace, each so sad he could feel the same wail of tears in their throats.

At last Michael came and kissed the motionless forehead on the pillow.

"Good-by," he said softly.

Still he waited.

"Why must I go?" he thought. But the words he had heard pushed him from the bedside and moved him across the room. Here he remained in the darkened doorway. He stood, thinking of the life begun in a basket on the steps of the orphanage, and knew it was finished. There was the cry in his heart that rises from all endings, the good-by of days that all too suddenly become the Past, and leave us exiled and forlorn in a new, strange hour.

A voice came from the pillow.

"Michael," it called faintly, "Michael, are you gone?"

"No," said Michael. Tears fell from his eyes.

"I see a light," the voice on the pillow whispered. "Take it away . . . take the last light away."

Michael smiled at the madman.

"I will always love you," he said.

He moved away and when he was in the hall he heard a new sound from the pillow. The voice wept.

Michael walked from the house weeping, for he had been cast out. In the streets his eyes searched the night sky as he moved.

The night sky grew large with his loneliness. So vast a darkness to cover so little a thing as his heart, he thought—so deep and far-away a mystery to haunt eyes so small as these looking up.

Michael stood on a dark and empty road beside the cemetery where Sarah was. Behind him lay a waste of land, and before him the trees where the dead lay. But it seemed to him that he was standing on a little bridge between Heaven and Earth, and that the way back for him was easy.

He walked under the trees where the dead lay, and stopped to look at the white stones that marked their homes in the earth. And it seemed to him as if a voice were calling to him to come back.

The moon on these white stones spelled out names and figures and words, and Michael thought, not of the dead who lay beneath them, but of the living still further from him who must come this way, of the dreams and powers and agonies that must speak finally only from a white stone.

"Michael," the Voice called, "Michael. You cannot see Me, though I am close to you, and My arms are around you. I am He, Michael, for whom you once toiled. You were My friend, Michael. Remember now that I sent you to this little place where you stand. Remember, Michael."

Michael remembered. He continued walking, and came to the grave that was Sarah's. The little white stone leaned erratically over the grass as if the careening soul of the old scrublady were in it. Michael stood remembering vividly all the tones and movements that had been hers, and a tenderness for the half-crazed smile overcame him, as if it were crying eagerly for him to bring it back to life.

Many voices came to him now. They seemed to surround

him, clamoring joyously and calling out his name, calling to him to remember.

Michael remembered. Many were the memories that came crowding around him on the little bridge between Earth and Heaven where he stood. The sky came close to him, as if the rope ladder that Dr. Rufus used to speak of had been let down. And names he had never known were known to him, and the stars were near. But stronger than all was the memory of Sarah.

He beheld her in himself as in a mirror, and before this mirror she postured and cackled and banged away with her pails and brushes. But as he looked closer into this mirror, her image became silent and the careening little body stood motionless. Michael looked into the eyes that were gone from the world and at the half-crazed smile that was nowhere except in this mirror. He saw not only Sarah but his love for her, as if it, too, were in this mirror, standing like a child with its hand in her work-battered fist. They were waiting, both of them, for him to speak.

"Mother, Mother!" he cried, and cast himself on the grave.

He had chosen Sarah's world.

He was glad.

"In the hearts of the living," he thought, "the dead have their little extra hour of life." He would not have deprived Sarah of this hour. And though he no longer understood the true bliss of the eternity he had forfeited, he remembered still the truth about himself, and knew that he would never go back to Heaven.

The sound of the Dove came to him.

And, looking at the familiar bird on a tree branch close to him, at last Michael knew. Human he was, only that God's truth was in him, and this, the white friend that had first danced on his foundling's basket, was truly God's spirit, and it was his mission to carry God's message throughout the world.

Soundless and far away, the Voice now came to him.

"Go and tell them, Michael. When you speak My name, I shall be there beside you. I will be there as a light for your eyes and a whiteness on your hands. You will not be afraid, Michael, for My light will lead you. My truth will make a road for you. I am God. Go now, Michael, and bring Me the world."

But as he walked away, Michael's eyes were wide and thoughtful. There was no exultation in them but a question and much sadness. His heart did not exult with the memory of the Dove. It lay in the grave with Sarah, and beside Dr. Rufus moaning in his head.

When it was morning, Michael found himself on the outskirts of a small town, watching a little army of men raising a circus tent in a meadow full of daisies, butterflies, and the chirping of frogs. A ring of circus wagons painted red and gold enclosed one end of the field.

The summer dawn was a-scurry with exuberant figures. Tall blue painted poles rose magically out of the daisy patches. Ropes fluttered, pulleys creaked, and, to the accompaniment of shouts and of sledge hammers ringing, and a roar and whinny of hidden animals, a great spread of wrinkled canvas rose like a giant bird and became a circus tent, scalloped and minareted. Michael watched with delight. Everything around him hinted of gaieties, and the rough, unshaven figures assembling this toy world in the summer meadow reminded him of old Sarah as they dashed about with hammers, poles, and ropes.

As he stood enthralled by this little world that seemed to be hatching out of the daisies and the long grass, he heard a voice calling insistently. He turned and saw a preposterous-looking man standing in the doorway of one of the red and gold wagon trucks. The man was thin as a beanpole and naked to the waist. He looked like a huge insect with a gaunt human head attached to it. Michael stared at him and, never having been to a circus, was unaware he was being addressed by one of its Artists.

"Hey, you," called the man, shaking a finger, "what are you doing?"

"Nothing," said Michael, trying not to stare too much at the gruesome body. "I was just watching." And he began to move away, but the man laughed, and said: "What's the matter? You scared of me, kid? Come in here and give us a hand. Nobody's gonna eat you up."

Michael entered the wagon. The interior was a dark little house crowded with cots, chairs, a table, and innumerable chests. There was a little window with curtains. And there were three other figures. One, a huge creature who dwarfed everything around him, was sitting on the edge of a cot, his chin in his palms, and staring like a half-asleep monster out of the curtained window.

"Make yourself at home," the beanpole man was chuckling, as Michael, open-mouthed, stared at this and that. "We got some work for you. We're short-handed and want somebody to carry our stuff to the sideshow tent. We'll show you where. But first meet Mr. Henry Marblehead, better known as the Giant Munso—the tallest man in the world. What's your name, kid?"

"Michael," said Michael and smiled.

"O.K., Mike," said the Giant Munso in a soft boyish voice as if someone else had climbed up into his monster's head and were speaking for him. The huge man reminded Michael sud-

denly of a gangling, loose-skinned little chicken just hatched—
and wondrously enlarged.

"And this," said the beanpole, "is Captain Achilles."

A midget, with a round baby head and a face puckered as if it
were about to cry, bowed like a courtier and then extended a
puny hand.

"Allow me," continued the beanpole, who appeared to be
enjoying their visitor's wide-eyed interest, "Dr. Holmes, the
India Rubber man—a fascinating creature made of rubber bands
instead of flesh. Snap him, if you wanna, kid."

A man with a pirate's mustache sat up from under the covers
of a cot.

"What's transpiring?" he inquired dazedly.

"I've got us a valet," said the beanpole.

"How do you do, sir," said the India Rubber man and Michael
saw that his naked body was tattooed so completely that he
seemed clothed in a tapestry.

"I'm Philo, the Human Skeleton, as you have no doubt observed by this time," said the beanpole. "And now to your
duties, kid. We want all this truck removed to the sideshow
tent. And when you've done with your interesting chores, young
fella, breakfast will be ready for you in the cook tent. Just
follow your nose."

It was thus Michael joined the circus. For several weeks, as
the painted wagons rumbled from town to town, and the blue
and white tents rose in various summer meadows, Michael
remained more a spectator than a participant. He watched the per-
formances, the crowds, and the animals with undiminished excitement. He ran errands, was hustled about by acrobats and bare-
back riders, and slept at night in the wagon occupied by four
freaks. But gradually he seemed to enter the mind of the circus,

and he began to feel the painstaking and concentrated little talents out of which rose the daily illusion of glitter and gaiety.

It was in his relationship with the four strange men in the little dark house of the circus wagon that the major change occurred. In the mornings Michael still served them as he had on the first day—carrying their trappings to the sideshow tent. The afternoons he spent tidying up the wagon interior. But after their evening exhibitions, which were concluded long before the Main Performance, the four freaks would return to their wagon and stretch themselves in the grass around it. Michael would then talk to them as the music of the circus band came muffled from the lighted tent and filled the summer night with its dancing far-away sounds. He talked softly, and at first inspired no more than awe for his quiet eloquence and remarkable erudition. He discussed with Dr. Rufus's words as much as his own the activities everywhere in the world, explaining the tawdry secrets behind the bombast of the world's leaders. But in explaining these matters there was a gentleness in his voice, like a deeper vocabulary, that made even Dr. Rufus's philosophies sound mysteriously tender.

His four friends stretched on the grass grew nightly more eager for his talk. In his absence they took to strutting about with brooding philosophical looks on their odd faces. They grew proud of the things Michael had put into their heads, and looked down from their sideshow platform, like sages, on the pathos of the uninformed.

In the second month of his travels, Michael emerged from the status of mere philosopher. The Giant Munso became ill. A physician was called, and the tallest man in the world was pronounced in grave danger. He lay doubled up on his long cot, groaning through the afternoon and complaining of frightful pains in his groin. His large loose-fleshed face rolled on the pillow. That night, when the other three crowded into the wagon, Michael was absent. The freaks wondered at this, for Munso had always been kind to him. And now Munso kept calling his name like a frightened child. A great gloom lay on the three friends watching him. Each knew that the giant quivering on the cot was dying. Several years ago, there had been another giant among them who had lain just this way, doubled up and gray with pain. And though three doctors had attended him, he had died, refusing to leave the circus wagon. The band had played just as it was playing tonight, and this other giant had sat up and listened to it for a moment with a sudden childish smile on his huge face and then fallen back dead.

Michael appeared in the doorway, and the three heads turned miserably to him. He came to the cot and stood looking down on the enormous figure.

The Giant Munso opened his eyes and paused in his groaning as he saw Michael. The others also looked at Michael with a silence that became like fear. They saw a light in his face and on his hands.

Michael, looking into the pain-filled eyes of the stricken giant, kept smiling, for in these eyes he saw Sarah. He felt her withered muscular arm flung again across his neck as he slept. A great love seized Michael, and he felt that his heart, glowing with power, was in his hands; that his heart was his to give away. He placed his hands on the giant's head and continued to smile. This perplexed and pitiful giant seemed to Michael all he loved in the world, and his hands caressed the huge head as tenderly as if it were the little fledgling out of a chicken egg it had once seemed to him. And his eyes, smiling as over a crib, begged for an answer, as if they were saying aloud: "Deep inside you,

little giant, lies the secret of life—the child love for the works of
God. Love life, little giant. Be grateful. The night is your
mother, and all that lies hidden in the dark loves you."

The look of pain and perplexity passed from the giant's eyes
and he smiled at Michael.

It was thus the miracle was done. In the little dark house of
the circus wagon the four freaks sat in silence and looked at
Michael with fear. Munso, the world's tallest man, felt no more
pain and his face was no longer gray. He placed his feet on the
floor and straightened till his head touched the ceiling.

"I feel all right," he said in his soft, boyish voice. "I feel
mighty good."

Captain Achilles, the midget, climbed like a distracted infant
into the vacant cot and began slapping one little fist into the
other palm, which was his way of expressing wonder. And Dr.
Holmes, who was made of rubber bands and tattooed like a
human mosaic, pointed silently to the wagon window, in which
perched a white Dove, gurgling. Somehow the white Dove was
even more frightening than this strange Michael whose hands
had turned so white as they rested on the stricken Munso's head.
Philo, the Human Skeleton, covered his face in panic.

Michael spoke.

"It is the Spirit of God," he said.

The Dove fluttered to his hand and couched itself in his palm.

"He has spoken to me," said Michael, "and I know the Truth.
It is simple. I will tell it to you. But you must not repeat it, yet.
You must only dream of it and let it fill your hearts a little more
each day."

As the four freaks listened, the Dove in Michael's hand began
to shine with an unbearable light and for a moment all of them

felt that the entire night had burst into a single flame and devoured the earth. When they opened their eyes again, the Dove was gone.

Michael spoke to them until the dawn came. He told them it was his mission to redeem the world. He spoke of a Soul that was greater than the souls of men, of life and its meaning, and of the mystery of God.

All night long the freaks clamored to hear about Heaven, and if they were going there immediately when they died.

"I don't know," Michael said at first, unhappily—for it seemed to him there was a greater Truth than the tinseled Heaven for which they longed.

"I think we are the leaves on His Tree, and fall to make room for other leaves. Only the Tree that produces and destroys us is divine. We must resign ourselves to the mystery of the tree trunk, and the hidden roots that lend us life, and not try to see too much. That is the way God wishes it. He wishes us to live on this Tree, and shine in the sun as part of His mystery."

"But we die just the same?" asked Dr. Holmes.

"We die knowing we please God by being part of His plan," Michael said.

"It's hard to understand—if there is no Heaven," said Philo sadly.

"Maybe we're not smart enough to understand yet," said Captain Achilles.

"You don't have to understand," said the Giant Munso, who had just been saved.

But the others kept asking questions, and searching Michael's eyes, which grew sad and far away.

"Maybe we express ourselves too crudely," Dr. Holmes said,

calling the attention of the others to Michael's darkened face.

"Yes, we ought to do a lot of reading," piped Captain Achilles, anxiously, "and then we'd understand better."

In the end Michael, smiling suddenly, promised them the eternity for which they asked. He was young, and he was not sure of his words yet, and the Truth told him that it was better not to be too wise. For the wisest thing a man can do is dream, and dreams have no words. This he told them.

"Dreams," he said, "are the mists of Heaven brightening our souls for a moment. Some day," he said, "we shall be overcome by these mists, and instead of falling like leaves from the Tree, we shall remain eternally green, and rest like a crown on God's head."

When he had promised them this, the freaks were happy, and wished to know shyly if, when they went to Heaven, they would still be freaks.

Michael comforted them on this score.

And now they were excited by their new religion.

"What shall we do?" they cried, crowding around him.

"Love God, and you will know how to pray to Him," he said.

And he told them the following story:

"There was once such a good heart in a boy who had been born without the gift of speech. His parents were pious people, but as their child grew up they were ashamed to bring him into church because he was unable to speak. As he grew older his parents saw, too, that he was a backward boy without much sense in him and their shame in their misfortune increased. But their son was unaware of the trouble he caused them, for they were not bad parents. Left to himself, he learned happily a few simple and foolish things. Among the foolish things that he learned was how to play on a little fife made out of a willow-tree twig. It had three holes in it and he could blow three notes out of it as if he were a bird.

"One Easter Day the parents, seeing their son running about like a pagan when everybody else was off to church, decided to smooth his hair and wash his face and take him with them. They thought that perhaps his dumbness wouldn't be noticed by their neighbors while they were rejoicing so ardently over the Resurrection.

"So their son sat between them in the church, awed and thrilled by his first visit, and listened breathlessly to the choir and the priest and the exultant praying of the flock. And all this pleased him so that he reached into his pocket for his fife to play his three bird notes on—because he was unable to make any other sound. His father, seeing what he intended, grew angry and slapped his hand. The boy sat still for a time, but again the rapture of the prayers excited him and made him want to join in. And again he half drew his fife from his pocket. This time his mother slapped his hand and whispered fiercely to him to behave. Once more the boy sat silent and quivering. But the voices of the choir chanting of God's glory overcame him a third time and a third time he started to draw his fife from his pocket. His parents grew scarlet with shame, for the antics of their son had attracted attention. Fearful of offending both God and their neighbors, they rose piously. They seized their stupid son by his hands and started to lead him with flushed and apologetic faces from the church.

"And as they walked up the aisle a strange thing happened. A sound came piping out of their son's pocket. It grew louder. Its three notes trilled and rose above the choir voices and filled the church with sweeter sound than had ever before been heard in it. And the boy, afraid to move because of the disturbance his foolish fife was ·making in his pocket, stood still and stared around full of terror. But this time no one slapped his hand. His parents sank to their knees in the aisle, and all the devout and more gifted people thronged toward him and kneeled in silence as his willow-tree fife continued to trill its woodland hosannas from his pocket."

The four freaks wept at the miracle concerning one who was so like themselves. They assured Michael that they would know how to pray. They would pray humbly, like freaks.

"And God will love us, just as the public loves us, because we perform before them as freaks," Captain Achilles piped.

"If we pretended we were better than we are, God wouldn't love us," Dr. Holmes said thoughtfully.

Before the dawn came, they wished to know from their friend, the new Redeemer, how they would know when the world had been redeemed.

Michael explained to them as follows:

"There was once long ago," said Michael, "a great rabbi who was renowned among all the sad Jews of the world as one of their holiest men. When he was old he traveled to Jerusalem to look before he died on the place where God had once been kind to the Jews.

"While he was sitting at twilight in a room overlooking the lost wonderland of his race, a strange thing happened in Jerusalem. A madman, seizing a shofar, which is the ram's horn the Jews blow from their altar, ran to the top of the Mount of Olives and blew wild and terrifying blasts on it. The shofar calls echoed in the streets below, and the Jews, hearing the holy horn sounding, grew blissful and rushed out of their houses, crying that the Messiah had come at last and that the day of Redemption was here.

"As they rushed singing and rejoicing through the streets, they passed under the window of the holy rabbi, and cried out to him to join them quickly, for the Messiah was calling from a hilltop.

"The old rabbi opened his window as they shouted and sang in a frenzy below. Then he smiled and silenced them for a moment with his hand.

" 'Go back to your homes, my children,' he said, 'and wait a little longer. It is not the Messiah come nor Redemption calling.' The holy man pointed outside his window.

" 'Look at that little bird on the tree,' said the holy man. 'The little bird is not singing.'

"And he closed his window and went back to studying his holy books."

For several days the Giant Munso, Captain Achilles, Dr. Holmes, and Philo went about in a trance, and wherever Michael moved, these four were beside him. Alone, on the platform in the sideshow with the country folk gaping up as the barker described their remarkable abnormalities, Michael's disciples smiled giddily and went through their little routines as bewilderedly as amateurs. For their heads were in their promised Heaven.

This greatness, still extending their thought as they moved among others, brought smiles to the circus people. The sight of the midget at the long table in the cook tent closing his eyes and moving his lips in prayer as each dish was handed him began to stir chuckles. And Philo, the Human Skeleton, stealthily slipping notes into their hands reading, "Join Us and Be Saved," was also diverting. And for several weeks as the circus traveled among the prairie towns, there were only these smiles and good-natured comment among the performers. For these talented folk who could fly, tumble, balance, and caper in a hundred ways were fond of the freaks and had always treated them with a pleasant half-mocking deference that was part of the circus code.

But when the constant breakfast, lunch, and supper praying of the midget and the increasing flood of salvation notes from the Human Skeleton were climaxed by certain antics of the Giant Munso, a feeling of disquiet came to the circus people. Munso, who towered three feet above the tallest of them, took to extending his huge hands over their heads as they passed him, and uttering blessings. Finally Dr. Holmes completed their misgivings. The India Rubber man, heretofore esteemed for his wit and sarcasm, appeared one Sunday dressed in a frock coat with a priest's collar and his pockets filled with enormous quantities of feathers. These he threw by the handfuls at all he met, crying out that they were the Feathers of the Dove and that whoso wore one would be possessed of the Spirit of God.

The feeling that all four of their freaks had gone mad took hold of the circus people, and their smiles and banter gave place to irritation and then fear. Michael, who might have saved his four friends, for he was a sane and observant youth, had been too busy with his mission to notice the increasing anger of the artists and canvas workers. And when he did finally see the unhappy change that had come over his little world, it was too late to act.

By this time his four disciples, completely vanquished by his continued discourses, had disobeyed even his most important admonition. They had added to their other curious behavior the announcement that their valet Michael was the Saviour, and that God had visited them in their wagon in the form of a Dove and had filled their souls with light.

The sense that madness was among them began to unnerve the acrobats and tumblers, and so compact is the mind of the circus that its growing panic was felt in the animal cages. The cats took to roaring, the three elephants grew restive and pulled their stakes out of the ground at night, and even the horses leaped and bucked in the ring during their performances. These disturbances grew worse, and the circus, which had played happily in the summer meadows before Michael's arrival, became full of angers and plots and threats. One night while the management, consisting of two sawdust veterans who had trouped shows for a generation, was discussing possible ways of coping with the lunacy that had overtaken their freaks, a final and unforgivable event happened. Captain Achilles rose from his toy chair on the sideshow platform and addressed the astonished villagers gathered in the tent to behold the Wondrous Freaks of Nature. He cried out in a piping voice that Salvation was at hand for all who would listen and, falling to his tiny knees, raised his head in passionate prayer. The Giant Munso, seeing this happen, also forgot himself and began casting benedictions over the heads of the audience. In vain the barker's voice rose in its rhythmic twang of phrases. Philo, the Human Skeleton, attired only in his pleated silken trunks, was on his feet bawling that Michael was the Son of God, and Dr. Holmes, who had been snapping his rubber skin for the edification of a group before his section of the platform, reached for his frock coat hanging on a hook behind him and began throwing feathers.

After the performance, the circus management visited the wagon occupied by the four freaks and Michael. The four were given a week's salary and asked to leave the organization. Michael, who had received no salary for his many labors, was called a hoodlum and ordered never to show his face again.

Carrying their bundles, Michael and his disciples walked from the circus lot through muttering and menacing groups of those who had been their friends. The four freaks held their heads high. But Michael was sad and tears were in his eyes. For he knew this was only the beginning of his wretchedness.

In the hotel room where they arrived an hour later Dr. Holmes ordered up food and drink. Michael was unable to eat. He sat slumped in a chair and watched the others gloomily. No word was said. But when the meal was done, Dr. Holmes stood up and tapped his spoon against a glass. He made a speech.

"Gentlemen," he said, "we are the friends of God's Son."

"Yes, sir," Captain Achilles piped and beat his tiny fist into his palm. "We are the Four Apostles."

"We have followed Him where others cast Him out," continued the India Rubber man. "If He had wanted to He could have destroyed that tent and scattered that circus to the winds. But His heart is kind and He would rather pick up His Cross and walk away than cause any inconvenience. Am I right?"

The Giant Munso nodded his head.

"No use making trouble," he said softly.

"Now I want to ask Him Who we know is the Son of **God**, just what are His plans," concluded the India Rubber man.

"I haven't any," Michael said truthfully.

The four looked at him in silence.

Then Captain Achilles spoke.

"Yes, You have," he piped. "You ain't gonna let a lot of circus hoodlums get You down."

Philo left the table and came to Michael.

"You're in the dumps," he said softly, "which is only natural, considering the blindness and injustice of our fellowmen. But God's truth is in You. You can't say it ain't."

"You can't deny it," shrilled Captain Achilles.

"We saw it. We heard it. We know it," they all cried.

The midget climbed up into the giant's palm and leaned against his chin.

"We'll all go out in the streets together," said the India Rubber man, "and speak to the people."

"Not us, but Michael," said the giant.

"But we'll be there to draw the crowds."

"We'll give a free show."

"He needs us, just like we need Him," piped Achilles.

Philo raised his voice.

"What You got to tell the people, Michael, is this. You'll say: 'Looka here, folks, these were born wrong outside, but you folks are freaks inside. That's the Truth of God.' And that's where we come in."

"The Truth of God," spoke the giant. "I felt it. I was dying, and it cured me!"

"I was blind," Dr. Holmes cried. "All I did was cover myself with the false glory of worldly beauty—tattooed from head to foot—a living, breathing symbol of the world's vanity, Dr. Holmes, the golden calf himself! And then I saw the Dove!"

The freaks jumped up and down around Michael, calling his name, repeating their hackneyed phrases of salvation, urging him onward, to the cross if necessary, and crying out that they would stand by him to the end.

In their midst, Michael pondered on how to bring God's message to the world.

The next night Michael spoke for the first time to the world. It was a little world, gathered on a street corner to see the four circus freaks performing free of charge. The crowd laughed and applauded good-naturedly at the show.

When Michael stepped forward and began to talk, they listened, at first in curiosity, and then in silence. A great eloquence was on Michael's tongue this night. Though he spoke of God, he seemed like no minister of the gospel they had heard, but a poet making words come to life in the night street.

The simple rhythm and the insight of his thought stirred something deeper in his listeners than they usually brought into the streets with them. They stood a long time, moved by this strange emotion inside them and by the smiling, glowing face of the pale boy who spoke.

Throughout Michael's talk, the freaks too remained devoutly silent, proud of his gift and of his beauty too. To help detain the crowd, they had struck postures: Captain Achilles still smaller on his little knees; Philo, who imagined himself a symbol of mankind's distortion, holding piously a posture with his legs around his neck. Dr. Holmes held a torch aloft and let the light flicker over Michael's face. The Giant Munso stood behind Michael like a mystic bulwark. But the freaks went unnoticed.

Michael told the stilled crowd something different from what the freaks had suggested. It was a simple parable of a traveler who had found a field so beautiful that he paused to admire it. As the traveler stood thrilled by the beauty of this field, said Michael, he saw that the beauty came from wondrous stones that dotted it. These stones were radiant with many colors, and the traveler looking at them grew more and more filled with delight. He raised his voice and other men appeared. All came running into the field and all looked and saw the beauty of the stones and were overjoyed. For a long time this group of men stood thrilled and full of pleasure for the beauty around them.

Then the first man, overcome by the radiance of a particular stone, approached it and knelt before it. He picked it up, holding it in his hands that he might be closer to its beauty and feel it actually against him. At first the stone weighed little but as he continued to walk in the field, exulting over his possession, its weight increased. Finally it was so heavy he began to stagger and sweat under its burden. He could no longer look at the other many beautiful stones, so busy was he carrying his one prize and so exhausted did he become clinging to it.

Looking around after a long time he beheld a curious sight. The other men, like himself, had also each picked up a stone and, like himself, each was staggering and sweating under his burden. This angered the first man, who began to shout that all the others were foolish to pick up the stones they had, since his was the most beautiful that had been in the field and the only one worth picking up. Shouts answered him. All the burdened men cried out he was mad, and each announced that the stone he held clutched to his bosom was the only thing of beauty that had been in the field. Soon after this they all lost their tempers and began to hit each other with the stones they were carrying. Although exhausted by the growing weight of these stones, they found enough strength to wield them as weapons. And soon all the stones that had lain in the field as objects of breathtaking beauty had become dreadful things with which the travelers, panting and bellowing, slew each other. And as each man killed he cried out he was wiser than the others, and as each man died he lamented that all wisdom and beauty perished with him.

It was thus, said Michael, that man had turned the world of nature into a battleground for insanity and greed of ego he called wisdom.

"Return to the field," said Michael, in so strange a voice that many of his listeners felt tears. "Return to the field. Put down your stones."

This was the first of his talks to the world. There were many more. Week after week Michael and his four friends traveled from town to town. He spoke sometimes with humor and brought laughter from the little crowds on the street corners. And at times his voice sounded so fresh and childlike that women wept without hearing what it was he said but feeling that someone tender and innocent was asking for their love.

One evening when he had told again of the travelers in the field and asked his listeners to put down their stones, he was sought out as he walked back to the country rooming house with his four friends. A man seated in the rear of a large and shining automobile, driven by a uniformed chauffeur, called to him. Michael stepped into the road as the car stopped.

"I would like to talk to you, if you could spare a few minutes," this man said graciously.

"Certainly," said Michael.

"I'll take you where you're going—you and your friends," the man offered.

Michael called to the four, who came running, the Giant Munso carrying Captain Achilles under his arm. They stepped into the car, Munso doubling up to keep from sticking his head through its top. On the way, their new acquaintance said he had listened to Michael's talk and that he had never heard so moving and beautiful a sermon.

"You've got the gift," he said, smiling. "No ranting, no bad style. But something spoken from the heart that's beautiful. . . . It got me, young man."

The stranger reminded Michael of Dr. Rufus. He had the same stern and superior face, though without a beard, and the same almost coquettish charm behind the sternness and superiority. He was asking Michael questions as to who he was, where he came from, and what he hoped to do. Michael stared at him, thinking of Dr. Rufus. A pang passed through his heart and, looking at the man with eyes full of remembrance, he answered his questions simply, as if he had become again a child being catechized by his old teacher.

In return the man had given his own name, George Griswald. Pronouncing it, he paused to see if it was known to any of his odd passengers. But all five went on looking at him as if he had spoken no name.

"You'll call me George," he continued, "and I'll call you Michael, and neither of us will have any other names."

As they rode to the rooming house where Michael and his followers shared a single room, as they had once shared the circus wagon, Mr. Griswald laid a plan before Michael. The world, he said, was exactly as Michael said it was. And what it needed was exactly the message Michael was preaching, whether it was God's or man's. And what Michael needed was this world to preach to, not just a few handfuls of it on a small-town street corner.

"I can get you a great audience," said Mr. Griswald, "a great mass of human beings. And you can talk to them, night after night. And thousands will come from all over the country to listen. That's the way you'll be able to save them."

"Save them?" Michael repeated and looked confused.

"Bring them to God," said Mr. Griswald. "You tell me He has spoken to you. And your friends here have seen Him. Is that true? Or is it a parable? Something you've made up to explain some inner truth?"

"It's true," said Michael. "He has spoken to me."

"Well and good," said Mr. Griswald. His fingers trembled as he rested them on the arm of this tall, glowing boy. "I believe you."

The automobile had stopped near a sagging wooden house.

"Here's where we stay," said Michael.

"Just a minute." Mr. Griswald drew a deep breath. "I want to finish with my plan.

"I want you to come to Hegemish, inside of two weeks," said Mr. Griswald. "That's a town two hundred miles from here, or thereabouts. I'll have everything ready for you. I'll put on an advertising campaign, put up a tent large enough to hold thousands. Will you speak to them?"

"Yes," said Michael.

"There are a lot of poor bewildered people in Hegemish," said Mr. Griswald, "whom your words will straighten out. That's what you want, isn't it? To tell people they belong to God? And to tell them who and what God is?"

"Yes," said Michael.

"Well and done," said Mr. Griswald, and mopped his head with a large clean handkerchief. "I'll expect you in Hegemish on the nineteenth. Do you give me your word, you'll be there on that date?"

"Yes," said Michael.

"It's hardly a word any man can doubt," smiled Mr. Griswald, "since it comes from God."

Michael shook hands with his new friend after he had stepped out of the car. For a moment as his hand rested in Mr. Griswald's, something cold touched his heart and he stared intently into the man's eyes. They were frightened and kindly and returned Michael's look with so pleading an air that he smiled.

"Thanks," said Mr. Griswald.

"What for?" asked Michael.

"For smiling at me," said his new friend.

In the days that followed, Michael continued to preach. During this time, his friends rejoiced at the good fortune that was coming to them all. But Michael knew only that the way was dark. Each time he had spoken, and each time he had felt love for the faces raised to him, and made them the promises he felt they longed for, he had felt the truth grow less. At last it seemed to him that when he stood alone, and tried to remember the divine message, it was only Sarah he remembered. Then he refreshed his spirit, not by contact with God, but with Sarah.

"I loved her," he said to himself, walking alone in the night, "because she was close to God. He tells me this now, but I knew it by myself then. She was close to God because she was such an unprotesting bit of life. The street she walked in was all the world she needed for walking. And in her purity she made a delight even of the toil that had been assigned her. She delighted in her movement beside the scrub pail as a bird might be glad to fly. She found success in the polish of a floor. And without dreams or thoughts she was able to embrace life and love it. There was no hardship or injustice for her, because, like a child, she played a game in which hardship and injustice were her favorite companions, her familiars to be loved. They could not make her see with their eyes. She saw only with her own, which were full of simplicity, and loved that which she should have hated, and embraced that which sought to ruin her. . . . Yet she told me something more than that. She told me that there is a golden age in the heart, that there is a fairytale world in which life smiles forever like a happy visitor—a fairytale that lies under the feet of Miss Rufus and the rest of them—nearly all of them. Under their feet and trampled away. . . ."

He stood in a dark street and looked up at the white leaf of dawn falling idly from the night. "What of them . . . ?" he asked himself. "What of all those who have trampled too much and buried Sarah too deep in themselves? How am I to talk to them?"

It was of Sarah he decided he would talk to the people in Hegemish.

On the night of the eighteenth Michael and his friends boarded a train that would bring them into Hegemish before dawn. They had learned that Hegemish was a town where steel was made.

It was still dark when Michael and his companions got off the train at Hegemish, where his first tabernacle waited. Dr. Holmes had sent a telegram to Mr. Griswald telling the hour of their arrival, and he hurried with Philo now from the station to look for the automobile they expected. Michael, flanked by Captain Achilles and the Giant Munso, sat on the platform, his feet on the railroad tracks, and listened to the train roar become a whisper. The night, routed by the train, returned. Silence and darkness rode the tracks, but the breast of the coming day was to be seen beyond the moon. There seemed nothing more wonderful in the world to the young Michael as he sat on the platform than to sit this way in a strange place and smell the dark prairies and watch the dawn restore the world.

Three men appeared behind Michael. One of them spoke softly.

"Are you Michael the Evangelist?" he asked.

"Yes," said Michael.

"Come along," said the figure. The Giant Munso rose with Captain Achilles under his arm.

"Not you," said the figure, "just the Evangelist. The man of God."

Michael smiled at the giant.

"You wait here," he said, and two of the men took him by the arms.

"Did Mr. Griswald send you?" Michael asked as he walked between them.

"Yeah," said one of them.

In the early gloom Michael saw that the three men were stocky and heavy-faced. Two of them were scarred. He heard Dr. Holmes calling his name in the distance.

"They're calling me," said Michael.

"Never mind," one of the men muttered and his fingers tightened on Michael's arm.

"Where are you taking me?" asked Michael.

"Shut up, you fink," the other man answered.

A fist struck Michael's face. He would have fallen but the hands on his arms kept him erect. Blood began to come from his nose.

"Keep your stinkin' trap shut and come along," a voice spoke in his ear.

Dizzied from the blow, Michael continued to walk as best he could. One of the men began to talk in a hoarsened voice.

"So you're gonna preach here, huh?" he said. "You're gonna set the workers right about God, eh? Well, try preachin' to this."

A fist struck him again, filling his head with sparks. A sting remained in his eye, and the side of his face grew slowly numb.

"You lousy strikebreaker," went on the hoarsened voice, "you and your fink God. Go on, yell for your bodyguard now. And your God too."

"What have I done?" asked Michael, blood streaming from his nose and from cuts over his eye. He felt choked and blinded.

"He don't know what he's done," sneered the voice. "He's innocent. He's a man of God."

"Listen, you sonofabitch," another of the three spoke. "Griswald brought you here to break the strike in his steel mills—and paid you plenty. So don't start claimin' you don't know what it's all about."

"A Judas, that's what you are," said the first man. "A Goddamn Judas. Comin' here to hop up the hunky workers with a lot of God talk. And take their fight out of them. I suppose you didn't know that, you fink!"

"I didn't know," began Michael and a fist struck his nose, again. He sagged between the two men holding him and heard a voice saying faintly:

"You know now, you louse. And you're gonna do no preachin' in Hegemish . . . after we get through."

Another blow struck Michael's mouth. A fist in his groin made him sag and scream. A third blow on his ear deafened him. He pitched forward, but a hand seized the collar of his coat and held him up with his head hanging. For several minutes Michael remained aware of fists beating at his face. He could hear and see nothing, but in the darkness that tasted of his own blood the blows continued. He dropped to his hands and knees. A foot smashed his fingers. Another foot stamped his face into the earth and a heel ground itself deep into his cheek.

The day was bright when Michael opened his eyes but he saw only a mist. He tried to rise but he could only crawl a few feet and then collapse. His right hand was crushed and he knew he was covered with blood. The blows seemed still to be echoing in his face. Each pulse of his blood tore at his eyes and ears.

An hour later Michael woke again. This time he saw figures around him, and with a childish moan he tried to hide his face in his arms. He heard Dr. Holmes's voice calling his name and through his swollen mouth he answered faintly: "Run away. Run away."

As he lay trying to understand through the battering in his head where he was, arms lifted him into a bed.

Michael lay in a hospital for two days. On the third morning he sat up. His eyes were swollen and patches of gauze covered most of his face. Two of his fingers were in splints. The door of his room opened and Captain Achilles looked in from under the doorknob. Michael saw the tiny figure and tried to smile. The midget gestured excitedly into the hall, and his three companions appeared. They walked cautiously to the bed. The eyes of the Giant Munso were reddened and his mouth hung loosely open. They stood beside Michael's bed in a long silence till Captain Achilles began to weep.

"Are you all right?" Philo asked.

Michael nodded.

"Never mind speaking," Dr. Holmes whispered quickly. "Come on." He prodded the giant, and to Michael he added in a low voice: "We'll be outside."

The four tiptoed out of the room and returned to the wicker couch in the corridor where they had been sitting for three days.

At the end of the week, Michael left his bed. His swollen and discolored face still pained, and occasional lightnings danced in his head, but he was whole and able to walk and speak. His four friends led him to an automobile waiting outside the hospital. Their eyes were full of pity, and a desperate friendliness was in their silence. But Michael, smiling at them, understood that they were confused. They had spoken to him of how the police were working to find the men who had attacked him, and of Mr. Griswald's great concern for his recovery. But of what was most in their minds they had said nothing. Michael knew that though they loved him and looked on his battered face with anguish, he had grown dim in their souls as a champion. Pity was a difficult emotion for these freaks who were Michael's disciples. As they rode, Captain Achilles finally spoke this disillusion.

"You should have smited them all," the midget piped, banging his fist into his palm. "You shouldn't have let them do that."

The automobile turned in at the opened gate of a tall ornamental iron fence, and followed a graveled lane flanked by boxed hedges. It wound through an area of lawn and gardens and stopped before the tall doors of a large house made of white stone.

"We got to wait outside," said Dr. Holmes. "He said he wants to see you alone first."

Michael was admitted through the tall doors. He was led up a curving flight of heavily carpeted stairs, down a stone-walled corridor hung with tapestries, and into a towering wood-paneled room. The room was full of books, and its floor was covered with glowing carpets. The late afternoon sun came dimly in through heavy red curtains over its windows. In this great and heavy room, Mr. Griswald appeared less a myth and more the prosperous owner of steel mills that he was.

Michael silenced this gentleman's greetings, his pained expressions of sympathy, and his profuse apologies by telling him he would not preach in Hegemish. Michael had figured out something during his days in the hospital. This was that, if he told the workers Sarah's message, of her love of life and simple-hearted abnegation, and if they believed it, it would be used against them. It would be used by Mr. Griswald and others to make their lives still harder, and to deprive them of more things.

In vain the capitalist pleaded, telling Michael he would be safe now, speaking of police protection, and of the tabernacle that would be more crowded now that the papers were full of news about Michael. In vain he apologized for not having told Michael of the strike, which was unimportant, he said. What was important, he cried out, was that there was something wrong with the world. A devil was loose in men, a devil of strife, people killing each other for ideals and ideas, and making the world a frightening place to live in!

The stern superior-looking man humiliated himself before the youth with the deep smile on his bruised face.

"Forget me," he said, "forget the strikers. Remember only that you've got something we all need. Not only your words, Michael, and your uncommon beauty, but I saw your spirit come over that crowd like an angel's wing."

Michael looked at him, knowing that even though he told the truth, he lied. He explained to Mr. Griswald that he would never preach any more, not in Hegemish or anywhere else.

The millionaire blurted out, in seeming sincerity:

"But your sermon, Michael—the sermon about the stones. Surely it can't hurt anybody if you preach that. It's true, Michael, it's so deeply true that it's haunted me every day since I heard it."

"You've got the biggest stone," said Michael. "Lay it down first."

"I can't," said Mr. Griswald, touching Michael's arm with trembling fingers. "Listen to me—please. I believe in you—just as those four freaks do. You can add me to them—the freak of a Rich Man who believes in God and His messenger. I swear on my soul, Michael, I believe the Truth of God is in you and there's some sort of divinity in your spirit. . . . Now listen, if you don't want to preach in the tent I've put up, well and good. But you've got to preach. You'll go somewhere else and preach."

"No," said Michael, "not here or anywhere again."

The steelmaker stared at him.

"You'll keep God's voice silent?" he said softly.

"Yes," said Michael, "God's truth is only one of the beautiful stones in the field we stand in. It is one of the heaviest and largest to pick up and it makes one of the most powerful weapons with which men kill each other."

Michael raised his head and stared at the carved wooden ceiling that stretched coffin-like over the handsome room. His bruised face and swollen eyes were full of passion. He spoke to God.

"I have a memory," he said, "of having heard somewhere that the Thought of Man is Your enemy, and that it has brought chaos into the world You created so well. I can see how true this is. I can see also what endless trouble this Thought must continue to bring into Your universe, where everything else is so serene and obedient. For this Thought is a smoke that cannot be chained. It will escape from the strongest dungeons of Your will. It will trickle out of the deepest disasters with which even You can smite it. And if with Your power You destroy not only Thought but its possessors, if You slay every human who walks the Earth, it will continue to coil and uncoil in the heads of dogs and birds, of simians and other forms that will continue to take Man's place in soil, water, and air. And if You destroy not only Man but his home, if You reduce to a funeral plume of dust the planet on which we live, our Thought will still hover in the particles that remain to darken the winds of space. It will not die.

"But if You want it otherwise, it is not I who will help You.

"For Your truth is of no use to men. I have no wish to preach it to them. As death puts an end to their lives, Your wisdom puts an end to their minds. And I have seen that it is not we who are Your enemies but You who are ours. For I have seen that those who have hated men the most and warred the most violently against their dreaming and thinking have been always such humans as have had a little of Your light in their souls.

"I have no wish to preach the wisdom You have given me," Michael said, and closed his eyes, "because I like better the fragment of wisdom, the shred of cunning, we have won for ourselves out of so much disaster. And because there is no reason for us to worship You, since You are interested only in our bodies and never in our souls.

"The bird at sunrise may sing to You," said Michael, "but we do not step into light and space when we leave our bed in the morning. We do not enter a universe perfectly made for us. We awake into a world created by our own Thought. Miseries and injustices dawn for us with each sunrise and no light floods our spirit as the day brightens. Our Thought has built for us only darkness and phantoms. But if You would have it otherwise, I will not help You.

"If I did what You have asked me to do," went on Michael more softly, "I would end perhaps as another of Your redeemers once ended—in agony on a Cross. And I would be remembered as a Son of God who had suffered and died a miserable human death in order to call men's attention to Your truth, Your glory, and Your mastery over Man.

"I am not afraid of being Your redeemer and of dying on a Cross. But in the world where I live Your Cross is a little one and to die on it is a little death.

"For if You want Crosses, look down, O God, not on any son but on man writhing atop the world, and hear his cries of pain going up without end. Look on him hanging a little space above the beast's lair, nailed to time by his philosophies and crowned by his thorny dreams.

"I do not understand the mystery of his suffering," said Michael after a pause, "or the goal of his Thought. But my heart leads me to his side in the darkness and I throw away the truth You have placed in me. I will never preach Your word or dream of You again. And if You would find me, come into the darkness where I live. And if You would see a Cross, come into that world beyond the bird song where Your enemy hangs."

Michael walked from the wood-paneled room, leaving the rich man for the moment paler because of the blasphemy he had heard. Outside he met his four friends. He said nothing to them. They rode to police headquarters. There he was shown the men who had beaten him into unconsciousness. Their faces were bruised almost as much as his own. One of them, under police beating, had confessed. But Michael lied to the police. He said his assailants were much taller and in no way resembled the three being held. After some discussion the police released the three men. Michael waited for them outside the station. Leaving his friends with instructions to meet him later, he walked with the three bruised faces.

The three sluggers looked suspiciously at their victim. Their swollen faces waited sullenly for some trick from this battered youth who again walked between two of them. Nothing was said until they had gone several blocks. Then one of the men muttered something.

"Here's where we get off," Michael heard him say.

"May I come inside with you?" asked Michael.

"Come along," the man said curtly.

Michael entered a saloon. Clusters of silent angry men stood at a long bar. They were the striking workers from the steel mills and, like all workers, looked ominous in their idle postures. The interior of the saloon was dim and smelled as if it were a cavern in the sour, wet earth. The workers looked at Michael. Despite the swollen face they recognized him as the man of God brought by their arch-enemy Griswald, to break their strike.

"Get out o' here," a voice spoke softly from the bar.

"What d'ye want in here, you punk?" another voice growled.

One of the sluggers answered for Michael.

"I don't know," he said, pausing at the bar, "he keeps folla-ing us."

"Slapped you around, eh?" A beer-drinker stared at the three.

"Yeah," said another of the sluggers, and then, with a look at Michael: "Not him. The cops."

The three ordered beer. Then one turned and suddenly seized Michael by both lapels and held him helpless with one hand as if he were going to punch him with the other.

"What do you want?" he demanded.

"I want to talk to you," said Michael. "I'm sorry they beat you."

The bar was silent. The angry workers sipped their mugs of beer.

"Cut out the Christ stuff," said the bruised slugger. "It don't go." He looked up and down the bar for corroboration and repeated loudly: "It don't go."

Michael nodded.

"I know," he said. "Could I have some beer?" he added to the bartender. He was served a glass mug of beer as the strikers stood watching him with their unwavering silence and anger.

Michael raised the mug.

"Here's to your strike," he said. "I hope you win."

He drank alone.

"What I wanted to say," said Michael, smiling, "is that God isn't on your side. That's one of the reasons I quit Him."

"Oh, you've quit Him?" sneered the slugger who had seized Michael by the lapels.

"Yes," he said and finished his beer. His face grew flushed.

"God doesn't know the difference between the poor and rich," Michael went on, "or between right and wrong or the good and the bad. He doesn't care about men's souls and the ideas in men's heads. I'm not preaching to you or anybody else again. But I wanted to tell you this. I want to tell you what He told me—that He hates you all."

Michael asked for another mug of beer. It was handed to him and he gulped it down. He felt happier when he looked at his listeners again.

"He wanted me to do something," said Michael.

"You mean God?" inquired one of the strikers suddenly.

"Yes," said Michael, "God."

"I see," said the striker and spat slowly and thoughtfully.

"He wanted me to do something," repeated Michael. "Not just beat your strike. But beat you. Everybody. Hand you all over to Him, like a boxful of bugs. The whole race. I didn't want to do that. That's why I quit."

Michael smiled dizzily at the blurred faces along the bar. They had moved toward him. Some of them were spitting and some were frowning violently. But Michael remained unaware of the wave of indignation he had stirred along the bar by his words. He turned to the three sluggers.

"You beat me up," he said softly to them, "but you were

really beating someone else. You were beating God. And you were doing right. That's why I lied to the police. Keep on beating Him."

Michael smiled again at all the frowning faces.

"I am not a Saviour," he said, "I'm a man. And I love men. I love you all."

Michael extended his unbroken left hand for the sluggers to shake. One of them took it and pulled him to the door.

"Outside," he whispered in Michael's ear, "before somebody starts pasting you again. You're drunk."

"Good-by," said Michael in the swinging door, and waved at the dim, odorous barroom. "Don't forget me. I'm your friend, Lucifer."

He laughed and was pushed into the street. Inside, the steel strikers stood silent and angry. The bartender, wiping the place where Michael had left his beer mugs, spoke.

"That's the yellowest preacher I ever heard," he said.

The sluggers ordered more beer. They were silent. They thought the preacher had gone mad from the blows they had given him.

Michael met his four friends. He talked to them for an hour, persuading them to go back to the circus. They finally agreed and all of them thought, like the sluggers, that the beating had driven Michael crazy.

Sitting together in the day coach of the train, the four friends were silent at first. Then Dr. Holmes removed some feathers from his pocket and began dropping them listlessly to the floor.

"Cut it out," said Philo, the Human Skeleton; "no use getting the conductor sore at us, now," he added practically.

"He threw us down," said Dr. Holmes, "a fine Saviour."

There was silence.

"Not very much like the former Saviour," Dr. Holmes resumed. "The former Saviour didn't take a runout powder."

Captain Achilles puckered his face.

"I wonder what he'll do about the Dove?" he piped. "That bird's gonna hand him a lot of trouble, whether he likes it or not."

The Giant Munso, hunched in his seat, sniffled and looked out of the window. Tears clouded his pale blue eyes.

"I got an idea," said Philo, "that the bird was an optical illusion."

"It was the Holy Ghost," shrilled the midget. "Let's be careful what we say about it."

"He sold us out," said Dr. Holmes, still dropping feathers. "He was scared, that's all."

"Who sold us out?" demanded Captain Achilles.

"Michael," said the India Rubber man.

"Oh, all right," said the midget with relief, "just don't say anything against the Dove. We don't want any wrecks on this train."

"I don't know," said Philo, slowly. "I keep wondering. His last words were there is a God but He's no good."

"That's not a new philosophy," said Dr. Holmes in a lofty tone.

"It's a shame," said Captain Achilles. "I would have stuck to him to the crucifixion."

The midget paused and then added in a frightened voice: "Maybe that was the crucifixion we seen."

There was silence as the train chattered on through the prairie. The Giant Munso wept with his face turned from his friends. Tears seemed to be coming out of his skin as well as his eyes.

"We ought to figure out what happened," the midget resumed. "We were the Four Apostles. And we ought to know what happened—in case somebody asks us."

"Nobody's going to ask us," Dr. Holmes muttered.

"You can't tell," said Philo.

"I say he was crucified," piped Captain Achilles.

"I take it you are speaking figuratively," said Dr. Holmes.

"Who crucified him?" demanded Philo.

"He did himself," cried the midget shrilly. "He crucified himself. I seen him! I seen him!"

Philo pushed the tiny man off his feet against the plush seat and spoke, ignoring the midget's exultation.

"He told me once," said Philo slowly, "he told me he had a feeling he was born in Heaven and brought to earth by that Dove."

"He told you that, eh?" Dr. Holmes snorted, and slapped his hands free of the last of his feathers. "Well, if I were you, I'd forget it."

"Why should he lie?" persisted Philo.

"Listen," said Dr. Holmes, "he lied to one of us. Because he told me his mother was a scrublady in New York. Now, I ask you, which of those two statements sounds like a lie? What did he tell you about where he was born, Captain?"

The midget jumped to his feet on the seat.

"He told me his father was a famous doctor worth millions of dollars," he piped.

Dr. Holmes snorted again.

"That's one of the troubles with religious-minded people," he said. "They always lie like hell."

"He sold out to the Devil," Captain Achilles piped, "and crucified himself for good measure. That's the long and short of it."

"Shut up," said Dr. Holmes. "I want to think this through."

The apostles sat in silence. The memory of Michael's battered face as they had looked on it the morning he was found in the ditch haunted them. And the thought came to them that they had not been the apostles of a messenger from God but the friends of a poor, weak boy. At length Philo spoke.

"I think the story is," he said, "that we all lost our heads. That's what people expect of freaks, anyway. So they'll forget it."

The Giant Munso continued to weep and sniffle as the train entered the night.

Michael's life after his last sermon contained only a single miracle and that was the miracle of his survival through the years of pain and misfortune that followed.

After he left Hegemish, Michael found work in a steel mill in South Chicago. Here he spent several years in the furnace rooms. His body, never powerful, grew gaunt and dry with the blasting heat of the furnace pits and crucibles.

In South Chicago, where he was unknown as an evangelist, he made a few friends, and this was a recompense for the day-dream that he had resolutely put away from him. Daily he moved only among these poor people, and what he saw filled and overfilled his heart with a great kindness and pity. It was this love that burned away the last shreds of the Angel Michael in him and that made him each day weaker and more human. In this love, all the powers he might have nursed as his heritage from Heaven disappeared.

Seven years of toil in the glare and burn of the furnace pits removed all of Michael's youth. He was turned into one of those gaunt hungry-eyed workers under whose strong muscles a per-petual weariness lies. This weariness finally dropped him exhausted out of the ranks of the laboring ones, like some over-used animal that had shed its vigor, and he wandered off. He moved through the snow, rain, and sun of the Middle West, helping out on farms and sleeping often in fields and under trees.

At times, lonely and hungry, he sat beside a dusty road and watched birds move in the summer sky, and wondered if the Dove would ever appear again. When he found himself looking eagerly at the birds he became shamefaced, and tried to keep certain thoughts out of his head. These thoughts were about his having been a Divine messenger and having heard God's voice. Although these things seemed to him still to have actually oc-curred, he began to attribute their seeming occurrence to some-thing wrong in his head. Remembering the Voice that had spoken to him, he would smile sheepishly. And if there were people around him he would smile at them quickly, hoping they would be unable to detect what he thought.

One day, after two years of wandering, Michael came on the circus he had known as a boy. It was a summer afternoon and the meadow was alive with the familiar sounds and movements of the toy world he had once known. He watched the people crowding the scalloped and minareted tent, their faces already happy with the promised wonders. He walked into the sideshow tent, wondering if his friends Philo, the Giant Munso, Dr. Holmes, and Captain Achilles would still be sitting on the plat-form. He saw a midget and an India Rubber man and a giant, but they were strangers. At first he was depressed. Then he felt relieved, for he would not have known what to say to the four freaks who had been his apostles—except that he had been a big-ger freak than any of them.

At night when the tents were being struck, Michael offered himself to the boss canvasman as an experienced hand. He was hired. Thereafter he worked in the circus as a razorback and traveled with it, as he had once done, from meadow to meadow. None of the few who had known him recognized him, for he had changed greatly from the tall glowing youth who had once brought God into their midst.

An hour of happiness came to Michael. He fell in love with one of the pretty girls who rode the horses. Her name was Josephine de Ballo. This young girl, walking at night with Michael and listening to the softness of his voice, and looking a great deal into his gentle eyes, fell in love with him—as she knew she should not have done. For, belonging to the lowliest of the circus personnel, he was no one for an aspiring young equestrienne to marry. Yet there was no resisting this sad and curious man who loved her, and who seemed as happy as a child at her side. And Josephine, who had always had an easy heart to give, gave it to Michael and overwhelmed him.

Some months later Michael's wife became pregnant and was forced to quit her work. She and Michael left the circus, and Michael, still happy, still full of gratitude for this hour of dream and sweetness that had finally come to him, grew ambitious. He found work as a waiter and kitchen helper in a country hotel. His child was born in an unpainted little wooden house on the edge of the village where he worked. It was a beautiful and healthy son. Michael's face grew smiling. He smiled on the world through the months that followed, and an endless spring-time was in his eyes. One day he brought his wife to the photographer's gallery in the hotel where he served and Josephine beamed over his son as he held them both in his arms and was photographed. This was the only gift Michael was able to give his wife, for there was hardly enough money for them to live on, and never any left over for gifts or pleasures. But it seemed to

Michael they needed none of these and that his wife and son were enough riches and entertainment for any man. Josephine talked sometimes of returning to the circus, but her figure had changed and idleness had taken away her girlhood ambitions. She continued to love Michael and her child, who was more beautiful than any infant she had ever seen pictured. This was truer than mothers' opinions usually are, for young Michael, as he took to walking and chattering, was as radiant as an angel. Unlike his father, whose hair was black, young Michael had blond clinging curls. He filled the days and nights with a marvelous excitement for his parents. For though she had given up her ambitions to become an equestrienne, Josephine grew very ambitious for her son. When he was two, she began training him to walk on his hands. He learned to tumble and to sit on a trapeze that Michael had rigged for him over the vegetable garden. Here he swung and yelled and tumbled, and Josephine watching him heard the far-away music of the circus she loved, and Michael dreamed of him growing up strong and agile and never having to feel the blast of the furnace pits or the humiliation of the waiter's apron.

Then tragedy struck the house in which the little family lived. When he was three, little Michael was run over while playing in the road. An automobile hit him. He was carried into the house by a policeman. He breathed for an hour, although his ribs were broken and his head crushed, and blood kept pouring from his mouth. Then he died, and Michael, who had come rushing home in his waiter's apron, wept. Josephine sat white and mute. She wept only when they lowered the little box containing her son into the ground. Here she remained kneeling, and tears shook her body. There was no comfort in Michael's arms. She raised her face to the chilly morning sky and began to pray wildly through her sobbing. She prayed to God to take her little

Michael in His arms, to see that he was happy and to preserve his soul forever.

Michael, her husband, looked at her in silence as she prayed. He tried to join her, but as he raised his head to the sky, a blankness came into his heart. Bewildered, he ran over the words of prayer he knew, looking for some he could utter. But he was unable to pray. Dim thoughts peered into his mind, and he grew confused. He fell forward on the fresh grave and buried his cheek in the newly turned earth and muttered the name of his son over and over into the ground.

Michael returned to his work as waiter and kitchen helper. His heart hung like a stone from his throat, but he smiled at the travelers around the dining-room tables and took their orders, and later washed the dishes they had emptied. There were a few who knew of his loss, and for a week or two were kind and softspoken with him. But after a short time they forgot and became unaware of the grief that hung in his throat. Soon no one knew his life was darkened, and he moved without the aid of human understanding through the painful days and nights.

But the tragedy had not ended for him. One day in the early spring when he came home from his work, he found the little wooden house empty. He waited till late at night for Josephine, thinking she had gone to visit somewhere. As the night deepened, Michael grew frightened and was going to run to the police, when he saw an envelope on Josephine's pillow. He opened it and read a letter she had written, saying she was going back to the circus and couldn't live with him any more because her heart was empty and their lives were too dull.

"Although I love you still," the letter read, "I can't stand to be buried alive like a nobody. It is driving me crazy, and when I look into the future, that drives me crazy too. You will be better off without me, in the long run. I will always remember you and little Michael and, oh, please forgive me. I can't help it. . . ."

Michael put the letter in his coat and it stayed there for several months. He read it two or three times a day as he continued to wait on tables and clean dishes, and again as he lay alone in the bed his wife had left. So deep was the pain he felt that he did not speak of it, even to himself. He felt as if something had been amputated from him, and he woke in the night crying. His tears wet the pillow on which his wife's head had lain, and when the darkness and the silence became unbearable he spoke her name softly, over and over. This would soothe him and he would fall asleep, as if her name, like a mother's hand, had taken the fright from his heart.

No curse ever came from Michael. His pain was as much for the pretty girl into whose life he had brought so much sorrow and trouble as for himself. He took to walking in the country roads at night, remembering their hours of sweetness together. His eyes stared at the star-brimming vaults over his head as he walked, and some of the heroic thoughts he had had as a boy returned to him. But he was diffident about thinking them, for they reminded him of matters too strange now and too dim to pursue.

One night Michael failed to turn back in his walking. He walked on into a field where he lay down and slept. And in the morning he was again a wanderer. From this morning on, luck seemed always against him, and his mind, inuring itself to misfortune, grew emptier and emptier of the Michaels he had been. Such jobs as he found he lost quickly, for the times had grown worse and the world of the workers appeared to be growing smaller, like the pond in which the ugly duckling swam.

At times, sitting around wood fires with other wanderers and looking into the night grown deep and large above him, Michael would remember some elation that had been his, and he would speak in turn to the disinherited ones around the little wood fires. But words were unable to unlock the hiding place into which Michael, his vision, and his youth had disappeared.

The New War came. This war, so long foreseen and so wildly babbled about by the terrified nation, swept up millions of men; cleaned, shaved, and dressed them in its insignia; and set them across the Pacific. Michael was among those who marched, drilled, and ended up lying in tropic trenches, cursing with fever and vermin, and heroically firing their guns and trotting bravely forward into death.

During this time no thought at all came to his head, but his heart surged with a desperate reawakening of the love he had felt long ago. His heart embraced his comrades as they lay cursing under the heavy blankets of sun, fever-ridden and with an incorrigible snarl and laugh for all that touched them—even death. They were of the same men he had known in the mills and in his wanderings, but here around him they no longer seemed the casual, drifting figures of those other days. They were men concentrated into a single mood. This mood was not of war or courage or anger against an enemy, but a simpler mood of manhood. They seemed, now that they lay fevered, cursing, and dying, to have for the first time become men, who had been only strangers and exiles before.

Michael was gassed in one of the attacks. A fire burned in his lungs and throat. He was carried into the trenches taken by his comrades. Later he was removed to a hospital. This time there were no bruises to be seen on him but inside, invisible, his organs were shattered with poison. He spewed and screamed through nights that lit and relit themselves like flames in his tissues.

But though he burned through months he was not consumed.

After a year he came out of a hospital in New York, pronounced cured, and for another year he crawled about the streets, a yellowed shrunken man clinging to the fringes of life. He slept in verminous beds, found food in charity wagons and on fly-covered saloon bars. But he was not consumed. Life trickled and then once more began to pulse hopefully in his maimed tissues. Michael resumed his wandering, working in factories, restaurants, and among cattle on farm lands. Wherever he went now, he heard the rumblings of deeds to come. The great and scattered body of labor was threatening to raise its fist.

When he was forty-two, Michael came back to New York, still spewing and coughing at night, but darkened by sun and wind. One evening, walking the city streets in the rain, he saw a familiar face. He stopped in the crowd, looked long at the face, and then followed it. It was painted but gaunt almost as his own and its eyes were ugly with a rim of charcoal. He came next to the face and said softly: "Josephine."

The face looked at him and its voice simpered: "Hello," and the charcoaled eyes smiled coyly.

"Come along, big boy," it said. "Let's get out of this damn rain."

"Josie," he whispered, "I'm Michael."

The face grew pale under its paint and Michael took the arm of the woman who had been his wife and walked on in the crowd with her.

"I got no place to take you," said Michael. "Where do you live?"

Josephine pointed to the west of the city.

The rain fell on the crowd in which they walked, and in the

wet twilight the city opened the huge umbrella of its lights.
They entered the house in which Josie said she lived, and she
whispered to him as they went in—as if it were a matter of great
importance: "My name ain't Josie in here. It's Belle. I had to
change it because they got two Josies already.

"We'll go upstairs," said Josie. "Maybe she won't see us."

"Who won't?" asked Michael, staring at her.

"Madam Hattie," said Josie, as she led him up a worn stairway. "I work here. It's a house, you know."

Michael nodded.

"She's pretty mean," said Josie, looking back at him and smiling with her mouth twitching.

In a dim lace-curtained bedroom that looked out on an alley,
Michael and the woman who had been his wife lay on the sagging white iron bed. Michael held the yellow curls against his
bosom. They reminded him in a hideous way of the little
Michael's head he had buried. Josephine tried to talk, and
Michael thought of questions to ask. But neither of them had
any words. They lay clinging to each other in their wet clothes.
The poison in Michael's tissues began to burn him. He coughed,
and Josephine begged him not to make any noise. After a long
silence, this woman, who had been so pretty and whom Michael
kept seeing in the photograph he had once had taken of him and
her and his son all beaming at one another, began to cry. As she
wept she made a heavy frightened sound that was like a wail,
half agonized and half idiotic.

Michael started coughing, and his coughing and Josephine's
wailing brought the dreaded Madam Hattie to the door. This
was a fat-shouldered creature with dulled black eyes. She stood
looking at the two figures clinging together on the bed and demanded to know what in hell was going on. Josephine sat up

and ended her wailing as quickly as if she had been only pretending her distress.

"He's an old friend," she began.

Madam Hattie interrupted viciously.

"If he ain't got any money he gets out," she said. "We ain't running no charity institution."

Michael would have argued, but a man with even fatter shoulders and duller eyes than Madam Hattie's appeared behind her. Josie whispered to him quickly to go away. Michael tried to take her in his arms again. But she jumped from him and stood screaming harshly for him to get out. Curses and foul words came from her twitching mouth.

Michael returned to the rain, but he was changed. He looked at the crowded street with rage in his heart. He was not angry at the faces he saw or at the eyes that looked curiously at his blazing expression as they passed. But at something else, something much littler and yet looming behind the crowd—at a Thought, an Idea, a Scheme, which seemed to him suddenly hideous. He walked slowly, and the towers that lined the streets became to him caverns in which a monster lurked. Although he had known misfortune and injustice all his life, he had never cried back at them before. Now the years of misery and the memories of his pain all seemed to explode in his soul.

He felt the face of the painted street woman, who had once been so sweet, wailing against his broken and poisoned bosom. And her wail and his own pain rose in him like a battle cry. He looked up desperately at the monster he had seen in the gleaming towers of the city. Why should this monster, coiling like a lighted dragon over the heads of the crowd, remain unchallenged? There was another monster in his heart and in the hearts of those like him—the monster of pain, dark and hidden.

Michael's heart opened and this long cowering beast emerged.

From this hour Michael became one of those who met secretly in halls, basements, and barns; who plotted and organized and inflamed one another with angry and prophetic words. He was never among the leaders but among those who listened and followed. But his set face, his wild smile, his curious concentration, as if he himself were a bullet aimed at that monster in the towers, won him a little place in the Revolution. He commanded a group of men when the first barricades went up. Again he lay under clouds of gas and the whine of shell, and again he fought. Desperate and heroic men fought beside him. Towers were tumbled, streets blasted, and fires lighted in many proud sectors of the Republic. For a year the Revolution ripped at the fabric of a society grown hateful and too painful to those who lay at its bottom. Driven from town to town by superior armies, Michael's cause stumbled into disaster. It went down, blasted by too many guns, and those who survived its last defeat were hunted.

Michael had not believed, despite all he had seen, that men could be so cruel as were these who came now in pursuit of his scattered comrades. Gone were the easy-spoken rulers of the democracy, and in their place angry and implacable minds scurried like hounds through the nation, leaping at the throat of every contradiction and every lingering hope. Michael, who had dreamed to make the world a better place, found himself unforgiven for his dream. He hid himself, and hid what was harder to hide, the very color and smell of his mind, from these hounds. And again, despite the poison still burning in his tissues and the despair emptying his heart of all hope, he survived.

He resumed his life of wandering, finding small tasks that kept him fed. He was now nearing fifty, and no longer tall or straight. His body was bent, his hair whitened. He coughed at night and felt his tissues grow weaker with the fire that never quitted them. He became silent, and for a few years longer kept himself alive with the aid of the government that had risen triumphantly over the barricades. This government was proud to take care of its citizens, and when citizen Michael, shuffling wearily from street to street, was called to its attention, it provided him with employment. He was given a flashlight, a stool to sit on, and a large empty warehouse to watch each night.

Now there was no more left of Michael than of a machine long dismantled, rusted, and discarded. Yet as he sat on his night watchman's stool, his flashlight on his withered thighs, there was one thing still Michael that remained and that had never changed. This was the look old Sarah had left him as a heritage.

Though his mind had long ago grown clumsy with disuse and disease, and what had once been the remainder of his wisdom had become as tattered as his clothes, this look of tenderness remained fixed as a star in his eyes. His eyes had always smiled on other eyes, and when Michael had lost the words with which to speak their meaning, they had spoken in their smile, saying always, life is sweet somewhere in the dark.

Toward the last of his life, his bad health almost entirely dimmed his perceptions and there came to his wrinkled face the same half-crazed smile Sarah had turned on him in his childhood. He came to work with the night, holding a flashlight in his hand. Coughing, he made the rounds of the empty warehouse, sending his light into its unoccupied shadows, and returned to sit on his stool in the doorway. Sometimes men older but no more battered than himself would join him and talk. Listening to them relate their tales of misfortune, and recite their own little tattered hopes for tomorow, Michael would smile at them and feel a warmth in his tired body. Though he no longer knew himself, he still knew life; and the less he became, the deeper grew the warmth of his heart in which he rested.

In the third year of his employment by the government of hounds, Michael caught a cold. He continued, however, walking through the shadows of the empty warehouse, fearful of losing his job if he stayed away. One night he collapsed. He was found in the morning lying on the floor, fevered and too weak to move. As he lay on the hard boards he remembered fists that had once battered him, gas and bullets and hungers that had continued this battering, and he sighed for fear this heat now in his head would be the last blow. He desired to live. When he was taken to the crowded ward of the city's largest hospital, where others like himself lay spent and fevered, he still desired to live.

On a bed surrounded by men moaning with pain and crying in delirium lay Michael, who had once been an Angel and who had been sent by God to redeem the world. He lay with his face shrunken, and whimpered in his fever like a little dog run over and left in the middle of the road.

His fever increased, and the interne who made the rounds of the hospital wards reported that the patient in Bed 9 would die in a day or so. This report occasioned no stir in the hospital. There was no little group of relatives pacing and chattering at the end of the corridor and waiting for the dreaded news. There were no friends to hear it over the telephone. The nurses passed with a perfunctory look at the chart that hung on Bed 9, and on which every two hours the thermometer and pulse readings appeared like the nearing footsteps of death.

Michael, unknown and unmourned, lay dying in the epidemic

ward of this overcrowded hospital. Nurse, interne, doctor, and orderly who looked casually at him saw no more than an old man with a bad medical history, as Michael's gas-shattered tissues and the many years of malnutrition were called; an old man such as must always be dying some time. They noticed the fear of death in his eyes, and the night nurse, who despite her youth was used to this look, wondered as she always did when she saw it, why people so shattered and friendless should be so frightened to die. What was there that could be worse than the darkness of their lives, thought this young nurse, and why did they want to hang on to nothing? It was true, they sometimes sighed when Death came, as if they realized in their last minutes the mistake they had made by living and desiring to live. And probably this white-haired old man, whimpering in his fever, would also sigh when his only remaining friend appeared.

The night nurse smoothed the pillows under Michael's burning head and looked over at the other beds in the ward. How alike they all were, she thought, all these half-dead brought in from the streets. Here in the ward their empty lives more than their disease made a circle around their beds, and they lay exposed in their loneliness—as unvisited as fish pulled out of some far-away sea. She wondered, as she marked another footstep on the chart, how long it would be before she would have to remake this bed. Then she straightened and listened calmly for a moment to the whimpering and moaning in the dimly lighted ward. It was like standing in a graveyard, she thought, listening to the dead going home.

The night nurse walked slowly out of the ward and closed the door on these little last sounds of life, and Michael, who lay near a window, continued his dying, as nameless and unattended as the grave into which he would soon disappear.

But there were eyes that watched. God looked through the window and searched for the Angel Michael whom He had loved. At His side were the two who had taken Michael's place —the Angels Malliol and Azriel.

"He is in here," said God, holding the epidemic ward of the hospital before their eyes, "but which of them is he? Their voices are all the same and their faces are like brothers', and they are without names."

The Angel Malliol pointed to one who tossed unshaven on a pillow.

"No," said God, "there will be something in his eyes by which to recognize him." Then He added softly: "There he is by the window."

The Angels Malliol and Azriel looked at a battered face with whitened hair.

"The one who has become silent?" asked Malliol.

"Yes," said God, "he is Michael."

"He is dead," whispered the Angel Azriel.

"No," said God, "he is listening to his brothers moaning. Look how tender his eyes are. There is a dream in his head. He hears someone laughing. An old woman's laughter is in his ears. And he sees her. He imagines she is in the room and he watches her move on her hands and knees from bed to bed."

"What is she doing?" asked the Angel Malliol.

"Scrubbing," said God. "She scrubs the floor and Michael watches her."

God was silent.

"He dies looking at her," He spoke at length, "he dies without asking for Me. Michael, Michael, turn your eyes to Me."

"He keeps smiling," said the Angel Malliol softly.

"Because he dreams," said God. And suddenly a great compassion came into His voice.

"He dies as My enemy," God spoke, "smiling and unregenerate. Look at him who was once so radiant. Now shrunken and miserable, discarded and unknown. All the terrors of life have burned in his soul. All the pain of unreason and injustice has ached in his heart. He has feasted only on defeat. Wounds and sorrow have tormented him. And now he lies among faces like his own. He whom I sent as a Redeemer dies as the lowliest and most forgotten of men. No eyes weep for him. No songs will be born for him. He will be buried and he will vanish and there will be none to speak his name and none will know that he was one apart and that My Truth was in him.

"Yes," said God, "he failed Me. He betrayed Me and blasphemed against Me. Yet My heart softens. For hidden in his blasphemy there are love and courage. Look how his eyes refuse to lift to Me but continue to smile on the world. Look how this man tormented and crucified by life still turns to it with love.

"O suffering one," said God softly, "for whom do you suffer? What gain is there in your agony? My Angel, once so wise, where is your wisdom?"

"He moans again," said the Angel Azriel.

Tears clouded the eyes of the Angel Malliol.

"I loved him," he said.

"I too," said God.

There was a pause, and then God spoke so sadly that a mist filled the hearts of the Angels.

"I remember," said God, "the hour of his betrayal when he threw away the truth I had placed in him and ceased to be My Son. And bade Me, if I wanted to see him again, come look for him in the darkness, hanging on a Cross as My enemy. There is that darkness, there that Cross, and there he hangs. My light is nowhere round him. And yet something dim glows about his head. It is the light of humanity."

"I can see no light," whispered the Angel Azriel.

"Nor I," said Malliol, looking eagerly.

"It is too feeble for your eyes," said God. And His own eyes wandered from Michael.

"Look," He went on, "this light is everywhere over the earth. A wretched little glitter such as hovers on Michael's head. Look, above the blaspheming of Me and tormenting of one another, this sad little light is everywhere."

"He once spoke of their souls," said the Angel Malliol.

"How long, Michael," God said softly, "how long, little man who has forsaken Me, how long will you stay on your Cross?"

God was silent.

"A long time," He said then more softly, "even as we reckon time. Ah, Michael, there is none who watches you but Me, and none to weep over you but the Angels. And you have not lived as I ordered or died as I desired. And none in the world is the better for your living or the wiser for your dying. None in the world.

"But I, Michael, hear a prayer and see a light, and I turn to all those on the Cross beside you, to all those who have left Me. I speak to you a last time out of My love. Michael, I have seen your Cross in the darkness. Michael, I shall watch that never-empty cross you have shown Me. I shall listen without anger to the blasphemies that rise from it. And I shall wait for a face to glow in the darkness.

"Only now, Michael, remember Me once, for I too am part of the wisdom you sought. I am a little part of Chaos. Michael, hear Me, you have not died in vain."

In the dimly lighted ward, the burning head of Michael heard a sound. His eyes turned to the window, and on the ledge outside he saw a white Dove. A faint gurgle came from its throat. He stared bewilderedly. As the Dove cooed, words came into his head, familiar and far away. He could not distinguish them. His fever converted them into echoes and caused them to sound as vague as music. But he kept staring at the white Dove outside the window whose whiteness seemed to fill the night. He smiled at the little throat ballooning with its curious gurgle of greeting and lamentation.

"Little Dove," said Michael, "it is cold outside."

Then he closed his eyes and died.

THE HEAVENLY
CHOIR

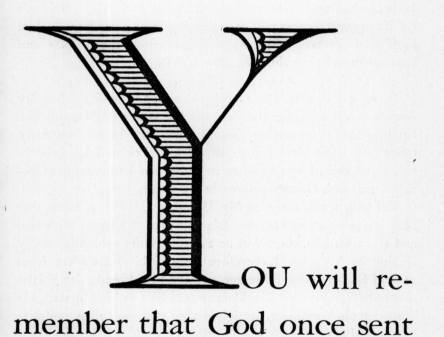

YOU will re-
member that God once sent

a flood to remedy certain matters He found distasteful in the world. I have here the account of another such Miracle. And if you have, mysteriously, heard nothing about it to date, I am sure this will in no way interfere with your believing it. It is as easy to believe in Miracles that haven't happened as it is to believe in Miracles that have. Only the most quibbling would dispute this.

But you will have to be patient and allow me a Prologue. Since the Miracle is to destroy a sector of civilization which you possibly, at this very moment, admire, it will be to your advantage to attend my preliminary cat calls, however involved-seeming or divergent. They may woo you from certain unthinking Loyalties and Admirations and kindle in you a bilious eye for these very matters you consider, heedlessly, so pleasant. And such new aversion will enable you to enjoy the Miracle and applaud rather than shudder at its havoc.

There is a certain Mr. George Woodyard who catches my attention as I assemble the data for this disaster. I behold him hanging by his suspenders from a chandelier in his impressive office, the suspenders being around his neck and he as wry-faced and out of wind as any highwayman I saw pendent beneath the Cook County gallows in my youth.

As I look at this dangling Mr. Woodyard, it occurs to me that here is a proper hero for my tale and that, if I begin with him and end with him, there will be a certain unity which is usually lacking in Miracles. I therefore remove his suspenders from around his bruised and sausage-stretched neck and with a false comradely slap on his shoulders restore him to his Heyday. He blinks at me a moment, straightens his vest, and then smiles as gently and reassuringly as if his presence were a Cathedral, likely to overwhelm any stray worshiper. Whereon he returns to his desk, slowly, as if he were approaching another Mr. Woodyard almost as remarkable as himself. It is obvious that he has forgotten the grisly matters that took him to the chandelier, for he sits himself down with air-cushion pomp; he regards sternly the Documents, Calendars, Inkstands, Push-Buttons, and Photographs on his desk as if he were reviewing a battalion of heroes passing in salute; and he then looks up at me and inquires with a sort of modest good-fairy humor:

"And what can I do for you, sir?"

This is a silly and even pathetic question, for it is I who intend to Do for Mr. Woodyard—and without further delay.

Mr. George Woodyard's kith and kin regarded him, very likely, as a Human Being—that is, as a Citizen full of distinctive appetites and odd little habits. They most probably saw in him constant, if minor, evidences of that caprice and illogic that convince one School of Psychologists that Man is a product of some Inner Deterministic Creation—a Blossom painted on Nature by a spirit brush. It is an old contention that the Breath of God blowing from the inside molds the human soul, and not the breath of platitude blowing from the outside. The truth lies, I suppose, with God, but I, for one, have an open mind in the matter.

I must insist, however, that as far as I could see there was no Inner Man to Mr. Woodyard. He was put together by contemporary winds like a sort of jigsaw puzzle blown together, and very inaccurately. His mind, his soul, his dreams, were made out of little vari-colored pieces of cliché and current bombast and slightly larger pieces of sky-blue Space. The whole thing didn't fit at all, though it was immediately recognizable as the Picture of a Leading Citizen.

Leading citizens have been immemorially, I am sure, like Mr. Woodyard. Nevertheless, they are difficult to describe. For how describe people who seem always on the side of Error and Bigotry when you look back at them, and on the side of the angels when you shake hands with them? It can't be that they are all villains. I prefer to think that they are the Cautious Ones, the Slow Ones, who make more money than sense, and who delay the world while they wring a last dollar out of its Yesterday.

Factually, Mr. Woodyard was the president of the Woodyard Advertising and Radio Service Company. This was an organization that spent some fifteen million dollars a year in pollination work for a score of Toothpastes, Automobiles, Laxatives, Tobacco Products, Beautifying Creams, and certain Life-Giving Cereals. I shall go into this more fully later.

Enough for now that the Woodyard agency was one of the largest and shrillest of the Pied Pipers in the land. Mr. Woodyard, under whose baton its varied choir of salesmanship assailed the earth and the skies, was in his fifties. He had a square jaw and bushy eyebrows, seemingly borrowed from an illustration for the *Art of Ruling Men;* pale Sunday School superintendent eyes, narrow shoulders, and a large pear-shaped paunch. His long legs tapered like a Brownie's into childish calves and small feet. He had warm, soft hands and artistic nails. His mouth was wide, his lips thin, his cheeks loose, and some wattles hung, statesman-fashion, from his chin.

He covered this fat-padded, old-womanish body with perfect tailoring, a little on the archaic side. His linen was starched. Gold-studded detachable cuffs protruded from his pressed sleeves, hinting of an elegant but cautious soul. He wore a stiff detachable collar and his ties never ventured beyond maroon.

But more than by these impeccable draperies, Mr. Woodyard was clothed in an aura of Right Thoughts.

Success had robbed Mr. Woodyard while he was still in his teens of whatever intelligence or Inner Man he might have possessed. Like all weak men who find themselves in positions of leadership, particularly in the leadership of Finance, which rolls its captains out like dice from its wantonly rattling box, Mr. Woodyard had one definite mental characteristic. He was opposed to Thought. Since no thinking had landed him on the throne he occupied, it was natural that he regard cogitation as an alien, dangerous factor.

However, Mr. Woodyard was not opposed to what he called "understanding people's needs." In serving the People—as all Rich Men piling up their dividends insist they are doing—Mr. Woodyard was never tired of saying, at banquets and board meetings, that you must give the People what they want and what is good for them.

What Mr. Woodyard meant, in a coarser manner, was that the easiest way for a peddler to get rich was to carry only a Line of Necessities. But this was no explanation of Mr. Woodyard's success at all. He carried no Necessities. He had nothing to sell that the Public needed and little of what was good for people. Although he talked like one, Mr. Woodyard was no honest peddler knocking on lonely farmhouse doors with packages of pins, thimbles, and beeswax. And when he pretended he was, he wasn't really trying to deceive, but merely being part of a pretense larger than himself and as beyond his talents to question as the Laws of Matter. This is, in fact, the secret of the non-Inner Man and his villainy. Having no contradictory vision of any sort, he has no need for pretending. The hypocrisies of his day, which he finds plastered on his tongue like circus posters on a fence, are for him the Truth. Success speaks out of him, glibly and innocently, like a Prince of Barnums. The great significance of Mr. Woodyard lay in that he was no peddler at all, though his entire dream of life was concentrated in salesmanship. He was a sort of mystic evolution of a peddler or, rather, a peddler's aide. Since the Peddler, whom I will now put in capital letters by way of promotion, had taken to selling things that were no longer necessary to the world and to hawking nuances rather than commodities; since he had burdened his pack with more gewgaws and gadgets than there were customers, more utilities than there were users, and more panaceas than there were ills, he had found it necessary to create an Assistant, even in the Pre-Radio Era. The duties of this Aide were simply to invent desires in the human soul, hitherto absent, and to inflame it with greeds hitherto dormant.

Abetted by brigades of Circes and Psychologists, Mr. Woodyard and his fellow-Aides had remodeled a generation. Theirs was a task to the horrid nature of which everyone closed his eyes, since in the emptying of the Peddler's pack, by fair means or foul, was said to lie the rainbow's end of prosperity for all. Unchallenged even by the most carping of sages, these Aides went about their work of palming off the over-enterprise of an economic system whose trimmings had outstripped its necessities.

Under cover of Art and Poetry and the great Democratic Credo that every man had a right to blow and market as many soap bubbles as he desired, the hawking of superfluities became the soul of the nation. Nobody attacked our Peddler's Aide. Even the Anarchists, who needed an advertisement or two to keep their Red Sentinels going, ignored him. Where find an editorial egg to throw at the golden goose who was apparently laying them for all? Unheckled, this drum-beating, fife-tooting, tambourine-banging, and whirling dervish of an Aide, leaping about with a million tin cans tied to his tail, devoted himself to reshaping the human innards.

I shall attempt no orderly survey of Mr. Woodyard's work, but touch briefly on some of his more obvious wiles and conquests. A cigarette habit, to begin somewhere, according to some doctors a habit almost as injurious as dope addiction, had been injected into the national consciousness by an appeal to the bounderism of the masses. Cigarettes had been revealed on a million walls and billboards as being the diversion of exquisite gentlemen, presumably young and old Dukes, lolling about on Yachts or attending the most exclusive of Social Events. And the opportunity to improve their own social status by aping the vices of their betters at the cost of a few pennies had proved irresistible to the masses. They took to smoking like mad, fancying themselves with their cigarette holders and snapping cigarette cases and mysterious preferences for this cigarette over that cigarette as part of a very dashing world.

Later, with the cigarette well launched and half the nation suffering from dry throats and jittery fingers and on the verge of realizing the cause of its troubles, a secondary compaign had been rushed into the field. Marvels of male and female athletic prowess, huntsmen, parachute jumpers, wrestling champions, lion tamers, racing drivers, and tight-rope walkers had been revealed as grateful devotees of nicotine who owed their steady nerves to the chronic use of the weed, and the tobacco industry had been saved from threatened collapse.

Other inflammatory psychological campaigns had been placed behind Automobiles, Washing Machines, Bathing Suits, Oil Heaters, Wrinkle Removers, and nearly all the rest of the con-

tent of the Peddler's pack. Bawdy wenches with breath-taking
contours postured for attention from billboard and printed page,
with deodorants, laxatives, and hair restorers in their hands—for
the Peddler's Aide had discovered Sex. Whereupon, in addition
to the bamboozling implication that he would share in the glories
of his Superiors if he bought certain brands of Underpants,
Whiskies, Shoes, Canned Soups, or Mattresses, the market Bo-
Peep known as the Consumer found himself the butt of such a
phantom attack on his libido as might have signaled the rebirth
of Sodom instead of the mere rise of Mr. Woodyard.

Bacchantes gamboled now on the billboards in juicy and provoking poses; glistening stockings drawn over Fragonard legs,
eager mouths moist and red and apparently hissing with passion,
bosoms bulging with concupiscence and eyes lurid with lechery
battered away at the sales resistance of the masses. The Psychologists had discovered not only Sex but one of its most pathetically fraudulent uses. Unable to embrace the superb strumpet
offering a new Sedan, a Kitchen Stove, or a Bottle of Pop, the
Consumer's libido—always a blind force in human history—was
very likely to embrace the objects themselves.

This salesmanship worked in another way but even more effectively on the women than on the men. To women it had the
deeper appeal of sympathetic magic. The plainest of housewives
was inclined to feel she partook a little of the seductiveness of
the lovely nymphs whose stockings and bloomers she wore and
whose deodorants and laxatives she used.

But this cunning business of selling not to the needs but to
the bounderisms, libidos, inferiority complexes, etc., etc., of the
simple-minded Consumer was only part of the shambles. Over
and beyond all these odoriferous ruses to set a public whinnying
for wares it did not want was the main drive of reiteration.

Although he was willing to experiment with clever lures and psychotechnic baits, the Peddler's Aide knew (as all great forces for the confusion and belittlement of mankind appear instinctively to know) that success lay less in the exercise of his wits than in the basic ninnyism of his victim. Accordingly he let loose a propaganda of signs, layouts, panegyrics, and beacons, the only purpose of which was to beat with some sort of hypnotic rhythm on the always available eye.

The process of wigwagging the public and shooing it like a brood of hens to a thousand and one bargain-counter corn cribs gave the land a false literary glow. Newspapers and magazines multiplied fantastically under the largess of the Peddler's Aide, to whom all periodicals became pretty carts carrying his pigs to market. As a result the Republic wore a rash of printed matter that would have looked like a Belles-Lettres Renaissance if it hadn't looked so much and so transparently like the drool-and-dribble partner of a sales campaign.

By this monstrous coaxing the Peddler's Aide succeeded in perverting the buyer into a giddy spendthrift. A restlessness overtook his pocketbook and an echo of this restlessness filled his soul. His fancies, lashed by Duchesses and Bacchantes, began to poke feverishly at the Peddler's pack. Be-advertised into a state of economic somnambulism, he bought where he needed nothing. And then, obedient fellow, he bought duplicates of what he needed not at all. And then he bought improvements on these superfluous duplicates. And then he developed a whole set of extra and exotic appetites and nibbled delicately away on every newfangled product, with not hunger but a hawker in his stomach.

As he had been hornswoggled into the cigarette habit, he was decoyed and nose-ringed into the automobile habit, into the gadget and thingumabob habit; into the redecorating his home with daffier and more strawberry-box grandeurs habit; into the medicating himself like a chronic scurvy victim habit. He was tobogganed into the new hats, new shoes, new pants, new dresses, and new buttons for every change of weather habit; into lotions, creams, shaving, muscle-building, dieting, fattening, hair-restoring, flavored-slop drinking and chewing gum habits and other habits too vague and too pervasive to catalogue. He bought not to have but to have the right thing, which was constantly being changed by the savants, scientists, and seers a-toil in the Peddler's backyard; not to possess but to be in style.

And though at first our Consumer had been a resisting victim of the sorceries loosed by the Peddler's Aide, he became now, together with his wife, who is always ninety percent of the American picture, a creature of fretful and wry-brained acquisitiveness. He blossomed as a sort of dumping ground and he wriggled proudly and patriotically under the accumulating hill of his gaudy refuse.

It was only by developing this stunned and capricious Customer that the Peddler's system based on the overstuffing of his pack could continue. And continue it did. But there was no joy in the Peddler's camp. There were, instead, doubt and apprehension and a group of Handwriting on the Wall experts. The Peddler and his backers became alarmed. It became apparent—and not only to malicious and unpatriotic eyes—that a system whose outlets depended on a perversion of human instincts was likely to lose its shirt, its pants, and its Stock Exchange.

Thus it was decided even among the Manna Makers that something would have to be done. Since it was inconceivable to the Peddler that anything so subversive and unhuman as a curtailing of his pack be attempted by way of remedy (such tactics led straight to Bolshevism, Cannibalism, and the Antichrist), there was only one other road open. This was to inflame, confuse, and behowl the already reeling Consumer into a more staggering materialism and connoisseurship.

And, lo, the new road was revealed to them quite as if God were a Stockholder. The Radio, blooming overnight like the dragon-teeth-sown army of the Mongols, offered its hydra tongue to the worrited Peddler.

Among the first to discover this new road to riches was Mr. Woodyard of the pink face and yet unsilvered hair. But, like so many who later became Radio Kings, Mr. Woodyard did not so much discover his Kingdom as find himself seated in its midst with no knowledge that it was a Kingdom or even a Duchy.

Mr. Woodyard was at the time in the Advertising business and busy as a flea on a cow's tail plastering the land with pornographia and proverbs in behalf of the Peddler's pack. He was, presently, of the opinion that radio was a silly medium for his Service and that money spent hollering at people over the air to buy things was futile and undignified. Would that he had been right.

It is usually the way with men who gibber-jabber of Vision and Progress that they are devoid of any instinct for either and that if you left the world in their hands it would still be flat and full of icebergs. Not that, as you will discover in detail very soon, I consider the radio the measure of any movement forward of anything. To the contrary, I greeted it in its crackling infancy and held it to its dramatic death as the ugliest of the inventions by which man had managed to bedevil and corrupt himself. This hydra-headed megaphone attached to man's greed, his vulgarity, and his infatuation for error had in my opinion already howled half the Arts out of existence as well as belittled the very source of wisdom—the human word—before God smote it. But more, much more of this later, for my tale, when I am finished with this drum-rolling and get to it, concerns itself with the Miracle that squelched forever this newly hatched brother of Bedlam.

Mr. Woodyard quickly altered his views, proving that the simpler the parasite, the more nimble he is at changing his spots. He became a Pioneer. He began to build up Radio Advertising. It would have been impossible, in the year 1923, to have imagined that the Peddler's Aide had only scratched the surface. He was already scribbling away with smoke in the sky, hanging bargain banners from balloons and dollar signs from flagstaffs. He had already plastered all the available fields, fences, walls, and rooftops with his visual tom-toms, and he already owned, spiritually at least, nine-tenths of our publications. (For the Consumer's stubborn inability to read only Advertising Matter still made necessary a sugar coating of magazine literature.) What other fields, indeed! we might have scoffed.

We had reckoned without physiology. Nothing more was possible for the Eye, but the Ear was virginal. The great American Ear, heretofore the property chiefly of snake-oil doctors and can-can spielers, was promoted to a place in big business. And what had seemed to such sensitive fellows as myself the last vulture cry in greed-propaganda seemed now to have been no more than a mannerly bit of buttonholing. The Peddler's Aide, howling up and down the air waves, became loathsome where before he had been merely objectionable.

The reason for the difference was this. There is a chastity to print that even greed does not dare bespatter too much. The written word grown hysterical loses its meaning, and to whatever idiotic enterprise or bargain it seeks to lure one, it must retain not only its grammar, but also some sign of dignity. The spoken word has no such handicap. It does not exist, aloofly, within its own content. It is not merely a symbol. Behind it the speaker can moan, gurgle, rumble with passion, sough with righteousness, and play the whole shameless orchestra of human emotion.

Mr. Woodyard was among those early Radio entrepreneurs to invest in vocal mountebanks to cry his clients' wares. He bought orators, elocutionists, and spielbinders to carry the message of his client's Good Will to All into the American ear. Venal and sonorous charlatans proceeded to invade the bedrooms, living-rooms, and other hideaways of the Consumer. They dumped their gewgaws on his bed, spread them on his dinner table, and pumped away at his poor little money bags with a suction that was irresistible.

There was immediately a major boom in panaceas, those investments most dear to the addle-headed. The Peddler discovered it was much easier to frighten the Consumer vocally into believing himself a vat of horrid odors, a creature endangered by a thousand decrepitudes, than it had been to convince him of these things in print. Where print, usually in shamefaced agate type, had been used to inform the victim of his wretched status—muttering pimp-fashion out of the corners of newspapers about all manner of magic salves and purges—now there came into his ear no mutter at all, but tones as firm and holy as any ever heard in the Vatican. Print is always print, but the voice can sound like Galileo that has only a truss to sell and echo like Pasteur that has no more than an itching powder to peddle.

Every box of cheese, bit of fabric, bite of food; every lotion, vehicle, toothpaste, cigarette, liver poker, colon swabber, electrical doodad, screw-on appliance and screw-off appliance—all the contents of our Peddler's bulging pack now augmented by a world of new fiddle-faddle discoveries—became forthwith the Heroes of Hymns. Cardinals (seemingly) intoned the vitamin wonders of cabbages. George Washingtons lent to hitherto humble hair-restorers a dignity of utterance unknown outside the pages of history. Sindbads panted of diamond valleys lurking in every neighborhood store and Ciceros declaimed the triumphs of stink-removers. There was turned loose such a quiver-quaver of piety tones, brotherly love tones, straight from the shoulder tones, America for Americans tones; such a throbbing of cello calls and swooning love cries, that one would have expected the entire nation to fall victim to a mass attack of *mal de mer*.

But the wheedling and bombastic voices fell on the Consumer's ear and sent him spinning to the markets. And as these nauseating histrionics began to lose somewhat their power, the Peddler whistled for his dancing girls. And now came a renaissance of entertainment—an irruption of jesters, yodelers, banjo players, thespian bawlers, and star gazers. A thousand gullets poured revelry hourly into the Home and a thousand orchestras all going at once in various glass-enclosed chambers bombarded and enfiladed, sniped and barraged at the Consumer's castle.

Parnassus was wheeled to the microphone and the apoplectic hawkers found themselves augmented by Beethoven, Brahms, and Orpheus himself—and what an Orpheus!—by braying bands with their machine-gun rhythms; by Stars of Screen and Stage knee-deep in goo; by Philosophers whose quivering tongues seemed more to lick than to speak; by pun pluggers, wit sockers, hilarity uhlans; by skits and sketches and comic-strip dramas out of the largest swill barrel ever to emerge from the alleys of Art;

and chiefly, and to a point of Walpurgian horror, by ballad sadists and aria flayers enough to strangle the whole of song.

And all this free fun and melody released by the Peddler, become suddenly a Cuckoo-Clock Maecenas, yielded wondrous dividends. For it was a simple psychology, as apparent as flies in a milk pot, which the Peddler's Aide had discovered or had wished on him. He would sell his wares by appealing to the gratitude of his victim. There being no other reason to buy a toothpaste, Mr. and Mrs. America would buy it because it had made them laugh, rendered their home a cave of echoes, or reminded them of their mother.

This abrupt raid on the Arts had effects other than the emptying of the Consumer's pockets. What it emptied most amazingly was the Arts themselves. The eclectic music of the world, long preserved for the high ornamentation of human mood and long but sparingly used as a ladle for stirring the soul of man, came pouring now out of several million cuckoo clocks, preceded and followed by voices chanting the virtues of Headache Remedies and Corn Plasters. And where we had once listened to the Great Composers in the hush of auditoriums, our very souls attuned to the mystic language of notes, we heard them now with ears only. They cackled like geese out of the Peddler's pond who had once sung like cherubim out of Heaven. Their nobilities grew less with the lessening of our moods as audience. And though it was Genius that still played beside the Peddler's pack, it was eventually only Simple Simon who listened.

For a time the Peddler's Aide covered himself with bay leaves. He was hailed as an Evangel by those sages who see in the democratization of anything, whether it be Bach or the Bastille, a step forward. He was, it was eagerly stated by authorities who should have known better, colonizing the Ivory Towers. He was bringing about, they decided, the long-awaited liaison between Beauty and the Beast. Not alone for the few would the loveliness of great music exist, but for the All. Well, this is a fine theory, but like most Samaritan-hatched ideologies, it exploded in the face of its theorists. It was not the Beast that underwent any marked alterations, but, as always, Beauty. For Beauty lying down with the Beast too often grows a bit cockeyed and contemptible herself. And though she still hummed and fiddled for us her homeland songs, we knew her for an exile from that homeland. She had lost her power over us. It was in this way that the Peddler's Aide gutted the art of music.

There were other as morbid results. The manufacture of tunes was speeded up beyond the penny-whistle talents of the tunesmiths. Ballads crowded on ballads until not garden larks but magpies sang. A boiler-factory jamboree of jingle and heartbreak assailed our ears, such a pother of yearnings and bedroom-frustrations that we soon stopped learning and remembering songs.

And finally, in this desperate feeding of our glutted senses, the cuckoo-clock maestros began to run amuck. They invented pompous and classical orchestrations for the rankest of hillbilly tunes. They laid hands on the Classics and twisted the great tonal pillars of art into penny pretzels of sound. Visigoths of the air, calling themselves by such titles as Jam Kings, Swing Kings, Jazz Kings, Jive Kings, continued razing and firing the Orphic domains, and ravishing and hamstringing their deities, to the delight of a growing mob of followers. These capered after their heroes, whooping and jiggling like a rabble on its way to a lynching bee.

I shall conclude with only one more phenomenon. This was

the intimidating of the Consumer by the radio Cassandras. News commentators came leaping out of the loudspeaker like bogeymen. Voices, trembling and ominous, dinned war scares and political warnings into the Consumer's masochistic ear, appalled him as he lay in his barber chair, hounded him in taxicabs, and disorganized his liver with terror at the dinner table. It began to seem to this brayed-at and goggle-hearted Consumer that he no longer lived in a civilized world, but in a house of cards. The effect of such subtle terrorization was all too obvious. Jumpy nerves began to generate a jumpy national and international politics, and politicians, wrestling with their immemorial scraps of paper in the high winds of the world, began to feel that disasters were demanded of them. Hysteria, an ally they had been able to evoke at the proper time for their own ends, sat now in an opera box demanding encores before the show was on.

How now with Mr. Woodyard, prime master of these Peddler Revels, Chancellor of Cacophony, and Boy Scout Monitor of Bedlam? Does he flourish, does he smile benignly at the millennium in his lap? Is he Prince of Cornucopia abroad in a Toga and has he found the Philosopher's Stone? Verily, all these happy augmentations of the Woodyard soul have so occurred. He is all the Arts. He is Ibsen and Pavlova, Bizet, Epictetus, and Shelley. He is Demosthenes and Harlequin and Cyrano. He is the wind in the trees, the eagle on the wind, and the feathers on the eagle. He is the Mandarin sage of the Hwang Ho; the thunder is his sigh and the lightning is his fan. But all these avatars are only his side line. It is with his left hand that he takes over the tasks of Barnum, Ziegfeld, Albee, Gatti-Casazza, Diaghilev, and Toscanini. With his right hand he still fills orders. His Consumer, saturated and pulpified by the maniacal cuckoo clock, now sashays to work covered with Glass Beads, bristling with

Feathers, Pomaded, Physicked, Deodorized, and Pedicured and Lord of all the Rubbish Heaps under his nose. He is now Prince of Consumers, a Village Idiot snooping about after shiny pieces of tin, and Mr. Woodyard is his Guiding Star.

So we come on Mr. Woodyard this particular evening, November 27, 7:45 p.m., bestriding his Castles of Caterwaul. Truly the pride that goeth before the fall was Mr. Woodyard's. As he sat at his dinner table this ominous evening, he seemed as devoid of cares as a toad of feathers. His pinkish face glowed and twinkled like an altar and his wattles were as commanding as a cluster of Field Marshals.

This being, all unbeknownst to its millennium-drunk head of the table, a sort of Last Supper, I shall linger on its last few minutes and reveal who were present. At the other end of this shining stretch of silver, glass, linen, and mahogany, loomed Mr. Woodyard's wife—a plump décolletée and bedizened matron with the chop-licking purr of successful matrimony. Of such wives as Mrs. Woodyard one can say little more than that they are a sort of appendage, a tail wagged by the husband; or a third leg sharing the pomp of his stride and contributing no more than a freakish look to it.

There were present also the son of the house and his youthful madam. This son, whose name was George Woodyard, Junior, was a vacuous and beefy youth, almost completely stunned by his sire's lordliness. A protracted education had passed through him like grain through a goose. His head was as hollow as his father's, but lacking the bay leaves. Where success had wreathed the parent, its shadow had reduced the son to a mushroom. George, Junior, hated nothing and loved nothing, and beyond lying in bed figuring out some practical joke he might play on some one of his semi-conscious friends, he had no plans for his tomorrow.

His wife, Madeleine Woodyard, unable to become a tail or a third leg to so negligible a biped, contented herself with a limbo-like glitter. She had once been in the chorus of a night club, where, parading her nudity under an Egyptian headdress, she had appealed to some mysterious mating instinct in George Woodyard the Second. Two years ago she had discarded her career with her headdress, and a year of concubinage followed by a year of marriage had given her that sloth-like and decorous look with which beauty reveals the vacuity of its keeper.

Of more interest than these family members were the other two diners, Mr. and Mrs. Charles Chaley. Mr. Chaley, a roly-poly abstracted gnome man with mustard-colored hair and a freckled, somnambulistic face, was the manufacturer of the Chaley Beauty Products. He had made several millions of dollars by persuading several millions of women to inflame, erode, and macerate their skins with nightly applications of his products.

Success, however, had only provoked Mr. Chaley, since it had made further expansion of his beloved industry more and more difficult. Behind Mr. Chaley's almost idiotic stare lurked a veritable business satyriasis. His huge income from his innumerable and worthless beautifiers left him as restless as a bankrupt. He had apparently no interest in money and was monastically indifferent to all the pleasure it might have bought for him. He disdained leisure, was contemptuous of possessions, lived as un-ornamental a life as a Pullman-car passenger, and appeared, like some coral-obsessed polyp, to have only a single reason for his existence. A fever such as sometimes seizes the gambler had burned away in Mr. Chaley all interests beyond that of increasing the number of jars and bottles bearing his name.

Just what satisfaction Mr. Chaley derived from this form of expansion is hard to fix. There was, obviously, something alive and bewitching in the continued increase of Chaley jars and Chaley bottles, and had they come out of his loins he could not have been prouder of them. He daydreamed continually of ingenious sales campaigns, and after twenty-five years of strenuous familiarity with the ins and outs of every Chaley jar and bottle, there was still nothing so beautiful in the world for him as a window display of Chaley products.

Having determined to increase his output beyond its present colossal, but to him doldrumish, proportions, Mr. Chaley had turned to Mr. Woodyard—that peerless Peddler's Aide—for assistance. This evening, as a result of scores of conferences and months of artistic travail, was to hear the inauguration of a new Coast-to-Coast radio hour sponsored by Mr. Chaley and offering one of Mr. Woodyard's most masterly ensembles of wit, melody, and Peddler Cries to the Public.

Mr. Chaley sat beaming abstractedly over his coffee. He was thinking of the ten million homes into which, in a few minutes, the wonders of the Chaley products would be brought on the wing of song and jest.

As for Mrs. Chaley, nobody at the table had yet addressed a word to her and for the good reason that as far as it was possible for anyone to be non-existent, Mrs. Chaley was more mist than matron. She was a delicate-voiced, gray-haired little woman with an intimidating abstraction in her gentle eyes. She had, shortly after her marriage, endowed a Theosophy Center in her home city of Cleveland. Her subsequent preoccupation with the Occult fitted in nicely with Mr. Chaley's qualities as a husband. She sat now, facing the Lotion King, but looking thoughtfully, as was her habit, into certain problems of Transmigration which she carried like a menagerie in her head.

Mr. Woodyard put an end to the sporadic tittle-tattle by announcing that the Chaley Hour was at hand. The diners entered the Woodyard library, and, except for the coffee, the Last Supper was practically at an end.

The picture of these six folk agog in the Woodyard library, eyes focused on the little silk-covered hole of the Woodyard de luxe radio, is one which has already become a nostalgic part of the world's yesterday. And as the years festoon it with the charm of Things-No-More, it will gather further those nosegay qualities which so improve the looks of the world in retrospect. As one of those who found the reality always irksome, I can report the scene with no fiddle music beclouding it. And not this scene alone, but the millions of similar scenes which at this hour dotted the land, unaware that they postured before a final curtain.

In the Woodyard library a gong now sounded out of the radio, such as summons lamas to their devotions, and a voice trembling with joy sang out like a rescue party on a mountain peak: "Chaley! Chaley's Beauty Products are on the air! Chaley! The name that all the world over stands for feminine loveliness! Feminine Charm! Feminine Desirability! Chaley presents to you tonight the first of a series of all-star broadcasts featuring Mr. Willie Watts, King of Swing, and his Merry Andrews, Madame Olga Sweitzer, the world's highest-paid prima donna, and last, and by no means least, the great comedian Jimmy Carter, famed favorite of stage, screen, and air."

Dropping from these exuberant tones to one of vibrating intimacy, the Voice continued, in a rush of sotto voce passion:

"Chaley means Beauty. A Chaley bottle in your boudoir means an enticing skin on your face and bosom. A Chaley jar in your hand means ten years off your age. Use Chaley lotions and Chaley creams to smooth, liven, and beautify your skin. Chaley Products remake the Face of Womankind."

Whereupon the Voice returned to its Mountain Peak. "Introducing," it cried, "Mr. Watts, King of Swing! And remember, folks, Beauty is as Beauty does. Swing it, Henry."

Mr. Watts's orchestra, timed to the instant, dashed upon the ether like a cavalry charge.

The six in the library listened like relatives at a Confirmation, or rather five of them so listened, for Mrs. Chaley seemed not to be listening at all. To Mr. Woodyard the music, like all music under his auspices, seemed very personal, a series of glamorous sounds given off by the Woodyard Advertising and Radio Service; and to Mr. Chaley the whole thing seemed a hymn to his jars and bottles. He was very happy and nodded approvingly at his host and took to winking at anyone who caught his eyes.

Mr. Woodyard's pulse beat a little more rapidly. He thought of the ten or twenty million ears listening throughout the land to the delicious sounds of Mr. Watts's troupe, and a sense of mystery stirred his vitals. It was not the mystery of how this cuckoo clock worked that touched the Woodyard depths, or any wonder by what devilish legerdemain Mr. Watts's orchestral ravings were emitted in a sort of invisible dust to settle instanter on myriads of ears. It was the Mystery of these Ears that held Mr. Woodyard spellbound—of this Kingdom of Ears cocked in rabbit-like salute. Whatever troubles there were in the world and whatever tragedies and confusions, here in these ears lurked the True Humanity—the man or woman Ready to Buy.

The music ended and Mr. Woodyard beamed at the group as if it were he who had just laid aside the talented baton, for it is the ancient delusion of Entrepreneurs, even the dumbest of them, that they are the show. Mrs. Woodyard was about to wag vocally at her husband's achievement, when he arrested her with a good-natured finger of warning.

"Quiet, please," he cautioned, and just in time, for the Voice of the Mountain Peak filled the room.

"Chaley!" it cried out, so passionately that the owner of that name blushed to his toes. "Chaley!" it repeated, shaking with excitement. "The Name that belongs in Every Woman's Life!"

And at this moment the Unbelievable happened; a thing happened that opened Mr. Woodyard's mouth wide and left it open —in fact it was never really to close again—and that lassoed the woolgathering Mr. Chaley out of his daydreams. As for the others, they heard it too, and stared first at the little silk-covered hole and then at Mr. Woodyard's open mouth.

What had happened was that Another Voice was on the air, speaking in a kind of idiotic duet with the one on the Mountain Peak. And though this Other Voice was gentle and flute-like and wondrously tender, it was nonetheless horribly distinct.

"I am so happy," it said, wailing the words like a far-away peanut whistle. "Oh, so happy." Then it added a far-away little laugh by way of corroboration.

"So very, very happy," it continued while the Mountain Peak, as yet unaware of this competition, thundered on about the Chaley Products.

"Pure!" it cried. "One hundred percent Pure! No deleterious chemicals to leave their marks on Milady's face."

Which serious misrepresentation even a jury of scientists

would have ignored, for the Other Voice continued like a nightingale.

"It is wonderful here," it quavered tenderly. "Oh, wonderful, wonderful. And I am so happy. So happy. I wanted you to know."

Mr. Woodyard, mouth still open, was now on his feet.

The Mountain Peak had evidently now been signaled that he was not alone on the microphone, for a tremble hinting of protruding veins and beads of sweat had come into his tones. "Chaley," he quavered, "waits for you like a Friend in every Drugstore, like a Magician in every Beauty Parlor, like a Lover in . . ."

"Can you hear me?" wailed the Other Voice wistfully, and brought a bellow of rage from Mr. Woodyard by this offensive question. "I want you to hear me," it explained gently, "because I am so happy. Oh, so very happy."

Mr. Woodyard was at the telephone. The rest of the group gaped, wrinkled their brows, squirmed in their seats, glowered and perspired in embarrassment; all except Mrs. Chaley, on whose blank face a little smile had bloomed. Mr. Chaley had removed his watch from his vest pocket and was twirling it dangerously by its chain.

The Mountain Peak Voice had teetered for a moment on its last metaphor and then toppled into silence. The Happiness Boy was left alone on the air.

"Everything is so beautiful here," his swooning voice continued, and slid moodily into a whistling solo.

"There are smiles that make you happy," it whistled, "there are smiles that make you sad . . ."

The whistling trailed away and there was nothing to be heard on the radio but blurred sounds and some crackling indicating

an impromptu studio conference, and in the room Mr. Woodyard's voice shouting into the telephone to be connected immediately with a Mr. Aikens. The others in the library, excepting
Mrs. Chaley, sat as if under the first breath of calamity. Mr.
Chaley was the grimmest.

Then a crash of melody came out of the silk-covered hole,
signifying that Mr. Watts had rushed his men into the breach.
They played "*La donna è mobile.*"

Mr. Woodyard, thrusting a finger into one ear, cried into the
telephone: "What do you mean, sir, you don't know who it is?"

Mrs. Woodyard tiptoed to the radio and lessened its volume.

"It's some joker," Mr. Woodyard continued savagely, "or it
may be somebody from the Eversweet Hour." This was a rival
Beauty Products Program.

"Call the police," went on Mr. Woodyard, "and have them
comb the building. Get the head engineer on it. You have? Well,
where's Mr. Aikens, then? Indeed! I see. Hold the wire a moment." Mr. Woodyard turned and listened to the music and
then replied over the instrument. "There's no interruption now.
No, not a sound of him. It's coming over fine."

Mr. Woodyard hung up and smiled on the company as he
mopped his face.

"The situation is in hand," he said. "It was either a pitiful
attempt at a joke or pure sabotage. We don't know which yet.
We'll have a report on it in a few minutes."

Above the orchestra now rose the siren-like and tobogganing
tones of Madame Olga Sweitzer, the world's highest-paid so-
prano. The great warbler was singing with that added exuberance that characterizes the artist in action against odds. She filled
the library with a veritable festival of melody, raising the old
hurdy-gurdy tune of fickle womanhood into a compelling aria.

"Everything will be all right now," Mr. Woodyard whispered at the brooding face of his client. He was lowering himself into his armchair as into a throne of Normalcy when the Unbelievable thing happened again—and just as Mrs. Woodyard had increased the volume of the radio by turning a little wheel. Mr. Woodyard remained crouched in midair, his bottom for the moment abandoned by his brain. The Voice of the Happy One, gentle, far away, but incredibly distinct, had joined Madame Sweitzer in song, albeit of a different genre.

> "Sweet Genevieve, sweet Genevieve,
> For you I pine, for you-oo I grieve,"

sang the Voice as the diva's throat hurled rival cadenzas into the field.

"Ta taa ta tumm, tum taaa ta tummm," continued this Other Entertainer, who had evidently run into a memory snag and was now merely baying after a lost melodic trail. Then, with a triumphant lilt, the eerie Voice doubled on its tracks and located happily the beginning of its ballad once more.

"Sweet Genevieve, sweet Genevieve," it resumed, "for you I pine, for you-oo I grieve."

But again it floundered, revealing a haunting but diminishing knowledge of the ballad's structure. Throughout its efforts Madame Sweitzer's voice remained a-soar above the whoopings of the orchestra. But in vain were all its rafter-shaking powers. In vain she sang the little Verdi tune as if a herd of Valkyries were hallooing it at the Fire Gods; that is, in vain, if her intention was to drown out her quavering colleague and his faltering but nostalgic cries for Genevieve. Madame Sweitzer achieved volume and tonal beauties such as had never before come pouring from her larynx. But by some astonishing twist of sound perspective, the Voice of Genevieve's mourner remained brilliantly audible. It continued in its fragile but indelible tones to sing, having for a third time become re-entangled in the opening of its ballad.

"For you I pine, for you I grieve," it inverted the couplet by way of emphasis, "sweet Genevieve, sweet Ge-hen-evieve."

Mr. Chaley, with a cold look at his open-mouthed host, marched across the library to the de luxe radio cabinet. He snapped off the current. The silence that followed was truly golden.

"That's not going to do my Product any too much good," said Mr. Chaley stiffly. "I'm kinda disappointed in the Program, Mr. Woodyard."

But Mr. Woodyard was glued to the telephone, where he had been hoarsely at grips for several minutes with a busy signal.

"You can't blame Mr. W. for that nasty fellow," said Mrs. Woodyard.

"Keep it going," Mr. Woodyard commanded; "we don't want to miss any of it. It's all evidence."

"I don't enjoy it, whatever it is," said Mr. Chaley angrily.

The Woodyard daughter-in-law, finding herself confronted by the Lotion King, who was pacing swiftly from one end of the library to the other, made a sweet effort to distract Mr. Chaley from his troubles.

"I wanted to talk to you ever since we met," said the young matron, "about that new Boudoir Cream of yours."

"Some other time," said Mr. Chaley and continued his pacing churlishly.

George Woodyard, Junior, always a fascinated student of practical jokes, sat with his nail tapping his lower teeth and his eyes raised in meditation. He was trying to figure out from a cursory knowledge of radio construction how the thing could be done.

"I keep getting the busy signal," Mr. Woodyard said raspingly.

"Hang up," Mr. Chaley flung back; "the whole thing's a filthy mess."

"Somebody evidently pulled a secret hook-up," Woodyard, Junior, offered, removing his finger from his mouth. "I've been figuring it out."

"Oh, do tell us!" his pretty wife cried. "Georgie has figured it out," she added, tapping Mr. Chaley's elbow. Mr. Chaley paused.

"It was a hook-up from outside the studio," said George, "because you will remember that the voice of the Main Singer, what's her name, was the furthest off, although it was the loudest by far. Whereas the little Voice, the one that we heard doing the Genevieve number, was in reality closer, almost in our ears in fact. By God"—he beamed suddenly—"I wouldn't be surprised if it was somebody in this room—right here!"

"What the hell are you talking about!" Mr. Chaley demanded.

"One of us"—the junior Woodyard lifted his beefy frame out of the chair with difficulty—"that's it! By God, one of us is a ventriloquist!"

He looked searchingly at the little gray-haired figure of Mrs. Chaley and inquired boldly: "How about it, madam?"

"Don't be a fool, Junior," his mother spoke sharply. "It came over the air. I heard it."

"She hasn't answered," said Junior.

"Listen, young man"—Mr. Chaley dropped his hand on his wife's shoulder—"we'll have no insults."

"Sit down, George," Mr. Woodyard commanded, still jiggling his telephone bar. "Besides, they heard it at the studio, so it can't be just in this room."

Junior was silenced.

"Whoever it was," Mr. Woodyard went on, enunciating distinctly from the telephone, "they will be arrested and prosecuted to the full extent of the law."

"I hardly think so," Mrs. Chaley said quietly.

The others looked at her with surprise.

"Go on, darling," Mr. Chaley answered with unexpected deference; "I'd like to hear what you have to say on the subject."

"I'd rather not," Mrs. Chaley smiled, after a pause.

"Please," insisted Mr. Chaley. "Why do you think they won't be arrested, sweetheart?"

"Well," Mrs. Chaley sighed, "it's really something I very seldom talk about, as you know, Charles. But if you insist . . ."

"I do," said Mr. Chaley.

"Well," Mrs. Chaley went on, smiling at the company, "the reason they won't arrest anybody is that there's nobody to arrest. You see, it's not a human being that did that—I mean, as we understand people to be human beings."

"I don't follow you," said Mr. Chaley.

"It's a ghost, Charles, very likely an earth-bound spirit caught between Transmigrations. It frequently happens."

At the end of this flow of words Mrs. Chaley sighed and looked eagerly at the radio.

"I wish you would turn it on again, Charles," she said. "He may still be hovering. And—it's really very instructive."

"Why, the idea!" exploded Mrs. Woodyard. "A ghost on the radio! Did you hear what she said, George?"

But Mr. Woodyard chose to ignore the vaporings of his client's wife.

"Listen," he snarled into the telephone, "it can't be busy all this time. I demand to be put through."

The library door opened and a visitor, pale and out of breath, strode into the room. This was Mr. William Aikens, president of the Trans-Continental Broadcasting networks, used by Mr. Woodyard for all his major programs. He was a thin, witty-looking man.

"Hello, folks." Mr. Aikens nodded automatically at the group. "Hello, George. I got here as fast as I could. Almost wrecked my car. Had to run the last two blocks on foot. Never mind the telephone, George." He waved at the instrument still in Mr. Woodyard's hands. "You won't be able to get the studio for a month. There are at least twenty million people on the phone. The biggest drawing power I ever saw any program reveal," he added with a clever look at Mr. Chaley.

"What in God's name . . ." began Mr. Woodyard.

"Let me get my breath," Mr. Aikens pleaded and slid into a chair.

"Well, Mr. Aikens"—Mr. Chaley stared at him—"so that's what you call radio advertising, is it?"

"Listen, I'm as much at sea as you are," Mr. Aikens answered adroitly between gasps.

"I want this distinctly understood, gentlemen." Mr. Chaley raised his voice. "You've made a laughing stock out of Chaley Products. And that's unforgivable."

"Nonsense, Chaley," Mr. Woodyard said. "The whole thing will react in your favor. It always does."

"What always does?" demanded Mr. Chaley. "Gentlemen, name me one possible way in which this doesn't make a fool out of Chaley Products."

Mr. Woodyard mopped his face and turned to Mr. Aikens.

"What steps have been taken," he inquired, "for the arrest of this fellow?"

Mr. Aikens had now recovered his wind and wanted a drink.

"It's the Goddamnedest thing," he said, pouring himself one. "I put the whole engineering force on it, the minute it started. They've gone over the entire system. Not a screw loose."

"The Eversweet Hour," Mr. Woodyard interrupted.

"I thought of that," said Mr. Aikens, nodding. He swallowed his drink and, with a glance at his wrist watch, walked to the radio. He snapped on the current.

"I left orders to resume the program at exactly 8:30," he said. "Our experts will have been all over the machinery by then."

The radio remained silent.

"Three more minutes," said Mr. Aikens apologetically.

"Can't we try some other station?" Mrs. Chaley suggested quietly. "He may have switched over to some other studio, you know."

"Who's that?" asked Mr. Aikens.

"The ghost," said Mrs. Chaley.

"She has a theory it's a ghost," Mrs. Woodyard explained and patted the theorist good-naturedly on her arm. "There, there, dear—there's no reason for any of us to get hysterical."

Mr. Aikens stared at the little gray-haired woman as he poured himself a second drink.

"A ghost, eh?" he chuckled. "That's very funny."

"I don't mean to be funny," Mrs. Chaley answered. "I would never have mentioned it if Mr. Chaley hadn't insisted on hearing what was in my mind."

"Baloney!" Mr. Aikens exploded, his nerves severely tried by the evening's confusion. "That's what's in your mind, madam."

"That's my wife." Mr. Chaley came forward.

Mr. Aikens blinked.

"Terribly sorry," he said, and extended his hand. "Glad to meet you, Mrs. Chaley. You must forgive me."

Mrs. Chaley nodded and shook hands.

"Oh, it's all right," she said. "I never expect to find any believers."

"She's up on those things," Mr. Chaley explained proudly.

"Well." Mr. Aikens took a deep breath, ignoring this hint of Mrs. Chaley's erudition. "Eight-thirty. Here it comes."

As he spoke, the Mountain Peak Voice charged into the room. But now it was a voice full of good humor and quivering happily as if but recently recovered from a round of merry laughter.

"Ladies and gentlemen, members of the radio audience," it cried gaily, "there has been a slight delay in our program due to an absurd and highly amusing mishap. I will not bore you with the details of what happened, good folks. I hope you have all been as amused as we have by our amateur friend whose pathetic efforts at entertainment tangled themselves in our wave length. Highly diverting though his contribution to our program proved, it will not be repeated. I thank you for your indulgence. And now"—the Voice clambered back on its Mountain Peak—"on with the Show! Introducing Chaley's Master Mind of Fun and Prince of Comedians, Jimmy Carter."

The orchestra, accompanied by a storm of studio handclapping, played the first bars of a song called "Here Comes Cookie" and the voice of the hilarious Jimmy Carter, familiar to the radio millions, uttered its zany chuckle like a tinkling of caps and bells. Mr. Woodyard, who was quivering, sat down slowly and shot a heroic smile at Mr. Chaley.

Jimmy chuckled again as if wrestling himself out of a blissful state of idiocy and then began to call eagerly for some comrade called Herman.

"Herman," he cried gleefully, "I know who done it. I know who done it."

"Who did what?" demanded Herman, none other than the Mountain Peak in a more artistic vein. "Who did what?"

"Made all that Genewieve twouble," lisped Jimmy. "I met him. He's a midget, the most terrible, blood-thirsty midget alive."

"A midget?" repeated Herman. "Well, that doesn't sound possible. Are you certain?"

"Am I certain! Ha!" Jimmy screamed in falsetto excitement. "I seen him, I tell you. With my own eyes. He was pointed out to me as the only midget gunman in the world. He's called," said Jimmy almost out of breath, "he's called Public Enemy Number Three-Eighths."

The studio laughter covered Jimmy's guffaws.

"Did he have anything to say to you by way of explanation?" demanded Mountain Peak Herman, apparently struggling unsuccessfully to keep serious.

"Yes," cooed Jimmy, imitating the tone of the recent interloper. "He said: 'I'm so-o happy. So very, very happy.' And I said: 'What are you so happy about, silly?' And he said . . ."

But whatever it was that Jimmy had learned was never heard by the listeners in the Woodyard library. For at this instant the Unbelievable returned with reinforcements. A Quartet of Voices, all flute-like and far away as the original's and singing in wavering amateur harmony, came valiantly out of the little silk-covered hole.

"Sweet Genevieve, sweet Genevieve
For you I pine, for you-oo I grieve,"

sang the Quartet.

"Turn it off!" Mr. Chaley cried. "By God, that's too much. I cancel my contract."

"Just a minute." Mr. Woodyard was on his feet and as out of of breath as if he had been run over. "We're all in this together."

"I never ordered a Quartet!" cried Mr. Chaley. "It's a distinct abrogation of contract. I bail out here and now."

"Hold your horses, Chaley," began Mr. Aikens, who was unable to take his eyes off the little silk-covered hole. The wailing Quartet was now a-flounder in mid-ballad. "We are not responsible for any acts of God."

"That Goddamn Quartet is no act of God!" Mr. Chaley shouted. "Any jury will bear me out."

Far away, Jimmy the comedian was still hard at work with his chuckles and his jests. But none of those in the library heard him. Panic entered their voices as the Quartet continued its wistful uncertain harmonizing.

"It can't be *four* ventriloquists," George, Junior, was saying reverently to himself.

"Please, everybody," Mrs. Woodyard cried out, "my husband will take care of it. Let's all keep our heads. George"—she scurried to his side and tugged at his arm—"there's no time to lose, darling. You must simply do something."

"Kindly mind your own business!" Mr. Woodyard bellowed and looked wildly for the telephone.

"Listen to them," Mr. Aikens demanded. "If that ain't the Goddamnedest most mysterious thing I've ever heard."

"There's nothing mysterious about it," said Mrs. Chaley gently. "He just went and told some friends."

"Who did?" asked Mr. Aikens, off his guard.

"The ghost," said Mrs. Chaley. "He brought his friends back and organized a Quartet. It's entirely understandable. There's nothing to be alarmed about. They're doing their best to entertain us. I doubt, however," she added, critically, "whether they were singers in *this* Vale."

"Sweet Genevieve, sweet Genevieve, for you I pine, for you-oo I grieve," the Quartet was reopening the ballad. The zany chuckle of Jimmy Carter deserted him.

A babble of voices followed, Jimmy's growing fainter as if he were being dragged from the microphone. In the confusion the Mountain Peak Voice appeared to be battling its way forward. Finally above the crackling and blurred sounds it boomed ecstatically out of the little silk-covered hole: "Chaley! Chaley! The Name of Beauty! Loveliness in every Chaley jar. Charm in every Chaley bottle. When you visit your neighborhood drugstore ask for . . ."

Silence fell on the Mountain Peak. The station had gone off the air. The Woodyard radio, an instant before an outpost of bedlam, stood now in wooden innocence before the eyes of Mr. Woodyard and his guests.

The newspapers the next morning carried accounts of the matter under various headlines. One reported: "Air Squatter Wrecks Broadcast." Another announced: "Hooligans Rout Chaley Program in Mystery Joke." Another stated: "Man in Moon Takes Charge of Radio Station. Angry Advertiser Investigating." A fourth maintained, though in a joking vein:

"Stage-Struck Ghost Raises Ruckus as Wave-Length Stow-away."

The narratives beneath these headlines were all written in that broad vein of whimsy affected by newspapermen when dealing with matters a bit too strange for belief. For there was no one like the Press, in those Pre-Debacle days, for poking fun at Mysteries. Although it occasionally reported a Miracle or a Miraculous Cure with a sober face and an eye to its devout Catholic circulation, it did not then regard God and His doings, or the secrets beyond the grave, as legitimate news items.

I know it is the fashion now to look back on the newspaper columns of the Radio Era and marvel at what seem the venality and cynicism of the then Fourth Estate. But the cynicism of the Press in such a crisis is not difficult to understand. Having to report from hour to hour with straight face and stern tongue the idiocies of the current politicians, having to ladle out in demitasses the Niagara of buncombe roaring around its ears, having to give credible dress to the decomposing and disheveled platitudes by which we manage to trick ourselves into a fairly orderly society, having to play usher to all the Political, Social, Artistic, and Industrial jackanapes whooping for front seats, is it any wonder that Journalism grows full of subterranean laughter? Not that its sons all rise above the litter of their columns or toil like Sages in Chains. But this constant flying of flags for Error, and keeping an endless twenty-one-gun salute going for the crackpot parade of existence, breed in them a need for sneering.

And yet this brings us face to face with the question: What can they afford to laugh at? What phase of existence is there sufficiently remote from their advertising columns and partisanships for them to vent this giddy cynicism on? Artists and poets, naturally, a few poor goats who pose as Casanovas, a Personality now and then with a feather too many in its cap; but chiefly it is the Supernatural that wears the safest motley. The Press, prostrate like a street Arab before every Altar, can usually afford a snicker for the miraculous.

In the case of the radio ghosts there was also in the happy chortling of the Press on that first day a less complex ingredient. This was a natural jollity regarding any misadventure that might befall an Advertising Rival.

Still, one might ask the newspaper gentry sternly how it was that they, as well as the millions who heard the Genevieve crooners, failed to know the truth at once. And worse, having heard these contented ghosts yodeling so benignantly of their condition, how could they ignore this tale of other worlds, as if by their indifference to that phase of the affair they outlawed its very existence?

I fancy I have answered as well as asked the question. It is by this Indifference that we survive. It is this Indifference that is our chief strength, our dike against the avalanche of the Unknown. The indifference of the public to the first whinnyings of the Radio Miracle was no greater than its heroic indifference to the numberless other Mysteries, Muddles, and Miracles that lie beyond each of its moments. Of the world we live in we know hardly more than the turtles; of the world that lives in us we know less the older and more complex we grow; and of the world beyond us, all we know is that its immensity is woefully unflattering, and that men have immemorially lost their wits merely from trying to describe it.

In short, though the Miracle had signaled, business went on as usual the next day, but not Mr. Woodyard's business—not quite. Mr. Woodyard appeared in his office the next morning apparently fully recovered, outwardly. Somewhere inside him, close to his solar plexus, however, his mouth was still open. He had received a great shock. Arriving, he skimmed through the reports of the Engineers, Electricians, and Physicists who had labored all night under Mr. Aikens's direction. They had been unable to figure out any possible way by which the Hooligan Broadcasters could have tapped the wave lengths of the Chaley Hour. This did not, however, cause them to alter their finding that such tapping by such hooligans had taken place. Being Scientists, they were a little more pompous about knowing nothing than ordinary people. They very nearly convinced Mr. Woodyard that the whole delicate investigation would soon end in the arrest of some hinterland playboy with a trick aerial in his barn.

Somewhat encouraged, Mr. Woodyard turned his attention to the Press reports of his troubles, including a daring editorial in the *Morning Inquirer* on the hazards of Air Advertising. As he read, Mr. Woodyard opened his dictograph and spoke sharply to his secretary.

"Get me the Advertising Manager of the *Inquirer*," he said. "Tell him I want him in my office between three and four this afternoon."

Then he closed the instrument, smiling for a moment at the retraction he anticipated. That Newspaper Ned would think twice before he ever plucked again at the Fabric of Society. He continued to smile, despite the nervous pulse that appeared near his liver as he read the data prepared for his morning's attention. His underlings seemed all to have been stricken overnight with an annoying jittery zeal. He learned that twenty thousand calls had been reported by the Telephone Company as having been made, unsuccessfully, to Mr. Aikens's broadcasting studio, and that five thousand more consumers had simultaneously besieged

the Chaley Main Office in New York, that forty thousand de-
rogatory postcards had already been received from truculent and
sarcastic listeners, and that these reposed already in files on Mr.
Chaley's desk. Mr. Woodyard felt that he was being annoyed
by Superfluities. There were a dozen departments for the consideration of such matters, and Mr. Woodyard called in his general manager, a Mr. Isaacs, and gave him hell.

Let it be said for Mr. Woodyard that he rose above all those
telephonists and postcard writers at this stage. Like all leaders
who mold Public Opinion, Mr. Woodyard knew there wasn't
any.

A few hours later he tried to explain this phase of the situation
to Mr. Chaley, who had arrived just as the repentant Advertising Manager of the *Morning Inquirer* was leaving. Mr. Chaley
had brought with him a suitcase full of the more unnerving postcards, which he could hardly lift, and which he insisted on regarding as so many death warrants for the Chaley Products.

Mr. Woodyard smiled at these alarmist views.

"You are welcome to withdraw your account," he said, "and
leave the Eversweet people in sole possession of the field. That's
up to you, sir. I will interpose no legal difficulties."

Mr. Woodyard calmly opened a drawer in his desk and removed a gold-sealed document as thick as a time-table.

"Here's your contract, Mr. Chaley," he said. "Tear it up if
you care to. It's my only copy."

Mr. Chaley accepted the ponderous document and stared
thoughtfully at his name, flickering in every tenth line as a sort
of clue.

"What I would like to say to you, Chaley," went on Mr.
Woodyard as casually as if he had handed his visitor a blotter
instead of a million-dollar contract, "is merely this. The Con-

sumer Always Forgets. That fact is the soul of all advertising. If the Consumer were able to remember anything, we wouldn't have to spend these millions reminding him hourly of things he already knows, now would we? I can sum up all I have found out in years of studying the Advertising Problem, in these few words—the Consumer can't even remember his own name. That's the long and short of it. He not only forgets *what* he wants to buy, but *why* he wants to buy it. He has to be reminded constantly. As for remembering the virtues of any Product, I assure you that's ridiculous. If you asked the most intelligent Consumer you could lay a hand on why he smoked a certain cigarette that spent twenty millions a year advertising itself, that Consumer wouldn't be able to tell you. And if he did tell you, ten to one he would be quoting some rival cigarette product. Well, it stands to reason, Chaley, that if they forget the good, they must forget the bad. In a few days not a single listener who heard that trouble last night will remember whether it happened to you or the Eversweet People or the lamppost. I sincerely think you're frightening yourself with a molehill."

Mr. Chaley hummed a few minutes and then tapped the suitcase at his feet.

"I brought these over," he began.

"I know, I know," smiled Mr. Woodyard, "the usual flash-in-the-pan resentment. It means nothing. I've been through it too often. If you're wise, you'll just burn them. They're a side of the Public you'll get nowhere listening to. They don't mean a thing by the time the ink is dry on them."

Mr. Chaley sighed with hope. He had been unable to sleep, convinced that the Chaley Products were ruined and that laughter would forever dog the aristocratic heads of his bottles and his jars.

"Tear up that contract, if you want to," said Mr. Woodyard coolly. "You're your own boss. I don't think I can advise you any further."

Mr. Chaley looked at the many-paged document and hesitated.

"Woodyard," he said slowly, "I couldn't afford to have another of those joke programs. I didn't sleep a wink."

"Well, that's one thing you'll never have to worry about again." Mr. Woodyard beamed, aglow with his victory. "We'll start over again tomorrow night and——"

Mr. Woodyard looked up in surprise. General Manager Isaacs had come through the private door at a run.

"Turn on the Magic Coffee program," Mr. Isaacs panted. "Something's going on."

"I must ask you not to come running in and out of this office as if it were a lavatory," Mr. Woodyard began, but the whiteness of his general manager's face and the glitter in his eyes halted him. "What are you talking about?" he added nervously.

"Turn it on," gasped Mr. Isaacs and stood pointing at the radio behind Mr. Woodyard's desk.

Mr. Woodyard's hands had grown cold. Magic Coffee was one of his Key Clients. He wheeled slowly in his chair and snapped on the current and dialed quickly. Paul Whiteman's orchestra was playing handsomely a medley of jive favorites, but Mr. Woodyard failed to hear this part of the entertainment. What he heard was a Voice wailing, not the Voice of the Chaley disaster, but a brother to it—a little hoarser and less tender.

"Hello, everybody," the Voice was saying in that maddening far-away sing-song these hooligans appeared to favor. "How are you, everybody? I want to say something. Don't go away. I want to say something nice."

Mr. Whiteman's bandsmen, although apparently aware of the new welkin squatter, continued with fine musical indifference, being made of sterner stuff than the entertainers who had lost their heads on the Chaley Hour. Mr. Whiteman, himself, ad libbed gaily to the audience during a pianissimo passage.

"Pay no attention, folks, to our little unseen friend," he said and then, addressing this Ether Pirate, added: "How are you anyway, brother? Are you very, very happy this evening?"

Mr. Whiteman's first violins were heard to chuckle at this sally of the maestro. To Mr. Woodyard's horror the peanut whistle Voice replied:

"Oh, yes. I am so happy. But I want to know how Irma is. How are you, Irma? Are you happy, Irma?" And without waiting for any reply from either Irma or Mr. Whiteman, the Voice slid tenderly into song.

"When it's apple-blossom time in Normandy," it sang, "in Normandy, I long to be."

Mr. Woodyard snapped off the current and looked foggily at Mr. Chaley and then at his general manager.

Mr. Chaley said: "Say, that's kind of serious. What are you going to do, Woodyard?"

Mr. Woodyard looked accidentally at the ornamental chandelier in the center of the ceiling. It had come out of a Florentine palace.

"Have the police been notified, Mr. Isaacs?" he inquired weakly.

His phone rang and he lifted the receiver.

"Hello," he said, "this is Mr. Woodyard speaking."

An expression of pain, which gave him suddenly a childish look, spread over all the Woodyard features as a voice crackled in his ear. It was the voice of Andrew Watterson, head of the

United Cereal Products Company, and even more than Magic Coffee, a Key Client.

"What the hell is the meaning of this, Woodyard!" Mr. Watterson was demanding. "There's some Goddamn buttinsky on the Golden Flakes Program hollering and singing like a lunatic."

"Just a minute," said Mr. Woodyard. "I'll see what the trouble is." Turning, he said hoarsely to Mr. Isaacs: "Golden Flakes."

Mr. Isaacs dialed the program in. Mr. Woodyard knew in a way what to expect. Nevertheless, his mouth opened again with shock. A Handel oratorio was being beautifully chanted per schedule by the St. Peter's Episcopal Choir, Mr. Watterson being religiously inclined in his sales campaigns. It was not these soul-stirring tones that Mr. Woodyard heard, however. What he heard was a woman, obviously a Negress, wailing away tenderly and, like the other hooligans, wonderfully distinct.

"Oh, Joe," she said, "why did you shoot me, Joe? Ah neveh loved nobody but you, Joe—so help me, Joe. That other fellah neveh got to fust base with me, Joe. Neveh got to fust base, Joe. Neveh got to fust base; honest, honey. Why did you go and shoot me, baby?" And with a little far-away sob, the speaker slid into a song.

"Who broke the lock on the backhouse door?" she wailed tunefully. "Who let that wind come blowin' in . . . blowin' in . . . ?"

Mr. Woodyard heard the telephone crackling on his desk and picked it up.

"Hello," he said.

"Tell them to take off that program!" Mr. Watterson screamed. "I ain't sponsoring any Southern harlots. Shut off that program and keep it shut off, or I'll throw you and your whole Goddamn organization into jail."

"My God!" said Mr. Chaley softly. "I got off lucky. Just listen to her."

"I'm putting through a call to the Federal Radio Bureau," said Mr. Woodyard into the telephone. "Personal messages are absolutely against the new code. We can get them on that."

"Get who?" Mr. Watterson howled so loudly that Mr. Chaley could hear.

"You better tell him the truth," he whispered.

"Just a minute," said Mr. Woodyard into the telephone. "What truth?" he demanded shakenly as he covered the mouthpiece with his palm.

"That it looks like ghosts," said Mr. Chaley quietly, "as you were informed right off the bat last night. If you had followed Mrs. Chaley's suggestions you might have gotten somewhere by this time."

Mr. Watterson had disappeared when Mr. Woodyard removed his palm from the instrument. Mr. Isaacs silenced the radio.

"Well," said Mr. Chaley. "I guess that's that."

Mr. Woodyard sat glassy-eyed as Mr. Chaley began slowly to tear up the contract foolishly placed in his hands a half-hour ago.

The Press on the following morning was divided between jolly descriptions of the two wrecked Programs and a stern curiosity as to the future of Radio as an advertising medium, now that irresponsible and malicious amateurs had found a way to join the entertainment personnel of the broadcasting studios.

"There is no telling where this unfortunate discovery, which evidently enables any Tom, Dick, or Harry to tap the wave lengths, may lead," one of the Editorial pages observed soberly.

"From what has happened, however, it begins to look as if no Artist or Advertiser will be safe from the vicious, if often amusing, raids of these new Ether Pirates. The matter calls for immediate action by the Federal authorities if the great field of radio diversion and propaganda is to be preserved."

In its news columns, however, the Press controlled its alarm over the radio's future. It dealt with the situation aloofly and with a beady eye for all its comic values. The thousands of inquiries asking for explanations and the thousands of explanations put forward by the more active-minded students of the phenomenon were a rich lode for the News Gatherers. And by noon the Press had, as if under some common baton, uncorked its full gale of laughter at the Supernatural. For out of the explanations advanced, the notion that ghosts were responsible for the confusion appeared to be gaining ground. Seemingly the entire lunatic fringe of news readers had taken to bombarding the editors.

This lunatic fringe, which includes the never-failing crop of Phantasts, Seers, Voodoo- and Spook-Mongers, Alchemists, Rosicrucians, Perpetual Motion Machine Inventors, crime witnesses and confessors, Hermits, Nudists, Whiskered Prophets, White and Colored Messiahs, Table Tippers, Frustrated Writers, and those who maintain there never was a Jesus Christ—this little but devout army of Unreason was generally ignored as a news source by the daily papers. A firm prejudice in favor of the utterances of the sane, or at least the pretenders to sanity, had been an ancient editorial dictum.

On this day, the Press, however, acting the facetious Master of Ceremonies, opened its columns to the crackpots. Interviews with basement savants, ferreted out among their witcheries, filled the papers. Members of Ectoplasm Societies and Swami Circles and End of the World groups were quizzed with mock serious-ness, and the great body of confused but normal readers was treated to a Mark Twainish holiday.

It is sad to relate that this laughter and calm, so rare a team of Editorial horses, remained but briefly in the field. For by seven o'clock on the third day the Press, with a volte-face more spectacular than any in its swivel-minded history, was on the streets baying the wild truth of the story. Headlines with less humor in them than a hangman's noose announced in fat slabs of ink that "Ghosts Rout Radio," that "Mystery Voices Fill World," that "Dead Orators Invade Air Fields," that "Heaven Speaks to Earth," that "Souls Stampede Radio." And there was one Editor who, finding the *mot juste* for the sudden rush of piety to the headlines, proclaimed: "The Heavenly Choir Is on the Air."

But these headlines were hardly news any more. For the news had already burst over every radio in the country. Beginning at five o'clock, thousands of voices, obviously under a sort of fal-tering organization, had joined the regular earthly programs. One group, seemingly numbering a thousand throats, came over WZX in a truly stirring version of "My Old Kentucky Home." Another group over WJY wailed in mighty chorus "Put on Your Old Gray Bonnet with the Blue Ribbons on It." Another calliope-like ensemble of heroic proportions took possession of WMX with "Old Black Joe." There were other units, evidently less rehearsed and only vaguely organized, that offered little but false starts and rallying cries from overzealous leaders.

Before a half-hour had passed, all efforts at any organized per-formances appeared to collapse, and the choirs seemed to grow out of hand both in numbers and in energy. Conflict obviously broke out in the wildly multiplying ranks of these unscheduled entertainers and a sort of anarchy overtook the whole Venture. Swarms of voices concentrating on a single tune were still to be heard, particularly one vast and dominant section which kept offering "It's a Long Way to Tipperary" in fine rhythm. This old tune came over station WOL and for ten minutes its swinging melody echoed sturdily out of the Other World.

By six o'clock the celestial program had degenerated into a hair-raising shambles. Over all the networks, drowning out the last desperate efforts at human competition, these increasing faraway hordes now whimpered, thundered, whistled, screeched, and hallooed, in a terrifying caricature of entertainment. All that was audible was a deafening surf of whooping and hilarious sound—and this surf rolled over the Great Dike.

This senseless booming and whistling out of Nowhere had the immediate effect of bringing half of Humanity to its knees to await the End of the World in the posture it had been taught was most pleasing to God. The other half of the world, which kept its feet, engaged just as earnestly in the various enterprises that bloom always under the nose of great disasters, such as Looting, Arson, and Rapine, while a minority who obviously did not believe in a Future Existence took to their beds in more concrete devotions than those of prayer.

And as in all routs, the horrible imaginings outstripped the present fears. For disaster is never disaster enough for the human mind, and whatever horrors chase it down the night it will multiply them by ten and recaparison them with the largess of hysteria.

By eight o'clock that species of hair-streaming information that travels the currents of mob thought had spawned the tale that an incalculable horde of wailing Dead had captured the radio stations; that vast troops of white-sheeted Spooks were marching through scores of cities and causing them to dissolve under their graveyard breath; and that it was only a matter of hours before these myriad Visitors would have reduced the world to a guttered candle. Harassing each other with these tales, droves of people came bounding out of their homes in quest of that last refuge against calamity—the touch, sound, and shiver of one another.

Now that we have come to accept the presence of ghosts as no more mysterious than that of other interstellar Gases, it is a little difficult to understand the wave of universal horror that swept these first hours. Apparently any modicum of Truth is enough to shake the world into insanity, as witness its behavior on first hearing that the earth was not flat, and on being apprised, more recently, that Man had not been pulled rabbit-fashion out of the Garden of Eden hat by God but was a creature evolved with heroic patience by Nobody in particular from some sort of Oyster.

The proof that Life existed after Death should certainly have come as no thunderclap to a race which had maintained just that since its earliest babblings. But there you have the weakness of human thought. However real it is, it never prepares us for reality.

By dawn the apex of the Rout had been passed. Most of the radio broadcasting stations had been burned and razed by mobs engaged in the traditional way of dealing with Truth by the stamping out of its mouthpieces. The churches in the morning were still doing a terrific turn-away business and streets were still full of demented groups hugging each other and bellowing hoarsely for the sight of Kingdom Come. But there was a recession of panic. For one thing, most of the radio receiving sets had been destroyed, thus removing the actual sources of the terror.

And for another thing, the Press began to take the situation in hand.

"Life after Death is not physical," one Editorial announced boldly. "We have nothing to fear from our Heavenly companions. We should, indeed, be overwhelmed with joy to learn that They are all happy and full of Song in their Home beyond the skies."

"They are still singing," stated another Editorial occupying half a front page, "and seemingly full of the comradely delusion that they are delighting the living by their efforts. Let us not tremble, but rather sit back and know that we are merely listening to Another Program, and one very close to God."

On the second day the Press bristled with statements from scientists and savants of every hue offering theories concerning the electrical composition of the human soul and its obvious affinity with other forms of electricity. And though these theories were too abstruse for the understanding of ninety-nine percent of their readers, they were greatly reassuring—as is anything that is couched in scientific words.

A statement from Washington revealed that the government, too, had not been idle. It announced that only one of the nation's broadcasting stations would be allowed to remain open and this only for the further study of the life-after-death phenomenon. A bill was rushed through both houses of Congress prohibiting all human radio broadcasting. The possession of radios was declared illegal. A special arm of the law was quickly created to confiscate all privately owned radio apparatus, with power to arrest and imprison citizens caught using radio sets.

And on the third day the debacle had spent itself. There was, apparently, no period of convalescence. Man recovered as he always does from these blows to his ignorance, instantly. He revealed, as he has so often done, that the basic meanings of human as well as divine activity by which he lives are of no actual importance but a sort of pretty scenery in front of which he playacts. Shift the scenery and he continues to perform the never-changing comedies and dramas of his daily life.

But no sooner had the Dead lost their status as a menace than they became the object of embittered controversy almost as menacing to the peace of the nation. The streets became full of men and women arguing in behalf of rival Interpretations. Innumerable Societies were hatched, each proclaiming itself the custodian of the Real Truth. Soul Worship Sectarians, crowding thousands of rooftops, took to howling back at the Invisible Ones in pious efforts to entertain Them. Their singing provoked the less demonstrative elements who were already back in office and shop. Police were finally called to dislodge these rooftop minstrels. Pitched battles were staged high in the air and hundreds of the Sect showed their determination to amuse the Dead by leaping from cornices to join the Heavenly Choir beyond the reach of infidel police clubs.

Driven finally from the building tops, the survivors took to parading the streets in the wake of large brass bands and singing frenziedly. For several days the racket set up by these worshipers threatened to disrupt the communities almost as much as the musical blasts of the Dead had done. Police and militia managed after some difficulties to scatter them into basements and other hideaways.

A tenderly worded but nonetheless stern document from the Vatican helped quiet the Holy Singers. The souls of the Dead, said the memorable announcement, must certainly be regarded as remiss in their duties to God and the Glories of Heaven in wasting their time listening to the profane music and questionable comedy of the world. The Living, it concluded, must not further their fall from grace by offering them tawdry secular entertainment and luring them from the superior bliss awaiting them at the feet of God.

Of the countless individual fanatics who took to chartering balloons and, equipped with mandolins, fiddles, accordions, and mouth organs, sailed off into space as pilgrims to Nowhere, never to be seen again, a great martyrdom literature is already extant.

More touching, however, than all these tales of aberration and confusion are the first accounts of the disillusion that overtook the nation. From the very beginning the knowledge that Heaven was no more than a raucous amateur hour began to depress the more thoughtful laity. Science, however, held out the promise of a great cultural renaissance. A process by which the myriad voices of the Dead still pouring out of the skies could be filtered through a sort of electrical sieve had been perfected in the first week. The achievement was heralded by the Press as opening unlimited vistas. It was eagerly announced that the boon to human knowledge from such orderly communication with the Dead as had become possible would be immeasurable.

In a few days, though, the Press began to abandon some of its first optimism. It became obvious that the Dead appeared either unwilling to contribute a mite to the reservoirs of the world's information or that they knew nothing. In reply to the most tender and patient questioning by a corps of scientists, priests, rabbis, and literary lights nominated for the task by the President, the Voices isolated by the electrical sieve offered only snatches of old songs or some pardonable but purely selfish interest in the status of some relative. A few of the fanatics who had leaped from the city's rooftops to join the Heavenly Choir were located and fruitlessly questioned.

The theory soon began to afflict even the most hopeful of the world that Heaven was as full of imbeciles and irresponsible souls as earth. And with this growing realization the great era of atheism in which we live today came upon the world.

But to return now to Mr. Woodyard, whose failure to survive the collapse of his Radio Empire I have already revealed. If you will recall, it was as a casualty hanging from the chandelier that I first introduced him. But before Mr. Woodyard was driven to this end, he struggled violently and with some heroism to restore Radio to the high estate from which it had been dashed and to rope and tie the vanished Consumer again. He threw his entire fortune into the laps of certain wizards and charlatans who were attempting to weed out what they called Ethereal Static—the new scientific name for the Dead. At the end of the first month of his labors he was joined by an unexpected ally, Mr. Chaley, who, it appeared, desired once more to advertise his products on the air.

"We'll show her," Mr. Chaley remarked slyly, referring apparently to his wife, "who's running the world—us or the ghosts."

For several weeks Mr. Woodyard, as is the habit of deposed monarchs, found solace in garrulity. He issued long interviews to the Press which were never published.

"In our rejoicing over the discovery of life after death," said Mr. Woodyard in one of these interviews, "let us not forget the Consumer. The fact that the Consumer has been deprived of that world of Music, Art, and Culture which he has come to regard as his fairest heritage is, indeed, a sad one. Personally, I shudder when I think of the silence in the American home."

In another unpublished interview a week later Mr. Woodyard "stated" a little more hysterically:

"It surely cannot be the will of God to wipe out the spirit of industrial enterprise which has been the greatness of America. But this is exactly what will happen if He allows the Souls who are His charges to overrun the radio. The falling off in national purchases is appalling, and forecasts inevitable depression and panic. Who are these so-called Dead that they should be permitted to fill the air lanes with their insane noises!"

Thereafter Mr. Woodyard, although he spoke to his few remaining employees of million-dollar war-chests, became subdued. He lacked any further capital for demonstrations. He was practically penniless toward the end. With his last seventy-five dollars Mr. Woodyard, abandoned by his friends as well as his family, hired a hall where he lectured to seats empty but for the loyal Mr. Chaley. What he said was that Mr. Roosevelt had shown himself a wretched coward in surrendering to the Radical Element in Heaven. In 1940, he roared at the happy Mr. Chaley, the Republican Party would put the Dead in their place! Mr. Chaley applauded wildly.

Shortly after this episode, Mr. Chaley, who had contributed two hundred and fifty thousand dollars to the radio war-chest, disappeared, having been committed to an upstate sanitarium on the plea of his wife. Mr. Woodyard lingered on. One of his last acts was to stop a taxicab in the middle of Seventh Avenue traffic and inquire pathetically of its occupants whether the Dead ought to be allowed to interfere with American business to the extent they were doing. At the end he wrote a letter. It was addressed to Mr. Chaley in the upstate insane asylum. It declared fervently that when he, Mr. Woodyard, reopened the air waves to industry, the Chaley products would be the single commodity advertised for thirty days. Alone and without competition of any sort he, Mr. Woodyard, would put on a new and greater Chaley program for twenty-four hours a day without pause.

It was at this point that Mr. Woodyard surrendered to the great beyond, via the office chandelier.

On the day that Mr. Woodyard joined the Heavenly Choir the scientists in charge of the Electrical Sieve succeeded in isolating three Soul Voices. Their report was submitted to the Congressional Committee for the Investigation of the Dead and added to the already voluminous archives of that body. It recorded that one of the three Souls had sung for several hours selections from *The Chocolate Soldier* and refused to answer any questions at all. The second was summarized as an obvious schizophrenic case unable to assemble into any coherent pattern whatever intelligence it possessed. The third Voice was discussed at length and quoted in full.

"We isolated this interesting Voice shortly after 2 p.m.," says the report, "and were pleased with its unusual clarity. It is one of the few Voices we have contacted that preferred expressing itself in speech rather than song. When caught in the Electrical Sieve, it was wailing loudly:

" 'Can you hear me? I am addressing the world of the Living. Can anybody hear me? I have something of vital interest to say.'

"We were able to assure the speaker of our attention. No sooner had we answered than the Voice uttered a curious shout.

" 'Chilly!' it cried. 'Chilly.'

" 'Tell us about it?' we inquired soothingly. 'What makes you chilly?'

"The Voice repeated with excitement: 'Chilly!' and for several minutes disappeared out of our Sieve. It returned, however, and began exclaiming violently:

" 'Chilly! Loveliness! Loveliness and Beauty! If you want to be beautiful be chilly!'

"Aware from experience of the confusion which overcomes the dead Souls, we spoke cautiously to it, pretending to understand its message and to be fascinated by all it was saying.

" 'Unearthly beauty!' it cried. 'Please don't interrupt me. Listen! Fairer than any dream of Heaven. Chilly! Am organizing Dead to be chilly. Stand by for announcement.'

"After some minutes of incoherent babbling which we were unable to decode, the Voice slid gracefully into song, as is the habit of the departed. It appeared to favor the old ballad 'Sweet Genevieve.' It was still singing its haunting notes when it fell out of our Sieve and joined the indistinguishable uproar of the Other Side.

" '*Vale*, sweet singer of Heaven's mysteries,' we called after it.

"As if in reply, we were able to catch a faint, far-away repetition of the word 'chilly.'

"At least this Soul has revealed to us," concludes the report, "that our old conception of Heaven has not been entirely false. From its happy cries Heaven seems to be, as we have always fondly imagined it, a white and snowy chaste domain. That the newcomer to its glories considered it a trifle chilly need not affright us. We must remember that the fevers of earth were still clinging to him."

There are, of course, still many who speak with nostalgia of the Radio Era, and there is always that crop of essayists for whom the past is tender copy. One hears and reads these unscrupulous romanticists moaning away about the Parnassian days of Soup Hours and Cigarette Programs, of the wit, melody, and drama that once throbbed ceaselessly in the ears of our citizens. And remarking these moony historians it would seem that another Golden Age had been snatched from, under our noses by the abolition of the radio.

All of which, as every semi-enlightened reader knows, is a thumping lie. Considered from the medical viewpoint alone the death of the radio is perhaps the greatest boon that has been contributed to the world by science. Statistics for the past decade show a fifty-percent lessening of gastro-intestinal ailments, particularly those due to distention, inflation, and subsequent dehydration by catharsis of the thirty-odd feet of bowel inherent in each human being. The public has slowly been weaned away from its wanton use of physics, deodorants, corn cures, pain killers, and nerve stimulants, with the happiest of results. The millions who were terrorized into alkalinizing their kidneys with proprietary medicines now report sanely to doctors when the occasion warrants, and feel better immediately. Our ladies, also, have taken to hormonotherapy, the latest of medical achievements, rather than to searching for youth in fancy bottles, beribboned salve boxes, and electric belts. Whether they have found it or not is beside the point. At least their faces have become cleaner.

The falling off in smoking, coffee- and pop-tippling, gum chewing, and other semi-pernicious habits has in general helped restore the public health incredibly.

With the disappearance of the impassioned hawker and his thousand and one dehumanizing gadgets and inventions the consumer has lapsed into comparatively human activities. Cooking, for instance, has been restored to the American home. In short, benefits too numerous to itemize have fallen like manna on the Republic.

But more than these concrete advantages has been the improvement in the mood of the world. The silencing of dictators and political dervishes has stabilized our governments. The return of music to the theaters and auditoriums has brought that oldest art back to itself. And there has been restored to man, particularly the workingman, whose leisure hours are precious, some measure of reflection.

A sort of peace has descended on earth. In the very first spring following the miracle many strange and unheard-of things began to happen. People picked flowers again, sat in the grass, read books and poems, or let their hands lie idle in the sun. And Youth took again to walking abroad in the night and raising to the skies that duet of silence which is most acceptable to love and the orderly propagation of the race.

THE ADVENTURES OF
PROFESSOR EMMETT

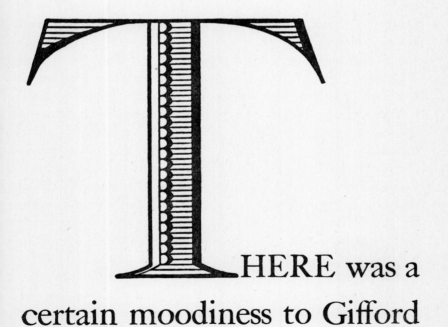

HERE was a
certain moodiness to Gifford

Emmett which he had picked up somehow while acquiring human shape in his mother's belly and which caused him to enter the world with a special lack of equipment for living in it. What he lacked chiefly was the desire to become a human being. Life sometimes produces these reluctant bloodstreams which, like backwaters without beat or destination, remain morbidly outside the traffic of existence.

Gifford Emmett spent his thirty-six years of life in a subtle campaign to return to his mother's womb. Though he matured physically, and his mind developed far enough beyond its fetal stage to earn him a full professorship at a university, Gifford actually never existed. He merely imitated the ways of life as one might the manners of a repugnant country. Like an exile in an undesired land, his soul retained nostalgic recollections. It yearned for its larval state, and all its subsequent stages seemed full of alarms and discomforts.

You will understand this matter better, perhaps, if you look back on your own birthday. Few of us arrive in the world with any real conviction or even positive attitude. We are inclined to squander our time in the womb, only to be dislodged at the last moment, and in many cases evicted. And with many of us, thus driven from our only Eden, there is a tendency to turn our tiny, half-simian backs on the world into which we are ejected. Even the best of us who later grow to assertive manhood come out protesting furiously at the miserable change of fortunes the forceps have to offer. Once out, we signal our despair with heartbreaking noises, or we lie stunned and unbelieving of the nasty trick that has been played on us by our mother's suddenly hostile muscles.

Our infancy is as much a time of readjustment as of education. During the first wretched months of our existence, we must inure ourselves to the repulsive oddity of a cradle vastly too large for us. We have been dethroned and our soul is full of complaints. As the days pass, however, we are wooed and purred into certain revaluations. We are kissed and fondled and made the focal point of this new and inferior existence into which we have blundered. A new if lesser ego is offered us. We are loaded with despot scepters and bedazzled with tyrant crowns. Whereupon, slowly and with many a night of sad weeping, which I myself can well remember, we reconcile ourselves to our second nests, and say farewell forever to our original dream of perfect living.

No such time of reconciliation or farewell, however, came to Gifford Emmett. The reasons for this I shall do my best to reveal.

Little Gifford was born on a December morning of the year 1902, in an old brick house that stood in the second nicest residential section of a small Wisconsin town. At the moment, the town was covered with snow, and in its streets lonely figures, booted and mittened, were prowling about in a blizzard. Under the cold beat of the wind, the Emmett house stood quilted and turreted with snow, its windows and doors half obliterated. In a bedroom too cold either for amour or for its public sequel, Mrs. Emmett lay doing her best to persuade little Gifford to take his place in a larger world.

After some seven violent hours, Mrs. Emmett finally triumphed, and little Gifford appeared, refusing to breathe or offer any tell-tale signs of life. His efforts to outwit the new and the horrible by a possum-like unconsciousness availed him nothing. The family doctor, a canny old gentleman aware of the ruses of the newborn, belabored little Gifford's bottom with a stout palm. Then he shook and rattled him about as if he were no more than a dollar alarm clock to be jarred into ticking. Eventually a tiny moan rewarded the scientist's work, and Gifford Emmett was declared officially in the land of the living.

At this vital and sensitive moment, a disastrous thing happened. The street door of the Emmett house was flung open, and eleven adolescents ranging in age from twelve to sixteen entered as if they were the spirit of the blizzard outside. They came in howling and prancing and fell to rolling on the floor and assaulting each other with snowballs scraped from each other's shoes and hair. Five of these arrivals were the moaning little Gifford's brothers and sisters. The other six were a species of local self-elected orphans who preferred the Emmett home to their own as an arena for feats of strength and budding musical talents.

The opening of the Emmett street door let in a wintry blast that scampered icily up the stairs and into the accouchement chamber. And since none of the eleven arrivals could find time to close the door, the wintry blast grew wintrier. It swirled and steamed up the stairs, and little Gifford, but recently induced to breathe, found himself swept by such frigid currents that he turned instantly blue and began to shake as if with palsy. He wailed once and then fell into that stoical, powerless silence that marked his demeanor for life.

There is no doubt but that little Gifford's aversion to life was fully developed when the forceps seized him. The opening of the door, the wintry blasts, the horrifying shouts of laughter, and the sounds of furniture toppling were merely details that instantly and forever verified his already full-blown conviction that he had been cast out of the best of all possible worlds into a nowhere.

Biologically, the facts are that little Gifford was the fruit of

an unexpected and autumnal flicker of parenthood. Mrs. Emmett
had conceived in her forty-third year, to the disquiet of her husband, himself nearing sixty. And though little Gifford had
emerged a fine infant, with a full quota of appendages, it is fairly
good science to conclude that he had been put together a little
tiredly. The elderly genes and chromosomes laboring at his fashioning had sighed at their work. And that cymbal crash of life
that inspires the newborn to shed its larval soul fell on tired ears
with little Gifford, if he heard it at all.

Whatever world he had been born into, it is likely that Gifford would have bloomed as a psychosis rather than a sultan.
Still the Emmett home did have its share in the non-development
of little Gifford's human side. There was no room or role for
this laggard little guest in the firmly established hullabaloo of
mixed quartets, juvenile sports, and endless riotings that were
the routine of this Wisconsin ménage. Gifford had arrived too
late to be of any use or interest to anybody. For his mother, no
new activities focused on his crib. His father instituted no
new regime for his sake. Nobody breathed or kissed or fondled
an ego into his consciousness. His brothers and sisters regarded
him with the perfunctory interest they had for all creatures who
fitted into neither football squads nor wrestling tournaments, to
say nothing of moonlight singing.

And from his first weeks little Gifford exhibited the detachment of one who knows himself an interloper. He allowed himself quietly to be stowed away in attics and back bedrooms and
other distant culs-de-sac where the banjo and piano banging and
other alarums of adolescence could not reach to break his hypothetical slumbers. He suffered sudden drafts, hunger, and terror,
without even the little comment at his command. And during
such naps as he was able to steal amid the hurly-burly of the

household, he dreamed happily of that land of warmth and plenty from which, like a peri, he had been expelled.

And so Gifford grew into a sober and unprotesting infant, well shapen but enigmatic. Soon he shuffled about on hands and knees, doing his best to avoid flying missiles, charging feet, and other hazards of life. He had no interest in living, but his intelligence had not yet encompassed the idea of suicide. In his second winter, he seemed to all the Emmetts but one a model child. He had by that time completely abandoned his small struggle to become part of life. No music or laughter could lure him now from his seclusion. He haunted the unwanted corners of the house, sitting on the floor and staring tirelessly into space with a sort of oriental calm. When summer came, he crawled into the currant patch behind the house, and lay in the cool dirt under the bushes. His mother, busy with stretching Mr. Emmett's weekly pay check (he was a chemist in the town's bottle works) over the seven days, smiled gratefully on his seeming ability to amuse himself. She misunderstood entirely the moods that sent him crawling under beds and into airless closets. There were times, however, when Gifford's eyes, looking intently at her, startled her and made her wonder if anything was wrong with him. It appeared to her then that the child Gifford looked at her with a most curious and desperate concentration, as if he were weaving a spell. Drawing him to her, she would ask kindly at such times what her little man wanted. But Gifford kept his secret.

The lone Emmett to whom Gifford seemed something less than a model child was Edward, the father. When Gifford was a few weeks old, Edward Emmett perceived that his son hated him. Mr. Emmett said nothing about it. He had long ago been elbowed out of any vital existence by his brood and their satellites, and converted into a fluttering, negligible shade of parent-hood who continued to drop lamb chops and fried potatoes on the Emmett table from his little perch as a bottle maker. This history had conditioned him to keep his thoughts to himself.

When the curious fact that Gifford fell into a fit whenever his father approached him began to be generally noticed, a number of theories sprang up as to its cause. Mr. Emmett defended himself vigorously against charges of clumsiness and unfriendliness. But Mrs. Emmett had still another theory that left him silent. His wife was of the opinion that the little creature objected to the smell of chemicals always rising from Mr. Emmett's person. And her husband recalled that Lily, as a bride, had once burst into tears over some chlorine gas lingering in his mustache, and concluded that Gifford had inherited from his mother this unreasonable distaste for antiseptic odors. Mr. Emmett took to bathing and cologning himself like a stage beauty, but, sweetened though he was, his effect on his son remained unchanged. The otherwise placid infant continued to have convulsions at the sight of him.

Such, without going any further into the matter, was Professor Emmett's childhood. Ignored by his brothers and sisters, misunderstood by his mother, and mysteriously outraged by the male collaborator of his being, Gifford tottered about at the age of three like a little ghost whom every dawn threatened to dissipate. At four he took to running away from home and hiding beneath neighborhood verandas, from under which he was dragged weeping at the frustration of his plans. At five he became a moody survivor of a vanished era, for his brothers and sisters and their hallooing intimates were then scattering to work and to college. Gifford haunted the once gay household like a little beggar poking around in the wake of a carnival. In the summertime, shooed out of the house to get some air, he spent long hours under the currant bushes, inert and moody.

It was in this retreat that Gifford, at six, discovered surprisingly a world that fascinated him. This was the world of insects. His child eyes became aware of ants and spiders, wasps, butterflies, grasshoppers, and earthworms. Lying on his stomach, chin cupped in his hands, Gifford would remain absorbed for hours by the busy ways of this wonderfully unhuman population. He began to see in the seemingly aimless careenings of these, his first friends, certain patterns of conduct. These minute creatures, in whose midst he sprawled like a Gulliver, became significant and interesting to him as human beings had never been, and he watched them as if they were tiny letters spelling out a new and breathless tale.

Through long summer hours he would lie this way, and sometimes, lured by these Pied Pipers of the garden, he followed them to sit like a guest on the thresholds of their curious homes. He learned many things. He became aware of the mother love of the beetle, of the precision and cruelty of the spider, and of the marauderies of the wasps. He grew to know the little wind lanterns of the glow-worm. The large head of the grasshopper, like that of a tissue-paper horse, became as familiar to him as if it spoke. The beetle, senile and saucer-eyed, and the paunchy spider, with its crown of legs, waiting owlishly in its hazy net, were his comrades. None of these diminutive ogres frightened him. Their ominous caricature of human limb and feature pleased him like a set of strange toys. He never tired of watching this little universe crawl and fly and dart, weave its homes and struggle murderously for its food.

Unguided by books, he created for himself a childish version of all he saw. The dark leafy tunnels of the overhanging currant bushes became a fairyland where eccentric-looking heroes performed for him. Dragons and helmeted knights battled on their twig arenas. Hobgoblins hung by invisible threads. Miniature witches leaped through the air, and the eyes of genii gleamed out of tiny holes in the ground. Troubadours, transported by summer, played their violins, and little scarecrow kings teetered on the berry clusters. The ants seemed to him like beaded acrobats of the grass blades. And over the bushes the darning needles fired arrows at the sun, and the butterflies swayed like tiny flags.

Like his friends, Gifford prepared himself for the winter months. He erected an insect zoo in his room. Glass jars containing ants and spiders, wasps, beetles, and flies, crowded his bureau top and his window sills. When the cold days came, Gifford tended his charges anxiously. He fed them and invented diversions for their welfare. He constructed exercise yards for them out of shoe boxes and built rickety mansions of mosquito netting. For the ants he modeled special hills of dirt so that they might not grow homesick.

It seemed unnatural to Mrs. Emmett that anyone should be interested exclusively in bugs. But her efforts to lure her child away were unavailing. It was the despised Mr. Emmett, whom Gifford still hated, but in an inactive fashion now, who rescued his son from the shadows of ignorance that seemed to be permanently enclosing him. Mr. Emmett understood that Gifford was a scientist. He was proud to have handed on to his son his own interest in this profound side of life. Diffidently, Mr. Emmett sat with his son and imparted to him his own theory of education.

"If you will go to Bible class and pay attention to your teacher in school," he said, "you will be allowed to study what you like when you grow up. I can't explain why it is, but you must study about angels and presidents before you can study about bugs. But I can promise you that after you've gone to school a long time, you'll be able to return to insects, and nobody will bother you."

Lured by the promise of this reward, Gifford submitted himself to the educational system. And long after Mr. Emmett's death, the prophecy he had made came true. At thirty-four, Gifford Emmett was raised to a full professorship in the university he had entered as a gloomy, gangling youth. Jars filled with insects, and elaborate cages teeming with his beloved coleoptera and arachnids, crowded his bachelor apartment just as they had his childhood bedroom. And for several hours a week, as Professor of Entomology, he lectured happily on the secrets of that Kingdom of the Little which he had first discovered under the currant bushes.

In leaping thus from the seven-year-old Gifford to the tall, thin, dark-haired, and goggle-eyed savant of thirty-four, I have omitted little of his life that calls for chronicling. During these missing decades Gifford was engaged chiefly in the moody but ungraphic business of receding from the world. He continued to hold himself like a bystander on the outskirts of its charms, its follies, and its adventures. He read tirelessly and studied deeply, and his mind evolved within the egg of inaction. It was a curious mind full of wit and learning. But it revealed itself to no one.

He had matured without tasting anything of life. Now he thrived like some specimen in a bottle, detached from his species and forgetful of them. Only one thing occasionally disturbed him. This was a periodic lapse into melancholia. The desire to die seized him each year of his life, and stretched him weeping and inanimate in his bed. These melancholic fits lasted usually through the week of his birthday. He suffered then from a sense of suffocation. The chill and contemptuous wit of his mind turned to fog. He lay staring at unbearable walls and listening to sounds of a life that tortured him. However, he always recovered quickly, and resumed his reading and his friendless ways of living as if nothing had interrupted them.

There are some of us, many more than are usually counted, who do not grow up at all. Life is unable to alter these little ones among us despite the plant-like increase of their bodies. In them the child persists not as a dim imprisoned ghost, but as a face always visible. All the trappings of age, its wrinkles, its wisdom, and its very largeness, seem like misfit clothes in which these children must stagger grotesquely about. And no matter what their lives or passions may be, there remains stamped on their reluctant adulthood the bewitched and pathetic contour of innocence.

Professor Emmett was of these nursery lingerers. His face glowed as if it were a shell that had never known wind or sun. So gentle and disarming did the smallest of his gestures seem that there was hardly a female student but felt an impulse to mother him. Men were equally charmed by his staccato wit and childlike simplicity. But Professor Emmett, who, if you looked closely, was still the little Gifford busy with his currant-bush comrades, evaded any intimacies.

In his thirty-fifth year, however, an adventure and a relationship befell him. And with it my tale of Professor Emmett's Homeric adventures in a sense begins.

Myra McKillup entered Gifford Emmett's life at that precise moment when he had decided to quit it. The melancholia that had assailed Gifford since his boyhood had subsided in his thirties. Now as he was approaching thirty-five it returned. Animation once more left him. Mysterious tears coursed out of his soul and overran his cheeks.

Of the diseases that touch the hearts of others, those of the subconscious are certainly the least. It is difficult to take seriously the nightmares which these oddly afflicted ones seem to parade as pets. We are inclined to regard them as impostors rather than martyrs. The fact that these impostors frequently leap from windows, hurl themselves under trains, thrust their heads into gas ovens, or blow out their brains is not enough to convince us of their reality. Their deaths come too late to impress us with their diseases. Even those who weep at the bier of the neurotic are inclined to withhold their sympathy for the secret agony that sent him to the undertaker's.

Thus, though I have come to a moment in my hero's life that might well call for a little tenderness from any reader, I feel it better to deal unemotionally with the matter. Of objective griefs such as we fancy drive folk to their deaths Gifford had no more than any of the grasshoppers he tended in their bottles. No amorous or professional entanglements beset him. No frustrations sawed at his nerves. Around him lay a little world of flattery, and he had no dreaded tomorrows awaiting him. Yet with all this well-being at his fingertips, Gifford sat ready to die. And if the reader will not cry over the fact he must at least believe it, and not assert that Gifford was behaving absurdly, as wives have been known to remark of husbands just before the latter leaped out of windows.

For a half-hour Professor Emmett sat inert and befogged. He held in his hand a small bottle of chemical which he was about to drink. Outside, it was a lavish spring morning. The windows of his study were open and through them came the shout of early vernal winds, colors, and odors. But this lean, goggle-eyed man remained insensible. Insensible, too, he stayed before another phenomenon. His spiders, hatched on this spring morning, had climbed the towering bamboo stalks provided for them and were escaping through the open windows, afloat on their silken rockets. Unmindful of this long-awaited spectacle, Professor Emmett blankly regarded the poison in his hand. Like any of his brothers in their bottles, he too sat separated from life by walls that obscured its breath. No tragic thoughts were in his head, and his reason for dying was no more than an oppression that called for death as thirst calls for water.

Occupied thus with the vague gesture which in a moment would bring about his dissolution, Gifford was unaware of a visitor until she had come close to him and removed the open bottle from his mouth. He looked up and saw dimly a dark-haired young woman with large trembling eyes. And at this moment Gifford was overcome with a misunderstanding of Myra McKillup that precipitated his first romance.

He saw her, this sad man pulled back to life, as a creature full of calm, beauty, and goddess-like radiance. A measure of his misunderstanding may be seen in the fact that Miss McKillup was a thin girl, undersized and meatless except for her breasts. These were not large, but, landscaped as they were by famine, they seemed plenty.

Because Gifford's desire to die had been only a temporary one he felt a surge of gratitude for this student who had entered his study by mistake, as she explained. Part of the need he immediately felt for her was probably due to her seeming to his bewitched senses a maternal figure. She had brought him to life, like a secondary mother, and Gifford's long campaign to re-enter his mother's womb transferred itself, a little more practically, to Miss McKillup. He stared at her from that first day with timorous, incestuous eyes, and she seemed to him a human being cast in a tender and superior mold.

This concept too was as completely unrelated to any image of the young woman as his first physical estimate. In addition to being as unmotherly as a hop-toad, Miss McKillup was actually a flibberty nerve-racking creature with a touch of pituitary emaciation. She owned a mind much like a sieve, through which her twenty-five years of life had passed leaving behind a froth of hysteria. She was an unstable and muddle-headed girl. She had a thin, forward-thrusting face like a bird's, bony hands, and a talent for breathlessness. She considered herself a superior person, for no reason that I can determine. It may be she fancied herself more sensitive than most people, and regarded her inability to talk rationally on any subject as a measure of some kind of mysticism rather than stupidity. She inhabited every cliché like an Archimedes yelling "Eureka." She was a-swoon with economics, art, and a bit of biology. There are whole continents of such women, who seem to feel that they master any subject they take up merely by sighing on it. Attracted by an idea, they belabor it with gasps and tremors as if they were coaxing it into bed with them. Usually, to do them justice, there is some sort of male attached to the idea.

Miss McKillup was of this inarticulate and oracular run of femininity. She was enrolled in a post-graduate journalism course under the not entirely erroneous impression that she belonged on a newspaper—as some kind of critic. Perhaps there was nothing more the matter with her than a need for seeming more intelligent than she was, which so often turns people into fools. Or perhaps she sought to reveal a beauty of soul as a lure for the opposite sex, there being little other bait at her disposal. Unsavory-looking girls often go in for this sort of spiritual cosmetics and flit about with over-rouged ideas and insane-looking mental coiffures.

I intend, however, to run no magnifying glass over Myra. That Gifford should have fallen in love with this lady at first sight and beheld her as a Demeter full blown with the blessings of the earth is a matter between him and his subconscious. My hero, who had never once felt the stirring of libido, was overcome suddenly by a mating instinct as implacable as it was mistaken. This movement of sap in Gifford, however, expressed itself only in a desire to talk. And the professor's many admirers looked on with surprise as their good savant devoted himself to addressing incessantly on the most abstruse of topics a young woman whom they knew to be as rattle-brained as a mongoose.

The curious couple was to be seen haunting all the lonely places that neighbored the university. Pale with long confinement in its bottle, the soul of Professor Emmett emerged and fluttered moth-like before the light it fancied lay in Miss McKillup's eyes. It filled the night with the colors of its wit and wisdom, for it is the habit of long-locked-away lovers to create themselves first before they fall to sighing for another.

It would be cruel to say that Myra understood nothing of what Gifford revealed to her during these trysts. Women usually understand what is said to them in courtship, but their listening has so much more coquetry than scholarship in it that the most Socratic of dialogues turn to valentines under their applause. Yet it is only fair to point out that if Myra listened with other organs than were meant for words to the wisdom of Professor Emmett, the latter was, in a sense, not speaking to her at all. She had accidentally removed the top of the bottle and the professor was emerging genie-fashion.

Gifford began his love-making with an attack on life. His aversion for living had spun many dark ideas in his head. His wooing of Miss McKillup consisted, to the end, of an effort to convince her of the infamy and absurdity of human existence.

For their first tryst, Miss McKillup had guided the professor to a little hilltop overgrown with tall grasses. This was the evening of Gifford's rescue from death. He had clung all day to Miss McKillup, allowing her to cool his head with icy towels and to induce him to eat. Still shaken by the double experience of attempting death and of discovering the first woman he had ever found tolerable, Gifford sat moodily on the hilltop. Now his melancholia thawed into phrase. The shawl of pain lifted from his senses and he spoke coolly and lucidly to his companion.

"I have always hated life," said Gifford, "and have found human existence a sort of calamity."

"You say human existence," said Miss McKillup with the air of a philosopher. "Is there any other?"

Gifford's romance almost collapsed under this insensate question. He looked coldly at the young woman.

"Human existence," he said, "is the least of the phenomena of Nature. The most rudimentary thinker must see us as a needle in a haystack. The history of the human race from its first grunt to its last sigh will be hardly more than a footnote to the story of life. We are less than a chirp in Bedlam."

"I know," said Miss McKillup sadly, "but don't you think there's some God who is aware of us, or some force?"

"God is aware of us only if He is a microscope," said Gifford, "or unbalanced. Our species will have come and gone too quickly to interest any sane Super-Intelligence."

Miss McKillup sighed and her face became full of compassion for the littleness of man.

"I've often wondered," she said, "what the end of our race

would be. Whether the insects would finally vanquish us—or what?"

"The insects are not interested in us," said Gifford irritably. "We are too vague and unimportant in the scheme of things to attract their attention. They bite us purely by accident. As for vanquishing us, nothing could be further from their thoughts. It is rarely that one species vanquishes another. The mind of the earth which we call Nature is so exquisitely balanced a pendulum of creation and destruction that even the most foolish of its children are able to survive."

Miss McKillup looked wistfully at the stars as if she were saying farewell to them.

"It is not the insects who will nibble our species into extinction," announced Gifford. "Our fate is more tragic than that. Man will be one of the few suicides in Evolution."

After a silence during which he continued to stare abstractedly at her knees, Gifford informed Miss McKillup that the dissolution of the human race already cast its shadow into our day. Thought, like a Walpurgis Night, was descending on man and the time was nearing when he would vanish on all the broomsticks of his philosophies. Luckily Miss McKillup was more stirred by his attentions than his assertions, or she might have become sincerely depressed.

Gifford launched into his first courtship essay. The human mind, he said, began very slowly. It took a long time to improve on its first growls. Why it began at all is a mystery. All we can be sure of is that it was intended as a serviceable bit of plasm. Let us say a sixth sense—a sense of knowing. Nature is full of similar compensating gifts for those of her children unable to run, fly, dig, smell, see, or hear too well. Each of these possesses the gift of some ruse by which it can outwit its enemies sufficiently for survival, like the spider's sting, or the glue arrows of the soldier ant.

Miss McKillup, listening, was surprised to find so much violence in this gentle and child-like man. Nevertheless, it pleased her, for it gave her a duty. She would make this morbid but delightful scholar change his opinions about life, which she was certain he would do under the influence of a little sweetness.

"For a long time," Gifford spoke up again, "the human mind fulfilled its simple destiny. It enabled us to outwit our better-equipped enemies. Primitive man was a very fortunate animal. But we are in no way related to him. We have been whisked out of Nature into the Alice in Wonderland realm of thought. Our mind has hatched a universe. It has projected a world of phantoms on the screen of our senses. We inhabit this world. We crawl on our animal legs into a mirror."

"Please go on," said Miss McKillup throatily.

Gifford remained silent.

After a pause Miss McKillup added wistfully: "I want to hear."

"I think you will understand me better," he resumed, "if I discuss the human mind merely as a parasite."

"Yes," said Miss McKillup breathlessly, "oh, yes. It will be much easier for me. Although everything you say is marvelously clear. Marvelously!"

Gifford nodded and waited for her to find a more comfortable piece of ground. She selected a place near his ankles and, lying down again, this time on her stomach, raised her face eagerly.

"The parasite mind," said Gifford, "is already nibbling at the biologic sanity of the species. Most of modern medicine is the record of the mind's ability to cripple the body. Modern history also has become a record of mental aberration on a grand scale. Intellectual quibbles now breed our wars. It's not difficult to foresee a world locked in a death struggle over theories for its improvement.

"But," mused Gifford, "I don't think the species will destroy itself in this coming struggle of Tweedledee and Tweedledum."

Miss McKillup sighed like a harp that is being plucked. All the same, the dissolution of the race disturbed her much less than the appearance of a slight flush in the professor's cheeks.

"It's so warm," she said softly. "Wouldn't you rather take your coat off?"

"Thank you," said Gifford mechanically and removed it.

"And your waistcoat," Miss McKillup insisted. This too was removed.

"No," Gifford resumed as she loosened his tie, "it will not be the war of man against man that will bury us in the grave of the dodo bird. Man against himself will be our finish. Not an honorable death, mind you, on the field of battle, but a gruesome suicide in the loneliness of the night, is the fate that awaits us. This suicide has begun. Thought has already crippled our nature. Our efforts to live by our ideas as if they were our bloodstream have rotted away half our health.

"Just look at us today," Gifford cried out to the seemingly fascinated young woman beside him, "us creatures who call ourselves the top of Evolution. Lords of the world, indeed! Why, the humblest beetle might laugh at us if it had time for the study of nonsense."

Gifford paused and stared at the night over the hilltop. How pleasant it was to speak thoughts, even the sullenest! He breathed excitedly. A new and exhilarating argument against life had just occurred to him.

"Our senses," he announced, "are caught in a net of reason. There's hardly a single thing we feel but we must busy ourselves misunderstanding or improving it. All our animal desires must crawl around on the flypaper of our mind and either die there or drag out an enfeebled existence breathing the poison of our ideals. All the magnificent functions of Nature are becoming confused in us. We can't sleep. Eating gets to be more and more complicated. Sex has become full of hazards and confusions. Morality and poetry have so bewildered the spinal cord that it has forgotten how to signal for a blood supply.

"Yes," cried Gifford triumphantly, "our search for the Ideal has converted our glandular system into a rubbish heap! Unable to transmute us into angels, our minds have turned us into invalids. Our last stand will be in the laboratories—as patients. Our scientists will toil away desperately at extricating our organs from the octopus of the mind. But I'm certain they won't succeed."

After a pause, during which he noticed with some surprise that Miss McKillup's head was now resting in his lap, Gifford continued.

"Have you ever noticed how the spider captures and destroys the powerful locust that leaps accidentally into its net?" he asked.

"No," Miss McKillup said, and sighed.

"The legs of the locust," explained Gifford, "are strong enough to kick the silken snare to shreds. But, as the spider stays out of reach, invisible to the procrastinating locust, it remains busy at work. It envelops the struggling bit of life in a flow of almost invisible thread. Round and round the locust the spider spins its delicate strait-jacket. Finally the locust is unable to move. Then our spider leisurely drains it of its blood, and the locust shell is left hanging in a net to rattle in the wind. We will end in a similar way. Enveloped by thought spun around us, our species will finally wither away to a few last neurotic husks, and then hang motionless in the web."

A little later the two strolled down the hill to the university, Miss McKillup clinging to Gifford's arm. She was pleased with what she called their first heart to heart talk, for she saw that it had made Professor Emmett extremely happy. He smiled when he said good-night to her, and she watched him walk off with a youthful spring in his long legs, trailing his coat and vest like a workman come home from a picnic.

A number of similar trysts followed, which I might report. But I shall hold myself down to the account of only one more. This took place a week later.

After they had dined together one evening, Miss McKillup— she was known to Professor Emmett as Myra now—guided him to a new rostrum, a little wooded river bank remembered from a previous love affair with a member of the university rowing crew. But Gifford ignored the loveliness of the spot, as he did for the most part the presence of his companion. For he was still too selfish in his pleasure to notice any contributing factors.

Just the same, he spent the first few minutes fidgeting and silent. This was because he suffered as always from the result of too much expectation. It takes time to adjust oneself to the reality of a Miss McKillup when one has walked with Dante's Beatrice all day.

Miss McKillup—Myra—did not allow herself to become discouraged by this ominous beginning. She smiled breathlessly as they sat in the little grotto once sacred to Venus and an oarsman.

"I've been looking forward so all day to this," she said. "I've lost interest in everything else in the world—except listening to you."

Gifford blushed, being unused to such bouquets. He remained silent and listened to the frogs and crickets singing everywhere in the spring night.

"I feel," went on Myra, "I feel as if we had known each other a long time. A terribly long time. I suppose that's because I can't remember ever having had any thoughts except those you've given me."

"The frogs sound very musical, don't they?" said Gifford.

"Divine," said Myra quickly.

"But it's a horrible music to others," Gifford said.

"Others?" cried Myra and looked around in alarm.

"I mean the insects," said Gifford. "Whenever I hear a frog I can almost feel the terror of the coleoptera and arachnids."

"Nature," said Myra, "is cruel, isn't it?"

"No," said Gifford. "That's a most ridiculous misconception. There's no cruelty in Nature. There are only necessity and precision. No animal tortures another animal. The frog devouring the spider acts out of an instinct shared by the spider. It is their stomachs and not their souls that are thrilled by murder."

"I hadn't thought of that," said Myra soothingly.

"Nature," said Gifford, "is a banquet board at which the feasters and the feast are one. This was shown to me once when I watched a praying mantis eat a grasshopper. The grasshopper had caught a caterpillar a moment before. It continued undisturbed to eat this caterpillar while the praying mantis munched on its own legs. Not until the mantis sank its teeth into the grasshopper's digestive organs did the latter abandon its own feast."

"It's all so frightening." Myra shivered.

"To me," said Gifford, "it is merely sane. I find our own

species vastly more terrible than the mantis, the spider, and the
humble caterpillar. Our mind is supposed to have improved on
the manners of Nature. But if you examine our activities you
will find that the mind has done little more with our animal
criminality than rationalize its crimes. It has added to the simple
murder-politic inherent in Nature the genius for depriving the
victim not only of his life but of his good repute. There's no monster, in Nature, whose fangs are as cruel as our ideas."

"We are all animals in exile," said Myra with a shiver.

Gifford thought it astonishing that she should not only understand him but share his point of view. He was also surprised that
this young woman's head in his lap failed to check the flow of
his thought, but somehow increased his desire to communicate
his ideas to her. Despite a slight numbness in his thigh, he permitted her to remain pillowed there.

"I'm afraid it's going to rain," said Gifford.

"Oh, no," Myra sighed, "I'm sure it won't."

"There's no question of it," said Gifford firmly. "I've been
watching that spider." He pointed to a bush overhead. "She refuses to repair her web. When the spider refuses to reweave her
web at night it's always a sign of rain."

"And yet," sighed Myra, "man believes himself the only
thinking animal."

"He is," Gifford corrected her. "Spiders don't think. Nor do
the bees or the ants. It's true some entomologists presume to see
in the precision of insect life human motivations such as love,
hate, ambition, or sacrifice. This is ridiculous. Take the case of
the Clotho moth. This moth, who sews so wonderful a nest for
her children, fills it also with materials out of which they will be
able to weave their first spring frocks. Without these they would
die of cold. Having laid out this wardrobe, the Clotho moth fin-

ishes her work of nest building by plugging up the last little hole in it with her own body. She dies with her wings spread as a barrier against her children's enemies. She might seem to be the most infatuated of Nature's mothers. Yet to call her a mother at all is to libel her. For the moth is unaware of what is in her eggs. She never lives to see them hatch. It is absurd to imagine that love for these never-to-be-seen moth infants animates her. They are, in fact, not her children but her ghosts. They are her future shapes. It is life she perpetuates. She is as devoid of personality as the wind that rocks her tiny body. Her loving and thinking are both done for her by a never-blundering hypnosis we must call instinct."

Gifford paused and looked lovingly at the night, and Myra wondered why he was trembling.

"How wise the insects are," he said softly. "Their learning is so great and their joy of life so intense it seems almost inconceivable that they have not evolved that foolish talent for comment which would destroy their Eden. How enviable their world is. . . . The bee, for instance, so industrious, and yet as devoted to capering and singing as any drunken troubadour. You might," he added wistfully, "call the bee a hymn to life."

He addressed the girl tenderly.

"You never see an insect becoming irrational or insane, do you, Myra? The reason for this, you see, is that her talent is not her own. It belongs to her species, and she can neither improve on it nor discard it. She feels the pleasure of living, but she has no ego with which to distort or exaggerate it. And so she doesn't confuse either herself or her species.

"For instance, the cicada is like some wonderful fiddler. When it emerges from the earth in the spring, it is overcome by the marvel of sun and air, and it strikes up a tune, playing on its wing with its saw-toothed right leg. But luckily it is stone deaf and doesn't hear its own paean to the spring. If it did, it might become a musician and cease to be an insect. It would devote all its instincts to music and disintegrate as a cicada."

Myra opened her eyes and smiled.

"You know," she said, "you have made me realize how much greater our spirit is than our so-called intelligence."

Gifford hoped she was using the word "spirit" in the right sense, but was fearful of inquiring. In a moment, however, he forgot completely the presence of his companion despite the fact that both his legs had now turned numb under the weight of her head. He sat looking happily at the scenery of the night. The rain was coming. Its smell arrived first. He smiled at the wise spider idling on the verbena leaf. The dark about him trembled as if awaiting a visitor. The leaves were stirring with the new pressure of the air. The night was full of microscopic traffic as his old friends fled for shelter or emerged to flit and dive in the film of moisture hanging everywhere. He remembered that in his childhood he had lain often under the bushes waiting for the soft explosion of the rain.

"It's amazing," said Myra, who had reached the collaborative stage of female pursuit, "but sometimes when you talk I almost feel that you're not really a member of our species, but an ant or a beetle or something."

Afraid that she had disparaged her admirer, Myra presently amended this.

"I mean with a soul of course."

But Gifford was flattered.

"It's hard to tell what we are," he smiled. "We have only our mind to figure with—and it's difficult to think out any of the mysteries of which we are only so small a part."

Myra had no such difficulty.

"I believe in the transmigration of souls," she said, throwing back her head.

"Fairytales," said Gifford, after a pause, "are likely to contain just as much truth as science. For, whatever Truth is, it seems to express itself as much in fantasies as in facts. Every movement of our mind is inspired by the Truth that exists forever outside it. Who knows but we will yet discover that our myths are the real science and that science is the only myth?"

"Then you do believe in soul transmigration!" Myra cried. "You do! Please don't deny it!"

"I never deny anything," Gifford said patiently. "All thought is the shadow of some truth we cannot understand. And since we can't ever see the Truth, I think it wise to study all the shadows it casts and to discount none of them."

"How wonderful that we should both believe in soul transmigration!" Myra chanted.

This was too much for Gifford.

"I don't know anything about soul transmigration," he said a little angrily. Then he added, more for the sake of politeness:

"However, Nature is so economical, it may be she uses her forces over and over. Perhaps she does this with the spirit of life, and perhaps this life force continues like a never-broken thread on which she strings the endless little brittle beads of our bodies."

"Oh, to come back to life again as a bird!" cried Myra, carried away by what she felt to be their mutual understanding. "Oh, to fly, to sing, to——"

"It would be terrible for the bird," Gifford interrupted in

alarm. "A bird with a human soul in it, even the remains of such a soul, would be a most ridiculous and incompetent fowl. I can't bear to think of anything in Nature so handicapped."

The rain came. A mist and an odor trickled into the little clearing. The roof of leaves resounded with the rain clamor.

Gifford was silent. It occurred to Myra that he was a very strange man. She sat up and looked at him. He was sitting, ears cocked to the wild hum of the rain. She watched his dark unflickering eyes and wondered what they were seeking in the night. He seemed to have fallen into a trance. She touched his hand to waken him, but his curious expression remained unchanged. The round black eyes protruded, empty and sage-like. The thin lips were curled inward over the teeth. The entire face glistened with so mad a preoccupation that Myra shivered. Gifford's face seemed for an instant like something brittle rising out of the grass and regarding the night with an ominous and secret understanding.

"What are you thinking?" Myra asked softly.

"Nothing," Gifford answered. "I wasn't thinking."

Myra drew nearer to his side.

"How foolish people seem in the rain," said Gifford suddenly, "as if rain were no longer meant for them. They've left the breast of Nature."

"Is there no way back for us?" asked Myra. "I mean, for those who understand?"

"No," said Gifford, "we're on our way somewhere else."

After its first gusts, the rain dwindled. Myra decided that the climax of their tryst had been passed.

They walked back arm in arm to the university. On this night Gifford was too preoccupied to smile when he left her.

After Myra McKillup had listened to Professor Emmett for a month she put an end to his talk by marrying him. There is no need to go into the tender and unscrupulous progressions at the end of which our hero found himself before the altar. He was a little amazed and considerably bewildered. After having been blessed by the minister and kissed by the bride, Gifford suddenly asserted himself. He refused to go on a honeymoon.

He announced, a little tardily, that he had been looking forward to these three summer months as a perfect time to investigate the stomach of the termite. He was determined, Gifford firmly told his bride on their way home, to solve the riddle of the parasites that inhabited this wood-devouring insect's stomach. It was these parasites that provided the termite, to Gifford's never-ending amazement, with a digestive apparatus omitted by Nature in its construction.

Seated in his apartment, now newly curtained and groomed out of recognition, Gifford did his best to explain the intricacies of the problem to his bride. And technical though this problem was, I feel its details are entitled to the precedence given them by the bridegroom. His investigations into the termite's digestive phenomena, started on the day of his marriage, were to mean more to him than the pathetic relationship into which he had been whisked. They were to outlast this union and even himself, and they were—in these pages at least—to place his name on the small scroll of heroes. I shall therefore join Gifford Emmett in elbowing aside his marital duties in favor of the colony of termites to which he hurried right after the wedding ceremony.

Gifford's interest in the parasites that served the termite in the place of digestive organs antedated by many years his wooing of Myra McKillup. He had, as he explained soothingly to Myra, often watched these microscopic mills at work. The parasites and not the insect converted into a nutritive pulp the otherwise fatal wood cellulose it consumed. It was indeed odd that the termite, considered by scientists the most essential mouth in Nature, should be lacking in its own digestive equipment. For it was the termite whose unique and diminutive jaws were the pestles that ground death into life. They transmuted the cadavers of trees into that womb of nitrate which is earth. Without this spectacular work done by the termites, as Gifford had often informed his students, the world would have hardened into a vitrified and unproductive crust long ago. The mundane detail that in their heroic task as earth-makers the termites also nibbled away a few wooden houses seemed to Gifford hardly worthy of consideration. The termites were of vastly more importance to the world than the handful of people they inconvenienced. Yet for this vast and scientific task, Nature had devised an incomplete tool. The stomach of the termite was incapable of the miracle assigned it. Its labor was contracted out to parasites.

Concerning this, Gifford had a theory which he admitted (to his petulant bride) was more romantic than scientific. He sometimes thought that the very importance of the task had inspired Nature to divide its execution so mysteriously. Thus, if something disastrous happened to the termites as a species, the parasites, much more invulnerable, would survive to seek out another ally within which to carry on the great work.

But the greatest riddle to him (Gifford also confided to Myra) was that of the parasite's genesis in the insect's stomach. For the termite was born innocent of them. They showed up later, a work-crew arriving as if by magic to take up the business of converting the earth's dead wood into life-giving soil. On the death of the termite they departed. Gifford was determined to uncover the secret of the parasites' arrival.

Two theories attracted him. Either the newly born termites acquired their work-crew from the excrement of their older fellows, on which they fed and which served as a transport service for the parasites; or the termites were part of a double birth phenomenon truly unique in Nature. It was possible that they were born with parasite eggs already in their useless stomachs and that these eggs contained their supplementary selves.

Myra was left during the long days of her honeymoon to contemplate these matters and a few others even more disturbing. But for Gifford his parasite hunt was the happier side of marriage. He secured the help of Professor Gerald Canning, an accomplished biological chemist, with whom he spent the greater part of his honeymoon.

But Gifford's home life can no longer be ignored. Even Gifford was becoming aware of certain challenging factors in it. The first and most disturbing of these was that in marrying the provocative Miss McKillup he had suddenly found himself locked away with a companion to whom he was totally unable to talk.

The explanation for this evaded our confused bridegroom. Like so many men Gifford had been lured into wedlock not by a woman but by a superior version of himself risen genie-fashion out of his bottled existence. It was, in a sense, himself he had married. He had taken a witty and exuberant Professor Emmett to the altar, and apparently left him there.

This hidden and evanescent self, which the most unlikely of women are able to evoke in us, is one of the chief causes of marital disaster. Its disappearance at the first breakfast table gives the groom the uneasy impression that he is bewitched. The phenomenon occurs most often to unsexual men in whom the mating instinct gives birth to personality rather than desire. Enchanted by their vivified personalities, these bridegrooms collapse like a jack-in-the-box at the first conjugal caress. The superiority born during their courtship is almost instantly deflated in the marriage bed. The former lover full of dreams and rhetoric vanishes like an impostor. There is left an inferior and useless husband.

Gifford was thus stranded. The situation of the incompetent male has long been a comic fixture. But it inspires less laughter today than in heartier times. There is a phase of sex of which the world is becoming sadly more and more aware. It is the fact that the generative organs have a deeper capacity for giving pain than pleasure. Normality, pleasing and diverting though it be, rarely lifts the soul higher than the bedposts. Abnormality, however, can plunge it down into Hell.

It is perhaps to insure our survival as a species—as Gifford might have explained it—that Nature places such a penalty on the absence of sex in us, and invests its lack with such irrational agonies and confusions. Though love, to the male, is usually a minor diversion, his inability to love becomes an entire career. It became, and quickly, the whole consideration of the loveless Emmett household.

The issue, at the beginning, was not of Gifford's making. Although cast down by his lack as a husband, Gifford was inclined to regard the matter in its perspective. It had no bearing on his labors of dissecting the termite stomach, which he considered his real lifework. The absence of any sensual interest in Miss Mc-Killup came as no surprise to him. Neither she nor any other woman had stirred even so much as curiosity in his head. He would have been as much astounded at any evidence of passion in himself as if he had grown horns. Accordingly he had weathered the first nights with more distaste than panic and hurried off to his termite colony with the childish hope that his incompetence would soon turn his bride's attention to other matters.

Although innocent, he had brought to his nuptial couch a curious sex lore gained from watching through a magnifying glass the libidinous moments in the lives of his spiders, beetles, and ants. His shyness before the swooning Myra was a little complicated by these memories of cohabitings studied since his boyhood. The hundred fierce little dramas of insect amour, whose details he had fully recorded in notebooks, bewildered him on his own bridal night as much as the memories of any rake. There was one scene in particular that kept recurring to him during his first days as a groom. It was the mating of a praying mantis observed seven times enlarged under his glass.

He had come upon the affaire mantis just as the female, lean and spectral, had permitted the woefully lesser male on her back. He had watched the tall and dreadful bride turn her serpent head and begin slowly munching on the passionately employed lover. The Romeo's head, wings, legs, and torso had disappeared under the razor-edged jaws of his mate. Yet this headless, legless, armless, but still enfevered swain had continued at his devotions. There had remained of him finally little more than a sexual organ. This, still alert and full of lubricity, had concluded by itself the act of love.

Gifford's imagination fastened on this spectacle the moment Myra emerged from her dressing-room in a creamy, green-dappled negligee with flaring sleeves, and held out her arms to him. The costume had instantly reminded Gifford of the hieratic and macabre wings of the mantis used by that ogress to bewitch her prey. He had said nothing of this to Myra. He felt during the following days, however, that he would be unable to embrace her as his wife as long as she reminded him, by coloration and gesture, of that cannibal insect.

On the fifth day of his marriage Gifford stopped on his way home from Professor Canning's laboratory to buy Myra a blue unpatterned negligee with tight sleeves. Myra, whose sex lore had not been acquired through a magnifying glass, accepted the gift without understanding. She kissed her husband gratefully, but appeared that night in the creamy, green-dappled, mandarin-sleeved transparency which she believed to be extremely seductive. Gifford shuddered, broke into a cold sweat, and clung fearfully to his own bed. After some minor caresses Myra retired to her pillows. She lay for a long time considering the various courses open to her in this combat with Gifford's virginity.

Left alone during the day, Myra preoccupied herself with what now appeared to her a tragic matter. She went over in her mind her own experiences. Though limited to the oarsman and a youthful cousin seduced during her own adolescence, these had left her with a workman-like knowledge of sex. She was also well read on the subject. Her thirst for wisdom of every sort had led her to devour numerous books on sexual abnormalities. Like most young women of the time she had substituted Freud for Browning and was as versed in the horrors of love-making as her sisters had once been in its poetry. But Myra's mind being a sieve, neither her experience nor her reading availed her. Her therapy was reduced to clumsy attempts at rape. All this rough-and-tumble wantonness failed to help the bridegroom. The impression only deepened in Gifford that if there ever was a praying mantis, here was one in his bed.

My attitude toward Myra is, perhaps, unfair. It occurs to me that the ex-Miss McKillup was a young woman lacking in malice or any of the villainies of temperament that wives so often bring as their sole dowries to marriage. She was neither possessive nor given to that home-wrecking preoccupation with her mirror which vainer faces, or prettier ones, adopt as a career. Her heart was kind, and her delusions of being a superior woman were for the most part harmless and inarticulate. She felt deeply on the subject of the professor's prestige and future, and was awed, as she should have been, by his talents. And no one could have asked of Gifford's wife a more hopeful scientific prognosis for his single but vital failing.

Yet with all these qualities I am inclined to accept Gifford's first nuptial glimpse of her as a praying mantis. She would devour him a little more subtly than that rapier-bodied, balloon-winged horror of the insect world. But devour him in the end she would. Stupidity is the cannibalism of the female. It is able, no less than razor-edged teeth, to devour men of talent.

Gifford Emmett did not live long enough to be either devoured or uncolored by the commonplaceness of the woman he had married. He underwent, however, some preliminary fading, just as Myra exhibited that first blossoming of a vocabulary enlarged by his phrases which would have resulted in time in that pathetic common denominator that Strindberg has named "the marriage likeness."

During this first and only year, however, Myra was too busy in other spell-weaving directions to have any influence on Gifford as a mind and an entomologist. She had fallen to work during the first flush of their honeymoon on turning Gifford into a male —which, by the way, is about the only thing women can't turn us into. They can clip our wings and turn us into barnyard companions. Or dip our sandals in the glue of their devotion and turn us into domestic statuary. But men they cannot make of us.

It seems a pity, too, that these alchemists who are able to transmute us into the gold of husbandhood can do so little about the simple backwardness of our glands. But the truth is that perhaps the only medicine that fails utterly as a cure for male impotence is a woman. Exercise, a change of diet, an ocean trip, diathermy, a confession to the police, a rise in the stock market—these are among the numerous therapies for a shy libido. At least they are harmless. But the female rampant as a panacea is not only useless but as menacing as the unrestricted sale of arsenic. In her avid arms, impotency, a minor disease if there ever was one, turns into lunacy.

Not that there was any hope for Gifford's insufficiency. My poor hero was as lost to the joys of sex as any parthenogenic worm. His spinal cord was as detached from the signaling female as if it were a-flutter in the wind.

Yet, there is this point—before his marriage Gifford had not suffered from his missing libido. He had been, I admit, the victim of a melancholia that had led him unassisted to the portals of death. But it was a poetical and uncrystallized melancholia. Neither a doting wife nor, later, medical science, had stripped him of his toga as a philosopher. Had he died at that time he would have been buried with his soul intact. It was a serpent's trick to give him of the apple to eat and to send him cowering and outcast to his grave.

Gifford's cowering began in the third month of his marriage. Before that time he worked feverishly over his termites. He filled scores of notebooks. He sought to hide his unserviceable masculinity in other industries. But there is no concealment for a man who has found a part of himself ridiculous. The canker will eat away his conquests, and his one little useless organ, like a worm, will devour his greatness. Finding himself night after

A Book of Miracles

night stretched beside a woman, and always as futile and absurd as if he were a bit of rotten cork, Gifford began to lose his character. The mornings found him more and more morose. He arrived at the laboratory with a clouded eye. Week by week the talents he had developed came to seem less than those he had been born without.

His impotence finally spread to the ants. He was as unable to deal satisfactorily with the termites as with Myra. Soon he was no longer able to eat properly. A tremor made his delicate research work impossible. Sleep withheld itself. Nightmares rode his bed. He grew gaunt and a little stooped. A harried look gleamed from his eyes. His desire to become a male, and his increasing psychic efforts toward that end, had been received apparently as a declaration of war by his well-armed subconscious. A conflict had started in Gifford, and his organs became a befogged battleground. He sat around twitching and bedeviled with the echoes of this hidden warfare.

In the fourth month Myra insisted that he consult a psychoanalyst. It was only fair to both of them, Myra argued, that he turn to science, since love had failed. Gifford resisted. His soul rebelled against this picture of itself being stripped like an onion in an analyst's office. His wisdom shuddered before the thought of being treated as if it were the layers of a disease. How foolish it seemed to him then to reduce the jewels of the mind and all its talents to the symptomatology of inert glands, to make of himself an enemy and harry himself like a traitor. But, as Myra pointed out, he *was* his enemy. His mind, brilliant though it was, must be regarded as the foe of Nature. And Gifford hung his head as his theories came home to roost. He saw himself as among the pioneers of disintegration. He was tasting the future of the species which must end, as he had prophesied, in the laboratory as patients. And so Gifford Emmett and all his wisdom and talents went to the doctor.

There has been in my generation such a blathering on the subject of psychiatry and its capricious twin—psychoanalysis—that I hesitate before this last phase of Gifford's life. I have no desire to reshuffle those new terminologies by which medicine has crept another millimeter into the vast dark of the human being. But this is hardly a time to desert my hero. And if we both sound a little befuddled, there is no help for it. The science of charting our subconscious—that secondary bloodstream that flows through us without arteries or tissues to mark its course—is a work so in its infancy that all who discuss it must sound in some way infantile.

The notion that it is possible to reshape our souls and play shoemaker to our tattered egos is perhaps the most ambitious project since the Tower of Babel. And at present at least its success looks as dubious. Its artisans are already screaming at one another in languages nobody can understand. But this may be only the disorder that attends the launching of all great tasks and not the confusion that marks their collapse.

I am not certain but, standing beside my hero in his travail, I am inclined to believe the former as the truth. In a time to come these Maestros of the Spirit Ducts may be able to reset a psychosis as easily as they do a bone. Chants, rituals, sesames may be discovered which, better than the scourges of our ancestors, will be able to drive the unwanted devils of Neurosis from their lurking places. A race of Mood Surgeons will attend our gall bladders, and medical Dostoievskys will operate on our dreams to cure us of such ills as stem from them. It may even become known and proved in the time that I foresee that all ailments, including the ravages of bacteria, and the accidents by which we

break our necks, are no more than visitations hatched by our
wills. And it may even be that on that day when Disease and
Death have been identified as the effluvia of disordered Thought,
we will seek for immortality on the analyst's couch.

There is of course nothing new to this theory except that it
has come to be regarded by organized medicine a little more as
science than imbecility. How sensible this change of attitude is,
only the layman will eventually be able to say, for he is, in medicine as in politics, ultimately the proof of the pudding. The prog-
nostications that doctors have to make concerning their own
business, their judgments of what is science and what is quack-
ery, can be more or less dismissed, historically.

In fact one would think that, confronted by a history so dubious as their own, so full of greed, bigotry, and organized outcries
against every bit of medical fact that has been uncovered, its
present custodians might feel hesitant about coming again to final
conclusions. They have only to look in the dusty corners of the
centuries to see them full of pale savants groping for mysteries
beyond the purgatives and operating tables of their day, and discovering these mysteries, only to be ridiculed and cast out by
Contemporary Medicine.

The biologist and his little umbrella-carrier, the doctor, have
always been slow to yield the small ground they have won for
the ever-befogged and uncharted spaces of the New—first asepsis,
then endocrinology, now psychiatry. The sons of Hippocrates
struggled violently enough against their elevation from barbers
to medicos. How much more will they battle against a fate that
now asks of them that they be geniuses!

The case of Gifford Emmett will, in a way, bear out what
sanity there is in their aversion to psychoanalysis, and mine—not
to mention the cases of my friends, who, with the aid of these

present-day soul searchers, are committing everywhere around me a sort of intellectual hara-kari in their efforts to outwit their ills. The condition of these friends—my contemporary neurotics —seems to me truly as pathetic as was that of the ancient lepers whom science sought to cure by the application of hot irons to the afflicted parts.

Our current lepers have their attention now scientifically directed to the obscene and idiotic waywardness of their souls. The rubbish heaps of their subconscious are turned over for their dazed inspection. Their wounds thus uncovered, and their hideous diseases thus exposed, they are handed diplomas that entitle them to cure themselves. Having given them a bad name, the scientist in charge washes his hands of them. It is presumed that, once a patient has located the sickening part of himself, he will vomit it out or rid himself of it elsewhere by virtue of some spiritual physic of which the doctor has no knowledge, but which he is sure exists in the pharmacopoeia of the patient. Thus the new therapy is placed in the hands of quacks and amateurs, for what else is a layman and particularly a diseased one? It is no wonder that most of these pathetically combined doctor-patients are bundled off to asylums to scream away their convalescence, or, more therapeutically, to put a bullet through their brains.

Dr. Oliver Jerome, the soul searcher into whose office Gifford was piloted by Myra, was an extremely talented man with an instinct for spiritual anatomy that soon won his patients. Gifford was immediately attracted by this new lens under which he was placed. His own keenness grasped quickly the manner of its operation. And instead of the repugnance he had anticipated, he felt himself being drawn into that friendship for the dark-eyed, placid-faced Dr. Jerome which is the first step of the "cure."

The human being has a remarkable and tireless gift for loving himself, or at least for being fascinated by himself, and he will fasten his gratitude on anyone who assists him in this direction. Within a week Gifford felt deeply attached to his ally—the analyst. The quiet-spoken, unemotional questioner seemed to him both guide and matchmaker. The analyst's eye that looked on human sins as if they were blood cells removed Gifford's social sensitiveness. He was able to experience the thrill of encountering the unknown in himself without embarrassment. He became oddly pleased to discover that his soul was as full of intrigue as a nest of spies and that the Gifford Emmett he had known was a sort of Character-President who had achieved office through the political chicanery of his subconscious.

This first uncovering of self is usually a delight to the neurotic. He embraces with elation the new features revealed, and sees in their often horrid and despicable aspect the mystic charm of kinship that our own always has for us. For a time he is actually happy to meet the disheveled Cromwells of his underworld, and he feels himself, giddily, as full of local color as a slum. Later, when this colony of gangsters and perverts on whom he opened a door loses its novelty, his elation is likely to give way to disgust. On his return to his capitol, the patient grows haunted by the chicanery and lawlessness of his own government. And sometimes in his disgust he abdicates.

This, briefly, was the history of Gifford's analysis. During the first days spent with the analyst, he fumbled nervously with his memories. In the second week, Gifford was in full cry after his past. Dr. Jerome, delighted by the eagerness and intelligence of his patient, explained they were trying to discover the origin of his aversion to sex. It was necessary to locate the exact moment in which the patient had decided on the criminal career of impotency.

Gifford offered his theory of the praying mantis, and related excitedly the many points in common which he had detected between that baleful insect and his wife. Dr. Jerome listened patiently to these somewhat lyric comparisons and then informed Gifford that the mantis religiosa was only a ruse to distract him from the deeper, darker truth of his ailment. Guiding him past the mantis, Dr. Jerome led his patient inexorably back to the scene of his crime. This turned out to be the windswept room in the Wisconsin home in which Gifford Emmett had been born. On the way back to this room poor Gifford ran the gamut of father-hatred and mother-fixation and a score of other criminal selves. Each day he was whisked along these byways and sent stumbling further into his past, until he arrived before the true and implacable enemy of his life. This was the tiny emerging infant that had, after a fashion, gladdened the Emmett home one snow-bound morning.

Dr. Jerome, aided by Gifford's memory of family tales, discovered that the little visitor had wanted none of this world. Spanked into existence, the indignant tot had devoted the rest of his life to a kind of suicide. Unable to get back into the womb for whose warmth he yearned, little Gifford had compromised on an aversion to all life outside it. Dr. Jerome was certain that if not for the currant bushes his patient would have willed himself into some form of idiocy. Gifford pathetically agreed that his learning was no more than a ruse by which he had evaded the world of reality. He agreed that his philosophy of hatred of humanity was the flowering of his original aversion to the doctor's forceps. As for his sexual impotence, Gifford saw that it was part of his fixed decision to remain, as much as was possible under the adverse conditions of maturity, a child in the womb. He was a little confused by Dr. Jerome's added hint that his frigidity toward Myra involved also a fear of committing incest.

In the seventh month of the analysis, Gifford was in full possession of his criminal history. His elation over his unknown selves had long since left him. He had returned to his capitol, and there he sat brooding and helpless. He mastered the conception of himself as an intricate and tireless suicide, and there he halted. He understood that his cure lay in his ability to dispatch his infant nemesis with some mystic *coup de grâce*. But how does one destroy one's oldest self? And with what weapons can one attack that which is deeper than the mind?

Gifford retired into himself and remained there with a futile, moody smile signaling defeat from his lips. His wisdom, silent since the first hour of his marriage, reasserted itself. It considered the quality and strength of his enemy. It measured him by all the science at his command and it came to certain conclusions.

I shall report Gifford's words on this subject because they were the last movement of his human-bound mind. Myra heard them excitedly, for she hoped that the analysis was bearing fruit. She was unaware that Gifford had risen finally from his analyst's couch only to speak his epitaph.

"I should like to believe," said Gifford, sitting with Myra in their lonely home, "that it is possible to re-educate the human soul. But I doubt whether even Dr. Jerome has been able to convince himself of this. For how can one re-educate the soul when it is obvious that it is impossible to educate it at all in the first place? The womb, alas, is the only university from which we may graduate with honors. The rest of our schooling adds hardly a credit to our standing. For the life particles of which we have been compounded have completed their studies before Nature entrusts us to the world. They have even completed our particular design. Our glands contain the full album of our photographs. The amount of our hair, its situation and duration; our height, weight, and coloring; our capacities for love and hate and even the nature of those who are to stir our emotions—all these are written in our embryos. The strength of our muscles and length of our bones, the very bent of our talents—whether we shall sing or be mute, whether we shall think brilliantly or dully or not at all; our politics and hobbies, in fact, are assigned us in the womb. Our thousand moods as well as many of our physical mannerisms are all predetermined for us by the quality of our thyroid, pituitary, adrenal, pineal, and other bits of tissue. We can move only in the directions charted for us in these glands. The distances we may cover are also fixed. We are, in the main, as predetermined as the insects—but less perfectly so. For there is left for us a small margin of chance and an even smaller one of effort. Within this little margin we are permitted to rattle around like peas in a pod. It is this pathetic movement we call our individualism, free will, divine independence, and so on.

"Seeing ourselves complete this way when we are born, with our destiny inscribed in every gland, I can't understand Dr. Jerome's theory that we are capable of rewriting our fate—that is, if he has such a theory.

"I am afraid," said Gifford, "that my cure lies in a more practical rebirth than our psychiatrist has to offer."

A look of torment came into his eyes and he muttered almost inaudibly: "It's not pleasant to be a human being."

Myra squeezed his hand tenderly, but Gifford continued to look fixedly at his shoes.

"Dr. Jerome's science is not impressive," he said at length. "But for that matter no science is very impressive. If you look back on what the Mind has thought since its first known statement, there's only one thing worth noting. This is the fact that its thinking invariably turns out to have been comic. Today's truth becomes tomorrow's jest. The Mind is always a hero to its own generation and usually a clown to the following. It is well to remember that we are in the midst of a constant yesterday of folly.

"The tale of who and what we are," Gifford said sadly, "is the tale told by a Peeping Tom flitting from one keyhole to another. Our knowledge is full of scandal and rumor, but none of it has seen the face of life or looked even for an instant into its eyes."

Gifford finished and stood up. He smiled for a moment on the alien woman whom he had married, and then went to his room. In the morning Gifford Emmett was found dead. Beside him was the bottle which Myra had taken a year before from his lips. It was empty. Myra, who had come into the room to waken Gifford, stood looking at his body with more amazement than grief. It was curled up, the knees clutched against the chin, and the head tucked down in a sightless and yet pleasant-seeming sleep.

II

Now that we know that the spirit of the tree returns to the earth, to be born again as loam, mushroom, or forget-me-not; now that we have discovered that when sea-water dies, algae appear to breathe back to it those very chemicals that had fled its dead and mighty cheek; now that we have mastered, however vaguely, the fact that all matter is a transitory display of eternal energy, and that there is no destruction but only renewal, it will be an aborigine of a reader, indeed, who sneers with incredulity at the bewildering fate that turned Gifford Emmett into an ant.

I say bewildering because, despite the assurances of science, there are some things I don't understand about it. I understand fully that the human spirit is chemically related to the sap of the vegetable and the whinny of the Unicorn and shares their fate. All that lives must ride and bob along on the same curving but unbroken seminal river. The headwaters of this eternal stream are unknown, and the Sea of Death into which it empties is another vast and unknown place. We know only the little landscape between that we call Nature. Having completed our brief excursion on this bright river, we very likely become part of some piece of legerdemain such as the sun performs on the sea. We, too, are probably lifted out of the Sea of Death and precipitated again into the hidden headwaters. And I can understand fully that this evaporation must be a fine democratic sight—that a man, a crocodile, and a gnat all evaporate, as it were, together into one great mystic cloud. And out of this far-away womb we come tumbling out again in an anonymous and intermingled cloudburst, hailstorm, or drizzle. We are returned to life as capriciously as weather. And out of this reservoir of vibrations or, at best, a sort of laboratory mist, we must not expect to emerge in the guise we entered. This would indeed be preposterous. We are re-costumed for our new excursions out of a most chaotic wardrobe. And it is our fate that any cap fits, whether it be a rooster's comb or a bishop's miter.

Of these matters I am fully cognizant and I can thus understand Gifford's reappearance as an ant. I could, if I wished to devote more space to the problem, explain it in considerable detail. But still one phase of it bewilders me. This bewilderment does not lie in the fact that Gifford became an ant but that he remained a human being. There I am a little at sea as an explainer.

I can only state categorically that Gifford's soul passed un-

changed into the newly laid egg of a termite in the low Sierras
to the southwest of the Republic. What the psychic and intellectual points were that made the new-laid termite still Professor
Emmett, I shall eschew for the time being. Also, if there is something more mysterious in Gifford's appearance as a California
termite than as a Wisconsin infant—in itself a very mysterious
matter if you stop to think of it—it is an increase of mystery on
which we had all better turn our backs if we wish to avoid too
much confusion.

The egg out of which Gifford emerged was one of some fifty
thousand that waited constantly, mob-fashion, for egress from
the belly of the termite Queen. It was the habit of this ovarian
monster to pump some five to ten thousand of her children daily
into the royal bed. Each of these remarkable litters contained, in
a ratio deemed proper, supplies of workers, nurses, agricultur-
alists, soldiers, and lovers. (Since Darwin and all the succeeding
biologists have failed to explain the phenomenon of an ant hatching a social system, I shall also ignore the explanation. It is obvious that Nature is not only a scientist but a magician too, and,
if she chose, cows would give birth to guinea-hens and Minervas
to tree-toads.)

Gifford arrived in the contingent of lovers. He was born a
male with the single destiny of cohabitation. All other insect
learning would be denied him. He would be unable to forage for
food. He would lack all equipment for toiling and fighting. Sex
would be his lone talent, his delirious and solitary objective.

In the beginning the Gifford Emmett who lay curled in this
tiny egg was scarcely any more related in character than in size
to his preceding status. There was no more in this egg than a
flickering consciousness of previous human estate.

For many days after he was born the new Gifford lay sightless, tiny, and content to be a grub. His human intelligence was the most delicate of obstructions to the perfect passage of time as the insect knows it. It existed like a bubble against which the great chemical currents of insect life swept and whirled. But, bubble though it was, they failed to dislodge or shatter it. The bubble persisted and within it, as within a secondary body, Gifford's human soul grew stronger.

When he had reached his third instar, having shed his chitinous exterior three times, and acquired the wings that identified him as one of the male reproductives of the kingdom, the human Gifford awoke sufficiently to become aware of his status and surroundings. But he experienced no shock, for what his mind saw appeared to him only the most fascinating of dreams. And, as one accepts in a dream the strange clothing and abortive geographies of the wandering Personality, Gifford accepted with no sense of panic his dwindled guise and amazing habitat. His dream of being an ant pleased him—though not entirely. He would have preferred in his dream to have been an early paleontologic insect with a wing-spread of two feet, and he made an effort to re-transform himself into such a redoubtable coleopteran. But while he could see himself as an elephantine gnat of some sort, the dream ant remained.

By the time of his fourth instar, Gifford had given up his efforts to alter the time and condition of his dream self. He devoted himself amiably to the study of this little phantom. Yet if it were an escape dream, why had he invented himself as a sexual ant? Here, Gifford thought, was something that would tax the psychiatrist's dream-book lore a bit.

He contemplated other things, among them the lineage of his dream figure. It had descended unchanged from lower Oligocene Tertiary times—as was evidenced by its identical amber-imbedded ancestors still in his college laboratory. It stood to reason, likewise, that the activities of the colony in which he lay maturing had also never changed since that far-away time. The government of which he was now a subject had not found it necessary to pass a new law for a million or more years. It had achieved social perfection when man was still lost in the anarchy-ridden debut of his evolution. This pleased Gifford and he was proud to be a member of a kingdom so hoary and glamorous.

In his sixth instar, curiosity beset Gifford. His dream seemed to him too static. He desired adventures. He was accordingly pleased to notice that his termite self was moving about. But even as he nodded with approval (an inward nod which the non-vertebrate termite in no way shared) he became aware of dangers now besetting this sightless and winged dream self. He recalled with a touch of fright that the status of the alate in the termite colony was a most precarious one. For this alate, who alone of all the castes in the kingdom was designed for love, inspired revulsion and rage wherever he appeared. Unequipped for foraging for food himself, he was ignored by the busy workers, who seemed intent on providing food for all mouths but his own. In fact these toilers seemed full of contempt for him and for all his sexual brothers, who lay about dreaming of their coming hour of love in the spring. And the soldiers too exhibited toward him the warrior's distaste for the sybarite. They were constantly decapitating and dismembering the defenseless, half-starved Romeos of his caste, tearing off their wings in what seemed to Gifford nothing more than the sadism of morality.

Wisely, Gifford accepted the fate of his kind in the kingdom, a sort of leper's fate. He must hide away from every one of his fellows, steal his food at the risk of his life, tremble before

every clanking troop of warriors that passed, and lead a bedeviled existence that was truly heartbreaking—all this because
for one hour in spring he was to enjoy the pleasures of love. It
would seem that the State, jealous of its metronomic soul, re-
sented even that exercise of individualism which insured its continuance.

Undeterred by the dangers that beset him, Gifford continued to study the swarming life around him. He saw the workers toiling at their thousand tasks, keeping the ventilator corridors in repair, hurrying down the spiral roads with food for the
combination store- and furnace-rooms. He could feel the
warmth rising from the decomposing provisions and calculated
quickly that winter lay outside.

In addition to the multiple domestic tasks of feeding, cleaning, airing, heating, storing, nursing, and all that occupied the
kingdom, there was the constant work of battle. Troops of soldiers were continually a-rush to the outer gates of the kingdom,
for here the enemy everlastingly threatened. The black and red
ants, scenting the stores of foodstuffs and hungering for the soft
bellies of the termites, were forever hurling themselves into the
kingdom and advancing down the ventilator roads.

Gifford watched a number of battles. He saw the warrior ants
march in formation to meet the enemy, and take their stand like
a praetorian guard barring the way of conquest. These armored
bullies, whom Gifford had come to hate because of their wanton and vicious manner toward his own daydreaming caste, now
became heroes whom even the alates must admire.

He had watched angrily these idling guardsmen standing
about so overarmored that they were unable to feed themselves.
A sycophantic worker class not only brought them viands but
stuffed them in their mouths while these robots stood glowering

like visored knights with iron-gloved hands clutching halberds that could never be laid down. But when the tocsin sounded in the termite land, and the alarm of the enemy at the gates was spread through the kingdom by the soldiers, and the corridors echoed with the beating of warrior helmets against enameled walls, Gifford, flattened against a ceiling, would see a rally and a march forward that were unforgettable.

The several battles Gifford witnessed were beyond anything he knew in the history of human heroism. He learned now that the courage of the termite warriors actually modeled their figures from birth, for they wore no armor on their backs. Since they would never turn tail to the enemy, no wasteful protection covered their rears, which were as vulnerable as the bellies of moths.

Calmly and precisely the soldiers advanced to meet the dreaded enemy now streaming down a ventilator corridor. Arrived in one of the vast chambers through which the zigzagging roads of the kingdom ran, the halberdiers would spread into a double-rank formation. Thus they stood barring the way into the interior. The enemy, usually sharp-fanged black ants, came rushing forward. They charged like a mass of little black bulls. Swifter than the termites, their armor more supple, they came in a deadly rain upon the defenders, whom they often outnumbered a thousand to one. Motionless against this tide of shields and sabers, the termite soldiers stood swinging their mace-like claws into the bodies of the swarming enemy. They fought erect. As long as possible, with their legs interlocked, they stood barring the way into the heart of the kingdom. On their courage depended all that was termite. Once past this barrier, the enemy would swarm triumphantly down all the roads of the kingdom, devouring the stores, the workers, and bursting into the royal chamber in murderous waves. Here, with the last of the royal guardsmen destroyed, the feast of the King and Queen would end their conquest. And the vandals who had found a kingdom would leave behind them a tomb in which not a tentacle was left moving.

This knowledge was in the halberds of the termite warriors. They fought on fiercely, piling the dead around them in great heaps. But from the top of these heaps, as from a thousand towers, the enemy continued to hurl himself in ever-increasing numbers. Losing ground, the beleaguered warriors sounded the signal for the reserves. The signal, like a high bugle note, drifted down all the roads of the kingdom, and in answer to it the waiting reservists moved forward. This signal was not only the warriors' cry for help but also their swan song. The reserves arrived, rank on rank of unarmored workers. With their arrival the termite warriors moved forward into the charging enemy. They had saved for this moment their last store of prowess. Erect and implacable, they held off the fanged host, and behind them the reserves worked desperately. They sealed the passage into the kingdom. Pumping glue and plaster out of their bodies, they walled off the battlefield. The road to life thus cut off for them, the termite warriors gathered themselves into a last phalanx. Left sealed in with the enemy, they were torn to bits by the thwarted hordes.

Gifford watched and admired these constant Thermopylaes. He grew to feel a regard for the clanking militarists in whom burned this great mood of valor and sacrifice which seemed to him a little nobler than his own dream of a spring cohabitation.

And still the half-delusion that these were all fantasies parading in his human sleep held Gifford's mind calm. The delusion remained until his seventh instar. On that day, full grown and finally winged, Gifford tasted for the first time the whole horror of finding himself an ant. His awakening occurred in the following manner. Moving furtively along the deep corridors, he had made his way through encampments of warriors and caravans of workers toward the place he knew existed somewhere in the kingdom and which he had not sufficiently observed in his first metamorphosis. This was the royal chamber of the Queen, where he discovered himself standing presently.

At first his human mind was fascinated by what he saw. But as he stood watching the hailstorm of termite life heroically brought forth in her bed, realization smote him. He became wildly aware that he was not dreaming this sight, that he lay in no bed of his own, hatching fantasies out of his subconscious. This tiny deviled termite standing on the Queen's threshold was himself. These pin-point features, this drop of matter was Gifford Emmett. His human mind was attached like some incredible fungus to an insect. It existed within its tiny structure. It was he, Gifford, who was the dream. And it was the ant who was reality.

With this knowledge, horror streamed through Gifford's mind. Despair erased for a time all his thought. His soul sought to hurl itself out of this minute and suffocating world in which it was trapped. But the insect in which it had its spurious seat clung to it with the clutch of doom. He sought to cry out and like some insect Samson to wreck the pillars of his prison and bring the kingdom crashing down on him and all its subjects. But no sound came from him and, though his mind vaulted, his midge of a body remained motionless. And he realized that he had no powers of expression other than those of an alate. His soul, complete with all its human senses, was not only without face but without talent of utterance.

Recovering slowly from this shock, Gifford found himself clinging to the wall of the great royal gallery and, philosopher that he was, he presently concluded that his condition and new environment were of minor importance.

There were many dead thinkers, mused Gifford, shaken but heroic, who occupied an even smaller space in the world than he did at this moment. And what, he argued, was the human body compared to the operation of reason but a cloud to the sun?

From this it will be seen that Gifford's former notions about the horror of Thought underwent a most thoughtless change no sooner than he had discovered that it was his only human possession. He clung to reason now like a survivor to a wrecked homeland. Despite his former infatuation for bugs of all kinds he refused to consider himself one, now that so ideal an opportunity offered. It was no doubt odd that Gifford, having become one of Nature's superior children this way, should cast his lot so loyally with a species he had always derided. But we are, perhaps, none of us ever ready to be what we dream.

His mind careening in the rapids of these revelations, Gifford opened his eyes again to the monster mother on her couch. Monster was a poor word, he mused, shuddering at what he saw. The termite Queen was no new sight to him, but it was one thing to have studied her as a scientist and another to look on her as one's progenitor. This new view held Gifford spellbound and nauseated. Two thousand times bulkier than any of her children, for she was six inches long, three inches tall, and as many thick, the Queen lay motionless like the figure of Mother Earth at the core of the world. Her great saucer eyes were sightless. Her legs hung from her as useless as feather fans. She was neither animal nor insect but a fount of life—a God-like ovary that hatched by itself an entire race. For there were no other mothers in her world. Within the great clay ball swarming with myriads of her progeny, she alone gave birth.

In the chamber all about her, several thousand soldiers stood guard. They were picked troops, taller and more unwieldy-looking than those of the corridor encampments. They stood immobile, as the workers fed them. A stream of caterers also attended the Queen. Her gigantic face, gray and bloated and lost in a spermatic dream, swarmed with subjects bearing food. These kept her mouth constantly filled, stuffing its monster jaws with cellulose pulp, dung, and the mangled bodies of her own children. She munched constantly as she lay. Another stream of attendants presided over her continuous accouchements. As the eggs issued from her in an unbroken larval ribbon, the medical caste hurried them off to the nurseries of the kingdom.

And Gifford, watching the horrid manner of his birth, saw too the ugly mechanics of his conception. He saw the pallid King, half the size of his consort, come dragging himself like some sack of concupiscence to the royal bed. The movement of this gouty Lothario made him more horrible-seeming than his inert mate. This, like the Queen, was no longer an insect but a mass of seed, an ugly and bloated servant of Nature, servile with lust. His very eyes were distended with sperm. Pale, crippled, and unrecognizable as one of his family, he dragged his volcanic loins toward his immobile bride. Slowly he mounted her and Gifford beheld the disemboweling deed of creation.

The cordon of warriors also looked on. Dwarfed by the occupants of the royal bed, they seemed like homunculi defending a throne. They watched the deed with awe, for it was the holiness of the kingdom, the chant to creation. There was no other sire in the land and no other such deed anywhere. The writing

Monarch astride the Queen was her single lover. From his loins poured the immortality of the colony.

The thought came to Gifford that this ritual before him was his own future. He had been born to breast the thousand hazards of death that lay on the way to the insect throne. If he survived them, he too would become a king. Even now these were the precarious hours of his apprenticeship. And hours even more laden with death awaited him. He would be among the thousands of kingly aspirants who swarmed out of the termite fortress into the world of spring. There in the open, he would seize on a mate. Around the multitude of bedazzled lovers that coupled in the maddening light of life, all Nature would be waiting, ready to devour. Lizards, spiders, black ants, frogs, everything that crawled or leaped or flew, would swoop upon the orgiastic nuptials and dine on them.

But there would be a few who survived. These would drag themselves wingless and exhausted into some burrow to found a new kingdom, to copulate endlessly, to hatch new myriads of workers, lovers, and soldiers, to grow into twin monsters of lubricity. Gifford, watching the bloated Monarch and his insatiable Queen, turned his thought coldly against such a future. His human aversion to sex was multiplied a thousandfold.

He left the royal chamber. Weak with hunger, he crept through a crack into an abandoned room recently the scene of some mighty battle. Around him he saw the disfigured warrior bodies all fallen forward on their faces, and the enemy dead. Gifford paused and feasted.

When it had gorged itself with its first full meal in weeks, Gifford's alate self started forward. It moved slowly, for it was burdened with food. Gifford's mind grew alarmed. He knew the fate that awaited the lethargic insect, and he turned his thought for the first time to the control of the alate's movements. For several minutes Gifford saw that both he and the alate continued to crawl slowly toward the distant corridors filled with clanking soldiers and inimical workers. But as he exerted what he hoped were hypnotic powers, the insect stopped moving. He remained uncertain whether his will had curbed the termite, or some tropism. Nevertheless, a sense of triumph came over him as the insect crept into a niche, where, safe from all dangers, it fell asleep.

At least, he exulted, he, Gifford, would not have to submit to being dragged about willy-nilly by an ant. He could bend it, evidently, to his own desires, even though the process by which he was able to dominate the insect seemed not only mysterious to Gifford but at variance with his learning as an entomologist. But whatever the situation was between himself and his ant self, he would soon determine it, Gifford assured himself. No entomologist had ever been so ideally equipped and situated for research.

Now there were other, more pressing, matters. These were his Thoughts. Like Robinson Crusoe's few possessions salvaged from the shipwreck, they must first be put in order.

He had just learned that he was an ant, and had survived the shock. Now he had to admit he was Gifford. For proof, he had been calling himself by that name. And otherwise, too, as far as he could make out, he was everything he had been before, even, he sighed mentally, to the point of being Myra's husband. Regarded externally, it is true, he seemed no more than an ant, but, observed from within, his learning, sense of personality, and human consciousness were intact as Gifford Emmett.

This raised the question—and one that might fascinate any psychologist, Gifford thought—of what constituted a man. Were he to crawl in his present guise before any group of scientists and address them to the effect that the human body was an unwieldy and superfluous masquerade, Gifford doubted whether a single one of the scientists would remain long enough to hear him out. And those who didn't bolt would identify him as a mass hallucination perhaps, and hurry off to some other scientist, maybe Dr. Jerome, to be cured of delusions.

On the whole, after musing for some time, Gifford was glad that the structure of the termite was too rudimentary to permit of speech.

Not that he feared he would drive any of his former colleagues into any serious aberrations. Considering the shocks he himself had just survived, the sanity of his former species seemed to him well-nigh indomitable. Besides, Gifford was too well aware of the propensity of orthodox science for ruling out unruly facts from their organized learning—thus making man's reason doubly safe.

But why, mused Gifford, when they had so much prettier theologies, should he attempt to substitute the promise of anthood for that of Heaven, if indeed such a metempsychosis as his own were the rule, and not the exception? (Since his courtship, Gifford disliked the word transmigration.)

This left him all alone with his immediate problem. This problem was to ponder, first, the generality of man's survival, then its relation to his own specific rebirth, and, finally, to compute, if possible, the various eventualities before him.

He eliminated as unimportant any question of the generality of rebirth. The immortality of the human soul was, after all, the most ancient of theories, and, *ipso facto*, he considered it proven.

As for his own rising from the grave as an ant rather than an angel, this was a more intricate idea. For one thing, it left him at least no closer to the bosom of God than he had been as a university professor. Then, it had not enlarged his wisdom according to the popular theory, but neither had it removed such enlightenment as he had, for which he found himself now wonderfully grateful.

In fact, closing his mind to any disputation for a moment, Gifford for the first time in his two lives repeated slowly and gently the words of a voluntary prayer. He pleaded with the Lord to accept a humble ant and open His arms to its wandering soul. And from this deed he learned the power of prayer as a bulwark against the extremely unusual.

At this point, although it was a far cry from his own Bible school Deity to the Hindu, his scientific mind obliged Gifford to take such a leap. He recognized in this older myth of the genus Homo a perfectly serviceable theory, according to which he was now scheduled for numerous incarnations. Death after death would probably be his, and also life after life. He would persist through these as Vishnu, Krishna . . . or, far more likely, he corrected himself, once he was through with the ant, as a moth, a lizard, and so on.

And here the disquieting question offered itself to Professor Emmett in all its darkness and bedevilment. Why, *why*, had he survived as Gifford Emmett? What possible purpose could Nature have had in fashioning an ant man?

The answer was inescapable. Professor Emmett found himself with no choice but to admit that something must have gone amiss with his death and the mechanics of his survival. He was no soul at all pursuing its normal orbit after death. He was a mistake. Owing to some aberration of Nature, he had entered this termite stage as Professor Emmett instead of arriving incognito as the pure spirit of life. Death had obviously blundered and forgotten to strip him of his useless human consciousness. He was at large in the Unknown as an interloper.

And now he faced the prospect of being doomed to exist—as a Professor Emmett forgotten by Nature—through an eternity of anthills and birds' nests and fish hatcheries. He might even find himself meditating amid the electrons of inorganic matter and forced to lie about for aeons as a stone. This thought that he was ordained to travel through the wonders of Nature like some perpetual tourist grew stronger in Gifford. Just as he had been born unfit for his former world, he had been reborn unfit for the Unknown. Gifford asked himself sadly if there was any profound and secret reason for his having been appointed eternal freak. Perhaps there was some pattern in his mismaking, some plot of which he was a mysterious part?

At this point, remarkable doings aroused Gifford from his scientific inquiry. A great commotion filled the kingdom. Gifford entered the senses of his termite self, now astir, the better to understand what was going on. A series of astonishing impressions smote him. Although blind, the alate was capable of a curious kind of sight. It saw reality as an inward dream. No objects existed for it, but it was as full of visions as a saint. Gifford applied himself eagerly to its sensory fibers as to a series of microscopes. Although still unable to translate most of its sensations into human understanding, he knew enough now to realize that the tiny body in which he resided was leaping about in a state of mingled exultation and panic.

A great noise filled the kingdom. From everywhere came the whistle of ants and a ghostly shout of song. The towering corridors were full of rout and revelry. Masses of ants appeared singing and leaping and rolling wantonly over each other. The once orderly roads had become the arenas of a Bacchanal.

Gifford moved forward into the hullabaloo. He saw the alate was no longer in any danger. Its status had changed. Bedeviled since birth, it was suddenly cock-o'-the-walk. And Gifford knew that the festival of Priapus had begun in the dark of the termite kingdom. The dreaded warriors greeted him with whistles of joy. They beat their helmets against the walls, and their cruel halberds had become castanets and tambourines. They had become an orchestra playing for his delight. Above the chant pouring from a million ant throats they sounded their delirious and compelling drum-beats. Gifford stood on his hindmost legs and danced.

Everywhere crowding all the roads the termites were dancing. They stood upright, swaying to the banging of the soldier drums. Now another wilder element entered the festival. A wind appeared, swirling and beating against the walls. Gifford perceived that the wind came from the swiftly moving wings of the alates. Above the heads of the mobs these males and females were now fluttering and leaping, heedless of everything but the joy of flight. They spun and dived into the press of orchestras and dancers, overturning whole ranks of them and scattering them fearlessly. And as he danced and hurtled with the rest, Gifford became aware that he was being fed. Honey-tasting morsels were being pushed into his mouth, and his head was covered with titbits as with garlands. Food rained down on him from everywhere. The armored bullies ran beside him, clearing the way for him. Garlanded and serenaded and preceded by hordes of dancers, the males and females were being escorted to their hour of love.

Swaying, chanting, and with a bullet-like urge in his heart, Gifford reeled along as part of the insect hallelujah. The writhing and screaming processions were moving toward some holy place that signaled from somewhere, and the subterranean kingdom was a single cry and its myriads were a single wave.

Suddenly the whirling spokes of some magical illumination overwhelmed Gifford. The chant around him was drowned by roars of light and sound that lifted him on their reverberations and tossed him headlong. The rush of the lovers out of the bowels of the kingdom to the couch of the sun was on. The exultation of air and light swept away all the memories of that dark termite land, and the alates, wings spread, were flashing toward its gates.

Gifford's mind removed itself from his insect self. He went to work again as a hypnotist. Desperately he exerted his will. He had set his mind implacably against any future that led to the royal bedroom. His human aversion to sex now gripped his insect self with a violence not to be denied. As he neared the little disk of sky at the end of the termite road, he struggled to command the clamorous instincts of his tiny body. Violently his mind proclaimed that he was not destined to couple with any of these million Myras, or to expire, still throbbing with pleasure, on a lizard's tongue.

The moment of exodus arrived. As out of a thousand rifle mouths the alates vaulted into space. Puff after puff of wings burst from the kingdom and remained like madly waving ribbons of smoke. Gifford was among them. He guided his insect self, however, to a leaf-shadowed twig. He knew that there would be neither bride nor enemy in the dark. And from his perch, he witnessed the prenuptial flight of his fellows. He saw that even the soldiers and workers had emerged to watch the spectacle. These stood thronged about the many gates of the

kingdom, as the once despised lovers filled the bright spring air
with the fiery prelude of their passion. Gifford's insect self
trembled, but Gifford held it firmly in the shadow.

Looking at the world above him, he perceived a mass of forms
whirling around as if caught in some overwhelming spout of sun
and air. And from these insect jets came the bellow of bulls and
the bugles of the chanticleer. The dance in the sun and air continued for a long time. Then, having saluted the mystery of
space, the lovers sought out one another. They embraced in midair. Gently they exchanged caresses, as yet too overcome by this
first taste of pleasure to dream of more. Clinging together, legs
and wings locked in a first innocent kiss, the lovers drifted
downward, seeking a couch. And Gifford saw that their couch
was the frog's toothless mouth and the spider's glue-dipped web.

Blinded to all but their dream of pleasure, the lovers died in
droves. Shining-backed bugs leaped at the double morsels. The
air and the earth became thick with murderers come to the carnival. Here and there a pair of lovers escaped for a moment the
gulp of the wedding guests. They lay coupled and creating. And
when the moment dreamed of through the dark year was done,
they threw aside their wings and started off for immortality. But
the locust and the cicada came to bar their way. The killer flies
swooped into the grass jungles after them. The snails and the
earthworms closed the roads.

Gifford watched this scene of bliss and death until the grass
grew still and the hum of slaughter was ended. Seemingly all the
lovers had been destroyed. But he knew that somewhere the road
to immortality had been left open. He thought of the two or
three royal couples, attended by the souls of the slain multitude,
crawling into the earth to continue the everlasting kingdom of
the termites. And his one-time admiration for the nobility and

cunning of the insect cosmos fell from Gifford as if only now that he was an ant had he become a man alive with human ego.

A contempt came to him for the manner in which Nature had just now handed on the termite scepter. The few alates who had survived to become Kings and Queens had earned their royalty neither by merit of their own nor by the operation of any law. Caprice alone had planted the crown of survival on them. And though he had always been aware of this lack of individuality in Nature, the fact seemed now outrageous to Gifford's mind.

Gifford recalled that in his human days he had been full of admiration for the Perfect State in which the termites and so many other insect species existed. But viewed now from within, this Perfect State seemed to Gifford a challenging and empty structure. There was, he mused, something revolting about the egomania of Nature, who, like some tireless dictator, demanded a kingdom of sleepwalkers to hymn her glories and never their own.

The perfection of Nature, thought Gifford, is made out of the imperfection of her subjects. The lower the slave the finer the state, was the secret of her ideality. The beautiful government of which he had been a part existed at the expense of a million individuals who had no existence at all. Their life and death were a command performance. And he thought of his termite brothers as somnambulists trapped in a monotonous dream. All experience was denied them, even that of age. They were permitted to learn nothing, for the wisdom of the tiniest grub and that of the hoariest grandfather were identical. They lived and died under a hypnosis that prevented them from ever changing or bettering the world into which they had been summoned. Their valor, industry, sacrifice, and even love-making were grimaces of obedience, and submission was their only genius.

It was a form of genius that occurred often among men, as a degenerative process. Whole nations of humans became capable of stripping their minds of all individual existence. Unquestioning and prostrate before Authority, their souls, identical and callous as so many beetle backs, offered the rhythm of their servitude as their greatness.

Those human groups like the Germans, the Italians, and the Japanese, thought Gifford, who seek for strength in the destruction of the individual, are operated by some dark and ancient ideal of Nature's. The lust for mass power is stronger in them than the dream of human development. By depriving the individual of a soul they are able to create an external and hypnotic soul called the State. Neither truth nor justice nor the graces of intellect become then the goal of the individual in it. But an ant-like metronomic existence allures these citizens. Their glory lies in being able to become by the surrender of self something more powerful and glamorous than lay in these scattered and struggling selves. These ego-castraters are the turncoats of evolution and they betray humanity back to its pathetic beginnings.

"I wish," added Gifford sadly, "that I had concerned myself a little more with the politics of the world when I was a human part of it. For I see now that politics is not the history of governments but the broad currents of biology. I was extremely stupid in admiring the spider and the termite above Lucifer and Prometheus."

In the midst of his musings Gifford became aware that he was crawling somewhat uncertainly down the tree in which he had been roosting. He quickly placed his Thought within his alate self and looked on the outdoors for the first time as an insect. What he saw bewildered him. He was plunging through ravines and craters which he recognized, after some hesitation, as the

bark of a tree trunk. Monsters beset his way and, holding his
breath, Gifford careened to the ground. Arrived at the foot of
the tree, Gifford felt that he had been suddenly translated to the
dead and awesome caverns of the moon. Around him loomed
shapes of infernal size and strangeness. Monstrous scimitars
waved over his head which, with difficulty, he remembered were
grass blades. Above the grass, the leaves of bushes floated like
vast domes. As from the floor of an abyss, Gifford looked up at
a gargoyle world.

Around him, as he crawled, rose the scream and roar of enemy
figures too gigantic for his vision to encompass. Disaster echoed
everywhere. Every bit of stone was a mountain inhabited by
ogres and every hollow was a chamber of death. Of all that
moved, he alone was without size. And Gifford perceived that
to an ant Nature was a storm blowing and a sky falling. Weaving onward, Gifford held his breath as if in the midst of panic.
No one thing threatened, no visible fate pursued, but he was part
of some general rout going on all around him. His ant was fleeing
aimlessly from life, scaling crags and tumbling into pits, scamper-
ing up waving roads that ended in nowhere and toppling from
these spiraled highways, moving ever without destination like
some pilgrim lost in chaos.

Then suddenly Gifford halted. He felt a warmth within his
body. And his ant self remained motionless in this bedlam as if before a friendly hearthstone. The warmth was some sort of signal.
Gifford recognized it presently as the rays of the termite kingdom beckoning. Flattened against the earth, Gifford refused to
move. The belly of a spider like a great cloud passed over him.
He watched the forest of its legs drift away. Huge and jagged
shapes leaped from the abyss with the noise of thunderclaps.
Meteor bodies flashed beyond the leaf domes and vanished. He

beheld horned creatures of incalculable lengths sliding down mountainsides toward him. Great heads protruded hissing and slimy from the earth, and Gifford stared into the chimera faces of the worms. In the midst of this paean of destruction the ant remained crouched as at some fireside.

Then it resumed its movement. But now it had discovered a road. Gifford realized that it had located the rays of the termite kingdom. He thought, rushing forward now, that here lay the secret of the homing instinct in nature's children. The air was honeycombed with radio-active currents. Placing themselves on these as on invisible rails, the unerring travelers of the sea, land, and air were able to return to their homes and homelands. It was obvious, mused Gifford, that this electric spoor was exuded by every species and that the seemingly trackless wastes of air contained a wonderfully organized system of vibrating streets. But this problem, which would have fascinated him in his human guise, occupied him only a moment in his present travels. He thought instead of the fate that awaited him on re-entering the termite kingdom. The warriors were undoubtedly still hovering about its gates, for it was their custom to assassinate such useless stragglers as returned unwedded from the field of love. Exerting his will, Gifford halted the termite and led it to the top of a vast stone. Here, he reasoned, it would be safe from its subterranean enemies. On this stone, with the warmth no longer in its body, Gifford's alate self submitted to his commands and lay motionless.

When he had rested on this stone for a long time, Gifford heard a sound different from all the noises around him. It was a muffled and continuous note, rhythmic as a purr. As he listened, Gifford grew frightened. This surprised him, for, being ringed everywhere as he was with the faces of death, why should he conceive of a sound coming from somewhere within the earth as unusually terrible? Surely there were no gradations to doom, argued Gifford against the terror-inspiring purr that filled his senses.

"It is not the ant who is frightened, but I," continued Gifford. "It lies with its wings folded like the toga of a Stoic. No hero was ever so calm in the face of disaster or so unperturbed before its many hideous heralds. Surely, I am as good a philosopher as an ant."

Thus, gathering courage from the termite's example, Gifford's mind grew calmer, though the horrible sound continued to come from somewhere in the earth.

"And of what," pursued Gifford, "have I to be frightened? If I am to be slain as an alate, I shall obviously make my reappearance in some other form. And no guise into which I am translated could be so distasteful and unflattering as this oversexed little somnambulist I now inhabit. My efforts to keep this priapic midge alive are absurd and short-sighted. Certainly there must be something more for me in Infinity than a post-graduate course in entomology."

Now entirely calmed by his musings, Gifford settled himself to wait for whatever doom lay in this ominous sound beneath him. But no monster came protruding from the earth or creeping over the edge of the rock. And as the sound continued, Gifford tried to locate and identify it.

"It is evidently something in the earth," he thought, "some monster of terrific proportions creeping along. Its eyes will be white, for it will be earth-blind. It will have a remarkably long and armored snout with which to dig and it will be possessed of countless shovel-like claws. And like all subterranean creatures it will smell disgustingly. But what monster is there," Gifford pondered, "that can creep through stone? For this noise is immediately under me. I can feel the vibrations of the creature's travels in this rock. I know of no animal or ogre who can crawl through the interior of rocks."

An enormous shape suddenly appeared and loomed on the stone. A vulture had alighted beside the professor. He stared at the arrival, pleased to be a morsel too insignificant for its powerful beak. The vulture was evidently resting, for its lidless eyes seemed full of weariness. Then, without warning, something astonishing happened to Professor Emmett's winged rock-mate. Gifford saw its legs disappear into the rock, and a moment later it had vanished entirely. It had fallen into the stone as if into a drum. There was a wild flapping of wings, and after some moments the vulture lifted itself out of this unexpected trap in a billow of dust. Without pausing to examine anything, the bird beat its way off toward the clouds.

Professor Emmett looked bewilderedly at the place where the vulture had stood, asking himself what sort of stone was this that collapsed under a bird's weight. Moving toward the hole, which was still smoking with dust, he beheld a sight incredible to his human senses. A multitude of termites was in the heart of the rock. Spread symmetrically before him like the spokes of a wheel, the insects were feasting. He watched the wheel turn and the stone disappear slowly before it, vanishing grain by grain into the bellies of the termites. They were eating their way into the rocky core of a mountainside, and Gifford realized that this was the monster at whose purring he had been eavesdropping.

Looking further into the stone he saw that this wheel was only a segment of the monster. There were other wheels turning. A series of circular tapeworms was moving like cogs of destruction within the flinty mountain base. Gifford looked up at the mountainside. The thought came to him that this whole towering and bouldered landscape was a shell similar to the rock through which the vulture's feet had plunged. And he remained for some time lost in wonder.

"I have come on a new species of termite," he reasoned, "that is able to penetrate rock as easily as its brothers penetrate wood. It is evident that these rock-eaters have evolved a new race of parasites as their digestive equipment, and that these hardier occupants of their stomachs are able to convert particles of stone into a nutritive pulp. Since nothing is impossible to the chemical genius of the insects, I must accept without further quibble the fact that they have mastered the secret of extracting nitrogen from a completely inorganic form of matter. As Newton said, one must not ask unfair questions of Nature. One must study her secrets not as if they were miracles but as the simple, visible links of a hidden chain."

Fortunately Gifford was able to bolster up his unbelievable observation with the memory that there were certain ants that had always been able to penetrate but not digest limestone. These ants were equipped with small tanks of formic acid that acted as a solvent. However, no species of ant had ever before been able to turn a whole mountain into a shell from top to bottom—a soufflé of earth and granite whose very existence would presently be threatened.

If this were to be the case—and he feared it would be—Gifford knew that it was a climax which was to be postponed. In the first place the ants were not likely to reveal their presence to their enemies, and in the second place they would be sure to devour the landscape completely before allowing any avalanche to interfere with their meal.

Pleased to be the first man in the field to view such a phenomenon, Gifford started on a tour of inspection.

"One can't help admiring the little beggars," he mused to himself as he toiled upward from rock to rock, listening always to the purr beneath him. "They know to a fraction the amount of material to remove without collapsing the structure they disembowel. This ability to calculate swiftly and with the most delicate precision the various stresses of a mountainside, the different pressures of its boulders, forests, and rivers, is an instinct containing in it information beyond all the engineering data known to man. Such a talent would be comparable in man to the ability for measuring the weights, distances, and constituents of the stars merely by looking on them with the naked eye."

This was backsliding toward his older attitudes, and Gifford knew it. And he knew, even in the midst of that vacillation so comically typical of the scholar, that there were greater duties before him than that problematical report to a scientific commission with which his fancy kept toying. What this tremendous adventure was to be, he did not know as yet.

Here, half-way up the mountain, he made another scientific discovery. He was resting from his labors on a high rock covered with frost, but the alate was apparently undisturbed by the chill of his lofty roost. Gifford couldn't help marveling, for the termites of every known species perished in a temperature below fifty degrees. This astounding fact, and his present certainty that the whole mountain, from peak to base, was alive with the insects, led to only one conclusion. The termites were engaged in some sudden evolutionary spurt. They had not only acquired new talents—for eating stone, resisting cold, and so on—but they had obviously increased fantastically their rate of reproduction. (Any numerical estimate was impracticable.)

Gifford paused at this point in his musings and observed that a storm was gathering around the mountain peak. He noted also that the purring within its heart had ceased. Full of apprehension, Gifford watched the black clouds massing and hurrying forward like armadas. Great gusts of wind came from their careening hulls and then the rain leaped down. Thunder crashed and the lightning brandished its quicksilver knives over the mountain peak and hurled its broken spears into its forests.

Gifford waited wretchedly. The mountain was quivering all about him. With each thundercrash it seemed to breathe and swell as if it were coming to life. Under the beat of wind and rain its sides shivered like rattled drumtops, and a rumble issued from its heart that drowned the noises of the storm. The din from the earth increased and the pulsing of the mountain grew wilder.

Then Gifford saw the mountain vanish. Bellowing and screaming, the great hill turned to dust. Its boulders exploded, its ravines and gullies opened into great umbrellas of dust. The mountain roared in the darkness. Cavernous night filled the air. Through the darkness Gifford beheld the forests raining out of the sky. Trees were shooting past him. Like a great rocket that had burst in midair, the mountain plunged out in every direction and collapsed in a thousand avalanches. Gifford leaped to a falling bush. Tossed far into the air by winds and gases, the bush parachuted to the earth. It lay on the edge of the smoking shattered mountain base.

Gifford looked out at the disaster. The rain had ceased. A cloud of vultures was drifting toward the mountain corpse. Looking into the great pile of wreckage extending for miles, Gifford saw that all that had lived in this mountain had been destroyed. The fish in its streams, the animals, large and small, who had haunted its forests, and great colonies of birds had all perished. All had been crushed and entombed, all but the voracious little wheels that had devoured the great hill. These still lived. Gifford saw the termite regiments racing undisturbed through the mountain remains, like vandals abandoning a razed and alien house.

Then suddenly Gifford realized the full import of what he had beheld. He had seen a new war lord launch a world conquest. The vision of all the cities of the earth devoured by termites came to Gifford as he lay staring at the mountain corpse. It was the insects who had conquered the Greeks (despite his argument to Myra), for that valiant race had degenerated through malaria. But how much greater a conquest this would be than all the plagues and epidemics of the past! These termites, whose numbers were already incalculable, would multiply within a year into great moving deserts of destruction. They would spread like a quicksand. As the mountain had fallen, so would all the steel and stone towers, all the homes and factories topple. The structures of the world would become a dust drifting away.

Gifford pondered the vision of civilization ravaged. Man would be stripped of all his inventions. All his refuges, instruments and machines, all his books and his seven-league boots would end in the bellies of the termites, ground to dung by a horde of parasites. The great human house of toys would be devoured and man would be left like an infant, naked and resourceless, on the inhospitable doorstep of Nature.

For a time Gifford lay motionless with his vision. He thought of the shout of panic as the first great structures toppled in the cities, carrying millions to their deaths. He imagined then the next inevitable downfall—civilization collapsing like a row of dominoes; art, beauty, and achievement vanishing in a rain of dust and splinters.

How long, he wondered, would it be before all man's systems of philosophy were swept from his soul as he returned again to the caves and campfires? How long before all wisdom and delicacy of spirit would be outlawed as incompetence? A month, a year, at most a handful of years, and power would be seized by sinew and sadism. And would the spectacle of man struggling in the savage state for which he had so vaingloriously unfitted himself be his final deathbed scene? Would he be able to repeat the great conquest of his near ape ancestors and come marching triumphantly out of the jungle mists once more? No, thought Gifford, he is a poor creature now, incapable of defending himself against the climate alone. The sun, moon, wind, rain, and snow would do for him without any other enemy's helping.

And Gifford thought of what a tragic little rabble of bad spearsmen all the politicians, preachers, industrialists, poets, and philosophers would make. How quickly Nature would close in on this child who had bartered his animal birthright for a fragment of soul.

There would be a battle against the ants, of course, before all this came to pass, for the human species was not without weapons and courage. It would mobilize all the chemicals in the world, and fall upon the termites with poison and fire. But all this would be futile against the overwhelming numbers of termites that Gifford foresaw at their present rate of increase. Also, the chemicals would give out, for the manufacturing plants would be destroyed. And, courageous though man might be, the ant was possessed of a heroism beyond his. Death had no meaning for the ant, for it was only a cell that died. The termites would attack as a single monster, invulnerable and immortal. Villages, farms, and cities would disappear—a scattered rubble heap of a decomposing species.

Here the thought that had been haunting him came into Gifford's mind like a thunderclap. It occurred to him that he could save the world. He could carry news of the coming conquerors to the scientific outposts of the race, and give man time to prepare for the termite raid. He could, somehow or other, guide an army into this unpopulated land where the conquerors were still hatching. Attacked quickly here in the desert, the termites could be destroyed. The entire mountain range which they now inhabited could be blown up, the surrounding desert irrigated with poisons, and the human race saved.

"I could save the world," Gifford repeated to himself, and lay staring as if under a spell. Then he began irrationally to move. For several minutes he darted about, climbing through the branches of a tree.

"I could save the world," he kept repeating as he climbed the tall tree. Arrived on its uppermost leaf, he hung from its pointed tip and was silent as he looked at the sky.

"I could save the world," he resumed finally. "I can save the entire world of Thought. It is something I must consider. A few hours ago I was full of sentimental memories of the human race. I felt indignant at Nature and her hordes of somnambulistic children. But let me think now of man. Where is his worth? For instance, is there a single thought worth saving? Is there one dream or scheme that has not brought misery to the species? Where in all its history is there an idea that, once launched, has not crippled and tormented it? What have its philosophies and religions been in the end but the means for the creation of new victims? And what is the mind of man, seen as a whole, other than the ghost of his fangs still tearing at the throat of life?"

And, looking back into the world, Gifford denounced it from his high leaf as an ugly place.

"Ah," he said, "if only thought were perfect, or half as perfect as anti-thought; if the human mind were not so eager to surrender its little handful of questing words to every charlatan who crossed its path!

"Unreasoning, malformed world," he cried, "world that fills its governments with witless, howling tyrants, that is forever driving reason into caves and placing ogres on its thrones, what is there in such a world to save?

"Remorseless and inhuman world, that postures like a parson and roars like a beast, wherefore save this world? Intolerant, cowardly world, that mangles its weak and spits upon its poor, what is there in such a world worth preserving?

"Wherefore save this world," Gifford cried to himself, "that has from age to age torn at its brother's face? This mocking, gall-souled race that denies solace to itself, that allows itself to be everlastingly conscripted into the vile armies of unreason, what is there in its soul worth the preserving? Stupid and clamorous race that can be bled of all honor so easily by any mountebank and brought crawling on its belly to cheer at every crucifixion—it will be well for itself to end. For what is there to rescue," demanded Gifford, "what is there to man but a little mask, a bit of silly lace that covers the tiger's eyes, a dainty little glove that hangs tattered from tiger claws?

"I shall stay here," pronounced Gifford, "and wait till all the pretense and vileness that has come to be called civilization shall have achieved the honest pattern of termite dung. And from some place astride a grain of sand I shall witness the extinction of the human race with the equanimity that befits an ant."

Gifford was silent. The matter was ended. Within the body of this termite high up in a tree, the fate of man had been decided. Let the termites multiply and devour man—his soul and his works. Gifford would not move from his leaf.

A little awed by the situation, Gifford decided to put the whole matter out of his mind and devote himself to the business of being an ant. And returning to his termite's senses, Gifford observed the scene. He noted that the sky and the leaf were of equal size, and that the tree in which he roosted was like a limitless sea whose waves roared and tumbled beyond the rim of the world. Thus occupied with the cosmos of an ant, Gifford suddenly heard a faint voice, a little sound of words that rose from his innermost self. It was his own voice, coming out of a buried self, that spoke. The humanity he had condemned was speaking in him, as if lingering in the court of his mind to whisper against the verdict it had heard.

We have not done so badly, it said, not if you care to look at us a little more closely. Considering everything, we have not done so badly. Before you condemn us, look on us again. Not on our pomp and murder, not on our governments and gibbets, nor racks nor righteousness. But look deeper and beyond these. The list of human evils is long and humanity's record of honor is small and scattered. But it is worthy of survival.

Gifford listened to the voice of the world he had found intolerable during his residence in it, and a sadness overcame him.

Consider, it went on softly, consider who we are, and the darkness out of which our mind was born. Consider how ancient the beast is beside the little furrow of thought that has come to mark its brow. Though we have in our ignorance spilled a great deal of blood, we have also wrested a little wisdom out of the dark. In the midst of our lusts and bigotries we have found time to draw maps of the heavens, to examine the roots of plants, to peer through microscopes at our bacterial fore-fathers, and to pry open a fraction or two the doors of mystery.

And listening to this cajoling voice in him, Gifford beheld slowly another vision of humanity. He looked at its science. Be-hind the political diseases of its centuries, hidden in the ugly shadows of its religions and conquests, he beheld the isolate mind of man—a never-dying light that gleamed through the ogreish history of the race. How valiantly it twinkled even in the darkest corners, how steadfastly it shone out of the ever-dreadful shad-ows! No wind had ever blown it out. No tyrant with whip and sword and exile but had left it glowing more brightly.

Consider, he mused, how great was the ignorance with which we were born and how many priests and captains have held us forever chained in this ignorance. Though we have come for-ward only a small way, it is a noble inch we have moved.

There are a few, continued Gifford, who do not merit my judgment. They are those who have preferred the search for truth to the banners of tyrants. They are the few who devoted themselves to something other than the making of crowns for bigotry and hysteria. Amid all the great hunger for applause and power which has wrecked each age, there have been always these humble ones.

And Gifford thought of the scientists, of the eyes that had kept everlastingly peering out of the human shambles at the ways of the moon, the sun, the stars, winds, birds, beasts, and all the elements and exudations of Nature. Even in the day when piety was feeding infants to the god Moloch there had been eyes to look beyond the fires of sacrifice at the meaning of the heavens.

And Gifford recalled these immemorial heroes of the mind whose names were written on the small scroll of wisdom. Where the many others had butchered and lusted and left behind the gaudy, vanishing tracks of conquest, these few had toiled and died and left only some tiny fact to mark the small road of learning. But how much brighter this little way shone than all the tracks of glory. And how much sweeter was the fame of these everlasting little plodders than that written on the arches of Triumph. Their names were inscribed on bugs and insects, on the skeletons of sea monsters and on the petals of flowers and the sacs, vesicles, and fibers of all physiology. Atoms and gases kept their memory green, and in every chemical and computation their laurels bloomed. They had striven for truth and not for greatness; died in poverty but bequeathed riches. And their honest names, unknown to the changing crowd, had found immortality in a spider's genus or a bit of human tissue.

And how far and tirelessly, Gifford thought, these had journeyed in their quest of truth, dissecting the eyes of butterflies and weighing the flaming bodies of the stars, ever a-tinker with mice and lichens, sea bottoms and cloud tops, and pursuing God or Nature into the invisible and marching on with their mathematical lanterns where there was neither light nor matter to guide them.

These are the mind of man, thought Gifford; these are the law-givers and the rulers of the world. These are the soul of the race. All the rest is a froth of hunger and ego, lust and lies and actors sick with the need of applause. The light of these remains to deny the most abominable darkness. I have judged wrongly. That grim and suffering face of humanity that finds solace in torturing its fellows is not to be judged, for it is only the rudimentary face of man. The list of human evils is long and the record of human honor small and scattered. But it is worthy of survival.

Having come to this conclusion, Gifford trembled on his leaf and began to glow with excitement.

It is possible, he thought, that I am not a freak but a Messiah and that I have been appointed to save the human race from extinction. That is, if there is a God it may well be that I am a Saviour, and that . . . But here Gifford paused and frowned at his own musings.

Such a theory is nonsense, he resumed coldly. It would seem that whoever allies himself too fully on any side, be it even that of reason, becomes forthwith full of the rankest delusions in its behalf. Obviously, if there was a God who had selected me to be His Saviour, He would now invest me with some sort of divine power, or some sense of His existence other than this worrisome quibble at present in my mind. At least He would not rely on an ant to rescue Mankind, if such a rescue was His intention.

Perhaps, added Gifford, I should pray. Whether I am a Saviour or not, it can do no harm.

And Gifford prayed for some metamorphosis which would enable him to speak and enlighten the race as to its impending doom. Trembling within his ant body, he tried to make the prayer sound as unselfish as he could. He murmured humbly that he was content to be an ant but that his desire to serve God's will made him long for increased measurements and some means, denied to the hymenoptera, of expressing God's word to the human race. Nothing came of his prayers, and Gifford found himself convinced neither one way nor the other by their failure.

The history of God, Gifford remembered, as written by His most infatuated admirers, reveals Him as too busy to give more than a glance at any of His problems. He has never asserted Himself in other than an incalculable way. He smiles out of Infinity like a coquette, and turns His back on anyone smitten by

His light. As a result His messiahs usually end up in bonfires, crucifixions, or as mince-meat.

"Whether or not I am part of some divine pattern for the saving of mankind," Gifford smiled, "of all messiahs, false or true, I am surely the most pitiful and futile to look at."

These confusions finally passed from Gifford's mind, and the decision he had made sent him helter-skelter down the tree. During his descent he kept looking about him with his human senses and wondering where he was.

"It is going to be very difficult fulfilling my mission," thought Gifford, "with or without divine assistance. And until I receive some revelation I will approach the career of Saviour as scientifically as I can. This desert around me may be part of Africa, Asia, or America. It is too bad I am such a poor geologist. Professor Wallachek could have told at a glance where he was. My ignorance is unbecoming both to a scientist and to a Messiah. However, I will not waste time bemoaning it. My first problem, wherever I am, is to find some human habitation and then figure out some means of attracting human attention and imparting my Message to human intelligence." And without further debate Gifford started forth.

For forty days and forty nights he continued to dart aimlessly over desert sand and hills. The bewildered but obedient ant plunged about this way and that, and no Saviour of mankind ever turned so many circles as did this termite. During this time Gifford was tempted often to give up his search and abandon the human race to its doom.

"It would be so much easier to be a Messiah," he mused wearily as he pursued his desperate journeyings, "if there were a God." And he paused time and again to pray, excusing the vagueness of his supplication by thinking: "If my piety is uncertain, it is not nearly so uncertain as God's interest in me. However, I should be a fool if I ignored altogether the possibility that I am a Messiah. In the midst of so many miraculous events as have befallen me, prayer is not entirely out of place.

"It will be easier to persuade Americans to save humanity than it would be to interest other nations in such a project," mused Gifford, "for Americans are about the only people left still amiable enough to be interested in preserving the race rather than in exterminating it."

On the fortieth morning Gifford emerged from the wilderness. He came upon a road. Urging the bedraggled ant to its edge, he surveyed the enormous stretch of concrete. The perfection of this road, the symmetry of its seams and smoothness of its surface, gave him a feeling that he was in his native land. A few minutes later an automobile swept by and he recognized it as American. At least his mission lay in a familiar country.

For several hours Gifford remained thus at the edge of the road, while a half-dozen dust-caked American automobiles appeared and vanished. The sight of the doomed but heedless human beings in them filled him with a sense of compassion. Gone now were all the doubts that had assailed him during his wanderings in the desert. Instead, his mind was full of plans. Foremost was the decision to go to Washington and reveal his news. Since the destruction of the termites would undoubtedly be a Federal project, much time would be saved in bringing the menace to the attention of the White House itself.

Gifford thought hopefully of the Chief Executive, famed for having surrounded himself with men of vision. Surely, he jested to keep his courage up, there would be no difficulty in adding an ant to the Cabinet, particularly in these times of social experiment. As each car passed, he looked desperately up at it.

"It is too much to expect," he decided presently, "that any of them will stop to give me a lift." And he began to crawl along the road.

Hour after hour he crawled, until, finding himself lying flattened against the hot concrete and no longer moving, Gifford realized that the inevitable had happened. His ant body had collapsed. Gifford remembered its hysterical scramble through the desert with death everlastingly looming and roaring around it, and was not astonished at its exhaustion. The termite, like a toy wound up, had run its course. His will was no longer able to budge the spent creature.

"How pathetic it seems," thought Gifford, "that the fate of the human species should depend on the fragile legs of an ant. For without its body to transport me I am powerless."

Studying his alate self closely, he saw it still breathed. The only thing left to do, he thought, was to signal some passing car. And Gifford's soul took its position on the road's edge and fell to sending out thought waves at each speeding vehicle. Toward nightfall the miracle happened. The despairing ant saw a car come to a halt in front of him. It was a lowly and battered conveyance, snorting as if in the last stages of mechanical existence. Smoke poured from its hood, and its doors were tied shut with pieces of cord. It had broken down, and its driver had alighted and started repairing the engine. There were two elderly women in the back seat. Gifford crawled slowly toward the car, mounted the hot wheels, and deposited himself on one of the four shoes. Here he lay listening eagerly to the conversation of the travelers. He learned that he was in the State of California, route 9, spur 52; and that the mountains some thirty miles to the south were called the Navajo range.

As these were the hills in which the termite hordes were toil-

The Adventures of Professor Emmett   449

ing, Gifford memorized the information carefully. Eventually he heard the sound of the motor and the rush of wind and knew his journey of salvation had begun again.

During this journey Gifford changed automobiles a number of times. Hitch-hiking from tourist camp to tourist camp, he remained loyal to his mission. Daily he listened to groups of mindless people debating the ways of the world and in the nights, as he lay tiny in the dark, he was shaken with doubts as to this civilization he was so desperately intent on saving from the termites' bellies. And though he saw that his fellow-travelers were as untouched by the three thousand years of science, art, and philosophy to which they were the heirs as if they had doffed only yesterday their nose rings and skirt feathers, and that if every statue, painting, book, idea, and instrument of learning were to disappear from the earth overnight these people would experience no more sense of loss than a backward child for a school that had burned down, he kept alive his ideal.

"I am riding to the rescue not of humanity but of a few of its dreams," thought Gifford. "I must bear this in mind lest everything I see and hear disillusion me and turn me back. It is a pity in a way that to save so little that is good so much that is stupid must be allowed to flourish. But a Messiah cannot afford to be critical."

On the afternoon of the eleventh day Gifford arrived in the city of Washington, which he found full of alarums. Crawling to a newsstand, he learned that the hysterical aspect of the capital was due to five recent attempts on the life of the President, all within the past ten days. The government, as a result, was full of panic, and the press was lucratively occupied with the horrors of the would-be assassinations. Gifford read a more or less cool account of the events in a Republican (anti-administration) newspaper. The criminals, this gazette reported, had all been captured. Four of them were men, and the fifth a scullery maid in the White House. The latter had poured a bottle of arsenic into the President's soup, endangering not only his life but the lives of his entire family. The others had concentrated on shooting and hurling bombs.

Under questioning, the five were revealed to be suffering from what several psychiatrists (Republican) identified as a New Deal psychosis. All five of them considered themselves in the light of saviors. The scullery maid submitted in defense of her action that she had heard on excellent authority that the President intended to close all the churches and banish all the priests, as had been done in Russia. She had acted solely in the interests of the Church, and felt certain that if she were executed for her so-called crime God would receive her with grateful arms as a valiant foe of the present administration.

One of the bomb throwers, a professor of economics at a boys' prep school, had acted out of the delusion that the President had tried several times to break into his study and set fire to it. And on two different occasions he had, in the nick of time, discovered fires lighted by the President in the main dormitory. He regarded his deed not only as one of self-defense but one in defense of many thousands of lives.

"I have nothing more to say," he declared, "except to express my regret that the pyromaniac President is still alive, and, what is worse, at large."

The third would-be murderer, a sergeant of police, appeared to be suffering from a misinterpretation of the finest Republican thought. He had read hundreds of editorials proclaiming that the President was seeking unscrupulously to retain his power by drugging the lower classes. The sergeant had conceived the idea that the nation's Chief Executive was head of a gigantic dope ring and engaged in distributing narcotics to a demoralized Republic. He had accordingly sought to remove him. From his cell this zealot called indignantly on other patriots to rally to the rescue of their country. Otherwise, he announced, the United States was doomed to share the fate of drug-ridden China.

The other two assailants refused to give any reason for their attempts to shoot down the Chief Executive. Informed that they would be tried for high treason, the penalty for which might be death, they answered proudly that Germans knew how to die in defense of their Fatherland.

Gifford digested these matters and all their sidelights from the journals. He realized he had come to Washington at a difficult time, for with all these attempts on his life the President was bound to feel a certain prejudice against any Saviour, however authentic. Just the same, that afternoon Gifford crawled down the policed and deserted street leading to the White House. Undeterred, he scurried up the wide steps and entered the Mansion. The vestibule too was crowded with Secret Service men. Lingering among them, he learned that the President was in his study upstairs preparing his message to Congress. Gifford zigzagged up the steps, located the study door by the presence of four armed guards, and entered through a tiny space over the threshold. A few minutes later, Gifford, from behind a towering inkwell, looked out upon the face of the Chief Executive, who sat in his shirtsleeves. He had a far-away look in his eyes and was chewing on a pencil.

Gifford observed that there were three other figures in the study. Two were obviously guards, for they remained stiffly looking out of the windows. The third was evidently someone very close to the President, for, like his Chief, he also was in shirtsleeves. After a period of silence, this friend of the President spoke.

"It isn't necessary to finish the message today," he said. "You've got a whole week."

The Chief Executive nodded. He addressed the two guards and Gifford was surprised by his whimsical tones.

"Any more assassins lurking about?" he inquired.

The guards answered solemnly that the coast was clear.

"It's damned hard trying to write with a lot of hecklers around," pursued the President.

"Hecklers!" cried his friend. "That's a fine name for those murderers."

"They didn't murder anybody," said the President amiably. "I guess, along with my other shortcomings, I'm a pretty bad target."

"Listen," said the friend, "I'm dead set against joking on this subject. And, what's more, I'm not going to let you pull any grandstand plays about those assassins. There's going to be no humorous attitude or official clemency. If you let them off easy, it'll just encourage every poisoned mind in the country to take a shot at you."

"That would be a lot of shooting," the President chuckled. Then he added: "How do you like this paragraph?" And he started reading from the penciled manuscript on his desk.

"We must bear in mind," he read, "when we listen to our great industrialists proclaim that they are motivated only by an interest in the welfare of the working classes, that these same gentlemen achieved their high estates by a complete indifference to the welfare of these same working classes." The President smiled apologetically. "That's all I wrote today," he said. "And I guess we better get fixed up for dinner."

"O.K.," said the friend, and turning to the guards at the windows he ordered them to remain at their posts until they were relieved in the morning.

"I don't think that's necessary," the President objected.

"There's no telling what some poisoned mind will do next," his friend insisted. "One of them might hide himself in your study and lay for you."

"Take it easy, boys," the President said.

Gifford watched the President and his friend leave. He had long before decided on his method of communicating his information, but he waited now patiently behind the inkwell. Knowing the literary obsession of the President, Gifford was fearful that he might return for another bout with his Congressional message. Accordingly he allowed hours to pass.

At one o'clock Gifford moved. He crawled quickly up the inkwell. On its edge the ant paused. Gifford urged it on but it remained obdurate. It refused to plunge into the ink. This unexpected mutiny delayed Gifford a half-hour. At the end of that time his will overcame the termite's reluctance and the insect, quivering for a last second on the edge of the inkwell, dropped into its black contents. A moment later Gifford came crawling out of the well. He moved with difficulty, being half choked and blinded with the ink. Down the side of the inkstand he crept and on toward the President's message. Here Gifford pressed his belly firmly against the paper and began to write. The writing required a score of trips to the inkwell and constant use of his human will. At the end of his labors, however, he had completed the first of a series of carefully contemplated messages to the President. In a wavering thick script, full of erratic deviation caused by the termite's inability to move in a straight line, Gifford had spelled out with his belly the first words of his Message: *Beware the Ants!* The warning covered the entire page of the manuscript.

When it was done the ant sank into a stupor, and Gifford waited for the dawn. He was not worried, for he felt that with practice his ant body would improve as an amanuensis. He felt certain, too, that despite its present exhaustion the ant would survive the hardships of composition.

The President entered his study at eight o'clock in the morning. He greeted the guards amiably and sat down before his desk. Gifford, who had stationed himself under a blotter edge, watched eagerly. He saw the President glance at his manuscript and start to sharpen a pencil and then pause and stare.

"Mr. Sykes," said the President sharply. "Come here, please."

Mr. Sykes came to the desk.

"Who wrote this on my manuscript?" the President asked quietly.

"I don't know." Mr. Sykes frowned. "There's been nobody in this room since you left."

The other guard came to the desk.

"Are you sure of that?" asked the President.

"Absolutely," said both guards.

"If you didn't write this, and there's been nobody in this room since I left . . ." began the Chief Executive, but gave up the logic of his case with a thoughtful "Never mind."

"Thank you, just the same," he added abstractedly.

The incident made a small stir in the White House. The President's friend pointed out that there could be only two explanations: either the guards had dozed off, permitting some vandal to enter the room and deface the manuscript; or one of them or both of them had done it themselves in a fit of aberration.

"It goes to show," said the friend, "that we can't be too careful. Even the White House is overrun with poisoned minds. I'll have those two guards questioned by a psychiatrist at once."

The President worked until late on his manuscript. When he left, it remained on the desk. But four new figures stayed behind this time to watch the premises. They had been carefully selected from the Secret Service ranks by the friend himself. Their instructions were not to leave their posts at the windows and door for any reason, except to apprehend an intruder.

"Nobody moves," repeated the friend. "We don't want suspicion falling on any of you four. Just keep away from that desk and keep your eyes open."

The following morning there was a greater stir in the White House. For the President had found on sitting down to his desk that his manuscript had been defaced once more. Across its top page was a wavering scrawl as if some infant or idiot had trailed an ink-dipped match over it. The scrawl read: *Termites now eat stone.*

A number of officials were instantly summoned. The four guards were removed to military headquarters. Here they were grilled by the Secret Service head, flanked by two psychiatrists. They persisted, however, in their original statement. None of them had moved from his post and no intruder had entered the study.

This absurd but mysterious sabotaging of the President's manuscript appeared to all concerned as something sinister. It was regarded as the beginning of a sixth plot against the President's life. Investigations were started within the White House. Every inmate and every inch of space were gone over by squads of detectives. After several conferences, the President stated, late in the afternoon, that he had something more important to do than chase a will-o'-the-wisp. He settled down again to the writing of his Congressional message. It was eight o'clock when he quit his desk. Six men remained behind, among them the Secret Service chief himself. Guards had been placed outside the windows, and at every door of the Mansion. The garden shrubbery was jammed with detectives. The President himself took the further precaution of placing his unfinished manuscript in a desk drawer.

"I don't think," he smiled on the group guarding the room, "that we'll have any more trouble with that scribbler."

The next morning the Chief Executive entered his study at the unusual hour of six. He was accompanied by his friend and an unknown man whom Gifford designated as his Chief of Staff. The guards and their leader greeted the President with smiles, and the latter was pleased to be able to report that there had been no vandalism during the night. The President unlocked the drawer of his desk and removed his manuscript. A frown came over his face as, without comment, he pointed to the ruined top page.

Scrawled in smaller letters that wavered less than those of the previous messages were the startling words: *Civilization in danger. New ants coming. Eat stone. Trillions. If think mankind worth saving hurry up.*

Several hours later the President, his Chief of Staff, his Secret Service head, and various wise men from the Military Intelligence Department were still in conference. A clue had been discovered and the best analytic brains of the nation were wrestling with its significance. Traces of ink had been found in the keyhole of the drawer in which the manuscript had been locked.

The men confronted by the mystery were all agreed on one theory. This was that some mechanism involving perhaps radioactivity and controlled from some point outside the White

House had been used. The motive, it was decided, was a plot against the sanity of the President.

"But I am not at all likely to go insane," the President protested. "And besides, most of the Opposition think I am already crazy."

"The Opposition," his friend answered, "has underestimated you for eight years. Let us not underestimate them."

"What's more," said the President, "I am convinced that no mechanism is being used."

Pressed for further opinions, the Chief Executive remained glum for a space.

"I would dislike this to get out," he finally offered with a sigh, "but there is such a thing as Revelation."

The friend was the first to speak in the silence that followed.

"Well," he said, "the plot is working."

"What plot?" demanded the President.

"You can see the effect of such a notion on the country," explained the friend firmly. "They're bound to crucify you for it."

"Me?" cried the President. "Crucify me for what?"

"For thinking that God is writing you letters," cried the friend.

"I have not referred to God or made any statement involving Him in this mystery," said the President coldly.

"Indeed," said the friend and lit a fresh cigar, "you said it was Revelation. And who else can make revelations besides God?"

"I don't know," said the President.

Although every effort was made to keep the bizarre events of the President's study hidden from the world, news of the White House mystery spread. It was garbled news, to be sure. The rumor that billowed through the nation concerned itself with the uncovering of some monstrous plot against the President's life.

In Republican circles, the tale ran that several members of his Cabinet had turned on the President, as in the case of Julius Caesar, and had tried to stab him as he was taking a walk. Another rumor swept through brokerage firms and other strongholds of conservative thought. This had it that the White House had been undermined, and numerous caches of dynamite discovered. These rumors and others reached the editorial desks of a thousand newspapers and set a thousand editors bristling with expectancy. By nightfall the reports had reached such proportions that a new and corollary whisper became current. This was that the President was dead. Oddly enough, gossip agreed he had been strangled by a close friend while in the White House study. The New Dealers, however, were in a plot to keep the news from the country in order to insure, for a while at least, the continuation of their policies.

Despite the absurdity of this last rumor, it had gained such circulation by midnight that the press took to clamoring through its representatives in Washington for the President to show himself and be photographed then and there—if he was alive.

This the President, ever ready to outwit the Republican press, was glad to do. At twelve-thirty he appeared in one of the larger drawing-rooms, and allowed a dozen photographers to take flashlight pictures of him. He was in evening dress, having been to a state dinner. Of the curious matters that had thrown the Secret Service and Military Intelligence into so obvious a panic, he refused, however, to make any explanation.

"If anything of any importance happens to me or to the country," the President smiled, "I or my survivors will inform the press immediately. Let me assure you, though, that nobody has shot at me, tried to poison me or blow me up for five whole days, and that if this armistice continues I shall have my message to Congress done on schedule."

The journalists were quick to note that the White House was a veritable encampment of generals, detectives, and bodyguards, and that the rugged face of the Executive was pale, and his large eyes far away. Leaving, they spoke to one another furtively of these impressions, and of the grave and ominous events that were obviously in the offing. Some of them doubted that they would ever take the President's picture again, and decided secretly to save the plates of these "last" ones.

The President's mind, so apparently elsewhere, had actually been fastened on the scene in his study upstairs. Here some twenty-five officials, scientists, and Secret Service operatives were assembled. They were standing in a regularly spaced circle around the room and their eyes were intent on the President's still unfinished message to Congress, which lay exposed on the desk. There was no light in the room other than that of the moon in the windows.

The twenty-five vigilantes were armed with various devices as well as weapons. The army had brought over its most recent radio-activity detectors. Three of the scientists present were world-famous psychiatrists on the *qui vive* for evidence of mass hypnosis.

At last the President hurried upstairs. A dozen guards made way for him. He entered the study as smiling and eager as a boy finally arrived at a circus.

"Well, gentlemen," he blurted out, "any more messages?"

There was a stir in the unlit room. The officials in charge assured him nothing had happened and urged him to leave the premises. They hinted that danger lay in the room and that the conspirators had most obviously planned some final *coup* for this night.

"Well, if you don't want me to go insane," smiled the President, "you'd better let me hang around here. After all, it's my study and it's my writing that somebody is defacing and it's to me that the warning about those ants is being given. I'll just sit here and wait with the rest of you."

The Secret Service chief explained that they had decided to make everything as easy as possible for the villain controlling the radio writing, as the mysterious warnings were now termed. Therefore the vigil would be kept in the dark. All the conditions prevailing at the times of the previous defacements would be duplicated. No one was to go near the desk. The President's message was to lie exposed as it had on the first night. And nothing was to be done to prevent the scrawling of the gibberish. However, a new type of radio-active camera had been trained on the desk. This camera, able to photograph in the dark, was even now taking pictures of what was going on on the desk.

"We are remaining here until dawn," concluded the Secret Service chief.

"So am I," whispered the President, and there was a note of glee in his voice.

Silence had been agreed upon, and the occupants of the room remained without sound. The white page of the manuscript on the desk shone faintly in the dark. Every half-hour the President's friend tiptoed over to examine it, and returned to whisper that nothing had happened yet.

At five o'clock in the morning the Secret Service chief rose from his chair. Dawn was coming.

"Nothing," repeated the friend, after a trip to the desk. He moved toward the President, who had dozed off in his chair.

Alarm was in his voice as he asked: "Are you all right?"

Immediately five Secret Service men turned their flashlights on the Chief Executive. The silence became suddenly full of hissing breaths and a hum of awe and consternation. The voice of the President's friend rose sharply.

"Nobody move," it ordered. "Everybody stay just where they are. I'll take care of him!"

"Take care of whom?" muttered the President, opening his eyes.

"You," said the friend. "Be still, please."

"Lights!" the Chief of Staff demanded.

The study became bright with electricity. The twenty-five figures stood staring excitedly at the Chief Executive.

Rubbing his eyes, the President looked about him and demanded nervously: "What's happened?"

"It's on your shirt front," said the friend hoarsely.

"What's on my shirt front?" the President began, and looked down. "I'm sorry," he added after a pause, "I can't read at this angle."

"It's a message in ink scrawled on your shirt front," repeated the friend.

"I know that," the President answered irritably. "The point is, what does it say?"

The friend looked at him strangely.

"Don't you know?" he asked.

"I told you I can't read it," said the President. "I'm no contortionist."

"Do you have to read it?" said the friend meaningfully.

The President burst into a guffaw.

"Are you suggesting," he managed to say presently, "that I have been writing on my own shirt front?"

"You have had access to it," began the friend, but the President interrupted him.

"Listen," he said in a low but vibrant voice, "use your head. Why would I write a message on my shirt front? Why would I try to confuse the country with that kind of shenanigans?"

"There's some ink on your collar!" cried out the Secret Service chief, who had been examining the President closely during this discussion.

"There are some ink blots on the third bookshelf!" spoke a detective, who, among others, had been combing the room, inch by inch.

"Will somebody kindly read what is written on me," demanded the President, "or must I undress?"

The Chief of Staff stepped forward and saluted.

"It's the same general type of message, sir," he said. "It reads as follows: 'Hurry, hurry, Mt. Navajo, route 9-52, or world lost. Send ant expert. Hurry. Consult atlas.'"

"There's some more of it on the back of his collar," the Secret Service head spoke up.

The President grinned.

"Well, that exonerates me," he said. "I'm no good at writing with the back of my head. What does the collar say?"

"It reads," said the Secret Service chief, "'Can't keep this up much longer. Hurry, for God's sake.'"

"Well," said the President, "the whole thing sounds very impressive to me. This makes the fourth warning about ants. Did anybody ever hear of ants that could eat stone and steel?"

A psychiatrist present who had studied entomology smiled at this absurd layman's question.

"There is no such ant," he stated with scientific finality. "The thing is a hoax from beginning to end."

"I see," said the President and added: "Did anybody see any-body writing on me?"

The Secret Service chief replied nervously after a pause.

"No," he said, "but we expect a number of arrests within the next few hours."

"Mt. Navajo, Mt. Navajo," muttered the President. "Sounds like the Southwest."

He walked toward the bookshelves, where an officer guarded the new ink blots.

"Keep away from those books!" cried the friend and several others.

"Gentlemen," said the President, "if we are to be afraid of books, we may as well resign as human beings."

The room remained silent as the President removed an atlas.

The vigil keepers watched him as he turned the pages of the large, heavy volume. At length the President spoke.

"Here's a Navajo mountain range," he began and then paused, open-mouthed.

"Quick, somebody come here," he whispered.

"What is it?" cried the friend, and the Secret Service men drew out their revolvers and stood in a ring about the Chief Executive.

"An ant," said the President softly. "Somebody pick it up." Both his own hands were occupied. "Look. It's sitting on the Navajo mountains."

The Secret Service chief reached for the volume. By a slight miscalculation the President removed his hands from it before any others received it, and the book fell and slammed shut as it hit the floor. The Secret Service chief picked it up.

"Page two hundred and sixty," said the President.

The atlas was carried to the President's desk and opened.

Page two hundred and sixty revealed a detail map of lower California.

And on the map near the Navajo mountain range lay splattered a blot of ink. The squashed remains of an insect protruded from it.

"Was that ink there when you looked at it first?" asked the Secret Service chief.

"No," said the President softly, "there was only an ant."

Two days later, the first telegraphed report from the Federal Mount Navajo Investigation Committee arrived on the President's desk. It read: "Fifty thousand men needed here at once to fight new species stone-eating termite. Termites already undermined several hills and moving northward in incalculable numbers. Will devour nation if not stopped here. Scientific survey of situation follows."

Of the remarkable battle that took place in the Navajo Hills between man and the termites I have little new to add. The two-thousand-mile ditch dug around the enemy's domain and filled with two-thirds of the nation's supply of petroleum appears to have checked, for the time at least, the termite conquest.

As for Gifford Emmett, of him there is no further record. After several conferences between the President and his advisers it was decided that no reference be made to the blot of ink on the atlas page. The President made a brief address to his Cabinet on his reasons for silence.

"Whoever that Saviour was who came to the rescue of mankind," said the President, "it will be best, I feel certain, to let him die unhonored and unsung. For history shows that only confusion arises from the worship of God's emissaries. We are in the midst of too much confusion today to add to our troubles the hysterias and dissensions which this miraculous ant would bring to our nation and perhaps to the world. If it is God who saved the race, let Him be content that it is saved. And if it is God who sent a Son to us in the guise of an ant, we may well believe He did it in order that we might ignore the Messiah. The Almighty could not very well have sent us a more inconsequential Saviour and one calling more for our indifference—if He desired any practical results. A gnat or a microbe would have been physically incapable of the Divine warning given us. I say, therefore, that we should continue to worship God's previous representatives without adding an ant to the galaxy."

Thus Gifford Emmett's cross was oblivion, which he may well have preferred. I am moved, however, to add an epitaph to the blot of ink that lies in the President's atlas. Of this little blot of ink I write:

Here lies one who hated life, who shuddered before the scurvy inhumanity of the world, who considered with revulsion the record of its endless injustice and triumphant cruelty.

Here lies one whose soul was wasted by the stupidity and barbarism of his fellows, and whose mind, looking out upon the earth, saw it overrun by the inane, the unscrupulous, the aberrant, and the sadistic children of the beast.

Yet here in this little blot of ink lies one who in all that he hated beheld the bright and beleaguered face of tomorrow and died full of hope.